THE GALILEANS

Mary jumped back from the door to escape being bowled over as the angry slave girl stormed in. "You were looking," the girl cried, panting with anger and the effort of dancing, her eyes darting fire. "Did Gaius Flaccus try to catch the girdle?"

Mary shook her head. "It would have hit him if he had not moved."

"You!" The dancer turned suddenly, feet apart and hands upon her full hips. "He refused me because of you—with your clinging robes and your talk of being virgin!"

"You are wrong!" Mary protested. "I came only to dance. . . ."

*Are there paperbound books you want
but cannot find in your retail stores?*

FRANK G. SLAUGHTER

THE
GALILEANS

A Novel of Mary Magdalene

A KANGAROO BOOK
PUBLISHED BY POCKET BOOKS NEW YORK

THE GALILEANS

Doubleday edition published 1953

POCKET BOOK edition published April, 1977

With the exception of actual historical personages
identified as such, the characters are entirely the
product of the author's imagination and have no
relation to any person in real life.

This POCKET BOOK edition includes every word contained in
the original, higher-priced edition. It is printed from brand-
new plates made from completely reset, clear, easy-to-read type.
POCKET BOOK editions are published by
POCKET BOOKS,
a division of Simon & Schuster, Inc.,
A GULF+WESTERN COMPANY
630 Fifth Avenue,
New York, N.Y. 10020.
Trademarks registered in the United States
and other countries.

ISBN: 0-671-80987-3.

Printed in the U.S.A.

Author's Preface

OF all the women who appear in the pages of the Bible, few have aroused so much interest as Mary of Magdala, usually called Mary Magdalene. That Mary loved Jesus deeply is self-evident, for Luke tells us quite early that she was among the women who ministered to Him and to the Twelve. What seems equally self-evident is that the Master Himself felt a special bond of affection for this woman from whom He had "cast out seven demons," for He singled her out from among the entire body of His followers as the first witness to His resurrection from the dead.

When in the closing chapters of *The Road to Bithynia* I introduced Mary of Magdala quite by accident as a minor character, a strange thing happened. It was as if this magnificent Christian woman of Jesus' day stood before me in the flesh, demanding that her story be told. This is the story of Mary of Magdala and her fellow Galileans, who left homes, work, security, and friends to follow a Man who taught a wonderful new thing, that every individual is important in the sight of God, whether black, white, or red, rich or poor, thief or saint. It is also the story of how these Galileans except Mary, who seems to have known from the start who Jesus really was, came to recognize Him as the Christ.

Many legends have come down through the ages about the woman of Magdala. Of some of them, the Encyclopaedia Britannica says: "Mary of Magdala has been confounded (1) with the unnamed fallen woman who in Simon's house anointed Christ's feet (Luke vii:37); (2) with Mary of Bethany, sister of Lazarus and Martha." A number of so-called "biographies" of Mary Magdalene are in existence, most of them based upon this false assumption that she is identical with Mary of Bethany. Actually they are fiction, for nothing is known about this woman who loved Jesus, except the few references to her in the New Testament.

Wherever Jesus speaks in this novel, His words are taken directly from the text of the Revised Standard

Version of the New Testament. I am deeply indebted to the Division of Christian Education of the National Council of Churches for permission to use this text. Portions of the Song of Songs and the Book of Ruth which appear in the body of the novel are used with the kind permission of the publishers of *The Bible Designed to Be Read as Living Literature,* Messrs. Simon & Schuster. I learned of the legend of Pilate's crippled son, Pila, while reading Catherine van Dyke's delightful little book, *A Letter from Pontius Pilate's Wife,* published by the Bobbs-Merrill Company. According to the author, it is "from an old traditional manuscript first found in a monastery at Bruges, where it had lain for centuries."

The description of Jesus given by Nicodemus in Book Three is from an ancient Latin manuscript in the form of a letter written by one Publius Sentulus, presumably a contemporary of Pontius Pilate, to the Roman Senate during the reign of Tiberius Caesar. I am indebted to the Reverend Carl Dobbins of High Springs, Florida, for bringing it to my attention.

Comparative studies between the Gospel of John and the three Synoptic Gospels make it evident that Jesus visited Jerusalem several times during his ministry, and not just once, as a superficial reading of Mark, for example, makes it appear. For the chronological sequence of those last months of Our Lord, I am deeply indebted to the article, "The Life and Ministry of Jesus," by Vincent Taylor, in the Interpreters Bible, published recently by the Abingdon Cokesbury Press, Vol. 7, pages 114-44.

My continued thanks go to the staff of the Jacksonville Public Library and the Library of the Florida State Board of Health for invaluable assistance. Most of the information on the fascinating culture and civilization of first-century Alexandria was placed at my disposal through the kindness of Dr. Lawrence S. Thompson, librarian of the Margaret I. King Library of the University of Kentucky, and many knotty problems were unraveled personally for me by him, for which my heartfelt thanks. My court of last resort, as always, was the staff of the Encyclopaedia Britannica Research Service.

To those who read this book it is my sincere wish that the times, the places, and the people of Jesus' ministry may come alive for them as they have for me.

And that they, too, may come to know Jesus, the Risen Lord, as did my friends, the Galileans, on the road to Emmaus.

FRANK G. SLAUGHTER

Jacksonville, Florida
May 28, 1952

Contents

Book One

MAGDALA

1

To the young man hurrying his mule through the streets of Tiberias late one afternoon, the voice borne across the city on the breeze from the lake was so startlingly beautiful that he stopped the animal to listen. It was the voice of a young girl singing in purest Greek, soft, gentle, sweet, and clear, with a bell-like quality that held the listener spellbound.

Joseph of Galilee had been studying Greek in the university of Herod Antipas' newly built city of Tiberias here on the shores of the Sea of Galilee, called by fishermen the Lake of Gennesaret, so he easily understood the words of the love poem first sung by the Greek poet Meleager to his beloved Heliodora of Tyre:

> *"I'll twine white violets and the myrtle green;*
> *Narcissus will I twine, and lilies' sheen;*
> *I'll twine sweet crocus, and the hyacinth blue;*
> *And last I'll twine the rose, love's token true:*
> *That all may form a wreath of beauty, meet*
> *To deck my Heliodora's tresses sweet."*

Joseph was only twenty-one, but tall and slender, with dark eyes and a mobile, expressive face already marked by a seriousness beyond his age. His high-bridged nose and cheekbones showed the purity of a bloodline that went in uninterrupted sequence back to the time of David and beyond. Living with his mother in the city of Magdala, only a few miles away on the heights overlooking the lake, he was close enough to attend the new univeristy at Tiberias. There Greek teachers instructed students of all nationalities in the lore of medicine and science developed by Hippocrates, Thales, and other great minds when Greece had been the center of the world of knowledge.

To earn bread for himself and his mother, Joseph was apprenticed to the famous Jewish physician of Magdala,

2

Alexander Lysimachus, while working also at the more lowly occupation of leech, draining poisonous humors from the besotted Romans whose villas lined the waters of the lake here at Tiberias. Being a devout Jew, he could not live in the new city, labeled unclean and cursed when Herod's builders disturbed the rest of the dead in the cemetery that now lay beneath its streets, but here was nothing to prevent him from taking good Roman gold for applying his leeches. Even now two of the dozen or so in the bottle hanging from the mule's back were fat with the plethoric blood of Pontius Pilate, for the Roman governor of Judea spent as much time in his pleasure villa at Tiberias as he did in his capital at Caesarea on the sea-coast, ostensibly because of the climate, but also to keep an eye on wily Herod Antipas, Jewish Tetrarch of Galilee.

Drawn to the girl's voice as iron was attracted by the black stone called *magnes,* Joseph moved closer to the source of the music along the granite-paved street of Tiberias. So new was Herod Antipas' city that the dirt was not yet packed hard between the stones of the pavement, and the pedestrian must walk carefully lest he stumble over rough edges and uneven stones. Turning a corner, Joseph came into the open square before the magnificent new Forum. A crowd had gathered there and was still applauding the singer, showering coins at her feet as tokens of their praise.

Joseph climbed upon the pedestal supporting one of the granite Roman eagles adorning the Forum. His pious Jewish father, had he been alive, would have cried out against this action as blasphemy, since it was unlawful for a Jew to make any graven image such as the Romans used to adorn their buildings, or even closely to observe it. Herod the Great, grandfather of Antipas, had earned the marked displeasure of his people by thus flaunting the emblems of his Roman masters in order to curry favor. Only by building the beautiful new temple in Jerusalem had he partially expiated the crime. Now this later Herod, more Roman than Jew, had assumed his grandfather's arrogance without his intelligence. From where he stood, Joseph could see the great citadel of the king's palace upon the acropolis, rising from the black basalt cliffs of the mountainside and dominating the whole shore line as a grim symbol of military might and kingly power.

The singer sat on the curbstone, holding a lyre against her breast as composedly as if she were in her own home.

3

The crowd, largely Greeks and Romans, was arranged around her in a circle. She was young, perhaps eighteen, Joseph thought, and tall for a Jewish woman. Although her body was slender, it was already filling out with the promise of a womanly beauty that could not be denied. Her hair was covered with a shawl, as befitted a Jewish woman in the open air, but no mere fabric could hide its lustrous beauty. As red as the copper dug from the mines of Cyprus and burnished in the forges of Paphos, it shone in the afternoon sunlight, framing her face in a halo of rich color.

The girl's features were a curious mixture of Greek and Hebrew lines, giving her face an almost stenciled perfection of classic beauty. The cheekbones were moderately prominent, the chin pointed slightly, and the forehead high, marking an intelligence that shone also in the cool glance of her deep violet eyes. They searched the crowd now, as if she were estimating just how many more coins could be extracted from the men applauding her so vigorously. Her skin was clear, almost translucent in its smoothness and its beauty, and lit with a faint tinge of color as she responded with a smile to the plaudits of the crowd.

To Joseph's observant eyes, the pallor of the girl's skin was further evidence of the mixture of Greek with Hebrew in her blood, as was her daring to sing a love song, however beautiful, before a crowd like this in a city shunned as cursed by the Jews. Her dress was of good material and beautifully made, but although neat and clean, it was worn and frayed, as was the leather of the sandals upon her lovely slender feet.

The four musicians with the girl seemed to be Nabateans, for their skin was dark and their profiles sharp and hawklike. Their dress, too, was the long flowing robe worn by the sons of the desert who roamed the sandy wastes to the south and east of the Jordan and the Dead Sea, where lay the great city of Petra. The leader, taller than the others and with striking face and graying beard, held a large cithara in his hands.

One of the other dark-faced musicians held a long pipe of Egyptian reed and another a trumpet of brass. A fourth carried cymbals strapped to his hands, and upon his feet were the reasonant boards called *scabella*, which were stamped in rhythm to the melody. It was an odd group, more like the bands of itinerant musicians sometimes seen with dancers than the accompaniment one would expect for a singer. Such bands were not at all uncommon in the thriving, populous cities around the lake, but Joseph did not remember one before with a girl singer, and certainly not a girl whose voice was itself a more perfect instrument than those of the musicians and whose beauty made her stand out like a lily among thistles.

"Who is she?" Joseph asked a Roman who was standing by, a fat man in a grease-stained toga threatening to burst at its seams.

The Roman looked at him scathingly, as if it were a sacrilege for a young Jew in a cheap robe to speak to his betters. "She calls herself Mary of Magdala," he volunteered grudgingly. "A *meretix,* no doubt."

Joseph knew the Roman word. The *meretrix,* or prostitute, was common wherever the Romans gathered, and women entertainers usually came from this class. A considerably higher group on the social scale, if not a moral one, was the Roman version of the famed Greek *hetairai,* courtesans who wielded a powerful influence upon their admirers and were highly regarded in Roman society. Devout Jews applied the word "Jezebel" indiscriminately to the women of their Roman conquerors, whether wives, daughters, or mistresses.

But to Joseph the girl of Magdala did not look like one of the women of the streets who thronged this beautiful new city. No paint or antimony whitened the translucent pallor of her skin. Nor could the henna of Cleopatra's Egypt have added anything to the natural luster of her hair. She was beautiful enough to be a courtesan, it was true, but something about her manner, notably the quiet dignity with which she sat there holding the lyre and accepting the plaudits of the crowd, told a different story.

"More! More!" the crowd began to chant now, and others took up the cry.

Mary of Magdala smiled and drew her fingers across the lyre, drawing a melody from the strings like the soft murmur of water flowing over rocks in some hidden place of beauty. Then she began to sing the melancholy lament of the poet Philodemus to his beloved Xantho. Joseph wondered how this girl knew so classical a poem and where she had learned her skill with the lyre, but never, he was sure, had it been sung by so beautiful a voice, not even in the palace of a king.

5

> *"White waxen cheeks, soft scented breast,*
> *Deep eyes wherein the Muses nest.*
> *Sweet lips that perfect pleasure bring—*
> *Sing me your song, pale Xantho sing . . .*
> *Too soon the music ends, Again,*
> *Again repeat the sad sweet strain,*
> *With perfumed fingers touch the string;*
> *Of Love's delight, pale Xantho sing."*

While she was singing, Joseph looked over the crowd. Only a few were Jews, for most of them avoided Tiberias. Actually Herod had been forced to import the scum of other cities to populate this gleaming new town. They had come eagerly, however, for much gold could be earned, and stolen, while serving the Romans whose pleasure villas lined the shore of the amethyst-green lake. From where he stood Joseph could see several of the elaborate villas, with terraced green lawns enclosed by high masonry walls and graceful marble stairways descending to the water's edge, where ornate barges awaited their masters' pleasure. The largest of the villas, except the palace of Herod Antipas himself upon the acropolis, belonged to Pontius Pilate, the Procurator of Judea.

All the emotions of man were betrayed in the eyes of those watching the girl. Some were lost in the beauty of her voice, the liquid notes of the lyre, and the contact with the sublime that beautiful music can bring to those who love it. Others had forgotten the music in admiring the youth and loveliness of the singer. But in a few there burned only a fire of lust for the slender body of the girl, and the most noticeable of these was a Roman officer standing to one side. He wore the purple-dyed uniform of a Tribune, and Joseph recognized him as Gaius Flaccus, favored nehew of Pontius Pilate and commander of the Procurator's personal troops. Already the whole region of Galilee buzzed with tales of the cruelty of this hated Roman to those who were unfortunate enough to come under his hands, his fondness for the wine-cup and women, and the saturnalian revels that were often held at the palace of his uncle.

Gaius Flaccus was tall, with a superbly proportioned body and a classic beauty of features almost feminine in its perfection. He could be an incarnation of Apollo or Dionysos, Joseph thought, then hurriedly erased the idea

6

from his mind, since it was a sacrilege for a devout Jew even to think of such hated pagan deities, still worshiped in Alexandria, Rome, Antioch, Ephesus, and many other cities of the Empire, with orgies and revels said to be scandalous in their abandonment.

The song ended and the musicians lifted their instruments. Then on a crashing chord from the leader's cithara they began a wild barbaric dance of the mountains and deserts beyond the Jordan and the Dead Sea. The flute wailed in the strange melody of the desert people, while the strings and the cymbalist took up the rhythm, set to the throbbing beat of the *scabella*. Stamped by the cymbal player against the stones of the pavement, the resonant boards produced a booming sound like the beat of drums heard afar off. Above this heady rhythm came the clear, commanding call of the long trumpet.

Mary of Magdala put down her lyre and stood erect upon her toes, poised with her arms uplifted, as if in adoration of something unseen. The music seemed to caress her body, creating in its lithe beauty a fluid rhythm in cadence with the clash of the cymbals, the throbbing beat of the *scabella* and the strings, and the wail of flute and trumpet. Slowly at first, then faster as the rhythm quickened, she began to move in a dance that, while not consciously provocative, set the onlookers to breathing hard with the grip of its allure. Like a musical instrument in itself, her body, slender and girlish, yet already seductive, seemed to vibrate in a wild melody all its own.

As she danced, the shawl about the girl's head came loose and was tossed aside, letting the glorious mass of her hair stream about her shoulders, enveloping them in a cascade of coppery gold. She was like a spinning torch, a veritable pillar of flame, and a roar of approval came from the audience. With an effort of will Joseph tore his eyes from the girl and studied Gaius Flaccus. Naked lust and a calculating light were in the Roman's eyes, and Joseph wondered if the girl had any conception of what her dancing could do to the souls of men, or of the dangers that might come to her because of it.

Mary of Magdala laughed exultantly in the midst of her dancing and, deliberately provocative now, whirled before the tall Tribune, her eyes mocking him. Faster the rhythm went as she moved about the open circle in the crowd, skillfully eluding those who tried to touch her.

Coins began to fall in a shower upon the stones as the music rose to its climax, then ceased upon a crash of the cymbals. Standing on her toes, her lovely young breast rising and falling rapidly with the excitement of her triumph and the effort of her dancing, Mary of Magdala poised like a statue of Aphrodite herself, eyes shining, cheeks bright with color, while the crowd deepened the spontaneous thunder of its applause.

Joseph was the first to see the rich color drain suddenly from her cheeks, leaving them marble-pale. For an instant she was rigid, as if truly transformed into a statue of the Goddess of Love, then she wavered and took a quick step as if to regain her balance. Sensing what was happening, he started toward her, darting between several men who stood between him and the open space where she stood. But he was too far away, and it was the Tribune Gaius Flaccus who caught the slender body of the dancer in his arms as she toppled over in a dead faint.

2

FOR a moment, as the Roman officer lowered the unconscious girl to the ground, the crowd stood paralyzed. Then someone shouted, "Away! She is possessed by a demon!" Those in front began at once to push back, for everyone knew that demons sometimes left those who were possessed, particularly during a period of unconsciousness, and entered the body of a well person. Only Joseph moved toward the girl and the kneeling Tribune.

Gaius Flaccus recognized him, for Joseph had often attended his uncle, Pontius Pilate. "You there, leech," he barked. "Help me with this girl."

Joseph knelt beside the unconscious dancer. As he felt for the pulse at her wrist, her body began to jerk convulsively, and he reached at once for the pouch at his belt, thinking to force one of the coins it contained between her teeth through the leather. Alexander Lysimachus had taught him early that the only thing to be done for an epileptic convulsion was to place something between the victim's teeth to protect the tongue from being bitten. But the girl's jaws were not tense; instead, a torrent of words poured from her throat. They seemed to be a confused jumble of childhood phrases and songs, then cries of protest, as if someone were punishing her, and finally screams of agony and a writhing of her body as if under the lash. The whole episode lasted only a moment, then as if the torrent of words had released some of the energy inside the slender body, she was quiet.

"Is it the Sacred Disease?" Gaius Flaccus asked. Epilepsy, variously thought to result from possession by demons or divine visitation, was often called the "Sacred Disease" even now, although Hippocrates had argued nearly five hundred years before it was no different from other diseases, having a natural cause in the diminution or loss of humors from the brain and nerves, leaving them in an uncommonly dry state. Watching the girl, Joseph thought there seemed to be much reason in the Greek view, for she was perspiring, and as she had begun to fall, her face had become suddenly very pale, showing that the body humors had indeed left the head where the brain was located. On the other hand, however, she had not bitten her tongue, there was no froth at her mouth, and no jerking movements, such as Hippocrates had described in what he had preferred to call the "Great Disease."

"Answer me, leech," Gaius Flaccus barked irritably. "It must be the Sacred Disease."

Joseph hesitated to disagree with the Roman, for his violent temper was well known. But on the other hand, he was not at all sure of the diagnosis. Just then, however, the girl sneezed violently.

"Hayim tobim umarphei," Joseph repeated automatically, for some said sneezing was connected with death, which might be averted by thus wishing the person who sneezed a "good and healthful life." Others felt, however, that *ittush,* the act of sneezing, presaged good fortune. In any event, it helped him to make the diagnosis, for he had never seen an epileptic attack end by sneezing. "I do not believe it is the Sacred Disease," he told the Roman confidently.

"What then?" They did not realize that the girl had opened her eyes and was listening to them.

"A faint perhaps," Joseph admitted, "from the dancing. Or she might be possessed," he added in deference to conventional Jewish belief.

9

Mary of Magdala sat up quickly, her cheeks burning with indignation. "Am I *cheresh* [deaf]," she demanded angrily, "that you speak ill of me to my face?"

Gaius Flaccus smiled. "No one speaks ill of you. The physician and I—"

"Physician! Zut! Joseph of Galilee is but a leech."

Joseph found himself squirming like one of his own leeches under the intensity of her indignation at being labeled possessed by demons. "I did not claim to be a physician," he protested. "You were dancing and fainted. The noble Tribune caught you and I offered to help."

The girl's anger seemed to depart as suddenly as it had come, like the quick play of emotions in a child. She smiled, but upon the handsome Roman, not the Jew in the dingy robe. "I regret if I have troubled you, noble sir," she said graciously in flawless Greek, and again Joseph marveled at her self-possession and her manners. Most girls of her age would have been dumb before the magnificence of the Procurator's nephew.

Gaius Flaccus bowed with equal grace. "If you still feel faint, my uncle's villa is only a short distance away."

But something else had claimed the girl's thoughts. "Hadja!" she called to the leader of the musicians, who waited nearby. "What of the coins? There should be many."

The Nabatean smiled and held out his cupped hands. They were almost filled with gold and silver. "We picked them up, O Living Flame, while you lay in the fit."

Mary stamped her foot. "How many times must I tell you I do not have fits?" she cried angrily.

"Then you have had them before?" Joseph asked.

"Sometimes when I dance I grow faint. It is nothing." She stood up but swayed, and Joseph caught her or she would have fallen. Her body was soft under his fingers about her waist, and he could not deny the stirring of his pulses at the contact.

"Let me carry you to my uncle's villa to recover," Gaius Flaccus suggested eagerly.

"I am all right now." The girl pushed away Joseph's supporting hand. "Thank you for your kindness, sir," she said graciously to Gaius Flaccus. "I must return to Magdala with my musicians."

"You can ride my mule," Joseph suggested. "I am go-

10

ing directly there." He did not stop to think that his patients in Magdala would be angry because he was late. Right now being with Mary of Magdala was more important.

3

THE road climbed sharply up the black basalt cliffs of the mountain above Tiberias, and Joseph had to lead the mule carefully because of the girl's weight upon its back. When they came to a level spot on the mountainside he stopped for the animal to rest, but the Nabateans went on ahead, since their long strides covered ground more rapidly than the plodding mule. Mary sat on a rock at the edge of the lake, with the white marble buildings of Tiberias below them. "How cool it is up here," she exclaimed, pushing her hair back from her face. "Tiberias is much too hot."

"Hot air breeds fevers for physicians to treat," Joseph told her. "I should like it, but I am always glad to leave Tiberias." Herod had failed to take into consideration the nature of the prevailing winds when he built this new city. While the flow of air through the mountain defile in which the lake lay kept the center of the inland sea and the cities around its northern curve cool in summer, it failed to stir the hot sultry air close to the western shore, where Tiberias was located. So for all its beauty, the magnificent Roman palaces, and Herod's own luxurious edifice on the higher ground of the acropolis, it was an unhealthy city.

"Who were you treating today?" she asked.

Joseph reached for the bottle containing his leeches and held it up to the light. Three of the sleek black squirming animals were fat and turgid. "My leeches are plump from the blood of Pontius Pilate," he said proudly.

She seemed entirely unafraid of the leeches, which was unusual for a young girl. "They say in Magdala that the blood of David flows in your veins, Joseph. Why do you work as a leech?"

"My patients pay me well. Meanwhile I am learning all that Alexander Lysimachus can teach me."

She wrinkled her nose at him impudently. "And it does not hurt your work, I suppose, for people to know that the richest merchant in Jerusalem, Joseph of Arimathea, is your uncle and you are his namesake?"

Joseph flushed at her raillery. Actually the recommendation of his uncle had secured him the Procurator as a patient. "When I have saved enough money," he told her, "I will go to Alexandria to study medicine."

"Why not Pergamos or Epidaurus?"

Joseph looked at her in astonishment. "How do you know of those places?"

"I know a lot," she said loftily. "Probably more than you do, for you see nothing but your medicine. I have seen you several times in Magdala, but you were too busy to notice me."

"I must have been blind," he said promptly.

Mary smiled at the compliment. "Demetrius has taught me since I was twelve years old. He has been everywhere and, besides, I read everything I can find."

"Demetrius? Who is he?"

"The maker of lyres. He lives on the Street of the Greeks, where the Via Maris passes. I live with him," she added matter-of-factly.

Joseph was shocked by her casual admission that she lived with a man. To cover his confusion, he changed the subject to Alexandria again, but to his surprise, she knew more about that city, too, than he did. When he told her of its university and medical school, acknowledged to be one of the best in the world and drawing students even from beyond the borders of the Roman Empire, she countered with a description of its magnificent theaters and arenas, the Serapeum devoted to the worship of the combined deity, Serapis, the ancient rites of Isis and Osiris, and the great lighthouse of the Pharos dominating the harbor, which was said to be all of four hundred ells, or five hundred and ninety feet, in height.

"When were you in Alexandria?" Joseph asked.

"I have never been there. But I shall go someday," she added confidently.

"Then how do you know these things? I have read much of the city, but you know more about it than I do."

"Demetrius lived there a long time," she explained. "And he still loves Alexandria. It will mean much to you,

12

Joseph, to say that you studied at the Museum. Few can make that claim, even in Jerusalem or Antioch."

What she said was true, Joseph knew. There were few really learned physicians either in Galilee or Judea. Those who went to Alexandria to study usually stayed there, for the Jewish community in that city was larger than the whole population of Jerusalem. But the hills and valleys of Judea and Galilee had been the home of Joseph's people since the days of the kings from whom he was descended. He loved the beautiful region around the lake and he knew it would always draw him back. For the most part, the healers of Galilee were either leeches like himself or mere Essenes, who relied upon prayer and a few dried herbs to treat the sick. Thirsty for knowledge, he had absorbed everything his preceptor could teach him, but a young physician could still learn much in Alexandria, where new medicines were constantly being used and some physicians even dared to cut into the body to cure disease.

"I am going to Alexandria someday." Mary's voice brought Joseph back to the present. "I shall dance and sing in the theater and become very rich." It was a calm statement of fact, not of hopes.

"You are very sure of yourself."

"I am beautiful. I have a fine voice and I dance well. Why should I not become a great actress? And I can also declaim the lines of most of the Greek comedies from memory."

"But you are a Jew," Joseph protested. "A Jewish woman should not show herself in the theater."

"Part of me is Greek," Mary said spiritedly. "And I was never happy until Demetrius took me into his home, where we live as the Greeks do."

"It is your affair." Then he smiled. "Is it not written of a woman, *'She openeth her mouth with wisdom'*?"

Mary tossed her head at the irony in his tone and the clever way he had turned her words upon her. She stood up. "Let's be on our way. You must have work to do, and I must buy supper for Demetrius in the market."

"And I must visit Eleazar, the seller of cloth," Joseph agreed, helping her up on the mule. "He is bedded with a painful swelling of the knee." Privately Joseph suspected the swelling to be of a character that would not be relieved by leeching, but he knew of nothing else to offer save the voracious appetites of his leeches. And at least the animals gave visible evidence that something was actually removed from the swelling when they sucked greedily and grew fat before the startled eyes of the patient.

With Mary riding the mule once more they began to climb the path leading to the heights upon which stood the city of Magdala. As he walked along beside the animal, past the aqueduct bringing water from the fountain higher up along the steep black cliffs that formed the mountainside here, Joseph was counting in his mind the number of coins he had saved in the earthenware jar at home. The contents of the purse hanging from his belt today would make a fine clinking as they dropped into the jar. And with a few more patients as liberal in their gratitude as Pontius Pilate had been, he might get to Alexandria sooner than he expected.

Mary of Magdala seemed lost in the beauty of the lake, which looked like a clear green jewel in its cup surrounded by mountains, with the snowy white peak of Mount Hermon gleaming like marble in the distance.

Against the steeply rising sides of the mountains at the end of the lake, beyond the Cities of the Plain and the beautiful Plain of Gennesaret itself, lay a ribbon of rock-paved road that ran between Egypt to the south and Damascus and Babylonia to the north and east. Joseph had once ridden as far as the ford, called the Bridge of Jacob's Daughters, crossing the swift waters of the Jordan where it plunged downward to the lake far below. Occasionally he had been called to treat the sick in the cities of Bethsaida and Capernaum along the northern shore of the lake, but in general he shunned them, as did many devout Jews, for they were turbulent places where many had turned away from the ancient customs to the newer and looser habits favored by the Greeks and Romans. It was a common saying in Jerusalem that "no good ever came out of Nazareth," which lay southward and westward toward the seacoast, but there was equal reason to say the same of Capernaum.

Mary's voice broke into his thoughts. "Who was the Roman that caught me when I fell, Joseph?"

"I thought you knew. It was Gaius Flaccus, nephew of Pontius Pilate."

"He is very handsome."

"And very evil," Joseph said sharply. "I hear bad things about him."

14

"How do you know they are true?"

"I have been in the palace of Pontius Pilate many times," Joseph boasted.

"Is it true that the Procurator has slave girls from the East who dance naked before him?" she asked breathlessly.

Joseph blushed. "A young girl should not say or even think such things," he scolded, shocked at her boldness. "Is it not written, *'Let her own works praise her in the gates'*?"

"I am eighteen," Mary said spiritedly. "I do as I please."

"You will get into trouble. Remember the law of Moses, *'Honor thy father and thy mother, that thy days may be long upon the land which the Lord thy God giveth thee'!*"

A strange look came into the girl's face, and her lips tightened until the lovely softness of her mouth was a grim line. "Do not speak to me of fathers and mothers, Joseph," she said sharply, "if you would be my friend." Then her entire manner changed in one of those mercurial transformations which he had first witnessed back there in the street in Tiberias. "And don't be so self-righteous, either. You can't be much over twenty-one or twenty-two years old yourself. If you don't watch you will be old without ever knowing what it is to be young." And she drew her mouth down in such a typical imitation of a disapproving old man that Joseph could not help but laugh. It was in such a mood that they entered Magdala.

4

Joseph had been curious to see where Mary lived and, if possible, the man she admitted to living with, but he was disappointed. At the very edge of the city she slid down from the mule and thanked him very sweetly for his help, but refused his offer to take her home. He stood watching her as she moved gracefully down the Street of the Dove Sellers, looking small and fragile, but somehow confident and self-possessed at the same time. Only when she was out of sight did he turn his mule toward the house of his patient.

The streets were thronged with travelers from both north and south seeking shelter for the night at the many inns the city afforded. To the north the Via Maris passed near Capernaum, a brawling little town where a traveler might easily lose his purse and have his head broken into the bargain. And to the east, where the Roman road passed through the Valley of the Doves, the narrow defile was pocked with caves harboring not only the birds that were trapped there daily for the temple sellers in Jerusalem, but thieves and robbers as well, waiting for a luckless traveler to be caught by darkness on the road. Wayfarers from both directions usually stayed in Magdala rather than be caught outside the city at night, and the travelers had to vie for the right of way with the dove trappers, who made up one of the main businesses of the city, returning to their homes in the evening, their mules piled with cages of cooing birds.

Eleazar, the seller of cloth, was in pain. "You are late, leech," he grumbled. "What kept you?"

Joseph busied himself in removing his leeches from the bottle, separating the lean ones from the fat ones, whose hunger had been satiated. "I was attending a girl who fainted on the streets of Tiberias," he explained. "A dancer."

"Mary of Magdala!" The merchant's wife fairly spat the words from the shadows where she was watching everything with grim-lipped intensity.

"Do you know her?" Joseph bent to pick up a leech he had dropped at her explosive outburst.

"Who in all Magdala does not know Mary of Magdala for a shameless hussy?" The woman's voice was shrill with the indignation of the completely righteous—in their own minds.

"Now, Rachel," the merchant protested. "You do not know that what you say is true."

"She is guilty of *abodah zarah!*" All Magdala talks of it!" *Abodah zarah*, one of the three deadly sins of the Jews, was literally translated as the taking up of heathenism. By devout Jews it could be applied to anyone living according to the ways of the Greeks and Romans, who were "heathens" in their eyes. Joseph could understand how the term would be applied by the uncharitable to

Mary of Magdala. He himself could even be accused of *abodah zarah* because he attended the "heathen" university at Tiberias, where Greek philosophers and scientists taught what a devout Jew would consider heresy.

Preoccupied by what Eleazar's wife had said about Mary, Joseph was not so deft as usual in handling the swollen knee. "By the prophets," the merchant squealed. "Must you treat my leg as a stick, to be broken across your knee?" And from the background his wife shrilled, "Most likely he has been bewitched. He is not the first to lose his senses over Mary of Magdala and the cursed demons that possess her."

In truth it did seem to Joseph as he lay trying to sleep that he must be bewitched. Or, he thought, one of the demons said to possess the girl might have escaped from her body into his. Whatever the cause, he could not get her out of his mind, and even in his dreams he kept hearing her voice and seeing her body spinning like a living torch in the dance. But just when he was going to take her in his arms, she was snatched away by a Greek named Demetrius, wearing the uniform of a Roman Tribune.

In the morning Joseph decided to go to the house of Demetrius himself and see what was the relationship between Mary of Magdala and the maker of lyres, even if he had to pretend interest in buying one of the instruments for which he had no possible use. He was spared the pain of pretending, however, for, oddly enough, one of the Nabatean musicians came while he was at the morning meal, with the request that he wait upon Demetrius in the Street of the Greeks.

While the messenger waited outside, Joseph bustled about, dipping a fresh supply of lean and slender leeches from the tank where he kept them, and renewing his supply of medicine. When he stopped to brush his robe carefully and comb his short beard, his mother asked curiously, "What has happened, Joseph? Why are you preening so?"

"I go to the house of a Greek named Demetrius."

"You did not make such a fuss as this when you were first called to the Procurator himself. Is there a girl at this house?"

Joseph's blush confirmed his mother's suspicions. "Who is it?" she asked slyly. "And how soon can I expect the visit of the marriage broker?"

The question brought Joseph up short. He could not

consider marriage before he realized his cherished dream of completing his studies at Alexandria, even if he thought of Mary of Magdala in that way. Which, he quickly assured himself, he did not.

"You are doing very well indeed for an apprentice physician," his mother continued with pretended innocence. "Just yesterday Alexander Lysimachus assured me that already you know more about healing than most of the physicians of Galilee."

Joseph easily understood her strategy. If he became interested in a girl he might give up the wild idea of going to Alexandria. So he did not doubt that his mother would welcome the visit of the marriage broker, if it meant that he would settle here in Galilee, or even Jerusalem. "Why should I want a wife when you take such good care of me?" he said fondly as he kissed her on the forehead. And gathering up his leeches, he was out of the door before she could question him further.

The home of the maker of lyres was fairly large, although not pretentious. Most of the Greeks on this street were artisans, silversmiths, or tailors, and lived well, but the sounds that poured from the house of Demetrius were foreign to such staid occupations. From the back came the uncertain plinking of a lyre, as if a student were practicing, and behind the musical sounds was the steady obbligato of hammers tapping on wood as workmen put together resonant frames and sounding boards upon which strings were stretched.

Mary was nowhere to be seen when the Nabatean escorted Joseph through the house into the garden. It was enclosed on three sides by the inner walls of the house, while the fourth side was the edge of a cliff. And since the roof of the house next below it on the hillside was well beneath the level of the shelf forming the garden, one had a sudden impression of stepping out upon a stage suspended between the blue of the sky and the amethyst green of the lake far below. It was easy to believe that Mary of Magdala lived here, for the flowers were gay and riotous with color, like herself.

"Come over here, young man." The speaker was a plump Greek about sixty years of age, sitting on a bench close to the edge of the cliff. He held a large cithara which he had apparently been tuning, for a delicately carved set of ivory pipes lay on the bench beside him. The Greek's eyes were deep-set in his round face and lit with intelligence and amusement, as if the owner saw only merriment in the world. Joseph felt an instinctive liking for the fat man, in spite of his soiled robe and the aromatic smell of wine that he exuded. "I was told that Demetrius wished to see me," he said politely.

"I am Demetrius."

"But Mary said she lived with——" Joseph stopped and crimsoned with embarrassment.

"Is there anything wrong in her living with me?" Demetrius asked.

"Of course not," Joseph said. "I am a fool."

"No more than almost anyone would have been under the circumstances," the Greek said equably. "When a beautiful girl says she lives with a man, you naturally think the worst, being human. Look at me, young man. Do I look like a debaucher of the young?" Demetrius suddenly began to guffaw, holding his vast belly as if he were afraid it might come apart with its shaking. Finally he stopped laughing and wiped his streaming eyes with his sleeve. "Alas," he added with mock sadness, "even if I longed for feminine solace, who would love a fat old man for anything but his money, of which I have next to none, anyway?"

"I did not mean that there was anything wrong in her living with you," Joseph assured him sincerely.

"Of course you didn't. But you must have heard other people insinuate things about her that are not true. Women envy Mary her beauty because men's eyes are drawn to her in the street. And the men, realizing how pale and insipid their own wives are beside her, label her *meretrix* so they will not feel so guilty about lusting after her."

"You are a philosopher," Joseph exclaimed admiringly.

"Nay. I am but a winebibber who has known many people, most of them bad. Because I acknowledge no God who would forbid me, I do as I please, but I harm no one except myself, which is my privilege. Since I like to see people happy and gay, I let Mary sing and dance that others may share her beauty and her talent. But to you Jews that is *shefikat damim.*" He sighed. "If you try to please everyone, you please no one. But sit down here beside me, young man. Mary has gone to Capernaum to sell some lyres for me and bring back a fish for our dinner from the stall of Simon and the sons of Zebedee. What do you think of the spell she had yesterday?"

19

"I do not believe it is the Sacred Disease," Joseph said promptly.

"Nor I. You have studied Hippocrates, I see."

"All of his writings that I could obtain, sir," Joseph said eagerly. "And those of Marcus Terentius Varro and Lucretius Carus too."

Demetrius lifted his eyebrows. "Your thirst for knowledge is worthy of the old Greeks, young man. There is a man in Rome, a friend of mine named Aulus Cornelius Celsus, from whom you could learn much, although he is a *philiatros*, a friend of physicians, rather than a physician. But getting back to Mary. What do you really think of these fits of hers?"

"I have seen them in some young girls before," Joseph said. "My preceptor, Alexander Lysimachus, believes they are possessed by a demon for only a short while, but I doubt if that is the answer. Most of them grow out of it with womanhood."

"Did she say anything yesterday when she was in the fit?"

"Only the babblings of a child. She seemed to be remembering a scene where someone was beating her."

"I was hoping she had forgotten all that," Demetrius sighed. "I took Mary when she was twelve years old, Joseph. Her father was a trapper of doves and a petty thief. He had beaten her many times and was on the point of selling her to a Roman, but I gave him a higher price. I adopted her legally and taught her all I know of music, philosophy, and the arts. Now the lyre is not so popular and I have been working to improve the cithara, so we have not fared very well. Mary loves to sing and dance, and since people will pay to hear her, I let her perform sometimes in the streets."

"Is it safe?"

"The Nabateans are always there. And Hadja would give his life for her."

"You trained her well," Joseph said. "I never heard a more lovely voice, nor saw a more graceful dancer."

Demetrius nodded. "Few can equal her, although she is still little more than a child. As a dancer and singer in the great cities of the Empire I am sure she could turn the heads of kings if she wished. But I place her happiness above everything else and so I hesitate to take her away from Magdala. . . . What would you do, Joseph?" he asked suddenly.

Joseph's first thought was that cities were wicked and sinful. Therefore Mary would be better off away from them, perhaps married to a good and serious young man, instead, who would love her for her beauty and charm and provide for her wants and make her happy. Such a man, he thought with quickening pulse, as a young and successful physician. But his own ambition had sensed a kindred spirit within Mary of Magdala, the same determination for success in the world of music and the theater that he felt for knowledge in the field of medicine.

"One of the proverbs of my people says, *'As a man thinketh in his heart, so is he,'*" he told the Greek. "I doubt if Mary will be truly happy until she has done the things upon which her heart is set."

"You have a wise head upon such young shoulders," Demetrius said approvingly. "I have been trying to avoid the same conclusion for many months. But since we have no money for traveling, we must stay here, for the time being at least." He picked up the cithara from the bench beside him. "Listen closely to the tones of this instrument." When he touched the strings, the air throbbed with a melody as soft as old linen.

Joseph recognized the touch of a master, even though the fingers of the lyre maker were pudgy and short. Mary had learned her lessons well, he thought, for she, too, possessed the same loving touch upon the strings. "I am not a musician," he confessed. "But the tones have a fullness and a resonance I never heard before."

"Exactly. And do you know why?"

"No. I know nothing of music."

"Plato warned against trying to separate the soul from the body," Demetrius told him. "Music is food for the soul, and when the soul is healthy, so usually is the body."

"I have noticed how grief and sadness can bring on sickness," Joseph admitted. "Some believe that the same demons—"

"Demons! Bah!" Demetrius spat eloquently into the grass at his feet. "The demons that possess man are born within himself, children of his own desires. Me, I drink too much wine when I can get it, which isn't often. And I eat too much when I can afford it, which is practically never. But I am happy, and so this blubber-fat body of mind runs as smoothly as a water clock. Can you say as much?"

Joseph smiled and shook his head. "Do you think I

should put down the *izmel*, as we Jews call the scalpel, for the lyre and the trumpet?"

"You might do as much good," Demetrius acknowledged. "But we were speaking of citharas." He plucked the strings again and a profusion of melody filled the garden. "The answer to the rich tone of this instrument lies in the body," he explained. "See how beautifully arched the sounding boards are, and the workmanship in these thin pieces forming the sides of the sound chest. The stupid musicians of Rome think of nothing save the size of the instrument and the loudness of the noise it makes. They even have citharas as large as carriages—that probably sound like carriage wheels, too." He laid down the instrument. "But I weary you with this talk of music. It is one of the penalties of growing old. Soon I shall be like Aristoxenus of Taras, who said, some three or four hundred years ago, '*Since the theaters have become completely barbarized, and since music has become utterly ruined and vulgar—we, being but a few, will recall to our minds, sitting by ourselves, what music used to be.*'

"We who look to the past are not always out of step with the present, though," Demetrius continued his lecture. "It was this same Aristoxenus who gave us our knowledge of harmony." He plucked a string, stopped its vibration by thrusting his fingers between the strings, then plucked another exactly an octave lower. "Listen well, young man. The answer to the mystery of the universe may well lie in the vibrations of these strands of lowly gut. . . ."

There was a commotion in the street outside and Mary ran in, plucking the shawl from her head so that her hair tumbled in a glorious torrent of living copper about her shoulders. In her excitement she did not see Joseph. "Demetrius!" she cried. "I brought Simon; he has been hurt."

Several people followed Mary into the garden. The tall musician, Hadja, was supporting a veritable giant of a man in the garb of a fisherman, whose occupation would have been betrayed, anyway, by the strong odor that accompanied him. The big man's face was white and he carried his right arm in a rude sling. Behind them was another man, slender and dark-haired, also in the garb of a fisherman.

When Joseph ran to hold Simon's arm while they eased him down on the bench beside Demetrius, Mary saw him for the first time. "I just came from your house, Joseph," she cried in astonishment. "Your mother said you would not be back until evening."

"I sent for him," Demetrius explained, "to thank him for bringing you safely home last night."

Mary tossed her head. "I am not a child any longer. I could have come home by myself." Then she smiled. "But it was nice of you, Joseph, and I did enjoy the ride on the mule."

"What was the disturbance about this time, Simon?" Demetrius asked. "You Galileans are always first in the fighting. And I suppose John, the son of Zebedee, here, was in it too."

"Some Greeks were arguing that the Jews will not rule the world when the Messiah comes," Simon explained. "We broke a few heads, but one of them had a club. You are the only sensible Greek I ever saw, Demetrius."

"Because I know better than to argue with you, my friend," the lyre maker said complacently. "Not sit still and let Joseph examine this arm of yours."

5

THE young physician knelt beside the injured man and gently felt his upper arm, where the trouble seemed to be. Simon flinched even from the light pressure of skilled fingers upon the arm, but not before Joseph had detected a slight grating of splintered bones rubbing against each other. "Can you make it whole?" Simon asked anxiously. "A fisherman has need of strong arms." The fishing establishment of Zebedee and his sons at Capernaum was a large one, and well known along the entire populous shore of the lake. Simon, Joseph thought, must be associated with them, for he seemed to be more than simply a fisherman.

" 'Healing comes from the Most High!' " Joseph said quietly. "I will do my best to set the bone straight, but the rest is in the hands of the Lord."

"Simon is a very good man," Mary said confidently. "The Lord is sure to favor him."

From his pouch Joseph measured out a dose of dried poppy leaves and mixed them in wine. Simon drank the mixture with a grimace. While he waited for the drug to take effect, Joseph began to prepare his bandages. Mary was sent to tear long strips of cloth from a winding sheet, while he trimmed short sections of the thin wood used to make the sounding boards of the musical instruments for splints. Water was also set to boiling in a pot over a brazier, and into it Joseph stirred flour to make a thick starch paste.

Demetrius watched the preparations with interest, and when Joseph sent for a chair with a high back and placed on top of it a folded napkin, the old musician could contain his curiosity no longer. "Why do you need the chair, Joseph?" he asked.

"The bar at the top will fix the shoulder and upper arm," Joseph explained as he seated Simon sideways on the chair, with his injured arm hanging over the back and the pad under the armpit. "Then a pull can be applied to the lower arm with weights while the bones are set properly and bandaged into place."

"And the flour?"

"Bandages moistened in starch harden when they dry, helping to hold the broken fragments in place and protecting the arm from further injury."

"By Diana!" the lyre maker exclaimed. "That is ingenious. Did you invent it?"

"You should study the medicine of the Greeks as well as their music," Joseph reminded him with a smile. "Hippocrates and other physicians were using methods like this nearly five hundred years ago. No doubt you remember what Idomeneus said to Nestor in the Homeric poems?"

"You may hoist me on my own spear, young man," Demetrius said triumphantly. "But that at least I know." He declaimed sonorously:

> *"A surgeon's skill our wounds to heal,*
> *Is worth more than armies to the Public weal."*

The poppy had exerted its effect by now, hastened by the wine in which Joseph had mixed it, and the lines of

24

pain were almost gone from Simon's face. He only winced a little as Joseph carefully removed the sling and showed Mary how to hold the lower arm so that the elbow was bent at an exact right angle. Next he wrapped a scarf around the elbow and arm, leaving the ends long, and attached to them a small pot from the kitchen. This was allowed to hang with its weight pulling upon the lower portion of the arm, and therefore upon the end of the broken bone.

Into the pot Joseph next poured sand slowly, increasing the weight very gradually. From time to time as the pull increased, he touched the upper arm gently in the region of the fracture, feeling with the sensitive fingers of the bonesetter for the positions of the broken ends. When finally he could detect no overriding of the fragments—the pull of the muscles being now overcome by the weight of the kettle and the sand—he gently pushed and adjusted the broken parts until they were in line with each other. To the amazement of the onlookers, Simon suffered next to no pain during this manipulation, for the steady pull on the arm kept the bones apart and in line with each other, so that no jagged ends cut into the flesh.

Now Joseph began to apply the bandage which must do the important job of holding the bone in place until it could heal. First the upper arm was wrapped in soft wool, and over it strips of thin wood were placed parallel to the bone as splints. Over this he wrapped turn after turn of the moist starched bandage, laying each one on carefully so that it was not twisted, rolled, or folded. At the shoulder he carried several turns around Simon's body and beneath the opposite armpit to hold the bandage in place, before continuing around the elbow and down the arm as far as the wrist. Thus the entire elbow joint was covered except the lowermost portion, where the ends of the scarf were attached to the small kettle furnishing the weight.

When it was finished, Demetrius waddled over and touched the white case. "By Diana!" he cried. "It stiffens already. To be able to relieve suffering like this is better than either philosophy or music, Joseph. I am properly humbled."

But it was John, the son of Zebedee, who gave the young physician a real accolade for his work when he said quietly, "It was well said by Jesus, the son of Sirach:

"Show the physician due honor, in view of your
    need for him,
His works will never end,
    And from him peace spreads over the face of the
    earth."

6

JOSEPH stopped at the doorway leading into the garden
of Demetrius when he came the next morning to visit his
patient, unwilling to interrupt the beautiful and peaceful
scene before him by making his presence known. Simon
was sitting on a bench overlooking the smooth mirror of
the lake below, where the boats of the fishermen with
their multicolored sails were already abroad. Mary sat on
the grass at his feet, with the morning sunlight turning
her unbound hair into a coppery cascade. She touched the
lyre in her hands with skilled fingers, and her voice filled
the garden with a paean of praise from the poet who had
loved this beautiful region around the lake, a part of the
Song of Songs!

"The voice of my beloved! behold, he cometh,
    Leaping upon the mountains, skipping upon the
    hills.
My beloved is like a roe or a young hart:
Behold, he standeth behind our wall,
He looketh in at the windows,
He showeth himself through the lattice.
My beloved spoke, and said unto me,
'Rise up, my love, my fair one, and come away.
For, lo, the winter is past,
The rain is over and gone;
The flowers appear on the earth;
The time of the singing of birds is come,
And the voice of the turtle is heard in our land;
The fig tree ripeneth her green figs,
And the vines are in blossom,
They give forth their fragrance.

Arise, my love, my fair one, and come away.
O my dove, that art in the clefts of the rock, in the
*   covert of the steep place,*
Let me see thy countenance, let me hear thy voice;
For sweet is thy voice, and thy countenance is
*   comely!' "*

"Beautiful!" Joseph cried from the doorway, unable to remain silent.

Mary jumped to her feet. "Joseph of Galilee," she cried indignantly. "What do you mean creeping up on us?"

"The song was too beautiful to interrupt," Joseph explained.

"The leech is right, Mary." Simon smiled fondly at her. "It was a lucky day when I found you weeping on the streets of Capernaum."

The girl's face sobered. "But mainly for me." She shivered a little, although it was not cold. "I was only twelve years old, Joseph, but already I had known what it was to be beaten without reason and to be stripped naked for men to set a price upon me. Simon was the first person who had ever been kind to me in my whole life," she added fiercely. "Do you wonder that I love him and Demetrius better than anyone else in the world?"

Joseph bent to examine Simon's arm. The bandage, he found, had dried into a stiff case that held the arm firmly, and the swelling had already subsided noticeably.

"Truly," the fisherman said, "if anyone had told me yesterday there would be so little pain today, I would have branded him a liar. It is well written in the Book of Ecclesiasticus, *'If you are taken ill, offer prayers to God and place yourself under the care of a physician.' "*

"Not all physicians would have treated you so well as Joseph did," Mary interposed. "Most people say he is better than his master, Alexander Lysimachus."

"How do you know so much?" Joseph asked with a smile.

"I go everywhere and keep my eyes open." Mary tossed her head. "Besides, men have no secrets from a woman."

"So you call yourself a woman now." Demetrius had come into the garden while they were talking. "Soon you will be eying young men and then there will be no more singing in the house of Demetrius."

Mary ran to him and put her smooth cheek against his grizzled one. "You know I would never leave you," she cried, and Joseph was amazed to see tears in her eyes, so quickly had her volatile emotions changed.

Demetrius squeezed her shoulder. "I was only jesting," he soothed. "Someday you will marry a rich man who will make old Demetrius the keeper of his wine cellar. Then I can die happy." He turned to Joseph. "The Street of the Greeks is buzzing with the miracle you performed upon Simon's arm, young man. Soon the whole town will know of it, if Mary has her way."

"I was just telling him that he is better than Alexander Lysimachus," Mary said. "But he is too modest to admit it.".

Joseph could stay no longer, but as he went about the city visiting the sick, his thoughts were full of Mary's gaiety, her beauty, and the way her mood could change from happy to sad and back again in an instant, like a child. He had seen no signs of prosperity in the house of Demetrius, but he had found there something more important, a quality often lacking in the homes of the rich where he went with his leeches, the happiness of people who loved unreservedly.

When Joseph arrived home that evening he was greeted by the fragrant aroma of a fish broiling on the coals of the cooking hearth. And when he came into the kitchen he saw that his mother was not alone. Mary was sitting on a low stool, watching the preparations for the evening meal and chattering all the while.

"Welcome to our home, Mary of Magdala." He gave the formal greeting. "Peace be upon you."

Mary's eyes twinkled. "I am part Greek and bear a gift. Do you not fear me?"

Joseph knew her too well now to be surprised at her learning. *"Timeo Danaos et dona ferentes,* I fear the Greeks when bearing gifts," he repeated, smiling. "No, I do not fear you."

"Look at the fine fish Mary brought us," his mother said proudly. "I have persuaded her to stay and help eat it."

"Will you dance for us afterward?" Joseph asked.

Mary held up her hands in mock horror. "Do you want your neighbors to say you are entertaining a Jezebel? Besides, does not Hippocrates warn that a physician must always be careful of his dignity?"

"If I remember the aphorism right," Joseph told her, "it was this: *'The dignity of a physician requires that he should look healthy and as plump as nature intended him to be; for the common crowd consider those who are not of this excellent bodily condition to be unable to take care of others.'* "

While his mother prepared dinner Joseph took Mary to the small surgery where he treated the poor of the city. It was little more than a covered terrace with a closet for his medicines and instruments. Magdala was not large enough to support a *medicamentarius*, as an apothecary was called who compounded and dispensed medicines only upon the order of a physician, so Joseph gathered most of his own herbs and ground his own medicines, plus those of his preceptor. Fortunately the hills of nearby Gilead were famous for healing plants, and the balm produced there was widely used by physicians everywhere.

Mary listened with intelligent interest while Joseph demonstrated the instruments and their uses. The bag he carried on his rounds was called the *nartik*. It contained the *izmel*, or scalpel, for incising abscesses; the trephine, a nail for letting blood; the *makdeijach*, a sharp pointed probe with which to explore wound tracks and other areas; the *misporayim*, a pair of scissors for cutting dressings or the sutures of horsehair sometimes used to close wounds; the *tarrad*, a speculum for exploring cavities; and the *kalbo*, a pair of forceps which had many uses.

On another shelf was the *kulcha*, for emptying the stomach in poisonings and for those suffering from overeating; the *gubtha*, a hollow catheter for cases of urinary stone or obstruction; and the *shel harophe*, the leather apron which was almost the uniform of the Jewish physician. In the corner stood the *kisei tani*, an iron box serving both as a desk table and as a place of safekeeping for precious medicines.

In the closet that served as a pharmacy and treatment room were the drugs: *borit*, a strong soap for washing inflamed skin, as well as the hands of the physician; *neter*, which was both a cleansing agent externally and a powerful kidney stimulant when taken internally; *tsri*, the healing balsam; *nehoth*, the gum of tragacanth; and *lott*, a powerful sedative made from opium. Next to them were various ointments labeled *unguentia: collyria* for washing infected eyes; and *pilulae* of various drugs, rolled into pellets of several sizes.

Below these another shelf was filled with jars of powdered poppy leaves for promoting sleep and relieving pain; the seeds of the *jusquiamus;* the *diachylon* plaster favored by Menecrates, personal physician to the Emperor Tiberius; the drug called "dragon's blood," because it was said to come from the blood of a dragon killed in combat with an elephant (although actually only the gum from an oriental plant); the preparation called *mithridaticum,* a favorite of the Emperor Pompey, and many others. At the end of the shelf was a pile of odd-looking roots. Joseph picked up one and handed it to Mary.

"Why, it looks like a man," she exclaimed. "See? Here are the arms, and the legs, and body. What is it?"

"The root is called 'mandragora.' Some people claim that it is actually human and shrieks when pulled from the ground." Joseph took down a bottle filled with dark fluid. "This is the wine of mandragora, made by soaking the powdered root in wine to extract the active drug. Some call it 'lovers' drink.' "

"Why?"

"They say because it strengthens love. Or maybe it got the name because disappointed lovers have been known to use it to bring on the sleep of forgetfulness. But the wine of mandragora is mainly used for relieving pain during surgery and in nervous afflictions."

"When the drug is used to bring on sleep," she asked, "do they ever wake up again?"

"Not always, but a very large dose is required to cause death."

Mary shivered. "You said mandragora was used for nervous afflictions. I only faint when I am excited. Would it help to prevent the attacks?"

"It should," Joseph agreed at once. "Let me give you a small bottle of mandragora wine to take home tonight. You can try a few doses when you are going to dance. It might keep off the attacks altogether."

The fish was perfectly cooked and the meal was gay, for Mary was as intelligent and witty as she was beautiful. Much of the time Joseph forgot to eat for looking at her. Afterward he walked with her across the city to the Street of the Greeks. "I love your mother, Joseph," she told him as they stood before her house. "And you are very sweet too." She stood on tiptoe and kissed him on the cheek, then was gone.

Joseph's mother did not miss the warm light in his eyes when he returned, still a little dazed by that feathery kiss.

"Mary is very beautiful, Joseph," she observed. "And her father was a Jew. Even if she was adopted by a Greek, she was brought up in the religion of our people."

"Why does it make any difference whether she is Jew or Greek?" he asked, but his mother changed the subject.

"She told me about the miracle you performed in healing Simon the fisherman."

"I only set the arm. The Most High must still heal it."

"But without your setting, the Most High would have let it heal crookedly," she observed with unanswerable logic. "The fish came from the establishment of Zebedee, so Mary has important friends. He is the richest fish merchant on the lake."

Joseph was beginning to get the import of this rambling conversation. "But she sings and dances in the streets," he reminded her with mock disapproval.

"Did not David the King, whose blood flows in your veins, sing and dance in honor of the Most High?" she demanded heatedly.

"Some call her a Jezebel and accuse her of *abodah zarah.*"

"Some women envy all girls with beauty and speak evil of them," his mother said with a sniff. "Mary has spirit and would make a fine wife for a bright young man. She likes you, Joseph; you should court her."

"There will be plenty of time yet to speak of marriage," he said more soberly then. "Today Alexander Lysimachus promised to take me in two months before the judges at Jerusalem. He thinks I am ready to be certified as *rophe uman.*"

"Aie!" his mother cried in delight. "My son will be a 'skilled physician.'" The title was conferred by duly appointed judges only upon those apprentices who had finished the prescribed period and were certified by their preceptors as able to practice in their own right. "Now you can forget all that foolishness about going to Alexandria," she added.

Joseph did not argue the point. He knew he had learned everything that Alexander Lysimachus could teach him and was probably as skilled as any physician in Judea or Galilee, perhaps in all of the province of Syria itself. But his studies in the works of the Greek philosophers and physicians had served to show him how small actually was the knowledge of even such eminent physicians among the Jews as his preceptor. The great

31

Hippocrates, Diocles of Carystus, the famous Alexandrians, Herophilus and Erasistratus—all had gone beyond the simple concepts of disease as a punishment from God, or the effects of possession by demons. And Asclepiades of Bithynia had even dared to state categorically that, since the body was composed of disconnected atoms in constant movement, health was dependent upon the orderly movement of these minute particles, while disease resulted from a standstill of the atoms, or violent clashes between them. His principle of *contrario contrariis* in treatment had earned him the favor of kings. More than once in his own experience, too, Joseph had felt that the derisive advice of *"Medice, cura te ipsum* [Physician, heal thyself]," was more truth than criticism.

Simon, the fisherman, improved so rapidly that soon Joseph could find no excuse to hold him in Magdala. As he left the house one morning, having promised that Simon could return to Capernaum following tomorrow's dressing, Mary came out carrying a lyre. "I am delivering this to the Street of the Dove Sellers," she said. "May I walk with you?"

He made way for her beside him, with the mule carrying his equipment following them. "I shall be sorry to see Simon leave tomorrow," he told her. "For then I shall have no excuse to visit the house of Demetrius."

"But you can come to see us whenever you wish."

"If I come without being called, people will say I am paying court to you."

"No one has ever paid court to me, Joseph," she said softly, and then her voice grew bitter. "The young men are afraid because their mothers call me Jezebel. Why is it a sin to want to be happy?" she demanded fiercely.

"My mother does not think you are a Jezebel."

"I know." She put her hand on his, and her fingers were warm and very much alive as they curled about his own. "She is sweet like you, Joseph, and I love her."

"I am going before the judges in about two months to become *rophe uman,*" he told her.

"Joseph!" she cried, her eyes shining. "That is wonderful!" Then her face grew sad. "But you will go to Jerusalem then; Magdala will be too small for you."

"My mother thinks I should marry and start practicing medicine for myself. She has already picked out the girl."

Mary did not look at him, but he saw her lips soften in a smile.

"She is a very lovely girl named Mary of Magdala," he added.

"Don't you have anything to say about the matter?" she asked demurely, her eyes twinkling.

They were crossing a little park and at the moment were screened from view by a clump of trees. Joseph pulled her around to face him. "You know I love you very much, Mary," he said.

"As much as Philodemus loved Xantho in the song?"

"That much and more," he said quickly.

"'Too soon the music ends,'" she sang softly, her eyes shining. "'Again, again reflect the sad sweet strain.' But you don't know me at all, Joseph. I am vain and forgetful."

"And very beautiful . . ."

"Greedy and thoughtless . . ."

"And lovable . . ."

She stamped her foot in mock anger. "Will you let me finish? I am telling you that I am not the kind of a wife you deserve. I would embarrass you, and people would talk about me."

"What would all that matter when we loved each other?" He drew her close. "Is it because you don't love me that you argue against me, Mary?"

"Oh, I do love you, Joseph," she said then, all in a rush. "I do. I do. But I love Demetrius, too, and he comes first."

"Demetrius himself told me he thought you might be happier married to the right man."

"He was only trying to protect me." Suddenly she clung to him and he held her there, asking nothing more, content to savor the sweetness of having her in his arms When she lifted her face from his breast, he kissed her and found the sweetness of her mouth mixed with the salt of her tears. Finally she pushed him away and wiped her eyes upon the sleeve of his robe. "We must be sensible, Joseph," she said firmly. "I can't possibly marry you. Not for a long time."

"But why?"

"It's a long story, but you deserve to hear it. Years ago Demetrius was the director of the Alexandrian Theater and the most famous musician in the Empire. He loved a girl named Althea and trained her to be the leading actress there. She was his mistress and he adored her, so he could not believe she would be untrue to him. But she took up with a rich Roman and tried to get rid of Demetrius by telling her lover that he was the leader in a plot against the Romans. Demetrius barely escaped with his life and a little money by joining a caravan going to Damascus, but some thieves robbed him in Capernaum and left him for dead in the lake. Simon found him and nursed him back to health. Since he had no money, Demetrius set up a shop for making lyres here in Magdala, but he lives only to return to Alexandria."

"Would it be safe for him to go back?"

"Yes. Althea's lover was really plotting to make himself ruler of the city, and both of them were executed, but it was too late to help Demetrius. From what Simon tells me, he was about to kill himself when I came to him. Since then I have been his whole life. He taught me everything I know, Joseph, and he lives only for the time when he can make me the most famous actress and dancer in Alexandria. It will be his revenge upon Althea."

"But Demetrius loves you enough to want your happiness, Mary."

"Don't you see?" she pleaded. "I have to do this for Demetrius, but I want it too. Kings have deserted queens for women of the theater. What girl wouldn't long to be as important as a queen?"

"But suppose you are not an instant success," he objected. "How would all of you live in Alexandria?"

"Demetrius says I am more talented than Althea was and that I will only need to sing and dance before the director of the theater to be accepted immediately." Remembering the living flame of her body when he had seen her dancing in the street at Tiberias, Joseph could understand the confidence of the lyre maker.

"This new cithara Demetrius has made is far superior to the old ones," Mary continued. "It is bound to be in great demand in a city the size of Alexandria, where there are so many musicians. We can live on what he makes from selling the cithara if we have to, but I would sing and dance in the streets to make him happy. No one but me can ever realize how much I owe him, Joseph."

Loving her as he did, Joseph could not find it in his heart to try to dissuade her. Having important plans of his own, he understood the inner fire of ambition that burned within her. "How much longer before you to go to Alexandria?" he asked.

Mary laughed and was herself again, gay and eager. "Who can tell? We have barely enough to eat now. But that day when I danced in Tiberias, the crowd threw more coins than I would earn in a week in Magdala or Capernaum, or even as far as Bethsaida."

"I wish you wouldn't go back to Tiberias, Mary," he said quickly.

"You go there yourself nearly every day," she protested. "If it doesn't make you unclean, why should it me?"

"I'm not talking about uncleanness. You are a beautiful girl, and you saw the way the Procurator's nephew, Gaius Flaccus, looked at you."

"Men look at me every day. Do you think I can't read what is in their eyes?" She wrinkled her nose at him. "The Tribune was a very handsome man and free with his gold. He gave Hadja twenty denarii."

"But you know how these Romans are. A young girl is not safe—"

"Joseph!" she cried delightedly. "You're jealous!"

"Of course I'm jealous," he admitted. "Didn't I just finish telling you I love you and want to marry you? But just the same, the Romans are evil and not to be trusted."

Her face sobered. "I know all about Romans; my father was going to sell me to one of them. But they pay well and we need their gold. Besides, I never dance without Hadja and his men, and any one of them could kill a man with his bare hands. Don't worry, Joseph. I will be safe even in Tiberias."

7

MARY was in the garden overlooking the lake a few days later when the messenger from the Procurator was ushered in. She had been learning a new song, and she put down the lyre as the visitor bowed before her. He was tall and imposing in appearance, but when she looked closer she saw that his ears were slit, showing that he was a slave.

"I am the *nomenclator* of Pontius Pilate, Procurator of Judea," the man said loftily. "Where is she who is called Mary of Magdala?"

Mary's heart jumped. "I am Mary of Magdala," she said. What could Pontius Pilate possibly want with her? she wondered.

"The Procurator bids you attend a supper to be given at his villa in Tiberias this very evening, to sing and dance for his guests."

"Are you sure he wants me?" she asked incredulously.

"Quite sure. He has heard of your dancing in the streets of Tiberias."

The thrill of being summoned to the Procurator's palace swept from her mind all memory of Joseph's warning a few days ago and the unsavory things she had heard about the orgies held in the Roman villas at Tiberias. She thought only that here was a chance to earn some of the money, perhaps a large part of it, that Demetrius needed to take them to Alexandria.

"Will you come?" the slave asked politely, although his manner said it was unthinkable that a Jew should refuse the summons of the Roman governor of Judea.

Mary had recovered her poise now. "You may tell your master that I shall be honored to dance before him and his guests this evening," she said with considerable dignity. "My musicians and I will be there at dusk."

The *nomenclator's* eyebrows rose. "The governor has his own musicians."

Now Mary remembered Joseph's warning. "I dance to no music save that played by my own troupe," she said firmly. "They accompany me wherever I go."

The slave shrugged. "Bring them then. Perhaps Gai— the Procurator forgot to mention them."

Mary did not notice the slip. She was too busy wondering whether to ask about money now or wait until after she had danced. As the slave was turning away she said quickly, "Could you tell me what my pay will be?"

"Entertainers do not ordinarily demand pay for pleasing the Procurator," the *nomenclator* explained. "It is enough to say they received a summons to appear before him." But seeing the disappointment in her face, he added kindly, "It is customary, however, to throw a purse to those he likes."

"A purse? How large?"

"No sum is set. A thousand sesterces, perhaps, if you prove particularly agreeable to him."

"A thousand sesterces!" Mary gasped, but quickly recovered her composure. "Of course I shall be honored to dance for your master, whatever the purse," she said graciously.

The *nomenclator* bowed again, as if he were enjoying this little farce. "Can you direct me to the house of the leech, Joseph of Galilee, here in Magdala?" he asked.

"What has Joseph done?" Mary asked quickly.

"The Procurator's lady would have the services of the leech at once."

Quickly Mary gave the necessary directions to Joseph's home. "If you see him," she added, "please don't tell him I am dancing tonight." She blushed. "I have a reason for the request."

When the slave was gone, Mary rushed to the room where Demetrius was bedded with a cold, solaced no little by a bottle of wine she had brought from Capernaum that morning. "Demetrius!" she cried excitedly. "Demetrius! The most wonderful thing has happened!"

"Simon has sent more fish," he groaned. "I am beginning to look like one."

Mary laughed and threw her arms about his neck. "Better than that. Would a thousand sesterces take us to Alexandria?"

Demetrius was accustomed to her rich imagination and her outbursts of enthusiasm. "A thousand sesterces might take us halfway—if we had them."

"Oh, but we do have them! Or we will, after tonight."

"Is King Herod bringing us his coffers?"

"Something even better. I am to dance for the Procurator, Pontius Pilate."

"For the Procurator!" Demetrius sat up in bed, clutching the wine bottle. "Where did you get this crazy idea, child?"

"It is not crazy!" She stamped her foot. "Pilate's *nomenclator* was here just now and bade me dance at a dinner tonight. And he mentioned a purse of a thousand sesterces if I entertain the Procurator and his guests well."

"A thousand sesterces!" Demetrius fell back on the couch. "I have not seen so much money since I came to Galilee. Let me see: two hundred will buy a mule stout enough to bear this besotted carcass of mine along the

Via Maris to Joppa. And another three hundred for baggage mules to carry our furnishings and the citharas to be sold in Alexandria. We could sell the animals at the seaport to pay our passage by ship."

"Then it would take us?"

He shook his head. "Not quite. But if Pilate likes you, others of the rich Romans and Syrians who have villas at Tiberias will want you to dance, perhaps even Herod Antipas himself. And it will not hurt to say you danced for the Procurator of Judea when we see the director of the theater at Alexandria." Then his face grew serious. "But is it safe for you to go to Tiberias?"

"You and Joseph are old women!" Mary cried in disgust. "I am not a child any longer, Demetrius. And besides, Hadja and the others will be there to guard me." She dropped to her knees beside the couch, and tears came into her eyes. "You must let me go, darling," she pleaded. "It will mean so much to us all."

"We do need the money badly," Demetrius admitted, smoothing the rich waves of her hair with his pudgy fingers. "But promise me that you will keep Hadja and his men with you always."

"I promise." Mary leaped to her feet. "Now what will I wear? I know, the white stola of silk you gave me for my eighteenth birthday. And the palla over it, the yellow one. I was saving them to wear in Alexandria. And Hadja must rent a cart and a mule for me to ride in, so I will not be too tired to dance well. And my hair! Oh, I have a thousand things to do." She was gone in a flurry of skirts.

It was just dusk when Mary and her party arrived at the villa of Pontius Pilate in Tiberias and tied the mule and cart to a tree in the grove outside the villa. Mary carried the package containing her silken stola and the yellow palla, plus fragile sandals of leather chased with a thin tracery of gold. A wall nearly ten feet high surrounded the elaborate, if small, palace. Most of the villas at Tiberias had such high walls running down into the water itself.

The Roman governor of Judea spent much of the time here in Galilee by the protected waters of the lake, where the winter climate was mild, rather than at his castle on the coast at Caesarea, which was buffeted by cold winds and storms from the Mediterranean, the Mare Nostrum of the Romans. It was common knowledge that Pilate's wife, the Lady Claudia Procula, suffered badly from asthma in Caesarea but was much better in the warmer climate of Tiberias and the Sea of Galilee.

An armed guard let them through the gate, and the *nomenclator* met them in the atrium, as the central room of the house was called. Even in the darkness they could see something of the beauty of the terraced gardens descending the hillside to the water's edge and the fragrance of flowers was everywhere. Slaves in white garments moved about through the open terraces, carrying dishes to and from the triclinium, the banqueting room, where the dinner was already in progress.

The *nomenclator* raised his eyebrows at Mary's rough dress. "Is that your costume for dancing?" he asked, then a knowing smile came over his face. This girl was smart indeed, he thought, in choosing to dance naked before the revelers. Her slim loveliness would be a welcome change from the more opulent charms of the girls who usually entertained Pontius Pilate and his guests.

Mary held up the package she carried. She had not seen his smirk, or she would have been angered by it. "I have my dress here for dancing," she explained. "Is there somewhere that I can change?"

"The entertainers dress for the performance in a room off the banqueting hall," the slave explained. "I will take you to it and show your musicians to the alcove where they will play." Through heavily curtained doorways on one side of the hall along which he took them came the sound of voices and laughter, the soft strains of the lyre and cithara, and the clink of glassware and cutlery. This was obviously the triclinium, and Mary judged that the doors across the corridor gave access to bedchambers.

The room to which she was ushered was small but tastefully arranged, with a door to one side giving access to the triclinium. An elaborate dressing table occupied one wall, complete with perfume and cosmetics, antimony to whiten the cheeks, kohl for the eyelashes, henna for toes and fingernails, and everything that a beauty would use in her boudoir. In an open recess hung a rack of costumes, some of them so diaphanous that they seemed not to exist at all. She had heard rumors that women danced in such costumes at the banquets of the Romans, while some were said to wear nothing at all. Now her startled eyes were seeing very real evidence that the tales were true.

Mary had not admitted to Demetrius or to herself that she felt any apprehension about dancing before Pilate and his guests. But now that she was alone, with the shouts of the drunken revelers coming from the next room, she could not swallow the lump that insisted upon rising in her throat.

Quickly, before her courage could desert her, she took off her dress and underclothes and hung them over a chair. In a sudden burst of exuberance she stretched her body luxuriously and whirled in a lithe dancing turn. Suddenly, though, she gave a little gasp and stooped quickly to hold her dress in front of her body. Only then did she realize that the lovely nude girl facing her on the other side of the room was her own reflection.

Timidly she crossed the room and touched the large mirror set into the wall, for she had never seen such a thing. Her whole body was reflected in it, the slender column of her head and neck, the lovely sloping lines of the shoulders merging with the taut fullness of small breasts, just now beginning to fill out with the promise of glorious womanhood, the sweet curve of a slender waist. No blemish showed anywhere in the perfect symmetry that faced her. Hers was the lithe grace of the huntress Diana, but ineffably feminine nevertheless, and as she loosened her hair and let it fall upon her shoulders, the whole white length of her body seemed to take fire from it and glow with a warmth of its own.

Reluctantly Mary turned from the adoration of her own beauty to open the package she had brought. She wished now that she owned a length of silken cloth to wrap about her loins for an undergarment, such as women were said to wear in Rome and the other rich cities of the empire. But silk was expensive and so she could only draw on the thin knit trunks worn by ordinary people, when they wore any undergarments at all. Over the trunks went a linen undershirt and then the silken stola, a sleeveless dress cut along classical lines and girt just beneath the breasts with a band of silver ribbon.

Some women wore broad girdles of woven metal mesh, or fine leather chased with a filagree of gold or silver design, but Mary's slenderness needed no such disguise. The clinging fabric of the stola caressed her bosom lovingly and fell in straight silken folds from her waist to her ankles. Over the stola went the palla, a mantle usually worn out of doors, which she would drop as she poised to begin her dance.

There remained only to buckle on the light sandals, tying the thongs about her slender ankles, and she was ready. She scorned the cosmetics with which even young girls had begun to paint their faces, for her virginal loveliness needed no such artifice. Picking up an ivory brush from the table, she brushed her hair until it shone like molten copper. Next she tied over her hair a white silken shawl that she planned to wear while dancing.

Suddenly the door from the corridor opened and a girl came into the room. At the sight of Mary she stopped short and frowned, "Who are you?" she demanded abruptly.

The girl was older and her figure more generously curved, but it was her costume that startled Mary, for she wore a loose robe wrapped around her body with careless grace, cut from the same gossamer stuff Mary had seen hanging from the racks. Beneath this revealing garment the visitor seemed to be wearing only a small girdle of gold held in place by delicate chains of gold drawn about her hips.

"Are you deaf?" the newcomer demanded shortly. "Or don't you understand Greek?"

"You startled me," Mary said politely, finding her voice. "I am Mary of Magdala."

"The girl who is to dance tonight? The *nomenclator* told me there was a peasant girl here, but you are hardly what I expected." She came closer and touched the palla. "Why haven't you undressed? They will be calling for you as soon as I finish." Without waiting for an answer, she sat down at the dressing table, elbowing Mary unceremoniously aside.

"I am dressed already," Mary protested as the newcomer began to paint her lips with carmine from one of the jars, laying on the scarlet dye with a small brush.

"In that?" The other girl put down the brush. "They will laugh you out of the room. Or maybe not." She stood up and peremptorily untied the ribbon about Mary's waist. Skillfully she adjusted the narrow bands beneath the younger girl's breasts and tied the ends again. When Mary looked into the mirror she saw with startled eyes that the silken fabric now clung intimately to the upper half of her body, sharply accentuating the contrast between the slenderness of her waist and the budding fullness of her

41

bosom. Stooping, the other girl also set the folds of the stola artfully, creasing the fabric so that it fell in many tiny pleats from the waist in front, but clung snugly to the curves of her hips. "I was not one of the *vestiplica*—pleaters of togas, in case you do not know the Roman word—for nothing," she said with some pride. "That is much better."

"You must be a dancer too?" Mary said.

"I am a slave," the girl flung over her shoulder. "They call me Thetis."

"Do you dance in—in that, Thetis?"

The slave girl stood up and smoothed the transparent fabric over her hips. "For a while. When the men are drunk enough they like to snatch at your robe while you are dancing. Look here." She came closer so that Mary could see how the fabric was held at her shoulder and waist by tiny silver clips, fragile and easy to loosen. "One good pull and the clips open," she explained. "The garment unwinds without tearing. This bombyx is costly; it can be woven only by experts."

"And you dance naked? Before men?"

Thetis laughed. "Has no man seen you thus?"

"Never," Mary cried in horror. "Not even Demetrius, my foster father."

"Then you must be a virgin."

Rich color stained Mary's cheeks. "Of course! I am only eighteen."

Thetis laughed harshly. "I was sold as a slave at twelve, and I gave birth at fourteen. Listen, little one," she said earnestly. "This is an evil place. Go back to Magdala and marry some nice Jew and bear him beautiful children. Believe me, the Jews are the only decent people I ever met."

"But all Romans are not evil," Mary protested.

"All I ever knew," Thetis said matter-of-factly. "Wait until you know what it is to be pawed by a fat man stinking of wine. Like your King Herod Antipas." She threw up her head and listened. "That is my music." And adjusting the golden chains about her hips with a lithe movement, she opened the door to the triclinium and shot through it, her body already writhing in the sinuous movements of her dance. A sudden burst of sound greeted her, maudlin shouts, the crash of an overturned goblet, then the door swung shut, leaving the small room unnaturally silent.

Mary felt a sudden, almost overpowering urge to take herself away from this place as fast as she could go. Tales of Roman orgies, heard second- or third-hand, were only juicy bits of scandal. But now she was face to face with reality; in a few moments she must go into the next room and dance before shouting, drunken men. Only the thought of the thousand sesterces that had practically been promised her kept her from running away then. She could not deprive Demetrius, she reminded herself, of the things tonight's purse, and the others that would inevitably follow if she succeeded here would mean to him. But she could not and would not compete with naked slave girls in sensuality, she decided firmly. Her dance must stand or fall upon sheer beauty.

Mary went to the door leading to the triclinium and cracked it open cautiously until she could see into the room. Its size startled her; she had never seen a room for dining so large. At one end were the couches upon which the banqueters reclined, arranged around a table like the spokes of half a wheel. The other end of the room was cleared for the entertainment, and here Thetis was dancing to music played by musicians hidden in an alcove.

The triclinium itself was beautiful, the ceiling inlaid with colored marble, the walls painted with scenes of a bacchanalia at whose frankness Mary blushed and turned her eyes away. Five couches were arranged around the marble table, from which the food had been removed now, leaving only wine goblets. Two slender, feminine-looking boys moved about with wine jugs, filling the goblets as soon as they were empty. They were fair-skinned, evidently Greeks, with painted cheeks and mincing gaits.

The Procurator's nephew, Gaius Flaccus, lay on one of the couches. Beside him was a heavy man with a weak, sensuous face whom she judged to be Pontius Pilate. The three other guests were older, and all quite obviously drunker than the host. One, a fat man with little eyes, Mary recognized as Herod Antipas, Tetrarch of Galilee.

Gaius Flaccus, strangely enough, did not seem to be as drunk as the others. He was watching the dancer with bored eyes, occasionally sipping from the goblet in his hand. Once more Mary was struck by his beauty. Reclining there, he might have been Apollo descended from Mount Olympus to revel with the mortals. But there was something repulsive about him, too, she thought, or perhaps it was only a part of her natural revulsion at his companions, the scenes on the wall, and the painted Greek boys.

Thetis was dancing to the throbbing rhythm of the music, and as she spun on the marble floor the diaphanous stuff of her costume stood out from her body like the petals of a flower. Dipping and swaying in voluptuous rhythm, she moved closer to the banqueters, then as they laughed and eagerly clutched at her dress, she leaped gracefully away, teasing them deliberately again and again. Once she came close to Gaius Flaccus, darting away as he reached negligently for the spinning hem of her costume, then moving in closer again with what was, Mary thought, deliberate intention, as if she were flirting with him, daring him to seize the hem of her garment. He grinned impudently at her, but waited until she was almost touching his hands. Then with a quick movement like the striking of an adder, he seized the filmy cloth in his fist and jerked. As Thetis had explained to Mary, the clips came loose, but the force of the jerk tore the fabric too. When Thetis darted away in mock surprise, the bombyx unwound itself from her body. Halfway across the room she poised, fingers over her eyes in pretended embarrassment, her body unclothed except for the girdle about her loins.

A roar of laughter rose from the reclining men, and a spatter of applause. Then as the music changed to a slower measure, Thetis lowered her arms and began to dance once more. Now she scarcely moved her feet. The expressive movements of the dance were limited almost entirely to her torso and to her arms and hands. It was the oriental dance of love, a voluptuous poem of amorous adventure, graphically portrayed by the body and arms, both repulsive and yet fascinatingly beautiful in its picture of animal passion, the age-old story of courtship, conquest, and fertility. Such a dance the Queen of Sheba might have done before King Solomon, or a favorite concubine in the harem of an Eastern potentate. Watching it, Mary felt her own body begin to quiver, while her cheeks grew hot and her pulse throbbed to the rhythm of the music.

The drunken revelers were beating on the table as the dance rose to its inevitable climax. "The girdle! The girdle!" they shouted.

It was a hoarse roar of passion whose sheer animalness frightened Mary, tempting her to flee. Yet at the same

44

time she could not take her eyes from the scene. Her heart was throbbing like the drumhead being beaten in the alcove, thrusting blood into her face until she felt as if her cheeks would take fire.

"The girdle! The girdle!" The shouts grew more insistent as the writhing of Thetis' body progressed to its inevitable climax. Strings and pipes wailed a sensuous rhythm against the throbbing of the unseen drum. On a crash of sound, the dancer's hands flashed down across her hips and came away bearing the fragile girdle in her fingers. She poised for an instant, then tossed the golden bauble directly at Gaius Flaccus, who alone among the men seemed not to be sodden with wine.

The handsome Tribune was forced to dodge lest the golden shell strike him in the face. But he made no attempt to catch it, and it was Herod who scrambled on the floor and came up holding it triumphantly. "I have the girdle," he bellowed happily. "The girl is mine for tonight." Then Thetis turned and ran from the room.

Mary jumped back from the door to escape being bowled over as the angry slave girl stormed in. "You were looking," she cried, panting with anger and the effort of dancing, her eyes darting fire. "Did Gaius Flaccus try to catch the girdle?"

Mary shook her head. "It would have hit him if he had not moved."

"You!" The dancer turned suddenly to face Mary, feet apart and hands upon her full hips. "He refused me because of you." In her anger Mary thought the slave girl would strike her. "You with your clinging robes and your talk of being virgin."

"You are wrong!" Mary protested. "I came only to dance."

Before Thetis could continue her tirade, a crashing chord of music came from the triclinium. In it Mary recognized the tones of the great cithara played by Hadja as the introduction to her own dance. Now that the reality of entering the banquet hall was upon her she felt herself grow faint with fear and excitement and swayed momentarily, unable to force herself to enter the other room. Were it not for the wine of mandragora Joseph had given her, she knew that one of the fainting spells would be upon her. And right now she would have welcomed anything that freed her from the necessity of going on. Then

45

with a strong effort of will she forced herself to be calm and put her hand to the door.

"A thousand sesterces! A thousand sesterces!" The words rode to her upon the rhythm of the great cithara, calming her fears and giving her strength.

"I will do this for Demetrius," she told herself. "I must. I must." And proudly confident, she opened the door and stepped out on the marble floor of the banquet hall to face Pontius Pilate and his guests.

8

As Mary dropped the palla, one of the Romans laughed. Remembering what Thetis had said, she stiffened and flushed with anger, but as the music took hold of her body, she tossed her head defiantly and launched herself into the dance.

This was no dance of provocation to inflame the beast in men. With the subtle instinct of an artist, Mary had realized that she should not try to compete with the unsubtle posturing designed to stir up base emotions that formed the stock in trade of the professional dancing girls. Instead her body was a vibrant poem in praise of the beauty of the Galilean country.

Now she was the wind storming through the mountain defiles to roil the waters of the lake and send the fishermen scurrying for home, the roll of summer thunder, and the majestic flash of lightning heralding the storm. Again, she was the rain of Marheshvan, swelling the taut skins of the grapes and wetting the freshly tilled soil in preparation for the falling seed from the hand of the sower, greening the grass and adding new life to the olive trees and the rich harvest of fruits and melons on the Plain of Gennesaret.

Next the scene changed under the merry lilt of the pipes and the glad song of the strings, whose tones were better suited for such a mood than the stirring blasts of the trumpet. Her slender, fragile, and utterly lovely body in its silken draperies now began to tell the happiness of children playing on the rain-wet grass, reveling in its coolness after the shower, their feet almost taking wings with joy and abandonment in the caress of the sun, freed once more from the prison of the clouds. The listeners could both see and feel the things her body and the music were saying, and even in their drunkenness they could not but share some of the emotion she was portraying. Only Gaius Flaccus seemed bored, for he stirred restlessly upon his couch, as if anxious for the dance to end. Herod Antipas had raised himself upon his elbow, and was watching Mary intently, his eyes soft with some memory of his youth, while even Pontius Pilate lost for a while the look of bored disdain that seemed to be his usual expression.

Now, so softly that it could hardly be noticed, the mood of the dance changed again. The sun was setting over the lake, and in the benign protection of the shadows a boy and girl, lovers, were meeting. Shyly at first, then with increasing boldness as hand reached out to hand and heart to heart, they told each other the story of their love, portrayed in ineffable beauty through the movements of the slender form upon the dance floor. The beat of their pulses rose with their newly awakened awareness of each other; the elation of their spirits was in every graceful step, every breath-takingly lovely posture. Mary's head was thrown back and her lips were parted, her mouth tender and soft as she portrayed without words the story of young love, its reaching out, its fears, its sweet encouragement, its tenderness, and finally its gentle surrender as the boy drew the girl into his arms and found her eager lips waiting for his own. As softly as it had begun, the music ended on that first sweet kiss, and Mary stood, lost in the mood she had created, poised like a delicate flower nourished by love itself and newly burst into bloom.

A roar of applause broke spontaneously from the audience as she sank gracefully to the floor, bowing before the couch where the Procurator lay. From the folds of his robe, Pontius Pilate drew a small pouch and tossed it to the floor beside her. From its metallic clink, Mary was sure it was filled with coins, perhaps even more than the thousand sesterces for which she had dared to come and dance. With a swift, graceful movement she picked up the purse and, running gracefully to the back of the room where she could see the musicians in the alcove, tossed it to Hadja, who caught it expertly.

Now the Nabateans lifted their instruments again and Hadja struck his great cithara with a sweeping stroke that set every string to vibrating. It filled the room with a throbbing burst of sound, reverberating from the walls and setting the beat for the other instruments, as the cymbalist crashed his polished metal disks together and stamped the *scabella* upon the floor, adding their booming rhythm to the sudden rush of sound.

This was the music of the wild desert dance Mary had performed upon the streets of Tiberias, and with a quick movement she loosened the silken shawl that covered her hair. It poured down upon her shoulders in a cascade of molten beauty against the pallor of her skin and the pure white silk of her pleated stola. Poised there, she was indeed, as Hadja had named her, the "Living Flame," a pillar of fire to set a man's heart burning, and a paean of savage beauty that was somehow also as tender as a maiden's first stirring of love.

Then, her body swept up by the throbbing beat of the music, Mary began the whirling, stamping dance of the desert people, the wild nomads who rode on the swift winds of the sandstorms and bedded themselves under the palms wherever a patch of green marked an oasis in the broiling wasteland. The dance itself was too strenuous to last long; soon her movements were so swift that the befuddled eyes of the Romans could distinguish them no longer. At its end she poised for an instant to receive the plaudits of the diners, then disappeared through the door into the dressing room.

Panting, all aglow with the thrill of her triumph, Mary leaned against the door. Thetis had gone and the room was empty. Nor would she have had it otherwise, for this was a moment to be experienced alone, the heady thrill of triumph that comes to an actress after a superlative performance. Moving over to the tall mirror, she stood before it for a long moment, savoring again the beauty of her lithe body. Her hair was tossed every way from the strenuous movements of the dance, and seating herself at the dressing table, she began to comb it with a fine ivory comb she found there.

Intent upon what she was doing, Mary did not realize that the door into the hall had opened, until her startled eyes saw reflected in the mirror the handsome face and tall form of Gaius Flaccus.

"Do not be afraid, little one." The Tribune smiled re-

48

assuringly. "I only came to tell you how well you danced and to bring you this." He held out another leather purse, also swollen with coins. Without taking her eyes off him, Mary took the purse and thrust it into the pocket of her dress hanging over a chair.

Gaius Flaccus pulled up a cushioned hassock and sat at her feet. "Your dancing was truly beautiful," he said.

"You are very kind." Her smile was wary.

"I mean it," he protested. "You made Thetis look like a cow."

"Thetis is very pretty. Mary's eyes twinkled. "She was angry when you did not catch her girdle."

Gaius Flaccus shrugged. "Who would look at her when he could see real beauty? Thetis has a fine body, but no soul. You have both, and therefore are perfection in itself." Then he smiled. "Enough of compliments. You must be hungry."

In the excitement of getting ready to come to Tiberias, Mary had forgotten all about eating. Now she realized that she was ravenous, but the thought of going into the room with the drunken Romans repelled her, and she drew back from the door.

Gaius Flaccus saw the involuntary movement. "Not in there," he assured her. "I have ordered a table set for you in a room close by."

"But my musicians. They will be ready to return to Magdala."

"They are eating now. I told them you would have supper here."

Mary hesitated, but there seemed no harm in staying for a few minutes, and she was very hungry.

"Are you still afraid of me?" Gaius asked with a smile. "I am not an ogre who eats up little girls."

She could not help laughing at the incongruity of comparing so handsome a man with an ogre, and took the hand he held out to her. "I must hurry, though," she insisted. "Demetrius will be worried until I return."

"The two purses you bear will allay his fears. Besides, you have four bodyguards, and big ones, too. They grow strong men in the desert."

Her fears were silly, Mary told herself as Gaius Flaccus guided her along the corridor. And it was thrilling to be waited upon by such a handsome man. Nor could she prevent a quickening of her pulses at the feel of his strong hand upon her arm and the touch of his silk-clad body against hers in the narrow space of the corridor. How Joseph would glower, she thought mischievously, when she told him tomorrow of her experiences in the palace of the Procurator.

The room into which Gaius Flaccus ushered her was not large, but it was luxuriously furnished. Heavy draperies hung at the windows and were pulled shut to keep out the night air so rightly feared in Herod's unhealthy city by Romans and Galileans alike. A broad, soft-cushioned couch half filled the room, and through the open door of a large closet Mary could see rows of the rich purple and white uniforms affected by the wealthy officers of the Roman Army.

"Is this your bedchamber?" she cried in sudden alarm.

"Yes, but you need not be afraid," he assured her. "See, your supper is already here." He took a burning taper from a bracket on the wall and went about the room lighting other candles, until the chamber was ablaze with light. "There," he said, smiling. "That should assure you of my good intentions."

Mary lifted the silver cover of one of the dishes arranged upon a low table and sniffed the delightful aroma. "It smells good," she admitted reluctantly.

"Go ahead and eat," Gaius Flaccus urged. "If I had worked as hard as you did tonight, I would be starved."

Mary hesitated no longer. Everything was here that a young girl would like, including many viands she had heard of but had never tasted before. On one plate was the *antecena* or *gustus,* strips of salted and smoked fish, tender radishes on tiny center leaves of succulent lettuce, and other dainties to stir the appetite. While she ate, Gaius Flaccus poured into a slender crystal goblet a mixture of mild wine and honey called *mulsum.*

Next was a large plate containing the *cena,* the main part of the meal. Tender slices of roasted and spiced beef were garnished with the rich and savory vegetables that grew on the fertile Plain of Gennesaret. Mary refused wine from a second flask, for her head was already light from the sweet *mulsum.* But she could not withstand the pastry studded with nuts making up the last part of the meal, the *mensa secunda,* as the Romans called it.

While she ate, Gaius Flaccus sat on a cushion at her feet, lifting the covers from dishes as she sampled them, and pushing them aside when she was finished. Finally, when she could eat no more, Mary wiped her mouth and fingers upon a napkin of linen finer than any she had ever seen before and took a deep breath of sheer content. Perhaps it was the wine or the heady effect of his admiration that made her feel dizzy. It didn't occur to her then that there might be another, a more dangerous, cause.

"Did you like your dinner?" Gaius Flaccus asked.

"Oh yes. It was wonderful."

"And have I offended you at all?"

She smiled. "Of course not, but I must go now. Demetrius will be wondering where I am."

He took her hands and pulled her to her feet. She was quite close to him, closer, she knew, than she should be. But a sense of exhilaration, a feeling of adventure, kept her from drawing away. As he smiled down at her, his broad chest touched her body and she felt the softness of her flesh give way against him. Her breath seemed to stop in her throat then, and she felt an almost uncontrollable impulse to press herself against him. "I—I must go," she stammered, but she could not draw away.

"Don't I deserve at least a kiss as a reward?" He held her hands still in his. "After all, I did help you get to dance before the Procurator. Both Pontius and Herod were enchanted with you, and their favor can mean much."

Deep inside she had known all along that Gaius Flaccus had persuaded Pilate to send for her to dance tonight. It was a part of the thrill of adventure, even of danger, that characterized the evening. Besides, the purse he had brought, plus the one she had tossed to Hadja, comprised more money than had been in the house of Demetrius for many years. And being generous by nature, Mary could not very well help feeling a warm glow of appreciation toward the handsome young man who had made these things possible. After all, she told herself to quiet her pounding heart, there could be no harm in giving him the kiss when, she was honest enough to admit to herself, she wanted him to kiss her.

Gaius Flaccus saw that she was tempted to yield and drew her gently to him. But when she would have given him her soft cheek, he claimed her mouth roughly and his arms tightened about her. Mary had seen passion in the eyes of men when she danced, but she had never been so close to it as this. Startled by the shock of Gaius Flaccus' mouth upon hers, his hands upon her body through the thin silk of her dress, and above all by the surging response of her own body to the purely animal lure of the Roman's embrace, she was paralyzed for a moment.

It was a strange new feeling, this pounding of blood in her temples and throat, this constriction in her chest that came only partially from the powerful arm holding her so tightly, this sudden whirling of her senses that was more than the effect of wine. And without realizing what she was doing, her arms crept around his neck and tightened, while her mouth softened and grew lax beneath his with the ready rush of ardor that throbbed within her.

Gaius Flaccus had planned with cunning, but now the surge of desire set off by her momentary yielding swept away all his restraint. Mary, herself, fighting against the stronge urge to yield and knowing that she must not, did not realize what was happening at first. Then, whatever response had been momentarily aroused by his ardor was swept away in a surge of revulsion and fear.

Forcibly she broke away from the demanding caress of his mouth and pushed herself clear momentarily of his embrace, but the man who held her now was not the same one who had waited upon her so gallantly while she ate. His face, so handsome a moment before, was swollen and distorted by lust, and his eyes were wild and bloodshot, like one suddenly demented.

While she struggled in a sudden rush of terror to break away from him Mary screamed again and again, but the thick hangings of the room dulled the sound. Her strength was failing fast and now she realized, in a rush of utter terror, why she had been a little dizzy. The effects of the wine of mandragora she had taken before leaving home had worn off. What she felt now was the aura preceding a fainting spell.

Mary could only resist feebly when she felt Gaius Flaccus lift her in his arms, for the strange paralysis that accompanied the fainting spells was already upon her. She could no longer move her limbs, and when she tried again to scream no sound came, for her senses had already begun to lose contact with reality.

Mercifully Mary of Magdala became unconscious.

JOSEPH was away when the *nomenclator* of Pontius Pilate called to request that he visit the Lady Claudia Procula. It was late in the afternoon before his mother found him at the house of Eleazar and gave him the message, and darkness had already fallen by the time he tied his mule to a tree outside the villa of the Procurator. As he was removing the *nartik* containing his instruments, medicines, and leeches from the mule's back, he noticed another mule and cart tied nearby but paid them little attention, for he was concerned lest the Procurator be angered by the slowness of his favorite leech in answering the summons.

The boudoir to which Joseph was admitted was small and exquisite, as was its owner. Pilate's wife was like one of the delicate figurines from the countries beyond the Eastern sea that were sometimes seen in the markets of Tiberias. Every line of her lovely features showed breeding, for she carried the blood of the Julio-Claudian line of Roman emperors. But there was also a warmth and understanding in her eyes which had not always characterized the often hated line. When Joseph saw that she was not angry at him for the delay, he drew a sigh of relief.

"I was treating the sick and did not get the message of the Procurator until an hour ago," he explained.

Claudia Procula smiled. "I should apologize for making you come to Tiberias after nightfall. I know how devout Jews feel about the city."

"The *chazan* of my synagogue might not understand," Joseph admitted. "But I am sure the welfare of the sick comes above the niceties of the law."

Procula looked at him keenly. It was unusual for a Jew to let anything come between him and his beloved law. This serious-mannered young leech was certainly well above the average of the Jews with whom she had come in contact, she decided. The breeding of a pure bloodline showed plainly in his clean-cut features.

"The trouble is here, with my left arm." She lifted a filmy sleeve and exposed an angry red swelling in the upper part of her arm. Joseph recognized the nature of the trouble at once, for such conditions were not at all uncommon in his experience. An insect bite, a small pimple, then in a few days a painful swelling and fever that lingered for days, unless it ended by rupture of the tense red skin and expulsion of the poisons which had somehow set up such a violent reaction in the flesh.

"Can you do anything to relieve the pain?" Procula asked hesitantly.

Joseph ran his fingers gently over the swelling. As he had suspected from looking at it, the skin was fluctuant, betraying the poisonous suppuration dammed back beneath it. "Hippocrates once said, *'Those diseases which medicines do not cure, iron* [the knife] *cures,'* " he told her.

"The knife!" she gasped. "But there will be a scar."

"Not as much as if it ruptures and drains by itself. And it will get well much more quickly if I incise it."

"Do it then," she urged. "And quickly. I have not slept for two nights."

"You will sleep tonight," Joseph promised as he opened his instrument case.

Testing his scalpel with his thumb, Joseph found it still of the razor-like sharpness that only the fine steel of Damascus could hold, for he honed it each morning before leaving his house. From the *nartik* he also took a pad of washed wool and spread out a clean towel beneath the inflamed arm. Then he nodded to Procula that he was ready. She set her teeth firmly in a soft red lip, and he plunged the blade quickly through the shiny red skin. Her gasp was more at the gush of bloodstained purulent matter that burst from the tense abscess than from pain, for the thinned-out skin had little feeling in it. Before Joseph withdrew the scalpel, he slit the skin well across the top of the swelling, laying it wide open so that it would not be sealed off again before all the poisonous material could drain out.

"Was that so bad?" he asked as he bound a pad of washed wool expertly over the wound.

"Oh no. I never thought anything could bring relief so quickly."

"If you will have your maid bring a little wine," he suggested, "I will mix you a sleeping draught. Then you can be sure of a good night's rest."

Claudia Procula ordered the wine. "And bring a tray for the physician, too, Letha," she added. "I'll wager you hurried to Tiberias without eating."

Joseph admitted that he had, and while he waited for the draught to take effect, he devoted himself to the excellent food. Under Claudia Procula's kindly questioning he found himself telling her of his ambitions to study medicine at Alexandria and return to Judea to bring enlightened medical knowledge to his people.

"I can remember when I was your age," she said with a sigh. "My dreams seemed easy to fulfill then."

"But the Procurator's lady could want for nothing," Joseph protested. "It is no secret that all who know her love her."

"You cannot know what it is to long for Rome and the things a woman who spent most of her life there yearns for, Joseph. Besides, the climate in Caesarea makes it difficult for me to breathe. Tiberias is better for me, but I am not free of it even here."

Joseph's interest was aroused at once. "Do you have the same trouble in the mountains?"

"Not as much. Once we took a trip into the desert and I was free of it altogether, but the Procurator of Judea cannot live in the desert. Sometimes I can hardly get my breath at all."

Joseph had seen many such cases. Some burned aromatic leaves and inhaled the smoke; others threw precious and fragrant oils, such as myrrh and spikenard, into boiling water and breathed in the vapor. There was no known cure for this sometimes fatal disease, and yet people sometimes became better for no reason at all.

Procula's maid went to get a purse for Joseph, and while he was repacking the *nartik,* a child's wail came from the adjoining room. He had heard of this child of Pontius Pilate who was never seen by the people, rumor said because it was deformed, but he had never known any real evidence before that the rumors were true. Now he sensed that there was indeed some mystery here, as rumor maintained, for a look of fear came into Claudia Procula's eyes. Before she could speak the door opened and Pontius Pilate came in. He did not see Joseph before he asked, "Has the leech come, dear?" Then he saw the bandage. "Oh, I see that he has. Does it feel better?"

She managed to smile. "Much better. Joseph is still here; he was just going."

Pilate turned and saw the young physician. "You took long enough getting here," he said sharply.

"I was treating the sick," Joseph explained. "As soon as your message reached me, I came at once."

The cry of the child came from the other room again, and the Procurator seemed to freeze in his tracks. Watching his face, Joseph saw a look of defeat, almost of despair, come into it and realized that there was some tragedy here, perhaps something that might hold a key to the behavior of this strange, moody man who ruled Judea for Rome. Pilate's gaze turned to Joseph. "Men have died for knowing less than you have just learned," he said slowly.

"No, Pontius," Procula cried. "Joseph is a good man. . . ."

"Tell me," Pilate snapped. "What do they say in Jerusalem and Galilee of Pontius Pilate? Are there stories that he has a child who is a monster?"

"I do not listen to idle talk," Joseph said quietly. "Life comes from the Most High; I do not question how He gives it."

Pilate stared at him for a long moment. "Perhaps you are right," he said heavily. "Come and see for yourself."

The adjoining room was fitted out as a nursery, and a small boy lay asleep on a bed in the corner enclosed by a low frame. He seemed to be about three years of age, and his face was beautiful, a miniature of his mother's with her delicate features and light-colored hair. Pilate's hand was gentle, as he drew away the light quilt covering the child's body, but Joseph saw at once why the Procurator felt so bitter about his son. The boy's right foot was deformed, the toes drawn until they pointed almost straight downward, a typical case of clubfoot. "You have some reputation as a bonesetter," Pilate said. "Can you make such a foot straight?"

Reluctantly Joseph shook his head. "I am told shoes can be made with a thick sole, however," he suggested, "so that such children can be taught to walk."

"The son of a soldier," Pilate burst out. "My little Pila! Hopping like a common beggar." His fingers clenched and unclenched. "Is this God of yours able to heal such

56

a thing as this?" He seized Joseph by the robe and shook him. "You are a Jew. Tell me, is he?"

" 'The Lord is merciful and gracious . . . as the heaven is high above the earth, so great is His mercy toward them that fear Him,' " Joseph stammered.

Pilate dropped his hands. Turning back to the crib, he took the quilt and drew it up again, hiding the piteously deformed foot. Joseph saw that his hands were tender and that he loved the beautiful child in spite of his bitter disappointment. "I fear no gods," the Procurator said slowly. "Because there are none to fear. Truth is the only God of man. But what is truth? Has this so-called Jehovah of yours the answer, Joseph?"

"It is said of the Most High," Joseph told him, " 'He is the Rock, His work is perfect: for all His ways are judgment: a God of truth and without iniquity, just and right is He.' "

Pilate shrugged. "Truth lies within man's soul, not in the gods he worships. I know the Jews say this thing was done to me because I crucified some of them who broke the laws of Rome." His voice rose in anger. "But I spurn them, just as I spurn your priests who plot to drive me from Judea and make Antipas king in my stead. I will show them yet who rules in Judea."

"My lord," Procula said softly. "Joseph has a long way to go. He has given me a sleeping draught."

"Of course, my dear," the Procurator said quickly. "We will leave you now." He took the purse the maid had brought and gave it to Joseph. "But see that you tell no one of what you have seen tonight, leech. I am generous with those who serve me well, but whoever betrays me dies."

" 'Whatever I see or hear in the life of men which ought not to be spoken abroad, I will not divulge,' " Joseph said slowly, " 'as reckoning that all such should be kept secret.' "

"The oath of Hippocrates." Pilate nodded. "See that you keep it then. You will profit by doing so."

Joseph's heart was light as he untied his mule in the grove outside the villa. He had been well paid indeed for tonight's work and, more important, Pilate had promised his favor in return for keeping the secret of the child called Pila and its deformed foot. The history of Pontius Pilate's term as Procurator in Judea had shown that his favor could be valuable, just as his anger could

57

bring sudden death and the agony of crucifixion, the favorite method of execution with the Romans. But Joseph had no intention of angering the moody Procurator. With such lavish patients as Pilate and his wife, he might have money enough to go to Alexandria much sooner than he had expected.

Seeing the other mule and the cart still tied to a tree as he led his own animal from the grove, he wondered again who might be visiting the villa of the Procurator in such a mean conveyance at this hour, but gave it little thought.

Then as he rode through the grove that surrounded the villa, a strange sound came to his ears. It was an odd noise, as if a man were groaning in pain. While he listened, it came again, apparently from the bushes beside the road.

Getting down from his mule, Joseph searched until he found a broken branch as long as he could span with his arms and, gripping it in both hands, approached the spot from which the groans had come.

Thieves often lay in wait for the late traveler along these roads, he knew, and a favorite stratagem was to pretend to be injured, luring the sympathetic wayfarer within reach of a long knife or a sword. It might have been wiser not to stop at all, considering the value of the purse he was carrying, but Joseph never passed by one who needed help without investigating.

Soon he made out a white form lying in the ditch. It stirred and a man's voice implored, "In the name of Ahura-Mazda, help me or I die."

The voice seemed familiar, and when he came closer Joseph recognized the swarthy face with its hawklike profile and graying beard and the white robes stained now with mud. It was Hadja, leader of the musicians who played for Mary of Magdala. The Nabatean appeared to be semiconscious.

Quickly Joseph knelt and ran his fingers over Hadja's skull, noting with relief there was no depression of the bone. A cut over the injured man's temple showed that he had been bludgeoned, a serious injury indeed if the bone were driven down upon the brain. The blood was still wet, although sticky, so it could not have been very long since he was wounded. The pulse, Joseph noted, was slow and strong, so he judged that no mortal wound was involved.

From his belt Joseph took a small flask of wine that he carried for emergencies such as this. The Nabatean swallowed automatically when the flask touched his lips, then gulped the wine down when he realized what was being offered him. "What happened to you, Hadja?" Joseph asked.

"Is it the leech, Joseph of Galilee?"

"Yes."

"Praise be to Ahura-Mazda! She whom you love is prisoner in the villa."

"Mary?" Joseph cried. "But how?"

Hadja told him then of the summons to the villa, of Mary's dancing before the Procurator and his guests, and of her great success. "Afterward," he continued, "we were told by the Tribune that the Living Flame was dining there and we were to wait, but they served us food and led us from the palace under guard."

Gaius Flaccus! This could be the work of no other. The stories he had heard about the libertine habits of the Procurator's nephew went racing through Joseph's brain. "Why did you leave her?" he demanded angrily.

"Two soldiers with drawn swords walked beside each of us. I tried to break away, but one of them struck me down with the butt of his sword."

There was no point in blaming the Nabatean. Only by the rarest sort of luck had the soldier used the butt of the sword instead of the blade, leaving Hadja alive. Joseph forced aside, too, the burning rage against Gaius Flaccus that rose within him, for he must think clearly now. It had not been long since Hadja was struck down; there might still be time to save Mary if he could somehow gain entrance to the palace. But since the high walls precluded any entry by that route, there was only one way, through the gate by which he had just emerged. The guard might remember that he had just left the villa and let him in.

"I am going inside to get her," he told Hadja.

"They will kill you." The musician stumbled to his feet, but swayed and was forced to catch hold of a sapling to keep from falling. He could only curse fluently, calling down the wrath of the supreme sungod Ahura himself upon all Romans and upon the Tribune Gaius Flaccus in particular. "I am but a blind man who must be led," he mourned. "Take this knife, Joseph. You may be able to slip it between the ribs of a Roman."

Joseph took the long weapon gratefully and thrust it under his robe. When he approached the gate, the guard stopped him with his sword. "What now, leech?" he demanded. "Were you not well paid? I remember a purse hanging from your belt."

"I left some of my medicines in the apartment of the Lady Procula," Joseph said, adding a silent prayer that the Most High would forgive him the lie. "Her maid knows me, so it will not be necessary to disturb anyone else. The medicine is very valuable."

The guard shrugged. "If it is worth so much, you will not mind handing over one of the gold coins from that fat purse she gave you to someone less fortunate."

Joseph would gladly have given the whole purse, if necessary, to gain access to the building without being observed. "See that you hurry," the guard growled, pocketing the bribe. "I will get the lash if it is known that I admitted you again."

Two corridors opened from the atrium, which for the moment was empty. One, Joseph knew, led to the apartments of Procula and Pilate, for he had just come that way, so he chose the other. He heard music and, cracking open a door, found himself looking into a triclinium. The course of the evening's revelry had taken its inevitable turn. Pontius Pilate and a fat Roman were declaiming in each other's faces, their golden wreaths askew. On the other couches Herod Antipas and another guest were embracing a pair of slave girls. Mary was nowhere to be seen, but one couch was ominously empty and Gaius Flaccus was absent, confirming his worst fears.

Closing the door to the triclinium, Joseph hurried along the corridor until he was stopped by a closed door, which he opened. The room was empty, but a woman's dress that he recognized as Mary's was hanging over a chair. Throwing the dress over his arm, he started out into the corridor, but, hearing the creak of another door, drew back just in time.

While Joseph watched, Gaius Flaccus emerged from one of the rooms, staggered across the atrium and out of sight. Quickly now Joseph opened the door through which the Tribune had emerged and stepped inside. A glance told him it was the Roman's bedchamber, for his sword and insignia lay on a chair. Then his eyes moved to the bed and he recoiled in horror, for a single glance revealed what had happened here. Mary was still unconscious, but the marble pallor of her skin, the signs of struggle in the room, the pitiful tatters of her clothing in a pile on the floor where Gaius Flaccus had dropped them could only mean that she had been ravished forcibly, in spite of her struggles to defend herself.

Eyes averted, Joseph covered Mary's body with the dress he carried over his arm. A quick examination showed that she was not seriously injured, although great dark spots already showed upon her tender skin. He knew that he must act rapidly, for the Tribune might return at any moment, but first he ripped a heavy drapery from one of the windows and wrapped it about Mary's body to protect her against the chill of the night if they were lucky enough to escape from the villa. All the while his thoughts were racing as he tried to decide what to do.

Going over the walls was out of the question—they were much too high—nor could he leave the way he had come, carrying an unconscious woman in his arms. One avenue only remained then, the lake. He had no way of knowing how deep the water was at the end of the wall where it entered the lake, but he must try to wade around the end of it. And if it was too deep he must swim, bearing the unconscious girl in his arms.

His decision made, Joseph lifted Mary from the couch. Then, carrying her in his arms, he stepped through upon the close-cropped green lawn outside. Next he worked his way slowly against the wall of the villa in the protecting shadows, until he came to the corner. The way seemed clear now and, moving quickly, he darted across the open space to the protection of the ten-foot wall that marched down into the lake itself. No outcry had arisen yet to show that he had been discovered, so he crept along beside the wall, steadying himself against it until his feet splashed in the water and a chill shot through his ankles.

The water was icy, fed by the rushing torrent of the Jordan, which swelled to a flood during the spring months from the melted snows of Mount Hermon and the ranges to the north. The chill of it threatened to paralyze him as he waded deeper, pressing his body against the wall on his left side so as not to leave it in the darkness, in case he stepped off into a deeper spot and needed something to cling to.

Wading was difficult, for he had to hold Mary high enough so that she would not get soaked by the icy water, an accident that might bring on unwanted complications with her body shocked and exhausted as it was. The water reached his waist, then his armpits. A few more steps and he must swim. Then suddenly there was no more wall against his left side, and with a thrill of exultation he knew that he had reached the end. Turning sharply to the left around the end of the wall, Joseph felt the bottom begin to shelve up as he waded ashore on the outside. A few yards more and he was out of the water, staggering up the shore toward the path where he had left Hadja, with Mary's unconscious body in his arms.

While Joseph was gone the Nabatean had recovered enough to bring the mule and cart in which they had come from Magdala down to the path beside Joseph's mule. Mary still showed no sign of consciousness when they carried her up the shelving beach and placed her on the rough floor boards of the cart, but although both were staggering from near exhaustion, they wasted no time in leaving the villa, knowing that the alarm might be given at any moment.

As they pushed along the path, Joseph explained to Hadja only that Mary had suffered one of her fainting spells and that he had found her in a room in the palace. Hardly half a mile beyond the villa, the road branched. The fork to the left ascended the hills past the great aqueduct bringing water to Tiberias and went on to Magdala, which overlooked the lake from a considerable height. The road on the right, however, followed the shore line to Capernaum and on to Bethsaida and the northern towns around the lake. They were turning into the left fork leading to Magdala, when Hadja said suddenly, "Wait, Joseph! I hear something behind us."

Joseph stopped at once. For a moment he heard nothing except the lap of the waves on the shore close by and the wind in the trees. Then faintly he detected the sound which had first reached the keen ears of the desert man, the sharp ring of metal on metal. Such a sound could have many causes, but only one was likely tonight, the ring of a sword on a shield.

Hurriedly they worked the cart and animals off the road and out of sight among the trees. The terrain was rough, but a fringe of trees grew just back of the shore line, so they did not have to go far to be completely hidden from the road. There they crouched, each with a reassuring hand on the bridle of a mule, lest the animals stir and betray their presence. By the time they had hidden the mules and the cart, the rattle of harness and the rhythmic tread of leather-shod feet were plainly audible. Shortly a party of soldiers with torches came into view, but without pausing at the fork they wheeled to the left along the upper road leading to Magdala.

The two remained in the darkness beside the cart on which Mary's body lay, until the Romans were out of sight and earshot on the heights above, then worked the cart back to the road. Joseph wiped his face and felt it damp with a cold sweat. Had not Hadja's sharp ears heard the soldiers in time, they would have taken the road to Magdala, he knew. Nothing, then, could have saved them from capture, for the road above was narrow, with no way of getting the animals and the cart into hiding.

"Which way now?" Hadja took a long breath. "We cannot follow them."

"They must be going to the house of Demetrius in Magdala," Joseph agreed. Then a thought struck him. "Do you know where Simon's house is in Capèrnaum?"

"Yes. I have been there many times."

"Good! We will hide Mary with Simon until it is safe for her to return to Magdala."

"The fisherman is a good man," Hadja agreed. "He will be glad to give us shelter."

With Hadja riding one mule and Joseph leading the one drawing the cart, they set out along the shore road to Capernaum.

10

JOSEPH stirred and sat up, rubbing his eyes. The sun was already bright upon the floor of Simon's house, but Mary still lay on the couch where he had placed her when they arrived around midnight. He had spent the night stretched out on a quilt on the floor, where he could hear her if she stirred from her stupor.

Simon and his wife had accepted without question

Joseph's story that Mary had been dancing for Pontius Pilate and had fallen in one of her fainting attacks, especially since he had taken the precaution of slipping Mary's rough dress over her body while Hadja rode ahead on the mule. The drapery from Gaius Flaccus' bedchamber had been discarded in the bushes beside the road. Hadja's wound proved superficial when Joseph dressed it, and he had been dispatched with the mule and cart to Magdala during the night to reassure Demetrius about Mary.

The sun was shining brightly on the shore outside the house. The soft lap of water against the sides of Simon's fishing boat drawn up on the shore with its bright sails furled about the mast, the chatter of gulls around the fishhouse of Zebedee nearby, and the myriads of small, intimate sounds that went with an awakening household made last night seem only a nightmare. But when Joseph looked down at the girl sleeping on the couch and saw again the dark angry bruises upon her neck and arms where she had fought against Gaius Flaccus, he knew in a sudden rush of concern that her own tragedy was very real indeed. Mary's hair was tumbled about her face and shoulders, and some color had come back into her cheeks, but her very helplessness as she lay there set a flood of tender concern rising within him. He wanted to take her in his arms and comfort her, letting her awaken in a safe haven that could always be hers if she wanted it. But she could not have heard these things had he been able to say them, and so he contented himself only with bending over and kissing her upon the forehead.

When he raised his head he saw that her eyes were open, staring at him with a puzzled expression. "This is Simon's house," she whispered. "How did I get here?"

Joseph gave her a quick account of his finding Hadja outside the villa and how he had taken her from Gaius Flaccus' bedchamber.

"You know what happened then?" It was barely a whisper.

"Yes. But no one else does."

"Why didn't you leave me there to die?" she said piteously. "There was a dagger in the closet." Suddenly she began to weep. Great tears spilled from her eyes and ran down over her cheeks, but her face remained a frozen mask of suffering and shame.

Joseph looked away, for somehow it seemed indecent to watch while she wept for the girl who had disappeared last night, never to return. He sensed that nothing he could say would diminish her agony now. It would do no good to tell her that others had survived an equal desecration and had gone on living. He could not possibly know, as kind and understanding as he was, what the terrible experience had meant. Only a woman who had been through it all could know that. But he could see how, overnight, the gay and carefree girl who had danced and sung for the sheer joy of it had become a woman.

The change was not only in the purely physical fact of defloration; it went deeper than mere flesh, into her very soul, a wound that would never completely heal. Not that she was outwardly changed, except for the bruises upon her body and the lines of suffering in her face. There was the same pale beauty, the same rich sheen to her hair, the same lovely body outwardly unchanged by the desecration it had survived. And yet the girl weeping there was an entirely different person from the gay and joyful Mary of Magdala who had loved to visit Simon and his wife here by the lake, the "Living Flame," as Hadja called her, who had danced on the streets of Magdala.

Finally the tears ceased to flow. "No one knows what happened last night except us, Mary," Joseph said, trying to comfort her. "I did not tell Hadja, or Simon and his wife. You must try to forget it; the memory can only bring you pain."

"Then let it," she said with sudden anger. "Let the pain keep me from ever forgetting I must be revenged."

" 'To me belongeth vengeance and recompense,' " he reminded her. "They are the words of the Most High."

"Where was He when I cried out to Him to save me?" she stormed. "Why did He not answer me then?"

Joseph was silent. The wife of Eleazar and most of the devout Jews of Magdala would have said God had deserted her as a punishment for her sins. But what was sinful about high spirits and courage, the impatience of youth for the conservatism of age, or the desire to be happy and share one's happiness with others? If this were sin, then God was indeed an unfair taskmaster.

"You think I deserved it, too, because you told me not to go to Tiberias," Mary accused, lashing out like a child in her pain and bewilderment, instinctively trying to allay the hurt and guilt she felt through hurting others.

"None of those who love you could ever think or say such a thing, Mary," he told her gently. "It is written,

'Hatred stirreth up strifes, but love covereth all sins.' "

"Stop quoting proverbs to me!" she snapped angrily, turning her face away from him. "Why don't you go away and leave me alone?"

"I thought I would go to Magdala this morning. . . ."

"Well, go then. Stop bothering me."

"Do you want to tell Demetrius anything?"

"Tell him I want to die." Her voice broke then and the tears began to roll once more, but her face still did not alter in its fixed mask of suffering. "Tell him to forget he ever had a daughter," she whispered and, turning over suddenly, buried her face in the pillow.

Joseph found Simon's wife and warned her to watch Mary closely, on the grounds that she might suffer another attack. Then, his heart heavy with concern for the girl he loved, he got on his mule and started up the hill to Magdala. There he learned that the soldiers had visited Demetrius during the night, seeking Mary, but had departed without troubling him when satisfied that she had not come there. The remainder of the musicians had drifted in during the early hours of the morning, but the pudgy lyre maker had been worried until Hadja arrived with the news that Mary was safe.

"What really happened at Pilate's villa, Joseph?" Demetrius asked soberly. "I am sure Hadja didn't know the whole story."

Joseph had no alternative except to tell the truth. When he finished, Demetrius' face was set with grief and self-accusation. "It is my fault," he said miserably. "I should have forbidden her to go."

"You were sick in bed," Joseph reminded him. "And you know her spirit; she would have gone anyway."

"None of us could have stopped her once she had decided she must dance at the villa to get money for me," Demetrius agreed. "I suppose I exaggerated my own importance in the theater at Alexandria, wanting to impress her favorably because I love her so much. And then the less certain I was that I wanted to go back," he continued, "the more Mary was convinced that I could never be happy elsewhere. And of course she wants to go very badly herself." He put his hand on Joseph's shoulder. "I wish she would marry you, Joseph. You are a fine young man and she does love you."

"But not enough to give up Alexandria."

"Enough, perhaps—once she has seen it and realized

66

the heartbreaks that go with the theater. But until then
. . . How is she now, Joseph?"

"Like another person, cold and hard. I think the only
thing that will carry her through all this is her determination to be revenged."

Demetrius sighed. "A woman is never quite the same
after she has known the embrace of a man for the first
time, even under the best circumstances. What a terrible
experience that must have been to a sensitive girl like
Mary. Bring her back to me as soon as you can, Joseph.
Perhaps I can help her through this ordeal."

Joseph shook his head. "I don't think any of us can
really help her, Demetrius, as much as we love her. She
must stay with Simon and his wife until we know whether
or not Gaius Flaccus will try to find her. I am going to
the Procurator's villa today to dress his lady's arm. Perhaps I can learn something of his plans."

Joseph approached the villa of Pontius Pilate with some
trepidation, for he could not be sure just how much was
known of his part in last night's happenings. The *nomenclator* treated him deferentially, however, and showed
him to the apartment of Pilate's lady. Claudia Procula was
in very high spirits, for her pain had vanished almost
magically. "Tell me the news of Galilee, Joseph," she
begged. "I have been inside so long because of this arm
that I have lost all touch with your people."

"There it talk of a dancer who was cruelly treated in
this very house last night," Joseph said as he applied the
bandage.

"What do you mean?"

"She was invited to dance before the guests of the
Procurator. Afterward her musicians were removed from
the palace by soldiers while the girl was held against her
will."

"Was she harmed?" It was almost a whisper, and the
color had drained from her face.

"The girl came here a virgin. But she is no longer."

"Not the Procurator . . . ?" she gasped.

"No. But she was brought here in his name."

"It was Gaius Flaccus then? . . . He promised us this
would never happen again," she cried, then she composed herself with an effort. "My husband's nephew is a
fine soldier and a favorite of the Emperor. But when he
takes too much wine, he sometimes becomes like an—an

animal, at least where young girls are concerned. My husband will want to pay the girl and her family well, Joseph. Do you know her?"

"I had asked her to become my wife," he said simply.

Claudia Procula gasped. "Joseph! How terrible!" She put her hand gently upon his arm. "Is there nothing we can do?"

"Gaius Flaccus sent soldiers to pursue her when she escaped last night," Joseph explained, "but she is in a safe place. Naturally she hates all Romans now."

Procula nodded. "I understand her hating us. What has all this done to you, Joseph?"

"I try to remember the teachings of the Most High," he told her. "But it is hard not to desire vengeance."

"I could not blame you for wanting to kill him," she agreed. "But you would only lose your own life. Rome does not always send its best representatives abroad, Joseph, and things like this only make us hated even more. But Pontius Pilate would never have condoned this. He is a good man at heart, although . . ." She did not finish the sentence, but Joseph knew she meant the weakness and indecision which had kept her husband from being one of Rome's great colonial administrators.

"I can assure you of one thing," Procula continued. "Gaius Flaccus will not harm the girl again. He sails in a few days for Rome; the Emperor has called him back to the royal household."

This was good news indeed, for then Mary could go back to Magdala and need no longer hide from her betrayer. Joseph hurried out of the villa to carry his tidings to Capernaum, but at the gate he was met by Gaius Flaccus himself. The Tribune was in full uniform, having just come from drilling the palace guards, of which he was commander. Joseph stepped aside, but the Roman called to him peremptorily. "You there, leech. I would speak with you."

Joseph stopped and waited. He was fairly certain that Gaius Flaccus had no inkling that he had snatched Mary away last night, for the guard could not have betrayed him without betraying himself.

"What do you know of Mary of Magdala?" the Tribune asked. "The girl who fainted while dancing in the streets."

"I took her to the house of Demetrius that day as she asked me to do."

"And you have not seen her since?"

"I see her quite often," Joseph admitted.

"Then you know where I can find her?" Gaius Flaccus asked eagerly.

"Have you tried the house of Demetrius in Magdala?"

"Of course." The Tribune made an impatient movement. "He will tell me nothing."

"Perhaps because he is not sure what are your intentions regarding her."

"I am mad about her!" Gaius Flaccus cried. "She runs in my veins like wine."

"Then you wish to marry her?"

"Marry! Does a Roman of the equestrian order marry a Jewess? You know better than that, leech. It is forbidden by your law."

"Our law forbids a Jew to marry a heathen," Joseph corrected him gravely. "For thereby a Jew becomes unclean in the sight of the Most High."

It took a second for Gaius Flaccus to realize that it would be the Jew who was defiled by marriage with a Roman, not a Roman by marriage with a Jew. He flushed, and Joseph saw his fists clench, but just then Claudia Procula came into the yard. Seeing them, she stopped to toy with some flowers, and Joseph understood that she had seen Gaius Flaccus' anger and was protecting him by her presence.

"Do you still say you know nothing of the girl?" the Tribune asked in a lower voice.

"I know that she is the adopted daughter of Demetrius, who is a Roman citizen," Joseph said deliberately. "He would be entitled to ask protection for her, even from the Emperor himself."

Gaius Flaccus was brought up short by the threat. A wanton act upon a daughter of a subject people might not bring punishment to a Roman officer. But a citizen of Rome had the right to bring charges against anyone below the Emperor himself and receive redress if his cause was just. And Tiberius was known to be very straightlaced in matters of this kind. "Are *you* a citizen of Rome, leech?" he snapped, his lips white with anger.

"No, I am not," Joseph admitted.

"Then see that you keep a civil tongue in your head toward your betters. The next time you may not have a woman to protect you." Turning on his heel, Gaius Flaccus entered the house.

11

MARY came home to Magdala a few days after Gaius
Flaccus departed for Rome, but there was little improve-
ment in her spirits. She remained in her room much of
the day, or sat in the garden holding her beloved lyre,
yet never touched the strings. Nothing Demetrius or
Joseph could do seemed to lift her spirits. The set cast of
her face betrayed her suffering and shame, but she said
nothing to show her feelings, speaking only when spoken
to, and then in a monotonous voice as devoid of feeling
as it was of tone.

And so the weeks passed and the time approached
when Joseph's preceptor, Alexander Lysimachus, was to
take him before the judges and doctors of law at Jerusalem, to be examined as to his competence to receive
the title of *rophe uman* and to practice as a physician in
his own right.

A few days before Joseph's departure Mary appeared
at his house early one morning. He was there alone, his
mother having gone to market. Mary's eyes had a strange
glow, and she seemed excited about something. His im-
mediate reaction was that she might have a fever, but
when he questioned her, she denied feeling badly at all.
"I came to get more of the wine of mandragora," she explained. "My bottle is empty."

While he filled her bottle carefully from the large jug
in which he kept his supply of this powerful and useful
extract, he noticed that Mary was looking at a large jar
at the end of the shelf. "My fortune," he explained with
a smile, and lifted it down. "See, the coins fill it almost
halfway now." The purses given him by Claudia Procula
had added much to the hoard, and Pontius Pilate himself
had needed the leech several times recently.

Mary lifted a handful of the gold and let it trickle
through her fingers. "You will soon have enough to go to
Alexandria," she said dully.

Joseph shook his head. "When I return from Jerusalem I shall begin my own practice here in Magdala."

"But you had your heart set on Alexandria."

"Is it news to you, Mary," he asked gently, "that I would far rather stay here in Galilee with you beside me?"

"Don't, Joseph," she whispered. "Please don't." She sank down on a bench and put her face in her hands, but not before he saw the utter hell in her eyes. Yet when he would have comforted her, she only pushed him away. "Go on to your patients," she whispered finally without looking up. "I will wait here and talk to your mother when she comes from the market."

Reluctantly he took up the *nartik* containing his instruments and medicines and left the house. His first visit took almost an hour, while he applied leeches to the swollen eye of a wool dyer. When it was finished, he hurried back to his home, for his mother sometimes lingered at the market in the mornings, talking with the other women who congregated there, and he did not like the idea of Mary's being there alone when she was so much disturbed.

The house seemed empty, and Joseph thought that his mother must have returned and walked with Mary across the city or into the small park nearby. Considerably relieved to find his fears groundless, he went into the surgery to drop the leeches that were fat with the dyer's blood into the tank and get fresh ones before leaving for his other calls. And there he found Mary, lying unconscious on the floor, with the empty bottle that had contained the wine of mandragora beside her.

For a moment Joseph could not believe what he saw. It seemed incredible that Mary would have tried to take her own life when that very morning she had showed more animation than she had for a long time. But then he remembered their conversation several weeks before, when he had told her of the power of the mandrake root to produce sleep and death.

Why had she done it? he asked himself as he picked up her limp body and carried her to the couch in his own room. She was still alive, but from the limpness of her muscles and the slow, shallow breathing, he was sure that a large amount of the drug must already have entered her body. He could have understood her trying to kill herself in the agony of shame following her experience at the hands of Gaius Flaccus. But almost two months had

71

passed now, time for the shock to wear off and let her become somewhat adjusted.

Joseph wasted no time in futile wondering, however. Only a little more than an hour had elapsed since he had left her, he calculated, so even if she had taken the drug at once there was an excellent chance that some remained in her stomach. If he could remove that, it would at least have no further power to harm her.

Fortunately he carried in his bag a *kulcha,* or stomach tube. What followed was not pleasant, but when he finished he had the satisfaction of knowing that at least a part of the drug she had swallowed was removed. Next he used the tube to pour into Mary's stomach a liberal dose of the mixture called *mithridaticum,* said to have been prepared first by King Mithridates VI, King of Pontus, to protect himself from being poisoned. He had claimed it to be "an antidote for every venomous reptile and every poisonous substance," and in various forms the mixture was used throughout the world.

When Joseph's mother arrived a short time later, he had wrapped Mary in blankets and was heating rocks on the cooking hearth to add more warmth. Everything possible had been done to remove the poison or counteract its effects. From now on he could only fight to maintain her strength in every possible way.

Through the day and into the evening Joseph remained beside the couch where Mary lay. The harsh cast of suffering in which her features had been set for the past weeks was relaxed now as she lay unconscious, and she looked once more like the happy girl he had first loved when he saw her dancing on the streets of Tiberias. Seeing her lying there sleeping peacefully, he found it even harder to understand what had made life suddenly so unbearable for her that she had tried to kill herself.

For a while, as the day receded into the shadows of the night, it seemed that Mary's spirit would leave her body. Desperately Joseph fought to save her, expending all the resources of his skill and his stock of stimulant drugs. Finally he fell on his knees beside the couch and prayed that God would let her live, and as night settled over the lake and the city he felt the pulse under his fingers grow stronger. With a rising sense of exultation then he knew that he had won his battle with death.

It was after midnight, and Joseph had long since sent his mother to bed, when Mary showed signs of returning consciousness. Suddenly she started writhing, seemingly in pain, drawing up her knees as if trying to find a comfortable position, like a sufferer from colic. And when Joseph put his hand on her body through the covers where the pain seemed to be centered, he could feel a boardlike tension of her abdominal muscles. Seconds later they relaxed and she stretched out her limbs, but almost immediately the spasm came again. This time she moaned and he thought for a moment that she was regaining consciousness, but the spasm ended and the lines of pain in her face were erased for a short time, until another bout began. Now, however, Joseph was able to make the diagnosis, and at last he understood why Mary had tried to kill herself.

How long since she first realized that she carried the child of Gaius Flaccus within her body, he could not know. But it must not have been more than a few days, or perhaps a week, he judged, for she had conceived less than two months before. Now he understood how the knowledge of her pregnancy during these past few days, coming after the shock of being ravished by a drunken Roman, had been more than she could bear. If he had felt anything of censure toward her before for seeking to end her own life, he could only pity her now. To one of Mary's proud spirit, this last blow would have been more than she could bear.

The inexorable forces of nature worked rapidly once they had begun, but fortunately Mary herself was still too deeply under the effects of the drug to be conscious of the pain or even of what was happening. When it was all over, Joseph removed all traces of the formless incubus and buried it in the garden.

It was morning before Mary awakened. She was pale, and great dark shadows showed beneath her eyes, but Joseph could see no other effects of the ordeal through which her body had passed. He had remained beside the couch all night and he was there when she awakened. "Everything is all right, dear," he reassured her. "I found you in time."

Slowly her face assumed its former harsh cast. "I wanted to die," she said bitterly. "Why did you stop me?"

"No one has a right to take his own life, Mary. You must live for Demetrius and for those who love you."

"And be labeled a harlot when I bear the child of Gaius Flaccus?"

73

"That is what I am trying to tell you," he said gently. "The conception has been expelled; your nightmare is over and no one knows of it except you and me."

For a long moment she did not speak. If she was relieved by the news, it did not show in the harsh cast of her face. And when she spoke it was only to ask, "What will you tell your mother?"

"She thinks you were suffering from one of the fainting spells. She was not here when I found you or when it happened."

Mary turned her face to the wall then, and Joseph did not try to say anything more to her. Telling his mother to give her some hot broth later when she felt like taking it, he went out to visit his patients. When he came back that evening, Mary's head was propped up on pillows and there was a faint color in her cheeks. He took her hand where it lay outside the covers. "I am going to Jerusalem soon, Mary," he said. "Perhaps for as long as a week. Promise me that you will not try again what you tried to do yesterday."

Her eyes met his, and the look of determination in them startled him. "I will not try to kill myself again," she said slowly and distinctly. "Now I have something to live for."

For a moment Joseph dared to let himself hope she could mean what he wanted so much to hear her say. But her next words dashed his hopes.

"Today I swore to the Most High a solemn oath," she told him. "An oath that I will not stop until I have killed Gaius Flaccus and am revenged."

Nothing Joseph could say had any effect upon her decision. In vain he pointed out that a member of a conquered race had no real chance against the conquerors, and that her resolve could only end in unhappiness, perhaps in death. But Mary's fiery Jewish blood had triumphed over the more logical Greek in her heritage, harking back to the implacable laws of the time of Moses, when God had said, *Thou shalt give life for life, eye for eye, tooth for tooth, hand for hand, foot for foot, burning for burning, wound for wound, stripe for stripe.*

Mary improved rapidly over the next several days. By the time Joseph was ready to depart for Jerusalem, she was walking about the house. She had sent to Demetrius for her lyre and strummed it off and on during the day, sometimes singing songs Joseph had never heard before,

as if she were working to enlarge her repertoire. But he
did not delude himself into believing this was the same
Mary of Magdala he had first come to love. An evil spirit
had taken possession of her, a demon of hate that would
not let her rest until she had accomplished her purpose
through the death of the man who had defiled her body.

12

As always on the few occasions when he had visited Jerusalem, Joseph stayed at the home of his uncle, the merchant, Joseph of Arimathea. Respected in the city for his
piety and his kindness even more than for his wealth,
the older Joseph, whose name the young physician of
Magdala bore, was a man of influence in the ruling council, the Sanhedrin. Joseph dined with his uncle on the
day of his arrival, and afterward the older man questioned
him carefully about his relations with Pontius Pilate and
his lady. When Joseph finished, the merchant nodded
approvingly. "You have done well in making a friend of
the Procurator and his wife," he said. "I can see that I was
right in recommending you to him." He pulled at his
beard. "Did you ever think of coming to Jerusalem to
work as a physician?"

Joseph smiled. "I suppose every leech or apprentice
dreams of being a successful physician here," he admitted. "But there are many here who treat the sick. I
would be but a small pebble in a rock pile."

"Perhaps so, perhaps not," his uncle said enigmatically.
"Now you had better get to bed. The judges will not be
easy on you, so you must have your wits about you tomorrow."

Actually Joseph had little trouble convincing the judges
at Jerusalem that his knowledge of medicine and his skill
in surgery entitled him to be designated *rophe uman*,
a skilled physician. Already his competence was far above
that of most physicians, even in the temple city.

The examination was held before a board of judges
and completed in one day. On the following morning

the formalities of issuing the necessary certificates were completed, but when Joseph was leaving the chamber, the chief of the judges, a venerable doctor of the law named Elias, who was also a member of the Sanhedrin, called him back. "What are your plans, Joseph of Galilee, now that you are *rophe uman?*" he asked.

"I will work on in Magdala for a while," Joseph told him. "At least until the Procurator goes back to Caesarea."

"It is good that Pontius Pilate has so much confidence in you," Elias said. "And after that?"

"When I have saved enough, I hope to study further in Alexandria."

"Why study more? You are more learned now than most of our physicians in Jerusalem."

"It seems that there is no end to learning," Joseph said with a smile.

"You speak truly," Elias agreed. "It is written, *'Give instruction to a wise man and he will be yet wiser; teach a just man and he will increase in learning'!*" He smiled then. "But it is also written, *'A wise man will hear and will increase learning; and a man of understanding shall attain unto wise councils'!* You could learn much here in Jerusalem."

"I am sure of that, sir," Joseph agreed, wondering just what this roundabout discussion could be leading up to.

"We of the council have known of you for some time," Elias continued, "through the excellent physician of Magdala who is your preceptor and through your uncle, who is my friend. We have heard, too, of your success in treating the Procurator Pontius Pilate and the Lady Claudia Procula. And since the blood of David flows in your veins, it is meet that you should serve in the temple of the Most High. If you will come to Jerusalem, Joseph, you will be given an appointment as *medicus viscerus* for the temple."

Joseph was so startled that he could hardly believe he was hearing aright. The honor of serving as temple physician was usually accorded men of age and standing in their profession and not given lightly, even then. Nor did he doubt for a moment that his association with Pontius Pilate and his wife had influenced the offer. The Procurator of Judea spent varying periods in Jerusalem in connection with his office, and it was well known that his temper was not good when he was in pain from his gouty toe. So it was perfectly logical for the Sanhedrin to want a physician who had been successful in treating the Procurator to be in Jerusalem during these visits.

Whatever the reason behind the flattering offer, Joseph knew it was to his benefit to accept. As *medicus viscerus* he would be assured the patronage of the wealthiest and most important people in Jerusalem and Judea and his fortune would be assured. It was a prospect he could not lightly refuse, and yet, although he had been willing to give up Alexandria to marry Mary, he hesitated to cut himself off from it since she had refused him.

"I had planned to study at Alexandria for at least a year," he said.

"No doubt that could be arranged at some future time," Elias agreed amiably. "No man can be blamed for wishing to improve his competence in his chosen occupation. Will a month be long enough for you to arrange your affairs in Magdala?"

"It should be ample."

"I will present your appointment to the high priest then. You will be notified of it in due course."

More than a week had elapsed before Joseph finally returned to Magdala, but as he hurried home he was bursting with good news. Now that he had incurred such good fortune and would be given such a high place, he hoped Mary might look with more favor on his suit for her hand in marriage. But at his home he learned that she had returned home on the very day he had left for Jerusalem, and his mother had not seen her since.

As he hurried to the house of the lyre maker Joseph reviewed in his mind the arguments with which he would bowl Mary over and make her agree to marry him. He had even figured how to take care of Demetrius, as Jerusalem would be a large market for the instruments the Greek made, since hundreds of thousands of Jews flocked into the city on pilgrimages every year. And with his position Joseph might even be able to arrange that Demetrius be designated instrument maker for the temple.

At first he could not understand what was changed about the lyre maker's house when he approached it from across the Street of the Greeks. Then he realized that he heard none of the usual sounds with which the building ordinarily rang, the tapping of hammers on resonant woods, the plink of strings, the unsure notes of a pupil practicing, and, above all, a girlish voice of incomparable beauty lifted on the mountain air. His spirits suddenly doused by a sense of foreboding, Joseph crossed the street and came up to the house. It was then that he saw the bars nailed across the doors and windows.

An old man passing in the street stopped. "If you are looking for the maker of lyres," he quavered, "he has gone. He and all his household."

"When did they leave?" Joseph cried. "Where did they go?"

The man shrugged. "A week or so ago. I only know they traveled southward on the Via Maris."

"Was the girl with them? The girl called Mary of Magdala?"

"The one with the red hair? Yes. She walked beside the mule that carried Demetrius." And then he cackled. "Or was it two mules? The lyre maker is too big for one."

Joseph could learn no more, either from the old man or from the neighbors, but all agreed that Demetrius' party had gone southward, so he could be sure their destination must be Alexandria. The southward arm of the Way of the Sea led from Magdala through the mountainous country to the west as far as Joppa and the teeming coastal cities. From there a traveler could take ship almost daily for Alexandria, reaching it in a few days' sail. Or a caravan could travel by the longer land route to the same destination. Undoubtedly Mary had somehow persuaded Demetrius to go to Alexandria at once, and Joseph was sure the decision was tied up with her oath of revenge.

But why had she gone without telling him? And from whence had come the money for the trip? Even with the purses she had received for her dancing before Pontius Pilate, she would not have had enough to take herself, Demetrius, and the musicians, as well as the skilled artisans of the lyre maker's household, to Egypt.

Joseph's every impulse urged him to follow Mary. By buying or renting a fast horse or camel, he knew he could pursue them along the Via Maris and probably reach Joppa before they took ship. Not that he could hope to persuade her to return; he knew Mary too well for that. But she did not know of his fine prospects since he was to be appointed *medicus viscerus* to the temple at Jerusalem. Knowing this, she might at least promise to wait for him in Alexandria. And as Demetrius had suggested, after living in Egypt for a while, she might be more willing to return to Judea and Jerusalem as his bride.

He would follow them, Joseph decided, and hurried back across the city to his home. It would take money to hire a camel or horse—they were much more expensive than the slower mules—but the jar in which he kept his coins held more than would be needed. Shouting to his mother that he was leaving for Joppa in a few minutes, he went to the shelf where he kept the jar that contained his savings. As he lifted it down, the jar seemed lighter than he remembered. But only when he turned it upside down, and saw that no coins fell from it did the truth burst upon him.

Joseph knew now where Mary had found the money to take her and the others to Alexandria.

Book Two

ALEXANDRIA

1

THE slaves at the carrying handles lowered the sumptuous sedan chair to the stone-paved quay. Joseph pushed aside the curtains and stepped out into a scene of bustling activity. The Procurator's own chair had brought him across the city of Caesarea to the harbor. As he stood beside it now, the sun gleamed on the golden eagles surmounting the standards at its corners, and the wind whipped the personal flag of the Procurator, borne by a burly soldier of Pilate's own guard. No one could doubt who ruled here—the stamp of Rome was upon everything —and for a moment Joseph was a little ashamed that he had given at least tacit approval of the conquerors by letting himself be carried in state, as it were, to the shipside.

The chair had deposited Joseph almost at the foot of the gangplank leading up to the deck of the great merchant ship—called "round" to distinguish it from the vessels of war, which were called "long." Protected by the great half-moon-shaped quay of massive stones with which Herod the Great had transformed an open roadstead into a protected harbor, the great ship hardly rocked at all as it rested quietly against the wharf. Slaves moved in long lines up and down the gangplank, but there was no confusion, for almost every day a ship from Rome or one of the other great cities of the Empire touched at Caesarea to load and unload cargo or bring messages and papers of state to the Procurator of Judea, Pontius Pilate.

Joseph had come from Jerusalem several days before, for a last visit with the Procurator and his lady before sailing to Alexandria for the year of study promised him five years ago, when he had accepted the position of *medicus viscerus* to the temple at Jerusalem. Much had happened in those five years. He was now a rich man whose fame as a physician had spread throughout Judea and Galilee, and even as far as the capital of the entire province of Syria at Antioch, where he had been called to treat the legate Vitellus.

Much of his success, Joseph realized, had come because of his relationship to the rich merchant of Jerusalem, Joseph of Arimathea, and to his sponsorship by Pontius Pilate and the Lady Claudia Procula. He was duly grateful, but although his relationship with Procula had always been a pleasant one, he had never been able to get really close to the Procurator himself, except physically to treat his gout and the other ailments which constantly plagued the Roman ruler of Judea.

Pilate, Joseph had come to know, was a strange man, given to bouts of abject self-pity because his son was a cripple and himself condemned to service here in what he considered a barbarous country, for whose inhabitants he had only contempt. As so often happens with the emotionally unstable, he swung sometimes to extremes. Then he could be cruel beyond belief, arrogant, haughty, trampling upon the rights of others, regardless of the freedoms that Rome guaranteed to those it ruled. Once he had marched the golden eagles of Rome into Jerusalem by night and confronted the people in the morning with the blasphemous spectacle of graven images at the very gates of the temple. And again his soldiers, their weapons hidden under ordinary clothes, had infiltrated among a crowd come to protest another of his indignities, then set upon the people and killed them without mercy. Knowing that some Jews conspired against him and hoped to make Herod Antipas king in Jerusalem, Pilate trusted no one.

The Jews had little cause to love Pontius Pilate, but he had always been kind to Joseph and by designating him as personal physician to the court at Caesarea and the garrison at Jerusalem he had enhanced Joseph's fortunes immeasurably. If there was a good side to Pilate's nature, Joseph knew, it lay in his consuming love for the boy Pila and the exquisite tiny patrician who was his wife. Only her influence over the Procurator kept him from becoming a complete tyrant.

Claudia Procula's asthma had brought Joseph to Caesarea frequently in the years since he had come to Jerusalem, although he had been able to help her but little. But the attacks had at least given him a welcome excuse to get away from the temple city every now and then and the tension that was a palpable thing there. As much as the

Jews hated the Romans and the man who was a symbol of Roman power in their country, there were always some who aped their Roman conquerors. In Jerusalem a small group called the Herodians wielded a considerable political power through allying themselves with the Sadducees, from whose ranks came the temple priests. The Pharisees, however, clinging stubbornly to the ancient customs and laws of Israel, had only contempt for both Herodians and Sadducees. Thus while the Pharisees swayed the mass of the people, who naturally clung to the old traditions and past glories of Israel, the Herodians and Sadducees were smart enough to see that, for the time being, the greatest future for the Jews lay with the Romans who were in power, although preferably with a Jewish king on the throne of Judea.

Now, as he looked about him at the bustle of activity on the great quay, Joseph felt a sense of relief that, for a year at least, he would be free of the constant bickering and tension of temple politics. He carried a letter from the high priest Caiaphas to Philo Judaeus, the acknowledged leader of the Alexandrian Jews, who actually numbered more than the population of Jerusalem itself. And Claudia Procula had also given him a letter of introduction to Cestus, Roman governor of Alexandria, a distant kinsman of hers. With these credentials Joseph knew he would have instant access to both Roman and Jewish society in Alexandria, but he did not plan to use the letters at once. It was as a student seeking knowledge that he was sailing to Alexandria, the greatest center of learning in the world of that day. Knowledge and something else, a girl whose hair was like a flame. And at the thought his pulse quickened again in the old familiar thrilling rhythm.

The captain of the vessel had not missed the arrival of a passenger in the personal sedan chair of the Procurator. Hurrying down the gangplank, he bowed low in greeting. "I am Marcus Quintus, captain of this ship," he said formally.

Joseph, too, bowed. "Peace be upon thee, Captain Quintus," he said. "I am called Joseph of Galilee, a physician."

The captain was a stocky man with an iron-gray beard and the keen eyes of a master mariner. "Your modesty becomes you, sir," he said as they climbed the gangplank together. "In the ports of Judea and even as far as Antioch, there are men whose lives have been saved through the skill of the physician named Joseph of Galilee. It is said that, although rich, you turn no man away from your door." He opened a door into the deckhouse and stood aside for Joseph to enter. "You will not be lonesome on this trip. A physician from the coast of Malabar is returning to Alexandria from Rome. One of my sailors was stupid enough to break an arm. He is setting the bone now."

Joseph had been looking forward to solitude and complete freedom from the problems of medicine during the short voyage to Alexandria. When he had arrived in Jerusalem from Magdala five years before, everything he owned was easily carried on the back of a mule. It had taken much longer, however, to set his affairs in order for this trip of a year's duration, for he was a rich man now, with many interests and an estate at the edge of the city, complete with vineyards, fields, and gardens as befitted the leading physician of the Jewish capital. They had been busy, prosperous, and pleasant years, during which he had matured greatly and for a while had almost forgotten his earlier desire to study in Alexandria.

And then one day three months ago a man had come from one of the banking houses of Jerusalem specializing in foreign exchange. With him he brought a purse of gold exactly equaling the amount Mary had taken from the jar in the house at Magdala, plus interest at the usual rate. Joseph could learn nothing about Mary from the banker, except that the money had been sent from Alexandria, but she had been constantly in his dreams and thoughts since. Finally he admitted to himself that he must see her again, if only for the certainty that she had stopped loving him and had given up all intention of returning to share with him this good life he had made for himself in Jerusalem. And with that decision had come a resurgence of his desire to study in Alexandria.

2

THE physician Bana Jivaka was a small, slender man dressed entirely in white, with a close-fitting turban upon his dark hair. His skin was a light brown, his features even and pleasant, and his dark eyes alert and intelligent. He bowed low when Captain Quintus presented Joseph, and acknowledged the introduction in excellent Greek.

The patient was a muscular sailor stripped to the waist. He was tattooed in the strange cabalistic designs favored by mariners who liked to boast that they had sailed beyond the Pillars of Hercules far to the west, where the Mare Nostrum of the Romans met the great sea that washed the shores of distant Britannia. The fracture was already reduced and bandaged in much the same way that Joseph had treated Simon the fisherman. What startled Joseph was the way the injured man sat bolt upright in a chair, apparently unconscious of everything about him. "What medicine have you given him to produce such a state?" he asked curiously.

"It is a trance," the dark-skinned physician explained, "produced by a method known to people in many parts of the world. We have used it in my own country for at least a thousand years, and in Egypt it has been known even longer."

"Would he not feel a touch upon the eye?" This was the ultimate test of unconsciousness, the front of the eyeball being the last part of the body to become insensitive before death.

Jivaka took a wisp of linen and touched the unconscious man lightly upon the eyeball. There was no response, no blinking.

"Remarkable!" Joseph cried. "How do you achieve such rigidity?"

"Through the same trance," the other physician explained. "If I desired, I could place him so deeply in a stupor that you would not be able to feel the beat of his pulse or see the movements of his chest. Only with a mirror before his mouth could you detect a film of moisture from his breathing. In India holy men have been buried alive for hours while in such a state," he added.

Joseph shook his head. "Had I not seen it with my own eyes," he admitted, "I would not believe such a thing could be accomplished."

"I can teach you to do it later, if you wish," Jivaka said courteously. Then he smiled. "There is a saying in my country. *The wagoner desires wood, the physician sickness, and the priests libation.*' If you will join me in emulating the priests, we can talk more of this." He leaned over the sailor and whistled sharply in his ear. Instantly the man was awake, looking about him dazedly.

"I have set your arm," Bana Jivaka told the seaman, "but see that you carry it carefully until the bandage is dry. And let me examine it tomorrow."

Over a glass of wine the Indian physician asked, "Are you going to Alexandria?"

"Yes. I promised myself a period of study there years ago. Now I am going to claim it."

"Good! We can be fellow students. I have another year in Alexandria before returning to Malabar."

"Malabar?" Joseph frowned. "The fleets of our King Solomon sailed to a port called Ophir centuries ago."

"Ophir is thought to have been either our city of Suppara or Muziris," Javaka explained. "Actually we of India have known the Jews for many years. I believe some of the precious woods used in building your temple at Jerusalem came from the coast of Malabar, and there were Jews among the learned men who accompanied the Greek general Alexander as far east as our inland city of Taxila, where I studied at the university."

"Are not mariners afraid to sail such distances?"

"Why should they be afraid? Someday men will sail completely around the earth."

"But the earth is flat!" protested Joseph. "In the ancient writings of our people God plainly said when he created the earth, *Let the water under the heaven be gathered together into one place, and let the dry land appear.*' "

"Perhaps there is another meaning to the words," Jivaka suggested. "In Alexandria you will see the very place where a Greek named Eratosthenes not only proved the world to be round several hundred years ago, but measured its circumference as well."

Startled, Joseph asked, "Could he walk upon the water?"

"The method of Eratosthenes was simple," Jivaka explained with a smile. "He learned from a traveler that at the city of Syene on the coast of Africa the sun shines directly into a deep well at the time of the summer solstice, showing that it is directly overhead. At Alexandria, Eratosthenes next erected a vertical pole and measured the angle of its shadow at exactly noon on the day of the summer solstice, finding it to be the fiftieth part of a circle. Then according to the propositions of Euclid, he deduced that if perpendicular lines through the well at Syene and the pole at Alexandria were extended to the center of the earth they would form the same angle as the shadow of the pole at Alexandria, namely the fiftieth part of a circle. Therefore the distance between Syene and Alexandria is also the fiftieth part of the earth's circumference. And since we know it is five thousand stadia from Syene to Alexandria, the circumference of the world is therefore fifty times that distance, or two hundred and fifty thousand stadia, roughly twenty-six thousand miles."

"Did he do all that without stirring from Alexandria?"

"Eratosthenes accomplished the entire calculation in the yard of the Museum," Jivaka confirmed.

"I must think more about this," Joseph said dazedly. "It is too simple to be easily understood."

Bana Jivaka laughed. "I suspect that is true of the most really great discoveries. After all, Archimedes was in his bath when he discovered that a floating body displaces a volume of water equal to its own weight. The Greek mind searches always for the simplest answer and arrives at the greatest truths."

"You were going to explain the trance you used just now," Joseph reminded him.

"It is simply a matter of the control exerted by the spirit over the body. When the spirit is rendered insensible, the body is made insensible too."

"But are you not afraid the *mazzikim*—the demons of the air—will fly away with his soul?"

Jivaka shook his head. "Our philosophers gave up belief in demons long ago. But we do know how strong is the control of the spirit over the body, for you saw an example of it just now with the sailor."

"How do you bring on the trance?" Joseph asked.

Bana Jivaka took a large emerald from his pocket and held it before an oil lamp that burned in their quarters. The jewel seemed to absorb the light, for it glowed like a ball of green fire. "This merely draws attention," he explained. "Any bright object will do the same. The rest is only a matter of imposing your own will upon another."

"When you explain it, the whole thing seems simple enough," Joseph admitted. "But I wonder if I could ever learn to do it myself."

"Of course you could," Jivaka assured him, "because you are willing to learn. Centuries ago a wise and learned physician of India named Susruta once said, '*He who is versed only in books will be alarmed and confused, like a coward on the battlefield, when confronting active disease; he who rashly engages in practice without previous study of written science is entitled to no respect from mankind, and merits punishment from the king; but he who combines reading with experience proceeds safely and surely like a chariot on two wheels!*'"

3

THE voyage to Alexandria covered only a few days, but they were a pleasant time for Joseph. His natural eagerness to learn had been submerged by his busy medical practice during the five years he had spent in Jerusalem, but now his curiosity returned full-fledged. He was amazed to find that physicians in India were far more advanced in both medicine and surgery than were the Greeks or the Romans, and that Susruta had actually performed difficult surgical operations centuries ago of which he had never even heard.

Most of all, however, Joseph liked to hear Bana Jivaka tell of the great unknown lands to the east from which he had come and the even more mysterious regions beyond the coast of Malabar, where yellow men with slanting eyes had progressed farther in science, medicine, and philosophy than had even the Greeks.

"Come with me to India when I return," Jivaka urged.

"We can sail when the monsoon blows eastward again next year, and you can return overland directly to Jerusalem by way of Babylon and Damascus if you wish."

"What is a monsoon?" Joseph asked curiously.

"A strong wind that blows across the great ocean between the mouth of the Red Sea at Adana and the Malabar coast, changing direction every six months," Jivaka explained. "When it blows from the east, ships make the trip from Muziris or Suppara to Adana and on up the Egyptian or Red Sea to Arsinoë in about eight weeks. Thence they travel by canal into the river Nile and downstream to Alexandria. When the wind changes direction, the return journey can be made as quickly."

On another occasion Jivaka showed Joseph a sheaf of sketches he had made during his studies in Alexandria and before. He had a great talent for setting down in simple drawings various aspects of disease. There were sketches of operations with the needle for cataract, a procedure Joseph had heard of but had never seen performed, extraction of growths from the eye, removal of tumors from the neck, and many others.

One set of the drawings in particular intrigued Joseph. They showed an operation for re-creating a severed nose that Jivaka assured him had been used in India for many centuries. In it a leaf-shaped piece of skin was raised from the cheek, with the end still attached, and moved across the face to replace the lost portion of the nose. Hollow reeds were inserted into the nostrils and the skin shaped around them and allowed to grow for a while, until it firmly adhered to the base of the nose. Then it was cut loose from its attachment to the cheek and shaped into an excellent substitute for the lost organ. Ears, too, could be replaced in the same way.

Other sketches showed the convulsions of epilepsy that Hippocrates called the Sacred Disease, a paralysis due to a horse's kick upon the skull, the distended ankles and swollen abdomen of plethora, and one picture that Joseph had seen several times. It was a girl with staring, prominent eyes, a slight swelling of the neck, and near emaciation. Having seen such cases, Joseph knew the face would have been flushed and perspiring, the pulse racing, and the hands shaking uncontrollably.

"I spoke to Celsus about the disease you are looking at now," Jivaka said. "He believes it is a form of the neck swelling called 'goiter.' He was surprised to learn that in India we treat it with dried seaweed."

"Seaweed? How does it work?"

Jivaka shrugged. "Who knows? But when the dried weed is fed to the patient, it sometimes brings about a miraculous cure."

Joseph smiled. "Thanks to you, I shall have much new to use in my practice when I return to Jerusalem. I hardly expected to—" He stopped, leaving the sentence unfinished.

Bana Jivaka looked at him quizzically. "You were going to say you hardly expected to learn anything from one you have been taught to look on as a barbarian, weren't you?"

"I spoke without thinking." Joseph flushed with embarrassment. "Forgive me."

"Of course." Jivaka smiled. "One should never be ashamed of knowledge, no matter from whom it is acquired." He glanced out the porthole. "It is dark and this is our third day out of Caesarea, so we may be able to see the light of the Pharos. The Alexandrians boast that it is visible all the way to the Hellespont."

The ship was moving smoothly over the sea when they came on deck. The great sails were taut from the brisk wind, and the galley slaves were resting at their oars or sleeping in their chains upon the benches where they sat. Overhead the sky was studded with stars, and to the southwest the horizon was lit by a warm glow.

"There is the light of the Pharos," Jivaka pointed to the glowing sky. "It guides all mariners to Alexandria. Nothing else man has ever built can equal it."

"I would place the temple at Jerusalem above it," Joseph said.

Jivaka looked at him in surprise. "Your temple is beautiful, but it is no such architectural wonder as the Pharos."

"The temple was built solely to the glory of the Most High," Joseph explained, "while a lighthouse serves only man."

"I am properly humbled in spirit, my friend," Jivaka said softly. "You Jews have worshiped a single God for thousands of years while the rest of us still grope futilely for Him among a host of impostors."

"But even the Jews do not agree entirely on the purposes of the Most High," Joseph admitted. "The Pharisees exalt the law until it becomes almost an idol. But the

Sadducees who make up the ruling priests of the temple would liberalize religious practices and center all power in the temple itself and the high priest."

"To which group do you belong?"

"As *medicus viscerus* of the temple, I am naturally expected to favor the priests," Joseph explained. "But the Sadducees do not believe in a life after death, as do the Pharisees. And I would hate to think that everything ended with death."

"You have no monopoly on that longing, I am afraid, Joseph. All religions have it. Here is a prayer from a very old poem of the Indian people."

> *"From the Unreal, lead me to the Real,*
> *From Darkness to the Light,*
> *From Death to Immortality!"*

"But the Most High chose the children of Israel to be His own people," Joseph protested. "He favors them above all others on earth."

"From the history of your people as I have heard my friends among the Jews of Alexandria recount it, the favor of your God would seem to be a heavy burden," Jivaka observed dryly. "They spoke of bloodshed, persecution, and enslavement."

"But that will not always be," Joseph insisted. "We have been promised a Messiah from the blood of David, my own bloodline."

"Messiah?" Jivaka frowned. "I do not understand the word."

"He will be a great leader who will set up the Kingdom of God here on earth," Joseph said confidently, "and elevate the Jews to rulership over all the people of the world."

"But that will mean battling against the might of Rome," Jivaka objected. "The Jews are few in number and scattered to the ends of the earth. How could you ever oppose Rome?"

"When the Messiah comes, His glory will be such that all the world will acknowledge Him," Joseph assured him.

Bana Jivaka shrugged. "I could believe in your God, Joseph, because I have been told that He reaches out to give men wisdom and help them over the rough places of life, forgiving them their errors if they will but ask

Him for forgiveness. But I cannot see why you compli-
cate your relationship with God by this talk of Messiahs."

Vaguely Joseph was sure this must be blasphemy, although he could think of no real reason why. Then he
remembered the words of the prophet Micah: *"What
doth the Lord ask of a man, save to do justly, to love
mercy, and to walk humbly before God?"* When he repeated them to Jivaka, the Indian only smiled.

"You see?" he said. "Like the measurements of Eratosthenes, the simplest answer is always the best, even between a man and his God."

4

JOSEPH was awakened at dawn by the shouts of the ship's
officers and the screams of slaves being whipped by the
overseers. The long oars groaned constantly now in their
leather collars, driving the vessel onward. And when he
came on deck Joseph found the sea illuminated brightly
although dawn had not yet broken. Captain Quintus told
him they were still almost ten miles from Alexandria.

The coast line of Egypt was so low in this region that
the great city itself was not yet visible, but the lighthouse
of Pharos was in full view, rising abruptly from the sea.
From the low island on which it stood to the top of the
giant mirror before which great fires were kept burning
from the setting to the rising of the sun, the tower was
nearly six hundred feet in height, a pillar of alabaster-
white stone directing all mariners to Alexandria. And although the fires were now dying down, the rays from the
great polished mirror still blinded one momentarily if
he looked directly at them.

Patterned after the Babylonian style of architecture, this
tallest of the wonders of the world consisted of four tow-
ers or stories, one atop the other, the lower ones square
and the topmost circular. The blocks of stone from which
Sostratus of Cnidus had erected the massive lighthouse
were said to be welded together with molten lead, since
nothing else would have been impervious to the salt

spray that dashed high against its sides during the winter storms.

"I envy you the sight of the Pharos for the first time from the sea," Bana Jivaka said. "It was not nearly so impressive from the Nile and Lake Mareotis when I approached it on my arrival from Malabar." They were standing in the bows of the ship while it breasted the surging breakers beating endlessly upon the shore, as if anxious to rush upon and engulf this city that was in Egypt and yet not a part of it. Behind them the overseers strode up and down the catwalks between the benches where the galley slaves sat, each chained to the great oar that he pulled. If one oar failed to move exactly in cadence with the others, the whip cracked and there was a scream of pain. Their seeming cruelty was not without reason, however, for a false move here could set the oars crashing into each other and send the ship, swinging suddenly under the unimpeded force of the long sweeps upon the other side, plunging to its death upon the rocks at the base of the great tower.

Soldiers parading along the balconies of the lower levels were plainly visible, as well as the windows of some three hundred rooms that the tall structure contained. Then, when it seemed that another sweep of the great oars would set them upon the rocks, Captain Quintus shouted an order. The slaves on the eastward side banked their oars, and the great vessel swung sharply, thrusting its prow into a narrow passage between perilously craggy rocks jutting from the sea and the end of the great stone breakwater on the left. Like an arrow directed at a target, the great ship shot through the opening into the wide expanse of the harbor itself.

The transition from wave-tossed sea to the glassy calm of the great harbor was astounding. In the protected quiet of the breakwaters the water was as smooth as a pond. Joseph could see white sand on the bottom and rocks here and there garnished with seaweed of various hues. Anemones floated in the gentle currents of the depths, swaying as gracefully as the sleek dolphins cavorting in schools on the surface. Brilliantly colored fish, their hues rivaling the rainbow, moved about in the depths, ignoring the great ship floating above them.

From the high prow of the ship the whole waterfront of Alexandria was spread out before their eyes. Not even in Jerusalem, for all its glory, had Joseph seen anything approaching this sight in magnificence and sheer man-made grandeur. To the left, eastward as he faced across the harbor, lay the curving breakwater called the Diabathra, a continuation of the Promontory of Lochias forming one boundary of the harbor. There the Royal Palace stood, and close beside it, shining in the morning sunlight, was the Temple of Isis. In the smaller and protected Royal Harbor great barges lay at anchor, thin gilded railings and colorful canopies gleaming in the morning sunlight.

The sails were lowered, and now the ship moved slowly across the broad expanse called the Great Harbor, to distinguish it from the Harbor of the Happy Return, which lay west of a great causeway called the Heptastadium, connecting the island of Pharos, upon whose eastern end the lighthouse stood, with the city itself. From the Harbor of the Happy Return, the Agathadaemon Canal led southward through the teeming Greek section of the city to Lake Mareotis and the Nile. Ships from the Nile and the seas to the east could proceed through it directly into the Mediterranean, making this narrow passage the water link between the storied lands of the East, the Great Sea of the Romans, and the unexplored mysteries of the Western Sea beyond the Pillars of Hercules. Bridged channels at either end of the hundred-foot-wide Heptastadium connected the two harbors of Alexandria.

The shore of the Great Harbor was lined with great stone quays to which were tied ships from all parts of the world. They were a district in themselves, called the Exhairesis, into which merchandise could be brought free of duty for transshipment to other lands. Thus Alexandria formed a most important focus in the distribution of goods and materials throughout the Roman Empire.

Joseph had never seen so many ships. Biremes, triremes, and quadriremes—named for the number of their decks—merchant ships and battle ships, coastal galleys and feluccas, lighters, barges, rowboats from which men seemed to be hawking everything under the sun—the masts were a forest, the bright-colored sails and pennants a riot of color.

Nowhere else in the world was there anything like this most colorful and interesting city, and Joseph's pulse quickened just at the thought that at last he was here. The quays were thronged with people. Sailors, merchants, street sellers carrying baskets of fruits and vegetables, wine sellers with the strange bulbous skins upon their backs, beggars of every nationality, priests in long robes with strange hieroglyphs on their foreheads, soldiers of every Roman cohort, faces, voices, and garments from every country of the world—all crowded the docks, milling about, it seemed, without purpose.

Most startling to Joseph, however, were the women. Accustomed to the habits of Jerusalem, where women remained for the most part at home, he was surprised to see them everywhere here, darting between groups of men or hanging onto sailors in frank invitation, chattering like magpies, their dresses every color of the rainbow, faces often shamelessly painted, and hair uncovered. Whatever of calm and dignity was to be found in this scene came not from the humans, but in the flocks of ibises, white, black, pink, and all shades between, who stalked the shore, oblivious of the people, apparently reflecting philosophically upon the foibles of mankind.

"We are docking in the Brucheion or Regia," Bana Jivaka explained. "It is sometimes called the Royal Area and is one of the busiest parts of the city."

"I never saw such warehouses," Joseph admitted. "Or so many people. Not even during the Passover is Jerusalem crowded like this."

"They are even larger on the other side, on the shore of Lake Mareotis. Shipping from the Nile and from Persia and the coast of Malabar is handled over there. Wait until you see the grain barges," he continued. "The life of Rome runs across this narrow tongue of land between Lake Mareotis and the sea upon which Alexandria lies."

Docking a vessel the size of the great round merchant ships from Rome was a tedious process, and the morning was half gone before Joseph and Bana Jivaka came down the gangplank. Their baggage was already piled upon the quay and a host of porters surrounded them, all jabbering at once, but Jivaka quickly selected two and gave them instructions where to take the baggage. A dozen sedan chairs waited to carry travelers into the city, but at the Indian's suggestion they chose to walk the short distance to his room in the Greek quarter, or Rhakotis, where Joseph would live for the time being.

Leaving the waterfront, they traversed the cool arcades of the Forum and found themselves upon the great central thoroughfare called the Meson Pedion or, familiarly, the Street of Canopus. Flanked by rows of colonnades, this main east-to-west artery of Alexandria cut through the city in a straight line for over three miles and was more than thirty paces in width. Beginning at the Gate of the Necropolis, giving access at the western extremity of the city's walls to an area of tombs, mausoleums, and a network of underground catacombs, the stone-paved ribbon led to the Gate of Canopus on the eastern side, where a canal led to the city of that name on still another of the many mouths of the Nile delta. Adjoining the Gate of Canopus, the Jewish Quarter occupied almost a third of the city, constituting the largest population group of this great metropolis, with their own officials and courts of law as well as freedom of worship in the synagogues.

The Rhakotis was not simply for the Greeks, but actually housed a mélange of people from every nationality. On the narrow streets tall Macedonians jostled blond descendants of the Gabinian army of occupation, made up mainly of soldiers from Gaul, who had married Alexandrian women and proceeded to add to the hodge-podge population of this most cosmopolitan of cities. Egyptians, Italians, Cretans, Phoenicians, Cilicians, Cypriots, Persians, Syrians, Armenians, Arabs, Jews, Indians, and occasionally a slant-eyed citizen of the empire of the yellow men far to the east walked the stone-paved streets and added to the jabberwocky of sound. In the babble of voices, only one language was common, the everyday Greek of the common people that nearly everybody spoke with one accent or another.

Finding Mary in this great metropolis was going to be far from easy, Joseph realized as they traversed the teeming streets of Alexandria, for nearly half a million people lived within its boundaries. His first disappointment came the day after his arrival, when he went to the famous theater in the Brucheion, just off the waterfront, and sought word of her. He was brusquely refused admission to the director's presence, and his inquiries brought only the information that no such person as Mary of Magdala was or ever had been employed in the Alexandrian Theater. And it was obvious, even without being told, that she had not realized her ambition to become the leading dancer of the Alexandrian Theater. Huge posters displayed everywhere about the city announced that the darling of the Alexandrians, a dancer called Flamen, would perform in the theater every afternoon beginning the following week, with a new group of dances never before seen on any stage.

Hoping to learn something of Mary in the Jewish Quarter, Joseph presented his letter of introduction to Philo Judaeus, the famed lawyer and leader of the Alexandrian Jews. He was received courteously and treated to spiced cakes and wine by the white-bearded patriarch who was counted the most influential Jew outside Jerusalem itself, if not in the world. But even Philo could tell him nothing except that no one named Mary of Magdala lived in the teeming Jewish Quarter of the city. The talk turned then to Jerusalem. "What do they think in Judea of John the Baptist, who preaches the coming of the Christ?" Philo asked.

Joseph shrugged. "There have been many such. Some even claim to be the Messiah himself."

"But none with the force of this man John. I talked recently with travelers from the lower Jordan who have heard him. They say he has a large following and makes much ado about baptism, claiming that men should repent of their sins and be washed in the water to make them clean."

"The Essenes have preached a similar doctrine for many years," Joseph pointed out.

"John is more than just another Essene," Philo said. "Some of his disciples have recently come to Alexandria and are living among the Therapeutae." Joseph had heard of this sect, a branch of the Essenes of Judea and Galilee, who lived on the shores of Lake Mareotis. Like all Essenes, these pious men observed the oral and written law in every detail, living together in commonly owned homes and obeying in every respect the motto of the Chasidim, *"Mine and Thine belongs to thee."*

"As a physician you should study with profit the methods of the Essenes and the Therapeutae," Philo advised him. "I have seen marvelous cures effected by them through prayer." He put his hand on Joseph's shoulder. "Come and visit with me again, my boy. While you are on this side of the city you might look for the girl in the Eleusis, although I should hate to think that a Jewess would have anything to do with the winebibbers and prostitutes who live in that village of sin."

It was still early when Joseph left Philo's house, so he decided to adopt the jurist's suggestion and visit the village of Eleusis. It stood on the shore of the sea just out-

side the city, with the cool green of the Grove of
Nemesis between it and the walls themselves. To reach
the village, Joseph had to leave the city by way of the
Canopic Gate along the road leading to the great
Hippodrome where horse races were held throughout the
summer months and in the spring. Here the pleasure-
loving Alexandrians flocked by the thousands during the
racing season, but the great amphitheater was empty
now.

Beyond the Hippodrome, by the shores of Lake Mareotis, where papyrus and rushes grew, was a village of low
white huts. When Joseph came nearer he recognized the
colony of the Therapeutae, of which Philo had spoken.
He had seen such colonies among the Essenes outside
Jerusalem, and this one, for all its high-sounding name,
seemed no different. The huts in which the holy men
lived were of wattle, woven from the rushes and papyrus
stalks that grew at the edge of the water and daubed with
a mortar made of ground-up shells from the nearby shore.
Garbed in spotless white, the Therapeutae moved about
their work, speaking only when spoken to. A few were
washing themselves endlessly in the lake, for all Essenes
made much of cleanliness.

It was obviously futile to look for Mary among the
Therapeutae, so he went on to the Eleusis. Devoted to
pleasure and named after the Greek city where the great
festivals of Dionysos and the other gods of the drama had
come into being, this small village was composed largely
of drinking and gaming establishments, plus a few houses
serving as harbors for women of small virtue. Joseph
had no real expectation of finding Mary there and so was
not really surprised or disappointed when no one knew
of her.

A small crowd had gathered at the edge of the town,
listening to an itinerant preacher, a wild-looking man
wrapped in a sheet such as the Therapeutae wore. Since
they blocked the road, Joseph was forced to stop.

"Repent!" the preacher was shouting. "For the kingdom
of heaven is at hand." It was a familiar exhortation, which
he had heard shouted many times by the fanatics who
thronged to Jerusalem on Feast Days.

A plump man standing in the crowd touched him on
the arm. "Are you not the physician, Joseph of Galilee?"
he asked politely.

"Yes, I am," Joseph admitted. "How did you know me?"

"You were pointed out to me in Jerusalem when I visited there last year," the man explained, "but I hardly expected to see you in Alexandria."

"I came here only recently to study medicine," Joseph explained.

"From what I heard in Jerusalem, the Alexandrians could teach you little about your profession," the other man observed. "My name is Matthat."

"Shalom, Matthat," Joseph said courteously. "May you have long life."

"And you," Matthat returned, bowing.

"Who is the preacher?" Joseph asked.

"He is called Eliakim, but he is a disciple of one John called the Baptist because he preaches baptism with water."

Joseph's eyes brightened. "I was talking to Philo Judaeus about John the Baptist not more than an hour ago."

"Men such as these are not fit to wash the feet of Jews like Philo," Matthat said contemptuously. "He is everything a Jew should be. These preachers are only fanatics."

"I come from John the Baptist," the preacher shouted, waving his arms. "His message to you is found in the words of the prophet Isaiah:

"The voice of one crying in the wilderness:
Prepare the way of the Lord.
Make his paths straight.
Every valley shall be filled,
And every mountain and hill shall be brought low,
And the crooked shall be made straight,
And the rough ways shall be made smooth
And all flesh shall see the salvation of God."

"How shall we flee the wrath of the Most High that is to come?" someone in the crowd asked.

The prophet shook a bony forefinger at them. "Bear fruits that befit the repentance. Even now the ax is laid to the root of the trees; every tree, therefore, that does not bear good fruit is cut down and thrown into the fire. He that has two coats, let him share with him who has none. And he who has food, let him do likewise."

"These wandering preachers are always willing to share the rewards of those who work, while they go about shouting of hell and damnation." Matthat spat upon the ground eloquently. "They disgust me."

"Is John the Christ?" a voice inquired from the audience.

The preacher held up his hand for silence. "I will give you these words of John himself: *'I baptize you with water; but he who is mightier than I is coming, the thong of whose sandals I am not worthy to untie. He will baptize you with the Holy Spirit and with fire. His winnowing fork is in his hand, to clear his threshing floor and to gather the wheat into his granary. But the chaff he will burn with unquenchable fire!'*"

The preacher had finished and now the crowd began to disperse. "At least John has the good sense not to claim to be the Christ," Matthat said. "Else he would have to be destroyed, like the other impostors who arose in Israel."

"But suppose he really is the Forerunner spoken of by Isaiah," Joseph suggested. "That would mean the coming of the Messiah is close at hand."

"Jews who live outside Judea and Galilee talk less and less of a Messiah. We may rule the world someday, as our prophets promised, but it will be through controlling commerce and money. With them, politicians can be bought and sold and power acquired to rule nations."

"You may be right," Joseph admitted. "Many have set themselves up as prophets and some even claimed to be the Christ."

"But none could prove they were sent from God," Matthat finished triumphantly. "Come, walk with me back to my place of business in the city. We will refresh ourselves with a glass of wine and talk of Jerusalem."

Matthat's shop was located on the Street of the Sun Gate, just off the Meson Pedion in the very center of the city. In the luxuriously furnished apartment adjacent to the shop a deft slave waited upon them and served them wine. "You are probably wondering what a man who operates an establishment such as this was doing in the Eleusis," Matthat said with a smile. "I can assure you I was not looking for a girl."

Joseph smiled. "If you asked me the same question, I would have to admit that I *was* looking for a girl."

The merchant's eyebrows rose. "Women are the cheapest of all commodities in Alexandria, and also the most expensive. If you want a woman you need only to shout from a window in the Rhakotis to find yourself overrun with them."

"You misunderstand me," Joseph said. "I am looking for a friend who lives here, or did at one time. She is a singer and a dancer, a very beautiful young woman named Mary."

"A Jewess?"

"Part Jewish and part Greek. She comes from Magdala."

"There is no Jewess named Mary of Magdala in the theater here, nor in the Jewish Quarter. I know the area well. But if you want to see dancing"—his eyes lit up—"you must let me take you to see Flamen when she begins her performances next week. Even a devout Jew should not visit Alexandria without seeing the most famous dancer in the Roman Empire."

"My purpose in coming to Alexandria was to study things I could not study in Jerusalem," Joseph admitted.

Matthat grinned. "Then we will call a visit to the theater the study of beautiful women. Believe me, there will be little to interfere with your vision." He put down his glass. "I went to the Eleusis this afternoon to meet a man who must be careful how he shows his face in the city."

"What do you mean?"

"Those of us who deal in gold and precious stones," Matthat explained, "buy from all who have such things to sell. Sometimes it is better not to be too sure of the identity of our clients."

"Thieves!"

Matthat shrugged. "If you would be so uncharitable as to call them such. I prefer to remember that the rich prey upon the poor by working them at low wages, and so it is natural for the poor to rob the rich. If I stand between them and make a profit by selling things stolen from one rich man to another, who is to say that I am either thief or profiteer?"

Joseph laughed. "Your reasoning would put a Greek philosopher to shame. I suppose many thieves are to be found in a city of this size."

"There are more living than dead in the Necropolis," Matthat said cryptically. "The police prudently stay away from the catacombs, for they know a man can get a knife in his back without seeing who struck him. But it is a good thing to know that one can always find a refuge from the Romans in the Necropolis, even with thieves. We Jews have had to look for cover more than once."

" 'Men do not despise a thief, if he steals to satisfy his soul when he is hungry,' " Joseph reminded him.

Matthat nodded. "The same prophet says, 'Whoso keepeth his mouth and his tongue, keepeth his soul from trouble.' Remember that, Joseph, and you may find that thieves can make valuable friends indeed."

5

A few days after his visit with Matthat a slave came to the house where Joseph lived with Bana Jivaka in the Rhakotis, asking him to come to the shop of Matthat at once and bring his instruments and medicines. The merchant would tell Joseph only that a friend was ill and he wanted him to give medical attention.

As they waited for an empty sedan chair at the corner of the Meson Pedion and the Street of the Sun Gate, by the square called the Omphalos, Joseph had an opportunity to see more of the activity of this great city from its busiest corner. On one side was the Jewish Quarter and on the other the Regia, giving access to the Royal Barracks, the Sema, as the temple-tomb where the body of Alexander lay in a coffin of gold was called, and to the palace itself on the Promontory of Lochias, with the Temple of Isis close by. It was nearing sundown and people thronged the streets, dodging through a constant stream of chariots, carriages, and sedan chairs to cross the busiest intersection in the entire city.

The hour was too early yet for the courtesans, who rarely showed their faces and as much of their bodies as they dared before darkness, but men were everywhere. Ruddy-faced Romans on the way to their homes from the baths, where they spent most of the day, jostled arrogantly against Greeks and dark-skinned Egyptians. A white robed prince of the desert tribes that lived beyond the Egyptian Sea, also called the Red Sea, strode through the crowd with haughty mien, until pushed aside arrogantly by a Roman officer in magnificently polished harness, followed by two soldiers with drawn swords, in case their leader became embroiled in one of the sudden snarling fights that often broke out here among the many nationalities making up this polyglot city. It was truly said that one could see here in an hour faces from every nation of the world. And of course the Jews were everywhere, for this was the richest of all Jewish cities.

Matthat had to shout at several chairs before one carrying double stopped before him. Four slaves were chained to the carrying handles, lest they drop the chair and run away after receiving the price. A few men controlled almost the entire public-chair concession in the city and thus were able to set the prices at which they rented their conveyances to those who needed them. Richer Alexandrians, of course, had private chairs borne by their own slaves, but any man could be carried about the city in a style equaling his fortune merely by hailing a conveyance that was for hire.

Along the Street of Canopus they were borne swiftly through the Brucheion. Swarms of people were moving toward the waterfront and its buildings, where much of the social life of the masses took place in the evenings. Already in the Forum a hundred separate groups of gesticulating citizens were discussiing as many subjects. And travelers from far-off lands were entertaining admiring circles of listeners with their thrilling tales. When darkness fell, the courtesans would saunter from their quarters in the high-tiered buildings along the streets housing the teeming thousands of the Greek Quarter, idling along the Heptastadium while the sea breeze molded filmy draperies to voluptuous bodies with calculated intent. There the gallants could write on the stone parapets with bits of charcoal their choice for an assignation, with the added forethought of the price to be paid. And seeing it, the lady chosen could hurry to the meeting or erase the offer contemptuously because the price was too mean.

Through the Rhakotis the chair moved slowly toward the Necropolis Gate, near where the smaller library of the Museum was located close to the Serapeum, the temple to the artificial god created by the Ptolemies to join the worship of Isis and Osiris. The streets of the Rhakotis were narrow, and they were stopped often by trains of mules bearing great bulbous wineskins and baskets of fruit to be sold that evening to the idlers thronging the waterfront.

In the center of the Greek Quarter was the open square of the market place, now almost depleted of provisions, for it was late afternoon. Here the stalls were loaded during the night, ready for the crowds that came shopping in the morning. But in the late afternoon it was a wild place of tumbled bales and wrecks of baskets, where squashed fruits and vegetables made the stones of the pavement slippery. In the booths, sellers cried the remaining wares, a few green beans wilted from lying in the open all day, too ripe berries passed over by discerning shoppers earlier when the produce was fresh, roots of lotus, wilted lettuce, baskets of olives, and all the thousand and one foods necessary to satisfy the varied tastes of so many nationalities.

Near the market were many open-fronted eating places, where attendants had already begun setting out viands to tempt the crowds beginning to throng the streets. Mugs of beer, preserved figs and dates, flat cakes, some spiced, some plain, preserved eels, smoked fish, something to tempt every appetite—all were temptingly displayed before the chattering crowd.

Women's voices shrieked from tier to tier of the high-fronted tenements and across the narrow streets, laughing, singing, shouting obscene jokes, or calling out a frank invitation to men passing on the streets below. They were like the varied instruments of a mighty orchestra playing a symphony in whose notes were the more earthy experiences and urges of human life. But no matter how intently he listened to the voice of the city, nowhere did Joseph hear the sound of a girl's voice as clear as the bell whose tones it resembled, or the twang of a giant cithara in the wild barbaric dances of the desert country.

Turning southward, the slaves bore the chair toward the Necropolis Gate that gave access to the City of the Dead. They crossed the Agathadaemon Canal leading from Lake Mareotis to the Harbor of the Happy Return, a narrow waterway looking far too small to perform its function of connecting the East and the West. Yet through it passed ships from Upper Egypt and the canal, completed by Darius I, between the Nile and the Red Sea, connecting the farthest eastern reaches of the world with the farthest western beyond the Pillars of Hercules, where the Western Sea washed the shores of Britannia, Hibernia, and Caledonia.

At the Gate of the Necropolis, Matthat dismissed the bearers and they emerged from the walls of the city itself on foot. To the south lay the stadium, scene of some of Alexandria's most magnificent religious festivals. The yearly Great Dionysia was held here in the spring, celebrating the resurrection of life through seeds after their death in the warm earth, and the breaking forth of new life from the ground that insured a good crop. And here, too, were held the games that the Greeks loved so well.

Matthat turned in the other direction, toward the resting places of the dead near the shore of the lake. Southward on Lake Mareotis was a suburb of palatial villas belonging to the very rich, but in the Necropolis itself the quiet peace of evening prevailed among the tombs. It was hard to believe that thieves lived here among the dead, but Matthat seemed to know what he was doing, for he led the way along a stone-paved roadway that passed directly through the vast cemetery.

Like all cities of the age, Alexandria had long buried its dead just outside the walls. Here, according to the earthly riches of the corpse and his relatives, the tombs varied greatly in magnificence. Almost a solid wall of marble mausoleums had been erected along the stone-paved central road, each with its tablet giving the list of those who occupied the tombs. Behind the rich marble facades was another and less expensive row of tombs, between which towered the tall spires of cypress trees and the broader expanse of green pines. As one moved back from the central road, the crypts were less and less imposing, and near the shores of the lake itself was a broad field dotted with graves, the resting place of those too poor to build a tomb or belong to one of the many burial societies. These last had tunneled long catacombs beneath the rising ground farther back from the lake, so that they could bury many at different levels and thus more effectively use the rapidly diminishing space left in the Necropolis. Any Alexandrian with a small coin to pay each month could thus insure a resting place for his body.

"I trust, being a physician, Joseph, you do not have the aversion of most Jews to the dead," Matthat said with a smile.

"'Death should be looked forward to if it takes the

spirit some wither where it will be eternal,' " Joseph quoted.

Matthat frowned. "I knew the books of the Law and the Prophets well as a youth, but I do not remember those words."

"A Roman philosopher spoke them. His name was Cicero." Bana Jivaka had introduced Joseph to the writings of the great orator, as well as to the opinions of Socrates and others among the Greeks. He had been startled to find that the views of these pagan philosophers on life and religion were remarkably like the things he himself had been taught.

Matthat stopped before a marble-fronted entrance bearing the name of a burial society. When he was sure no one was observing them, he opened the heavy door and motioned Joseph to follow him inside. They entered a narrow passage angling downward into the earth. Beside the door a taper burned, and above it was a rack of unlit torches. Matthat selected one of these and lit it from the taper; then, holding the flame above his head, he started down the passage with Joseph close behiind him. It was chilly here beneath the ground, and the floor was damp and slippery. "We are not very high above the sea level," Matthat explained, "so some water seeps through the walls."

"This place is truly fit only for the dead." Joseph shivered. "The living would soon die of phthisis."

"Better to risk consumption than be crucified by the Roman soldiers," Matthat observed. "Have you ever seen a man nailed to the cross, Joseph?"

"Once, in Caesarea. Pontius Pilate executed a fanatic who tried to kill him."

"From what I hear, Pilate is over-quick to crucify," Matthat said. "No wonder our people hate him. In this climate men sometimes hang for days on the cross before they die, with the flies torturing them and rats gnawing their bodies at night. The thieves are more merciful than the Romans. They usually manage to put the poor fellow out of his misery while the guards are not looking."

Deep underground they came upon a barred door. Matthat knocked twice upon it, paused, and knocked twice again. A few seconds later a small window in the door itself was opened and a scowling face peered out at them. "Who is it?" a harsh voice demanded.

"Matthat," the merchant announced. "Open up, Manetho, we are not playing games today."

The door was opened, but when they started to enter, a sword barred the passage. To Joseph, Matthat said in Aramaic, "This one is always suspicious. I will handle him."

"Have you come to cheat us again?" the man called Manetho demanded. "What scoundrel do you bring with you this time?"

"A physician to treat your father," Matthat said sharply. "Stand aside, buffoon."

"We need no physicians," the thief growled. "Today I sacrificed to Serapis. He will soon be well."

"Achillas asked me to bring a physician. Enough of this! I want Joseph of Galilee to see him."

"Bloodsucking Jews!" Manetho stepped aside but spat at the floor beside their feet in eloquent contempt. "We run the risk and you make the profit."

"And where would you be if I did not sell what you steal?" Matthat demanded urbanely. "Other bands of thieves would be glad to have me turn their takings into gold."

They entered a fairly large room, hollowed out of the earth and lit by oil lamps. Although the air was chilly it was not foul, so Joseph judged that there must be an opening on the surface above, perhaps hidden by another tomb. In one corner a brazier glowed with a pot over it, from which arose the savory odor of bubbling stew. Several men were gathered about the brazier, and in the corner of the room an old man with white hair lay on a couch. Beside him was a beautiful dark-skinned girl dressed in white.

"Shalom, Matthat," the old man said courteously. "I welcome you in the manner of your people."

"Shalom, Achillas," Matthat replied. "I have brought with me a skilled physician, Joseph of Galilee."

The girl's face brightened. She was quite beautiful, Joseph saw, with finely chiseled features, dark hair that fell to her shoulders, and a lovely figure. "This is Albina, Joseph," Matthat said. "She dances in the Alexandrian Theater."

"Welcome, Joseph of Galilee," the girl said in a low musical voice, bowing low. "Cure my father of this grave illness and you may call upon us for whatever you wish, even our lives."

Behind them Manetho snorted, "Jews!" but Achillas spoke sharply to him and, still glowering, he joined the men beside the brazier. "Forgive the rudeness of my son, I beg you," the old man said quietly. "He is a boor, and a disgrace to the Greek blood we bear in our bodies with that of Egypt. I have been grievously ill, and the fever is still upon me. If you have a potent medicine . . ."

"Let me examine you first," Joseph suggested courteously. "Perhaps I can do something to help you then."

He had little difficulty in making the diagnosis; the condition had been graphically described by Hippocrates nearly five hundred years before. First came an inflammation of the lungs, easily understandable in an old man who lived amidst dampness and cold. Then followed the exudation of fluid inside the chest and its change into a purulent accumulation, slowly poisoning the victim. Most physicians advocated waiting for the empyema to rupture through the lung, an event that occurred in far less than half the cases. But Hippocrates and a few daring surgeons after him had advocated a more direct treatment, draining the poisonous exudate by making an opening between the ribs directly through the chest wall. Joseph wondered if he dare advocate this procedure here, upon the leader of a gang of thieves, with the scowling son waiting in the background for an excuse to intervene.

He hesitated only a moment, however, for true to his profession, he could recommend only that treatment which seemed to promise some hope of a cure, regardless of the consequences to himself. Watching him anxiously from beside the couch, the daughter Albina said, "There is hope; I can see it in your face."

"Yes," he agreed. "I believe your father can be cured. But surgery is necessary."

She caught her breath. "The knife!"

"The knife is for embalmers," Manetho growled. "My father is not dead."

"There is an accumulation inside his chest," Joseph explained. "It must be drained away or he will be poisoned by it."

"I have felt the heaviness in my side for many days," Achillas agreed. "Do what you must, Joseph. But do it quickly. Already the poison is sapping my strength."

Joseph had brought the small case in which he carried his instruments and medicines, so little preparation was required. True to the description by Hippocrates, the spaces between the ribs on the right side of Achillas' chest were filled out, as if distended by the purulent accumulation deeper within the cavity. With the old man lying on his left side, Joseph tensed the skin between two of the lower ribs beneath the armpit and cut quickly through the skin and fatty tissue down to the muscle in one clean stroke, opening a wound about a hand's breadth in length.

Blood spurted from tiny vessels, and Achillas gasped with the sudden stab of pain. Had Bana Jivaka been there he might have induced the strange trance and thus prevented the old man from feeling pain, but Joseph was not yet adept in bringing on the stupor. Besides, he thought it advisable not to do anything startling in the face of Manetho's obvious suspicion.

Matthat had sickened at the first sight of blood, and it was the girl Albina who helped Joseph, handing him the pad of washed wool that he packed into the wound to stop the bleeding and holding an oil lamp where he could see. While he waited for the tiny vessels to be closed by clot, he could not help admiring the graceful way Albina moved. She reminded him of Mary, and then he remembered that she, too, was a dancer and made a mental note to ask if Albina knew anything about her.

Holding the wound open with the fingers of his left hand, Joseph now slit the whitish tough tissue over the muscles for the length of the incision, separating the pinkish muscle fibers with the handle of the knife. He could see a second layer of muscle running in the other direction, and this he cut through carefully, lest the crossing effect of the strands close the opening through which he hoped to drain the poisonous material.

Deep in the wound Joseph could now feel a tense layer that was like a drumhead. Slowly he slid the scalpel down along his index finger until it pressed upon the drumlike tissue. The point engaged the tough layer, and as he slowly increased the pressure upon the scalpel handle, he felt the blade cut through the almost gristly wall of the accumulated empyema. Then a sudden nauseating stench told him he had found his goal.

"Sacred Mother of Horus!" Albina breathed. "How could he live with that in his body?"

Joseph worked rapidly, letting the thick, foul accumulation pour from the cavity where it had been dammed up. When it was empty, he rolled a square of wool into a tube and slipped it through the opening, where it would act as a wick and keep the wound edges from closing together too soon. The whole thing had taken less than half an hour.

Achillas took a deep breath in spite of the pain. "Ahhh!" he exclaimed. "Already a great load has been lifted from me. You have performed a miracle, Joseph."

"Not a miracle," Joseph corrected him, "an ordinary surgical operation."

"But not one many physicians would attempt, even in Alexandria," Albina said warmly. "We owe you our lives for saving my father."

"I ask no fee," Joseph told them. "You are friends of Matthat, who is also my friend. That is enough."

"No," Achillas said firmly. "I know it is written in the ancient writings of the Jews that in all labor there is profit. Bring me the small pouch from the chest there in the corner, Albina."

Joseph was washing his hands when the girl returned. While he dried them, Achillas fumbled with the strings of the pouch and tumbled something out into his palm. "Take this," he said, handing it to Joseph. "It was to be Albina's wedding portion."

"You need not hesitate," he added. "It was bought, not stolen."

Joseph had no choice but to accept the gift, if he was to avoid offending the old man. It was a large pearl, almost as big as a small egg. "Won't you take this back as a gift from me?" he asked the girl. "I wish no pay for helping your father."

But the beautiful dark-skinned dancer shook her head. "My father's life is worth more to me than jewels. Take it, please, from both of us. You have earned it ten times over."

Joseph put the pearl into his purse. "I will sell it, then," he told them, "and give the money to the poor." As he gathered up his instruments and supplies he saw that the young thief Manetho's face was dark with anger. And when they were leaving the Necropolis, Matthat warned, "I may have underestimated Manetho, Joseph. He would gladly stick a knife between your ribs to get that pearl. Give it to me to sell and I will see that he knows you no longer have it. The money will be safe with a money-lender and will earn interest for you until you return to Jerusalem."

Joseph gladly gave Matthat the jewel, since he had no wish for his body to be found floating in the Agathadaemon Canal the next morning.

At the canal Matthat hailed one of the boats for hire that plied back and forth between Lake Mareotis, the Harbor of the Happy Return, and the main part of the city itself. Joseph left him there and went on through the Rhakotis alone. It was said of the Alexandrians that they slept by day and roistered the whole night long and, looking about him tonight, Joseph could well believe it. The weather was still warm, although winter was approaching and the babbling of voices in every tongue of the world filled the air. Brawny sailors and fishermen from the waterfront ranged the narrow streets arm in arm. Those they met were forced to scurry into doorways for protection or be knocked sprawling into the stone-paved street. On almost every corner was a drinking house from which came shouts and coarse laughter, mingled with the happy squeals of the women who thronged there with the men.

It was on just such a warm night as this, Joseph remembered, that he had walked across the city of Magdala to Demetrius' house with Mary and she had kissed him before going inside. Would he ever find her here in this teeming city? he wondered. The quest seemed hopeless now for she had apparently failed in her ambition to become an important figure in the theater of Alexandria, and he did not know where else to look for her. She might even have left the city in her disappointment, going perhaps to Ephesus, Antioch, or even Rome, all of which had large theaters.

Obeying an impulse to see if he could learn anything about Mary at the waterfront, Joseph turned along a street leading to the Great Harbor. The spars of hundreds of vessels were always visible where the streets opened upon the harbor, and if Mary had sailed for Rome or another city, it would have been from the great quay.

When he came out upon the jetty near the Heptastadium, Joseph stopped in astonishment. It was the first time he had come here at night, and he was not prepared for what he saw. A mirror reflected seaward the light of the great fires built nightly on the platform atop the Pharos, but the flames themselves were bright enough to light up the harbor and the great broad causeway leading across it to the island upon which the lighthouse stood.

Along the waterfront streets and the causeway itself a great crowd of people—the largest Joseph had ever seen —was moving in the nightly promenade of the Alexandrians, a sight to be seen nowhere else in the world.

In Judea women did not go out at night, except when accompanied by their menfolk. This crowd, however, teemed with unattached women of every nationality, every color, every social level, for the Heptastadium was in truth the meeting place of all Alexandrians. A haughty Roman wife walked idly along in her finery, perhaps to meet a lover, attended by a coal-black slave girl naked above the snow-white cloth wrapped about her body as a skirt. Almost touching the respectable matron, a courtesan ambled with the peculiar undulating gait of her tribe, cheeks painted with antimony, eyelids dripping with kohl, lips vivid with carmine, gazing boldly at the men she met and smiling an invitation to any who looked prosperous. Dark-skinned Egyptian girls walked with blond descendants of the soldiers brought here by Alexander and much more recently by the legions of Caesar. Actually, it seemed to Joseph that there were more courtesans in Alexandria than respectable women, which was not far from the truth.

In a Jewish community these painted women would have been stoned by an outraged populace, but although Joseph instinctively turned his head at the sight of them, he could not entirely still the quickening of his pulses at the sight of lovely bodies half revealed by diaphanous robes of bombyx, or draperies cunningly arranged so as to leave one beautiful breast entirely bare. Lest he find temptation stronger than his will, Joseph turned toward the quays themselves, where the work of loading and unloading ships went on both night and day. If Mary had left Alexandria, someone among the mariners who sailed regularly to all the seaport cities of the Empire might remember her and Demetrius, or at least the height and the hawklike profile of the Nabatean, Hadja.

He stopped to speak to Phoenician traders, tall men with long hair and jutting beaks of noses, guarding piled-up bales of the rich purple fabric used for Roman uniforms, but learned nothing. Then he went on to question sailors who had traveled beyond the Pillars of Hercules to the land called Britannia, returning with vast stores of amber and crude tin, but to no avail.

All the produce in which men traded the world over

lay on the massive wharves of this great free port, where no customs fees were charged on goods transshipped to other destinations. Silken cloth and cheaper cotton fabric from the far-distant domain of the Han emperors; apes, peacocks, and precious jewels from the ports of Malabar; spices and precious incense from the cities of Arabia; ivory and gold from the land of the blacks called Nubia —these and hundreds of other goods filled the quays and great warehouses. Long lines of slaves marched up and down the gangplanks under the whips of the overseers, handling cargo even at night. For the sea lanes of the world radiated from this teeming port, and from the bottomless granary of the Nile Valley flowed an endless stream of grain for Rome and its soldiers. But none of the ships' captains remembered taking as passengers a girl whose hair was as red as the sunset over Lake Mareotis, a fat Greek musician, and a man of the deserts.

6

ALTHOUGH Joseph was disappointed in his search for Mary, he was not unhappy concerning his other purpose in coming to Alexandria, that of learning more about his profession. Under the tutelage of Bana Jivaka he was able to go directly to the source of this rich fountain of learning, the great Museum that stood between the Street of Canopus and the waterfront. Actually the Museum was part of a larger building or palace that formed in its entirety a university for the study of science and other subjects. The teachers took their meals in a large hall from which opened a series of arcades where students walked and conversed with the professors between lectures. Nearby were rooms where the lecturers gave their discourses.

On higher ground between the Museum and the Lochias Promontory stood the famous Alexandrian Theater. From its upper seats patrons were afforded a view of the broad panorama of the harbor, a forest of masts from ships, scores of small boats, and the great white lighthouse on the island at the seaward boundary. Beside the theater towered the Temple of Pan, and to west of this, the great gymnasium, whose porticoes were more than a stadium in length. Just beyond the gymnasium were the Courts of Justice.

Joseph spent his days in the Museum, watching the physician-teachers treat the sick poor who thronged here from every part of the city. While the professors diagnosed and treated each case, they lectured to a semicircle of students standing around the patient. Less often surgical operations were performed, but in this field none of the teachers could equal the skill and daring of Bana Jivaka or the teachings of the great physician Susruta, whose precepts he scrupulously followed.

Afternoons were given over to lectures on science and astronomy, in which the school at Alexandria led the world. It was here that Euclid had proved his famous theorems in geometry. Here, too, Eratosthenes had accomplished the astounding feat of measuring the earth. And beneath the same cool arcades Aristarchus of Samos had studied the stars at night and evolved his startling theory that the earth and the planets revolved around the sun.

As the days passed, Joseph found that he was learning more from Bana Jivaka than he was from the teachers at the university. Under his friend's tutelage he became adept at inducing the strange trancelike condition by which the Indian surgeon was able to perform serious operations without pain. The subject merely gazed at a bright object, such as the jewel used by Jivaka, while the physician's will gradually overcame his through the repeated suggestion that he was falling asleep. From an Egyptian student he learned that this accomplishment was not limited to India, but had been known by the priests of the Nile for thousands of years.

Working together, Joseph and Bana Jivaka performed many feats of surgery, so much so that their reputation soon spread throughout the city and people came seeking them from all quarters. In this way Joseph came to make friends and earn the gratitude of high persons among the officials who ruled the great metropolis, merchants who operated the bazaars, traders in foreign exchange whose offices were in the great warehouses, people of his own race from the Jewish Quarter, and, following his

115

success with Achillas, even the thieves and petty criminals who were everywhere.

Achillas' recovery was steady and uncomplicated. Joseph visited him every few days for the first week, and by the second he was so much recovered that he no longer needed anything but an occasional examination of the operative wound.

True to promise, Matthat came a few weeks later to take Joseph to the theater, where the performances began in midafternoon and ran until darkness had fallen. The drama and dance were favorite diversions of the pleasure-loving Alexandrians, and a great crowd thronged the streets, moving toward the massive stone walls of the great theater near the waterfront.

"It is always like this when Flamen dances," Matthat explained as they were pushed about by the crowd. "The theatergoers worship her. There has never been another like her in Alexandria."

"Is she a courtesan?" Joseph had come to know that actresses in Alexandria, as in the rest of the world, belonged generally to this group.

Matthat shrugged. "Some claim she is not. Men who have sought her favors and been repulsed will wager she is a virgin. Whatever she is, her power over men is greater than that of any other woman in Alexandria. She is rich already from gifts by wealthy men who seek her favors."

"Why do they seek her if she refuses them?"

Matthat smiled. "You are a physician. You should know human nature well enough to realize that a man will beggar himself for a beautiful woman who denies him, when he would soon become tired of her if she yielded. Courtesan or not, this Flamen is smart and cold-blooded. Just last year the tax collector, Flavius, lost his position because he stole tax moneys to buy gifts for her. The day he was found out she turned to another, and richer, man."

Matthat had purchased tickets entitling them to a seat in the great *cavea,* or auditorium. They entered by the aisles called *paradoi,* separating the performers from the audience, and found their way along other passages radiating out from these to a row of seats only a short distance from the stage. The first several rows were reserved for the nobility and the very rich. Just over the openings where the crowd entered, two elaborate boxes called *tribunalia* were set apart for even more important dignitaries.

"One of the *tribunalia* is always taken by Flamen's current suitor," Matthat explained. "You can see that she caters only to very rich men. Nobody else could afford such a seat night after night."

Joseph looked about him curiously, for it was the first time he had ever been in a theater. Before the *scaena,* or stage, was a broad semicircular platform, the orchestra, on which the chorus sang and danced and before which the musicians sat. They were already tuning their instruments when Joseph and Matthat came in.

A great partition separated the audience from the stage proper, but soon after they found seats it was lowered into a grooved slot in the floor at the edge of the *scaena,* revealing the stage with its painted backdrop, or *skene.* Of stage machinery there was little except the *eccyclema,* a wheeled platform that was run out on the stage when necessary, bearing special scenes.

The auditorium was filling rapidly, and a steady roar of conversation filled the air. It was a brilliant scene indeed, for the vast semicircular theater was a riot of color from the tunics of the men and the vivid draperies of the women who sat with them. Hawkers moved up and down the aisles selling sweetmeats and small skins of wine with which a thirsty viewer might refresh himself. People shouted gaily to each other across the rows, relaying the latest bawdy story or the newest juicy bit of scandal.

The musicians soon began to play the opening chorus, but there was little letup in the hum of conversation. Fortunately Joseph and Matthat were close to the orchestra, so they could hear the music and also had a fine view of the stage itself. Shortly a group of jugglers appeared, tossing swords deftly to each other and catching them by the handles with amazing dexterity. After them a beautiful girl in jeweled breastplates and a golden girdle set a number of swords upright upon the floor and danced among them nimbly, missing the points, it seemed, by only a finger's breadth.

Now came the first play. It was a mime, one of those short scandalous dramas full of double meanings and frank asides spoken to the audience. The stock characters in these earthy dramas were the unfaithful wife, the handsome effeminate lover, the cuckolded husband, and the gay coquette. This last was played by a young lady who made a great hit with the audience by flirting up her skirts at every opportunity. The audience loved it all, shouting their approval and keeping up a steady conversation all the while.

Next a troupe of girls in filmy tunics ran out upon the orchestra with garlands of flowers in their hair and carrying golden lyres in their hands. They sang a tender love song, then, putting the lyres on the edge of the raised stage above them, began to dance. All were very graceful and made a lovely picture in their flimsy, revealing draperies.

After the dancing came another mime, this time the *Atellan Farce,* with its broad comic characters, the clown called Bucco, the pantaloon Pappus, a booby called Maccus, and the wise man, Dossenus. Next the musicians began a strange haunting melody which Joseph had never heard but which Matthat said was a song of ancient Egypt, and a dark-skinned girl ran to the center of the stage and bowed, her extended fingertips touching the floor. When she raised her writhing arms slowly and stood erect, Joseph saw with a start that it was Achillas' daughter, Albina.

"Next to Flamen, Albina is the best dancer they have," Matthat observed. "And a lovely girl as well."

The dark-skinned girl wore only a white silken cloth about her loins, but she was so lovely to look at that Joseph could not think of her as being wanton in the display of her body. Her dance was strange to him, a thing of stylized postures with fingers together and hands extended in many odd positions, but the audience, especially the Egyptians, loved it, and Joseph judged that it was a favorite of her people. When she finished, applause filled the theater and she came back once to bow to the audience.

On the performance went, for a regular program in the Alexandrian Theater lasted four hours. Finally a band of black women from Africa danced the strange, sensuous tribal dances of their people, their naked bodies glistening with sweat in the light of an actual fire built in a great copper pot on the stage.

"Flamen will be coming on soon," Matthat said. "Her current suitor is in his box."

Joseph looked across at the seat in the *tribunalia* which had until now been empty, and saw that a tall man with a cold hard face had taken his place. The Roman was graying at the temple but very handsome, a patrician in every haughty line of his face.

"That is the *gymnasiarch* Plotinus," Matthat explained. "I hear that he has already spent thousands of denarii on Flamen." Joseph had been in Alexandria long enough to know that the *gymnasiarch,* as head of the great gymnasium that was the center of the city's social activities as well as much of its political life, was one of the most important men in Alexandria.

"What does this Flamen do that makes her so popular in the theater?" Joseph asked curiously. "She can hardly wear less clothing than the dancers who have gone before her."

"She wears more. They say when she first came to Alexandria the director wanted her to dance naked like the others, but she refused. Wait until you see her, and you will understand the magic she uses upon a crowd, even when more fully clothed than many women in the audience tonight."

The last of the black dancers scurried from the stage and the massive curtain rose, creaking, from the depths beneath it. It was already dusk, and attendants began to light torches on either side of the stage itself while a hush fell over the crowd in anticipation of the main attraction. Then, as slowly and as ponderously as it had risen, the curtain descended again and a scene of fairy-like beauty was revealed.

A flower garden erected upon the *eccyclema* had been wheeled upon the stage while the curtain was down. A bench stood in the garden beside the little fountain playing there as naturally as if it were real, and flowers were cunningly arranged so that they seemed to be growing around it. The sheer beauty of the scene brought a burst of spontaneous applause from the audience.

When the applause had died away, a woman appeared from the flower-decked arbor beside the bench, carrying a lyre in her hands. She was dressed in a clinging gown of dazzling white, girt about her waist and beneath her breasts with silvery ribbon, and on her flaming red hair a circlet of jewels sparkled in the light of the torches beside the stage. Applause thundered through the building again, and she waited patiently for it to subside before plucking the strings of the lyre and beginning to sing. The song, when it reached Joseph's ears, was familiar, as familiar as when he had first heard it one day on the streets of Tiberias:

> *"I'll twine white violets and the myrtle green,*
> *Narcissus will I twine, and the lilies' sheen;*
> *I'll twine sweet crocus, and the hyacinth blue;*
> *And last I'll twine the rose, love's token true:*
> *That all may form a wreath of beauty, meet*
> *To deck my Heliodora's tresses sweet."*

7

LISTENING as she sang, drinking in her beauty with his eyes and his ears, Joseph could see that Mary had changed in the years since she had left Magdala. Not only had her body grown more womanly and less girlish, but her voice had matured as well. Where before it had been beautiful, the notes as clear as a bell of the finest silver ever struck by the superb artisans of Ephesus, whose peer did not exist anywhere in the world, the tones were now richer and deeper, a voice to stir men's pulses and set the blood pounding in their temples.

It was easy to see why she had captured the admiration of the jaded crowds of Alexandria, for looking around him in the theater, Joseph saw not a woman who could even approach her in beauty and sheer personal allure, although the most famous courtesans of all Egypt were here tonight. The *gymnasiarch* Plotinus was leaning forward in his box, and as she finished her song Joseph saw Mary glance up to the *tribunalia* where he sat and smile, before bowing to the thunderous applause of the audience.

"Is she not lovely?" Matthat asked.

"Even more than she was five years ago," Joseph said without taking his eyes from the white figure on the stage below.

"Five years?" Matthat's eyes widened. "Do you mean—"

"The woman called Flamen in Alexandria is Mary of Magdala, the girl I have been seeking."

The merchant's eyes popped. "Then why could you not find her?"

"She no longer uses her name. And she seems not to have let it be known here that she is a Jew."

Matthat nodded sagely. "She was wise. We Jews are not loved, even in Alexandria, where we outnumber almost everyone else. And no Roman would marry her if he knew she was a Jewess."

"She is only half Jew," Joseph explained. "And she was brought up as a Greek." But he could not repress entirely his disappointment that Mary had chosen to deny the Hebrew ancestry of which he was so proud.

"Flamen," Matthat mused. "The torch. She could hardly have chosen a more appropriate name under which to dance. Sometimes she does indeed resemble a burning brand."

"A Nabatean musician named Hadja gave her the name," Joseph explained. "He always called her the Living Flame. She would naturally take the name Flamen as an actress. I was stupid not to think of it before."

The applause had died away, and as the stringed instruments of the orchestra took up a soft lilting melody Mary began to dance. It was the same dance she had performed before Pontius Pilate and his guests, but Joseph had never seen it. As she moved about the stage, he could visualize the scene she was painting with the consummate artistry of her body as clearly as if he were once again on the shores of the beautiful Lake of Gennesaret, watching the lightning play across the dark thunderheads and hearing the drumming of the rain of Marheshvan sweep across the water and caress the shores with its promise of a bountiful harvest. The boy and girl might even have been himself and Mary back in Magdala, an eon, it seemed now, ago.

Matthat breathed deeply. "I have never seen her do this dance before. You can almost smell the rain upon the hills of Galilee again."

Finally the music faded away and the lovely flame-haired figure on the stage slowly sank to the floor with her arms outstretched before her while the crowd broke into a great thunder of applause. Men leaped to their feet and threw empty wineskins and the dried leaves in which sweetmeats had been wrapped into the air, shouting their approval. Mary remained in the center of the stage, bowing, waiting patiently for the tumult to subside. There

121

could be no doubt in Joseph's mind that as Flamen she had achieved the triumph for which she had longed. Idolized by the populace of Alexandria, with one of its most important citizens, the *gymnasiarch* Plotinus, her slave, she could want nothing more.

When the tumult subsided, the music began another melody, a wailing, sensuous beat. Now Mary's body was the promise of woman's eternal lure for man. Under its spell the very sound of breathing from the vast audience seemed to deepen and become turgid with desire, for the lure of all the delights in a pagan paradise was in her body.

"They say Salome, the daughter of Herod, dances like this for her lovers," Matthat said hoarsely. "And I have seen it danced many times by naked women from the East. But the clothing yonder Flamen wears makes her ten times more desirable."

Joseph glanced up at the box of the *tribunalia*. Plotinus was leaning forward, his eyes fixed upon the seductive undulating figure on the stage. The Roman's face was pale, and sweat stood out on his forehead. In a sudden moment of insight into the man's thoughts, Joseph knew that Plotinus had not yet possessed Mary of Magdala. A man could not desire with such overwhelming intensity a fruit he had already tasted. The thought, however, brought him little joy.

"How can you be so calm, Joseph?" Matthat asked hoarsely. "You love the girl. Are you not consumed by desire for her as is Plotinus up there?"

Slowly Joseph shook his head. "Flamen is more beautiful than Mary of Magdala ever was," he admitted. "But the woman dancing there is not the same. An evil spirit has laid hold of her."

"It is an evil spirit every man here save yourself would give his soul to possess then. No wonder she can do anything she wishes with men."

The dance came to its inevitable climax, and Mary ran from the stage. But the crowd shouted again and again for her, and she was forced to return many times before they would let her go. When finally the great curtain began to rise slowly from its slot in the floor, Joseph stood up. "I want to speak to her," he said. "Do you know how to get behind the scenes?"

"Of course. Albina sometimes dines with me after a performance."

Behind the great stage everything seemed to be confusion as they sought Flamen's dressing room. Scantily clad women hurried past, scenery was being moved, for there would be another performance tomorrow, and musicians were leaving the theater with their instruments under their arms. At the entrance to a short corridor leading to the dressing room of the principal dancer a picture of a torch had been painted on the wall. Beneath it stood a Roman soldier in polished harness with the *gymnasiarch's* personal crest upon his helmet below the eagles of Rome. He had a drawn sword in his hand, and as Matthat and Joseph approached, he held the blade across the passage, barring them from approaching.

"I would speak to the dancer Flamen," Joseph said courteously. "We are old friends from Galilee."

"No one visits Flamen except by permission of the *gymnasiarch*," the soldier said boredly, as if this happened all the time. "On your way."

"B-but—"

"Did you not hear the guard, Jew?" a harsh voice asked behind him. Joseph turned to see Plotinus standing only a yard away. At close range, the *gymnasiarch's* face was even colder and more forbidding than it had been from the box.

"I heard him," Joseph said in the same courteous tone. "If you would send word to Flamen that Joseph of Galilee is here to see her, I am sure she would admit me. We are old friends."

"Flamen would have no Jew as a friend," Plotinus said contemptuously. "I know this fellow Matthat is a thieving merchant of stolen jewels. Do you think to sell something to her by such a trick?"

"We have nothing to sell," Matthat protested, and Joseph added, "I tell you, I knew her in Galilee."

"Silence, Jewish dogs!" Plotinus snapped, reddening with anger. "Dare you insult Flamen by insinuating that she would even have heard of your cursed country?" He was wearing a mailed glove, and a sudden murderous light flared in his cold eyes. It did not for the moment occur to Joseph that Plotinus would strike him, and so he was totally unprepared for the smash of the mailed fist against his temple. There was a sudden sharp pain as the metal cut through yielding skin, then darkness engulfed him.

At first Joseph thought he was back in his own quarters, where he lived with Bana Jivaka in the Rhakotis section of Alexandria. It was night, for an oil lamp burned in a bracket on the wall and the room was just like that in which they lived, one of thousands of such rooms in the many-storied tenements making up the Greek Quarter. And yet something was different about this one, a distinctive touch in the draperies at the windows, the colorful cushions of the couch on which he lay, and the faint perfume in the air.

Something moved in the far corner, and he made out a graceful feminine figure in a white silken robe. For one thrilling moment he thought it was Mary, but as the girl came into the circle of light cast by the lamp he recognized the dark skin and cleanly etched features of Albina, the Egyptian dancer who was the daughter of Achillas, the thief.

"Have you decided to wake up?" Albina's fingers touched his forehead, and he realized that a bandage partially covered his head. Now he began to remember what had happened until Plotinus had felled him.

"Was I unconscious long?" he asked Albina.

"Almost six hours by the water clock. I saw Plotinus strike you in the corridor leading to Flamen's dressing room, and Matthat and I brought you here while you were unconscious"

"Who bandaged me?"

"Your friend, the physician of Malabar. Matthat went for him. He assured us that you were only stunned and would awaken later, so we thought it best to let you stay here"

"But it is night." He started to push himself up on his elbows, but the room began to reel. Albina stooped quickly and put her arm about his shoulders, lowering him gently back to the cushions. "It is almost morning," she said, "but what difference does that make?"

"Have we spent the night here alone?"

"Most of it." She smiled. "I do not mind. Why should you?"

"But your reputation?"

She shrugged. "I am a dancer in the theater. Everybody thinks we are courtesans, whether we are or not, so we soon stop worrying about what they think. You must lie still now."

"Did Ma—Flamen know I was looking for her?" he asked.

Albina shook her head. "Plotinus is insanely jealous. He posts a guard before her dressing room when she comes to the theater, and no man can enter it, not even the director. You should not have tried to see her at the theater, Joseph. Plotinus might have killed you if Matthat and I had not taken you away. He can do almost anything he likes here in Alexandria. They say even the governor obeys his orders."

"But I have been seeking her for weeks," Joseph protested.

"Then it is true, what you said about Galilee?"

Perhaps, Joseph thought, he had said too much already. If Mary did not wish it known here in Alexandria that she was part Jew, he owed it to her as a friend not to reveal the secret. "I may be wrong," he said lamely, but he was too honest to lie.

"I am one of the few who knows that Flamen has Jewish blood," Albina explained. "We were very close when she first came to Alexandria. I was the principal dancer then, and she was one of the chorus, but she soon stood above me."

"Most people would hate her for it."

The dancer shook her head. "Flamen is a great artist, the greatest I have ever known. No one could hate her for the gift the gods have given her. But she has no soul; that I could not forgive her."

"Why do you say that?"

"Woman was meant to fill a great need of man, Joseph. In her arms he can find release from the cares of the day, and she can give him strong sons and daughters so that his line may not die. But a woman who stirs up men's passions, not to satisfy them but deliberately to use them for her own gain, is dishonest."

"Then it is true that she does not give herself to these men who follow after her?"

A look of pain and disappointment came into her fine dark eyes. "You love her, too, don't you, Joseph?" she said softly.

"I have loved her for many years," he explained, "but not as the woman who danced tonight. She was a girl then, lovely and unspoiled. Now . . ." He did not finish the sentence. The thought of what Mary had become brought pain.

125

"It is hard to believe Flamen was ever thus," Albina said. "But you love her, Joseph, so I will tell you what I believe—that Flamen has been mistress to nothing but her own greed for gold and power."

"It is not greed that drives her," Joseph said, "but the desire for revenge."

"What need for revenge could be that strong?"

"She was cruelly ravished years ago by a man, a Roman," he explained.

"And she hates all Romans as a result? Yes, I could understand that. Any woman could. And you continued to love her even through that, Joseph? You must be a saint."

Joseph shook his head. "A wise man among the Jews once said, '*A friend loveth at all times, and a brother is born for adversity*'!"

Albina smoothed the bandage upon his head with gentle fingers. "I have never known many Jews, Joseph. And no man like you. If Flamen treats you as she does the others?" She took a deep breath. "Why do I find it so hard to tell you that I would be happy to bear you strong children? And to comfort you in my arms against the troubles of the world? I am a dancer and people believe me a prostitute, but I have lain with no man for his gold, or ever will. Still no good man would want to marry me because of this."

"I think you are wrong, Albina." He put his hand over hers. "Many men would want you for what you are, not what people think you to be."

"Men like you might, Joseph," she agreed. "But I have seen no other one. I would save you the sorrow I know Flamen will bring you, but if you must see her, I will tell you where she may be found. She dwells on the shore of Lake Mareotis outside the wall of the city and beyond the Serapeum, where many of the rich have villas. I have been told that Plotinus keeps soldiers always on guard there, but if you walk along the shore you can enter the garden between the water and the walls."

"How do you know this?" he asked.

Albina smiled. "You forget that my father is a thief. But take care that you are not taken for one yourself when you go to seek Flamen. The guards would make short work of you."

8

JOSEPH suffered no ill effects from his wound by the
mailed fist of Plotinus. In a few days the slight headache
which followed it was gone and the cut in his scalp had
healed so that he no longer needed a bandage. Late one
afternoon he set off for the villa where Albina had told
him Mary lived, but he was not yet sure of his way
through the teeming quarter of Rhakotis, and so darkness
was already falling when he reached the line of elaborate
villas on the shores of Lake Mareotis to the south of the
city.

The shores of the large inland body of water formed
by the mouth of the Nile were very fertile, and the luxurious villas of the Romans and the rich *hetairai* who
favored this sunnier side of the city were almost hidden
by trees and vines. Fruit gardens and vineyards flourished
and flowers grew everywhere, although it was early winter, for there was not a day in the year that something
did not bloom in Alexandria. Some of the streets led down
to the water itself, where boat landings had been placed
to facilitate traffic back and forth between the city and
the luxurious gardens on the eight islands outlined in the
early dusk against the reddish tint of the sky from the setting sun.

From the Agathadaemon Canal a regular line of ferry-
boats crossed the lake to the islands and on to the main-
land beyond. The glassy water was dotted with the masts
and bright sails of the Nile boats that plied the great
river and unloaded food for Alexandria and goods to be
shipped to other parts of the Empire upon the Mareotis
quays. Across the water moved an endless procession of
grain barges bringing corn for Rome and Alexandria from
the rich delta in the interior. Small galleys, graceful
pleasure boats with lateen sails, and light skiffs scurried
about seeking to reach their moorings before darkness
fell completely.

On winter days the winds often blew from the Great

Sea, bringing a damp cold miasma to the city that did not help the health of the inhabitants, but tonight was the kind the pleasure-loving Alexandrians adored. A soft warm breeze flowed down the Nile Valley toward its mouth, bathing the city in a pleasant warmth and wafting over it a fragrant aroma from the flowers and spice groves on the lake shore. Tonight a great crowd would be promenading along the waterfront, and a small army of people would be marching back and forth across the Heptastadium. And in the crowded native quarters people would lie outside the houses on mats and cushions while lovers huddled close in the shadows. But here on the lake shore there was peace and quiet.

True to what Albina had told him, two Roman soldiers guarded the door to Flamen's villa, identified by the same picture of a torch that marked her dressing room. Joseph knew better than to approach them after his painful experience in the theater. Instead he walked along the street before the waterfront homes and counted the villas until he came to a path running down to the water. Returning then near the water's edge along the shore in the dusk, he had no difficulty in locating Mary's home.

Pines, maples, and spice trees grew down to the water's edge, where stately white ibises stalked in haughty silence. A flock of ducks, disturbed by his passing, rose into the air with a whirring of wings and, as he turned along a path leading through the luxuriant garden that grew between the villa identified by the torch and the lake itself, a group of flamingos stared at him haughtily before moving aside for him to pass.

Joseph considered whether he should announce his presence in some way, but decided not to do so, hoping to surprise Mary and Demetrius. As he moved closer to the house along a winding graveled walk, a shadow suddenly darted from behind a tree and a brawny arm encircled his neck, bringing him up, choking, on his toes. "What do you seek in the garden of Flamen besides death, stranger?" a deep voice inquired. It was familiar, even after five years.

"Hadja!" Joseph croaked, for the Nabatean's massive arm was pressing on his windpipe. "It is I, Joseph of Galilee."

The pressure was released suddenly. "Praise be to Ahura-Mazda!" Hadja cried, embracing Joseph and

128

threatening to crush his bones again. "Why do you come through the garden like a thief?"

"I was knocked down by a Roman when I tried to see Mary at the theater several days ago," Joseph explained.

"It was Plotinus?" Hadja growled. "Someday I will slip a knife between the *gymnasiarch's* ribs! You have seen the Living Flame?"

"In the theater only."

"What did you think of her?"

"She has changed, Hadja, but she is more beautiful than ever."

"It is the beauty of evil. Sometimes I think as many as seven devils have possessed her," the Nabatean growled.

"Is she happy, Hadja? If she is, perhaps I should go away."

The musician shook his head. "She lives only to bring Romans to ruin. But come and see Demetrius. He will be glad to see you, Joseph."

Hadja led Joseph to a room at the back of the house. The villa was sumptuously furnished, beautiful paintings and expensive statues were everywhere, and deep rugs covered the floors. "The Living Flame is not here," Hadja explained, "but she will be home from the theater soon."

Only a small oil lamp burned in the chamber where Demetrius lay propped up on a couch, and the curtains were drawn so that the room was almost dark. Hadja ushered Joseph in and shut the door, leaving the two of them alone. At first Joseph thought the old lyre maker was asleep, but when he came closer he saw why the musician had not greeted him. The pupils of both his eyes were obscured by a dead white disk, the opaque growth of cataract. Demetrius was blind!

"I heard someone enter?" the old man quavered. "Who is it?"

"An old friend from Galilee," Joseph told him gently.

"From Galilee? Joseph!" he cried. "Joseph of Galilee! I recognize the voice."

Joseph embraced his old friend. "I knew you would come," the lyre maker cried. "How long have you been in Alexandria, my boy?"

"Several months."

"And you did not try to find us? How could you, Joseph?"

"I was seeking Mary of Magdala. How could I know that she is called Flamen in Alexandria?"

"Or that she does not let it be known she has Jewish blood, as if she were ashamed," Demetrius said bitterly. "You find us in a sad state, Joseph, my friend. This cursed desire for vengeance has made another person of Mary. She thinks of nothing but money and gaining power over Romans. It was an evil day when we left Magdala."

"Tell me about yourself,?" Joseph urged.

"What is there to tell?" Demetrius sighed. "I have all I want to eat and wine to drink, but what good is that when the light has gone?"

"Can you see anything at all?"

"I can tell night from day, but any bright light hurts my eyes, so I must live here in the dark. I cannot even see Mary, although they tell me she is more beautiful than she was as a young girl."

"She is. Much more beautiful, and in a different way."

"Then you have seen her?"

"At the theater. But when I sought to speak to her, a Roman forbade me."

"Plotinus!" Demetrius spat out the word as Hadja had done. "If she would only hurry with the job of getting his money and ruining him. The others were stupid, but Plotinus is dangerous."

"Have there been others?" Until now he had hoped all the things he had heard might not be true.

"A procession of simpletons who beggared themselves, hoping she would lie with them. Were I able to see, I might appreciate the irony of it, but I cannot help fearing for Mary herself. How long can you hate, Joseph, without your very hate consuming you?"

"I don't know. I never hated anyone very long."

"I know," Demetrius agreed. "You are a good man. God knows there are few enough of them in Alexandria."

A slave came in bringing two trays of food. While Joseph ate, the slave fed Demetrius, but the old lyre maker had even lost his appetite, something that could never have happened to him in the old days! His enjoyment of food and wine then had been limited only by the lack of them. Now the skin hung loose and flabby on his massive frame, and even his thirst for wine seemed to have left him, for he pushed away the silver goblet when it was still half filled. "Take the food away, child," he told the slave. "I have no appetite any more."

"Tell me something about your vision," Joseph said

when the trays were gone. "When did the cataracts start to grow?"

"Soon after we got to Alexandria; maybe they had really started before."

"And how long has most of your vision been gone?"

"Three years at least. Why do you ask? It makes no difference."

"It might," Joseph insisted. Bana Jivaka had taught him how to treat cases of cataract with the operation that had been used in India for almost a thousand years, one that brought sight to many cases such as this. Hippocrates, too, had mentioned it, but the Greeks had never been as skillful in such delicate mechanics as were the Indians. In the past several months Joseph had become as proficient as his teacher.

"Do not tease me, Joseph," Demetrius said wearily. "I know there is no hope."

"But there is; I have learned a way to treat cataract. If it is successful, you would regain your sight."

"And if not?"

"What do you have to lose?"

"As you say, what can I lose?" Demetrius agreed. "But if I could see, perhaps I could influence Mary away from this insane course she is following. When can you do it, Joseph?" he begged.

"Sometime within the next few days, I think," Joseph promised, and stood up. "I had better go now. Mary may be coming soon."

"But you are an old friend," Demetrius protested. "Why should you not be welcome in this house?"

"I did not tell you the whole of my experience with Plotinus the other day," Joseph explained. "He knocked me unconscious. I have no desire for a second dose."

Demetrius cursed savagely. Neither of them heard the door open or realized they were not alone until Mary cried from the door, "What are you cursing about, Demetrius? You sound more like yourself than you have in months." In the darkness she had not noticed that the lyre maker had a visitor. The night was hot, and when she came from the theater she had put on one of the diaphanous robes of bombyx that Roman women often wore in their boudoirs. Knowing that Demetrius could not see, she had not hesitated to come into the room in such a state of undress, with the sweet lines of her body almost fully revealed by the gauzy fabric as she stood in the door.

Suddenly Mary realized who was there with Demetrius. "Joseph!" she cried, and her face flamed as she tried to gather the wholly inadequate robe about her body. "You — Excuse me," she stammered, and was gone.

"What was the matter with her?" Demetrius demanded.

"She wasn't exactly dressed."

"That's the only sensible habit she has picked up from the Romans." Demetrius chuckled. "Their women go practically naked in hot weather, and it certainly makes life more interesting, even for an old sot like me."

Mary came back a moment later, wrapped in a long robe, and gave Joseph her hands. "Why didn't you let me know you had come to Alexandria?" she said.

"He has been here several months," Demetrius growled, "but could not find us because you have taken another name. And when he did, the guards would not let him see you. How long are you going to keep up this insane life, Mary?"

"We agreed not to talk about that, Demetrius," she said sharply. "Remember?"

"It is your life," he grunted. "Ruin it if you must."

Mary took a taper from its bracket on the wall and held it so she could see Joseph. "You have not changed," she said softly. "You will always be the same."

"I wish I could say as much for you, Mary."

For an instant there was a look of pain in her eyes, then she laughed, a brittle sound that was oddly like a sob. In an instant she was no longer the Mary he loved. "Of course I have changed," she said somewhat sharply. "When I left Magdala I was only a slip of a girl. I am a woman now."

"A very beautiful woman, Mary," he agreed. "Even more than you were in Magdala. You have come a long way."

"I told you I would be the leading dancer of Alexandria."

"I saw you dance several days ago," he told her. "And you deserve to have Alexandria at your feet. Are you happy with what you have accomplished, Mary?"

Again the look of pain showed momentarily in her eyes before she gave the same brittle laugh. "I am rich. The leading men of Alexandria are at my feet, and the people adore me," she cried airily. "What else could a woman want?"

"The love of a good man instead of the lust of these

accursed Romans," Demetrius growled. "It was an evil day when you left Magdala."

"It was not an evil day for you, Joseph," Mary said. "I hear that you are rich and the most famous physician in Jerusalem."

"Joseph has learned how to cure cataracts,'" Demetrius broke in eagerly. "He is going to give me back my sight."

"Is that true?" Mary asked quickly.

"There is an operation that restores sight to many who suffer from cataract," he told her. "I hope it will let Demetrius see."

Mary ran to the old lyre maker and put her arms around his neck. It was an impulsive gesture, such as she had often made as a girl in Magdala, and Joseph saw that she was weeping, for her shoulders jerked convulsively and she hid her face against the old musician's chest. Knowing her as he did, Joseph understood that her weeping was more than just for joy that Demetrius might regain his sight, and so did not interrupt.

Demetrius let her sob on his breast until finally she raised her head and wiped her eyes on the sleeve of his robe. "It will be a happy day when your eyes are whole again, darling," she said then. "I have a dance you have never seen. Joseph must take you to the theater and I will do it only for you."

Demetrius blew his nose loudly. "Run along now, you two," he said, "and let an old man rest. Visit me soon again, Joseph."

"Tomorrow," Joseph promised. "We can plan then about restoring your sight."

"How did you get into the villa?" Mary asked as she led Joseph out into the garden.

"By the shore. After my experience with Plotinus the other day, I did not risk the guards."

"He told me he had knocked down a tradesman who was trying to see me. Of course I had no way of knowing it was you."

"Would you have acknowledged me if you had?" he asked deliberately.

"Joseph!" she cried. "How could you say that?"

"You have denied your Jewish blood. . . ."

"I have not. I merely kept it a secret."

"But why, if you are not ashamed of it?"

She put her hand on his arm. "You must try to understand, Joseph. As a Jewess I would have had little chance

133

to succeed here in the theater. You know how the Romans hate Jews. And after all, I am part Greek."

"Have you also forgotten the God of your people?"

She laughed again, the same brittle note. "Why should I be concerned with the Most High? He would have let me be sold into slavery if Simon and Demetrius had not saved me, and He forsook me when I needed help that night in Tiberias."

"It is written, *'Say not thou, I will recompense evil,'*" he reminded her, "*'but wait on the Lord and he shall save thee.'*"

Mary kicked angrily at the trunk of a palm tree beside the path. "Don't quote proverbs to me," she cried. "Wait! Wait! Where would I have gotten if I had waited, or if I had stayed in Magdala?"

"Where have you gotten now, Mary?" he asked gently. "You are rich and famous, but no one is happy with what you are doing, not even you."

"I am doing what I want to do," she said sharply. "What I have sworn to do."

"And if what you have sworn to do is evil?"

"Then the evil will be on my soul. Why concern yourself with it?" She put her hand on his arm appealingly. "Please, let us not quarrel, Joseph, when we haven't seen each other in five years. Why did you come to Alexandria?"

"I came because I love you, Mary, to learn whether you still love me."

For a moment she did not speak, and he thought there were tears in her eyes. "And now that you know," she asked almost in a whisper, "why don't you leave?"

"But I don't know. You haven't told me yourself."

"You must not love me, Joseph," she said quickly, pleadingly. "It can only mean unhappiness for you. Go back to Jerusalem and forget you ever knew Mary of Magdala."

He took her by the arms, turning her until she faced him there in the darkness of the garden. "When you swear by the Most High that you no longer love me, Mary, I will go," he said. "It is the only thing that will send me away."

He heard the sob in her throat, and then her arms were about him and she was clinging to him, her face buried against his chest, sobbing unrestrainedly. Wisely he held her thus until she was quiet, then he took her chin in his hand and, lifting it, kissed her gently upon the lips. The salt of her tears was upon them, and she clung to him with her mouth soft and yielding beneath his own for a long moment before she pushed him away. Then she dried her eyes with the flowing sleeve of her robe and pushed the soft hair back from her face. "It has been a long time since I have wept like that, Joseph," she said with an oddly matter-of-fact note in her voice. "Nothing helps a woman more when she is troubled."

"You need be troubled no longer," he suggested. "Come back to Jerusalem with me as my wife?"

"You should know by now that I am not like other women, Joseph. I would not come to you as your wife when a part of me lived only to hate Gaius Flaccus."

"I might be able to show you the futility of hating."

Mary shook her head. "I could never be dishonest with you, Joseph. I love you too much for that." But when he would have taken her in his arms again, she put her hands against his chest in a restraining gesture. "Do you think it is easy for me to be what I am? Do you think I want to see Hadja and Demetrius—yes, even you— unhappy? But until I carry out my oath to kill Gaius Flaccus, I can never be the girl you loved back in Magdala. It's like a disease in my very soul, this hate for him and all the Romans. Nothing can purge it away except to kill him with my own hands."

"Hadja is right then. A demon has possessed you."

"Hadja claims there are seven." She smiled. "Perhaps he is right. But the demon of hate will possess my soul until I kill the man who put it there."

"Have you seen Gaius Flaccus since you left Magdala?"

"No." She hesitated, then continued: "Plotinus is close to the Emperor, though. He has promised to have Gaius Flaccus sent to Alexandria very soon, within the next few months at least."

"Did you tell Plotinus why you want to see him again?"

"I only told him I hate Gaius Flaccus and want to humiliate him. Plotinus is cruel himself, so he understands and sympathizes with that sort of motive."

"Then your using Plotinus this way is only part of your plan of revenge?"

"Of course," she cried. "Do you think I could love a Roman after what Gaius Flaccus did to me? They give me gold because they think I will give myself to them in return. But when I get their money I throw them aside."

"When will you be through with Plotinus?"

"When he brings Gaius Flaccus to Alexandria."

"Give up this madness, Mary," he begged. "You can't murder a man that easily."

"It will be difficult," she admitted coolly, "but I will do it. I would even lie with him, if it meant I could plunge a dagger into his heart."

"Would it be worth satisfying your hate to defile your body?"

"My body?" She laughed on that same harsh note. "Gaius Flaccus made my body a thing of dishonor. What difference does it make how I use it now? Nothing could defile me more than I have already been defiled. And besides," she added, "I was not without sin myself. I watched a girl dance at Pilate's villa that night, a slave. She stripped the clothing from her body and danced nude before the men, and I wanted to do the same thing, Joseph. I had to hold back to keep from tearing the clothes from my body and dancing there before them. Does that not make me guilty too?"

"The Evil One was tempting you."

"And when Gaius Flaccus held me in his arms afterward, I wanted to be there. He might not have done—what he did, if I had not let him kiss me. Maybe I wanted him to do what he did; I don't remember, I don't know."

For a moment he was given a glimpse into her very soul and the forces that strove there, torturing her. He knew now that, try as she might, Mary could not put out of her innermost being the teachings of God that all Jewish children learned early in life, without suffering from the implacable demands of her conscience. Ruthlessly it demanded a sacrifice in retribution for the sin of lust that had tempted her there in the villa of Pontius Pilate, as it tempts, at one time or another, every man and woman. Mary might kill Gaius Flaccus, as the demon of hate drove her to do, but the act would bring no peace to her soul afterward, no satisfaction in her revenge, for the implacable conscience would still be there. She was only deluding herself, he knew. And yet he could see no way to make this clear to her, no way to convince her that the only way to peace for her was through admitting her own sin and praying God to exorcise the demon of hate from her soul.

A sharp challenge came suddenly from the guard in

front of the villa. "Go," Mary whispered. "And stay by the shore. Plotinus has come to take me to a dinner this evening. I will tell him later that you are a physician treating Demetrius, so you can come here when you wish." She stood on her toes and kissed him quickly. "Heal Demetrius, Joseph, and then leave Alexandria. Believe me, it is best for both of us."

She was gone in a rustle of silk, leaving Joseph alone in the darkness. As he made his way through the garden to the shore and past the wall that ran to the very water's edge, he saw lamps being lit in the villa and heard the gay laugh of the woman called Flamen as she greeted her Roman admirer.

Seeing Mary once again, Joseph knew that his love for her burned now with an even deeper fire than it had in Magdala. And since she had admitted that she loved him still, he knew he must prevent her somehow from carrying out this insane scheme to kill Gaius Flaccus. It was not so much because killing him would be murder, but because by doing so Mary would be depriving herself of any chance of finding the peace she must find if she were ever to come to him as he wanted her to come, loving as unreservedly as he knew she could love. Her hate, her need for revenge had become a disease. And even if he had not loved her, it was his duty as a physician to cure it.

He had set himself a hard task, but an exciting one. And the prize? Could any man hope to win a greater one?

9

JOSEPH and Bana Jivaka operated upon Demetrius' right eye a few days later, and in two weeks they removed the bandages that had covered both eyes during the period, shutting out all light and stimulation to either eye, so that movement of the eyeball would be reduced to a minimum and healing promoted. There was some trouble in inducing the trance to shut out all consciousness of pain and, more important, allow the eye to be quiet during the delicate part of the operation, for Demetrius was so nearly blind that he could barely see the emerald. Finally Jivaka had been forced to use a bright flame at which the musician gazed, while in quiet, forceful tones the Indian physician gradually willed him to sleep.

The instruments on the table had seemed a pitifully small armamentarium with which to restore a man's sight: a slender metal rod with a tiny hook at the end, and beside it a long, sharp needle with one end embedded in a small wooden handle. Mary and Hadja had watched while they worked.

"The operation I am performing," Joseph explained as he took up the slender hook, "is very simple. Since the opaque growth of the cataract is confined to the small, spherical body of the eye, one needs only to dislodge that body from its normal position and let it drop down inside the eyeball away from the sight. Light can then enter the eye. The hook is first used to hold the eye still while inserting the needle." Carefully he inserted the point of the hook just through the outer side of the white portion of the eyeball, so that when he held it firmly the eye remained still.

"Does he feel no pain at all?" Mary asked.

"Pain is in the mind," Jivaka explained. "We have control of that."

Next Joseph took the needle by its wooden handle and carefully forced the point through the eyeball just at the border of the iris. The point appeared in front of the iris, and he drew it back a little, so that it slid back of the pigmented curtain in whose center was the opening of the pupil. "It is possible to go both in front of and behind the iris to reach cataracts," he said. "But the operation of Susruta goes behind it, and we will use that."

Joseph's movements were steady and sure, for he had done the operation many times in the past few months. He controlled the needle as if it were a part of himself, until he could feel the increased resistance of the cataract-filled spherical body when the point of the needle penetrated it. Next he moved it back and forth, tearing through the outer layer of the lens. As he continued, the point became visible through the small opening of the pupil, and the onlookers could actually see the tear he was making in the outer part of the cataract. Finally a dead white, round sphere, as large as a small pea. appeared just beneath the point of the needle. "It is the cataract," he explained. "I will push it down into the eyeball, where it will lie below the pupil and out of the line of sight."

Slowly, carefully, Joseph pushed the firm round cataract down through the jelly-like substance filling the back of the eyeball. Jivaka had examined the eyes of patients who had died from other causes after such operations and assured him that the dead white sphere was usually absorbed and disappeared after a while. As he drew the needle back, the upper rim of the white body appeared just at the lower rim of the pupil, and he waited expectantly to see whether it would pop back up in front of the pupil as sometimes happened. If it did he would have to replace it once more, or perhaps even cut it into pieces with the point of the needle, a job requiring considerable time and great danger of damaging the inside of the eye itself and bringing on an inflammation that often destroyed the good effects of the surgery.

But the cataract remained well below the sight, and it had not been necessary to do more. The bandaging was finished quickly and now, two weeks later, it was being removed. If the first operation were successful, the left eye could be treated soon.

Slowly Joseph unwound the bandages and removed the last layer of linen from before Demetrius' eyes. The room was in semidarkness, and as he worked he felt Mary standing at his elbow, her body pressed against him in her eagerness to see whether the operation had been successful. For a moment he was reluctant to remove the last bandage and break the spell. Then he gently took it away and saw with a thrill of satisfaction that the pupil of the operated eye was clear.

"By Diana!" Demetrius cried. "I see the light! I see! I see!"

Mary threw her arms around Joseph's neck and kissed him on the mouth. "You did it, Joseph," she cried. "You have given him his sight." Then, embarrassed by her outbreak, she said to Bana Jivaka, "Will you excuse my emotion, please? We Jews are easily moved."

"A man would be stone not to be moved by such happiness," Jivaka admitted. "The physician knows no greater joy than being able to bring light to the blind."

"We must have a celebration," Mary cried. "It will be like the old days in Magdala."

Wine and food were brought, and they sat around the couch on which Demetrius lay propped up, his eye bandaged again, for too much light was not good for it yet. The lyre maker was more like his old self now that he knew he would see again.

Mary filled the glasses and lifted her own. "To the heart's desire of each of us," she toasted. "May the gods grant its fulfillment."

The others lifted their glasses, but Joseph kept his by his side. "I cannot drink such a toast, Mary," he said quietly. "Have you forgotten that there is but one God?"

The rich color drained from Mary's cheeks as if he had struck her there. "It is a toast used by the Romans, Joseph," Demetrius said. "She spoke the words without thinking."

"Let us rather say we drink to the divine wisdom that guides the universe," Bana Jivaka suggested. "The wisdom that stands above and beyond any gods conceived by man."

"I will drink to that." Joseph lifted his glass. "For David said: *'Give thanks unto the Lord that by his wisdom made the heavens; for his mercy endureth forever.'*"

"You must not think badly of Mary because she speaks casually of gods as most Alexandrians do, Joseph," Demetrius said. "After all, Socrates said, *'To find the Maker and Father of all is hard, and having found him, it is impossible to utter him.'*"

"To the Jews there is only one God," Joseph said simply. "He is the God of Israel and no other."

"There speaks the hidebound Jew," the Greek twitted him. "But I would rather believe in the god of Socrates —whoever he was—who would let a man say, *'A good man in his dark striving is somehow conscious of the right way.'* In fact, I think that we are all seeking, like Socrates, *'that which, existing among men, is the form and likeness of God.'*"

"*'The form and likeness of God,'*" Mary repeated softly. "I never thought about the form and likeness before. We Jews have always thought of God as a being like ourselves.'

"We are told that we are created in His image," Joseph agreed.

"You might be wrong, though," Demetrius suggested. "Socrates taught that goodness and man's love for man have a real and actual existence. It could be that what we seek for as God is in reality not a being but a quality, a force we cannot comprehend except as we see it at work in our own lives."

Bana Jivaka had been listening quietly to the discussion but had not spoken. Joseph turned to him now. "What do you think of this problem of God?" he asked.

The Indian smiled. "Socrates also said of his own beliefs: *This may be true but also quite likely to be untrue, and therefore I would not have you too easily persuaded. Reflect well and when you have found the truth, come and tell me.* I wonder if you Jews would ever allow such a yardstick to be applied to your deity."

"Why should it?" Joseph demanded. "There is only one God, the Most High of the Jews. He cannot be doubted, for to do so is blasphemy. And He has promised to send the Messiah and set up the kingdom of God on earth in which the Jews will rule the world."

"I would not offend you, Joseph," Jivaka said. "But this talk of messiahs and kingdoms seems needlessly complicated to me. Socrates taught that the rewards of a goodly life are sufficient to themselves. One needs neither gods nor promises of immortality to justify right living."

"I can conceive of no life sufficient in itself," Joseph objected.

"Socrates was sufficient," Demetrius argued.

"But he was executed by his fellow men,'" Joseph pointed out. "Therefore, he must not have seemed sufficient to them. The Jew has only to believe in the Most High and obey his commandments. He needs no lofty philosophies."

"But think to what heights philosophy takes man," Demetrius cried. "And how close to God Himself. Just yesterday the slave was reading me the speech of Socrates to the judges who condemned him. I had him read it again and again, so that I could memorize it: *'Be of good cheer,'* he told the judges, *'and know of a certainty that no evil can happen to a good man either in life or after death. . . . I . . . see clearly that the time has come for me to die, and so my accusers have done me no harm. . . . And now we go our ways, you to live and I to die. Which is better, only God knows!'* Socrates did not even fear

141

death, as we all do, when he could say of it, *'Our venture is a glorious one. The soul, with her own proper jewels, which are justice and courage and nobility and truth, in these arrayed, she is ready to go on her journey when her time comes.'* "

" *'There is a life which is higher than the measure of humanity,'* " Jivaka quoted. " *'Men live it not by virtue of their humanity, but by virtue of something in them that is divine.'* You see, my friends, Aristotle came to the same conclusion as Socrates."

"But that something is the fact that they are the image of God," Joseph insisted. "So no man is really sufficient to himself. He needs always the presence of the Most High within him."

"You may be right," Jivaka admitted. "Although you allow no image of your God, you Jews seem better able to believe in an unseen divinity than those who need something they can see. That might even be one of the reasons for the eternal conflicts between the Jews and their conquerors. Being unable to believe in gods they cannot see and touch, people hate the Jews for the God that dwells within their souls. Naturally such people would indict Socrates as *an evil doer and a corrupter of young men because he does not receive the gods the state receives, but introduces new divinities.* Who knows, perhaps someday people will worship Socrates as a god himself, as some do the Buddha."

"The Buddha? What do you mean, Jivaka?"

"A man named Siddhartha Gautama lived in India about six hundred years ago," Jivaka explained. "He taught much the same things that Socrates taught later, and many of my people believe he was the Buddha."

"But what is the Buddha?" Mary asked curiously. "I never heard the word before."

"An ancient legend among the Indian people teaches that Wisdom returns to earth from time to time in human form, called the Buddha."

"Then your people, too, believe in a god who sends wisdom to earth," Joseph said triumphantly.

"Perhaps our religion is the same as yours in principle," Jivaka agreed. "We believe in the Buddha, you wait for a Messiah. Our Buddha might even have been your Messiah in a different form."

"But the Messiah will be a Jew!" Joseph insisted. "He

is to be sent only to the Jews and will come in the fullness of glory, not through ordinary birth."

"Siddhartha Gautama did not claim to be divine," Jivaka told them. "He lived and died like any other man. But some, refusing to believe that one so wise and considerate of man's foibles could have been born of an earthly father wove fanciful tales about his birth. They said he was miraculously conceived when his mother dreamed of a white elephant, which is also sacred with my people. Some even insist that Gautama was a god, but I have found no record that he so much as claimed to be the Buddha."

"What did he teach?" Mary asked.

Jivaka smiled. "Nothing that even Joseph could not subscribe to as a physician, such as that the miseries and discontents of life come from our own selfishness. We see that often enough in our work with the sick."

"I remember Demetrius once said something like that in Magdala," Joseph admitted.

"The babblings of an old man are hardly worth remembering," Demetrius objected. "He says one thing today and another tomorrow."

"We were talking of the *mazzakim*," Joseph reminded him, "and you said, 'The demons that possess man are born within himself, children of his own desires.'"

"Truer words were never spoken, I suspect," Jivaka agreed. "Thinking men everywhere seem to be searching for the same truths and often they arrive at the same conclusions by different routes. Gautama also taught that suffering is an inevitable punishment for greedy desire and an overpowering need to be greater than others," he continued. "These are the cravings he listed: sensuousness, a gratification of the senses; desire for personal immortality; and the desire for property or worldliness."

"But no one wants everything to end with death," Joseph protested.

"To overcome man's baser cravings, Gautama taught that he must no longer live for himself. Is the desire for eternal life anything but the wish to preserve self?"

Joseph was silenced. No one could deny such a simple and fundamental truth. "Cannot a man so deny self that he would be worthy of eternal life?" Mary asked.

"Gautama's teaching is very close to that," Jivaka admitted. "He said that when man has removed *I* from his thoughts, he reaches a higher wisdom called Nirvana."

"But that is no different from our idea of heaven," Joseph pointed out. "The Pharisees believe that those who love God and the law will live with Him there forever."

"The Nirvana of Buddha is achieved on earth," Jivaka explained. "Through it life itself is so complete and full that there is no longer any need for a life after death. The good a man does thus lives after him, forever immortal."

Joseph shook his head. "It is hard to put away the things you have been taught since childhood, Jivaka. I am afraid I shall never be a philosopher."

The Indian smiled. "You think so now, but only because you Jews in Judea have so studiously avoided contact with those you call the 'heathen.' Philo and I have discussed this many times. He thinks the Jews in other cities of the Empire than Jerusalem are losing the narrowness of thought that has kept your religion from being more widely spread. Both of us think your people will be the better for this emancipation. And the world will certainly be better off for being given a chance to worship the God of the Jews."

Joseph smiled. "I live in the center of what you call the 'narrowness.' And I can tell you there will be no revolution in our thinking without considerable turmoil."

"When was there not turmoil among the Jews?" Demetrius asked. "Sometimes I think they are bound to destroy themselves."

The color in Mary's cheeks heightened then and Joseph knew she understood that the barb in Demetrius' observation was directed partly at her. The discussion broke up shortly afterward, for Mary had to get ready for the theater. But as Joseph was preparing to leave, she said, "Come into the garden with me a moment, Joseph. I have something to tell you."

It had rained that morning and the trees and flowers were shining with moisture. A stone bench stood beside a small pool and the sunlight had already dried it. "Sit here with me a moment," she said. "I hardly see you any more."

"You asked me to go back to Jerusalem, remember?"

"It would still be better for both of us if you did. I am like your friend said of the Jews. Wherever I am there is bound to be turmoil."

"I am also a Jew," he reminded her.

"But you are wise and tolerant, while my emotions are as fiery as my hair."

"The girl I knew in Magdala was loved by all who knew her, but her emotions were fiery too."

Mary laughed, the same cynical note he had heard more than once here in Alexandria. "You forget easily, Joseph. The women in Magdala hated me because their husbands stopped to look after me in the streets. They knew what was in the men's thoughts, as I did."

"Does that give you a right to hate when men wish to possess you?"

"No," she admitted. "I suppose not. But I hate only Gaius Flaccus and the Romans."

"Remember what Demetrius said in there about Socrates?" Joseph reminded her. "Goodness is an end in itself. Our ancient prophets taught the same thing for thousands of years. You should remove hate from your mind."

"How can I? As long as he is alive?"

"Killing Gaius Flaccus and forcing Romans to ruin themselves because of their desire for you will never bring you peace, Mary," he argued earnestly. "I know the real Mary of Magdala, and she is not like that. If you do this thing you will regret it always, if you do not lose your life in the doing."

"What would you do in my place then?"

"You can only find peace through forgiving Gaius Flaccus."

"Forgive him!" Color surged into her cheeks. "How can you suggest such a thing and still claim to be my friend?"

"Because I *am* your friend I know it is the only way. Give up this insane plan, Mary," he begged. "Gaius Flaccus is a favorite of the Emperor Tiberius and a nephew of Pontius Pilate. You could not kill a prominent Roman like him and live."

"Not even when it is my right under the law?"

"What law gives you the right to kill?"

"It is written in the laws of the Jews: *'If a man find a betrothed damsel in the field, and the man force her, and lie with her: then the man that lay with her shall die.'* "

At the moment Joseph had no answer, for as she said, that was the rigid law of the Jews. "But it does not say you yourself have the right to kill," he protested lamely. "Execution of the law is the province of the council of the judges."

"The law says the life of the guilty man belongs to him

to whom the damsel is betrothed. You did not take Gaius Flaccus' life, Joseph, so I must do it."

"That would have been murder," he protested.

Mary stamped her foot angrily. "I was your betrothed," she cried. "But neither you nor the Jewish authorities would have dared to kill Gaius Flaccus because he is a Roman and you were afraid. The law of our people says he must die, and I am not afraid, so I will carry out the sentence myself."

She was magnificent in her anger and her determination, and yet he knew that what she proposed was folly, a rash act which could only end in death, whatever she thought the justification might be. And then he thought of a way he might prevent her. If somehow he could get her to reveal her plans, he might be able to foil her and save her life, although it would mean that her hate would be turned on him. Even that, however, was not too high a price for saving the life of the woman he loved.

"How do you propose to do it?" he asked.

Mary tossed her head. "Do you think I would tell you now? But my plans are made, and all of Alexandria will know the hour of my vengeance."

"Alexandria? I thought Gaius Flaccus was in Rome."

"What do you think I have been working for these past months?" she asked tartly. "Remember, I told you Plotinus would have Gaius Flaccus transferred to Alexandria. He is due here in a few weeks to serve as *praefectus vigilum,* in command of all Roman troops in the city."

10

KNOWING that he could do nothing to turn Mary away from her firm resolution to be revenged upon Gaius Flaccus, Joseph was tempted to do what she had advised, leave Alexandria and return to Jerusalem. But first he had to treat the cataract in Demetrius' other eye, and when the operation was followed by an inflammation that threatened to destroy the eye, he was forced to make daily visits to

Mary's luxurious home on the shore of Lake Mareotis until the inflammation subsided. It was a month before Demetrius was able to leave the house, and then he moved with difficulty because of a plethora and dropsy that caused his body to swell.

When the old Greek musician was able to be up long enough, Joseph took him to the theater to see Mary dance. From a seat back of the *tribunalia* Demetrius was able to see fairly clearly, since his vision was much better at a distance than closer up. Mary seemed to be inspired that night; never had Joseph seen her dance more spiritedly or with more grace. And watching her beauty, the slender loveliness of her body as she moved about the stage in the expressive rhythm of the dance, he felt a deep sense of depression and foreboding grip his soul. She had embarked upon an insane course, he was sure, and yet he could do nothing at all to stop her. She was truly possessed of a demon, but he knew no way to drive it out. And his depression deepened when he glanced at the box usually reserved for the Roman governor of the city and saw Gaius Flaccus sitting there, as handsome as a Greek god.

When the performance was ended they made their way to Mary's dressing room through the corridors beneath the great theater. She still wore the costume in which she had danced, and was sitting before her dressing table when they entered, while her maid, a dark-skinned slave from Cyrene, brushed her hair. Mary got up and ran to kiss the old musician. "I was dancing for you, Demetrius," she cried. "Did you like it?"

"There has never been one to equal you, child," Demetrius' voice was thick with emotion. "This is the crowning moment of my life."

"We will have other moments," she promised gaily, "many of them. The director has agreed to present the *Bacchae* of Euripides at the Great Dionysia, and I am to lead the dancers."

"I know you will triumph," Demetrius told her. "You have everything you wish for now."

"Not everything," Mary said, suddenly serious, "but I am very near." She turned to Joseph. "You saw him?"

"Yes. How long has he been in Alexandria?"

"Only a few days. Plotinus is arranging a dinner in his honor tomorrow night."

"What is all the mystery about?" Demetrius demanded.

147

"Gaius Flaccus is in Alexandria," Mary explained. "He was in one of the *tribunalia* tonight."

"How will you keep the two of them from flying at each other's throats?" Joseph asked. "Plotinus is bound to be jealous if you show much attention to Gaius Flaccus."

Mary laughed confidently. "I have learned a lot about handling men in the past five years, Joseph. You simply tell each of them that he is stealing your affections from the other."

"But suppose they compare your statements."

"When each distrusts and is jealous of the other? Hardly."

Joseph shrugged. "We had better go, Demetrius," he said. "Doubtless the lady called Flamen will have suitors wishing to visit her."

Mary flushed at his tone, but before she could say anything a sharp-voiced challenge came from the guard outside the door. A moment later the curtains were thrust arrogantly aside, revealing a tall man in the uniform of a Roman Tribune. It was Gaius Flaccus.

For a moment Mary was like a marble statue, then as the young Roman strode forward and lifted her hand to his lips, color came into her cheeks and she relaxed. "I could not wait until the dinner tomorrow to meet you," Gaius Flaccus said, kissing her hand. "Such beauty and talent deserve a more spontaneous tribute." And then, as his eyes met hers, a puzzled look came into his face. "Your face seems familiar."

"Does it?" Mary asked, still smiling, but her eyes were hard and cold.

Gaius Flaccus seemed to realize for the first time that there were others in the room. He turned to them, and his eyes widened in surprise. "Are you not the leech, Joseph of Galilee, that I knew in Tiberias and Magdala?" he asked.

"I am Joseph of Galilee," the young physician said quietly.

"And my name is Demetrius," the old musician added, "a lyre maker of Magdala, lately come to Alexandria."

Gaius Flaccus looked from them to Mary, and his eyes widened with amazement. "But you couldn't be the little dancer," he cried. "The one I knew in Tiberias."

Mary's voice cut him short. "In Alexandria I am called Flamen," she said proudly.

"Mary of Magdala," Gaius Flaccus said softly. "And

the streets of Tiberias. You have come a long way, my dear. And you are more beautiful than ever. No wonder they tell me the men of Alexandria are at your feet."

"And you?" Mary asked. Her voice was soft, almost coaxing. Hearing it, Joseph could understand her power over men.

The Tribune smiled fatuously and lifted her fingers slowly to his lips once more. "No doubt I shall be there too," he said softly. "Dare I hope one day to be first among your admirers?"

Joseph could stand no more. "Come Demetrius," he said, "I will take you home."

"Stay, leech," Gaius Flaccus said. "Do you have any news of my uncle Pontius Pilate and his lady?"

Before Joseph could speak, Demetrius said sharply, "Joseph of Galilee is no longer a leech, Roman. He is *medicus viscerus* to the temple at Jerusalem and personal physician to the Procurator Pontius Pilate."

Gaius Flaccus shrugged. "In Rome physicians are little thought of, being mostly Greeks." He made no apology for the contemptuous title, and Demetrius snorted angrily.

"I spent several days in your uncle's palace at Caesarea before I sailed for Alexandria," Joseph told him. "They were well, except that the Lady Claudia Procula is troubled with her breathing."

"She should stay in Tiberias," Gaius agreed. "She is much better there. Anyway, I will be seeing them before too much longer."

"I thought you were going to stay in Alexandria," Mary said quickly, then bit her lip with vexation at having revealed her knowledge.

But Gaius Flaccus was too taken by her beauty to notice the slip and apparently mistook her sudden concern for interest in himself. "I will be in Alexandria perhaps six months, then I will go back to Judea and Galilee," he explained. "Pontius Pilate has been too lenient with the Jews, which is always a mistake. And he needs someone he can trust in Sepphoris and Tiberias to watch Herod Antipas."

"Should you not go sooner," Joseph asked, "if you fear Herod?"

"A Roman procurator does not fear a mangy provincial tetrarch." Gaius Flaccus laughed contemptuously. "But it is good political practice to keep a watch over Herod. Besides, there is trouble in Judea and Galilee. I understand

149

the Jews are up in arms because of a man named John the Baptist."

"Do they know of John in Rome?" Joseph asked incredulously.

"Rome knows everything that happens, even in the provinces. The Emperor has always kept a close watch on Herod Antipas. Unless I miss my guess, Herod's patience will wear out soon and this John will lose his head."

"On what grounds?"

"What grounds does one need to behead a zealot who stirs up the people?" Gaius Flaccus demanded. "Herod reports that John the Baptist preached the coming of another king. You are old enough to remember when two thousand Jews were crucified in Galilee, Joseph, for supporting another of those upstarts who are always trying to take over your country from the Romans and their appointed rulers."

"But John the Baptist is simply a preacher," Joseph protested.

"You seem to know much of him," the Roman said sharply. "Are you a rebel too?"

Joseph shook his head. "All I know is that he is an Essene who preaches the coming of the Messiah."

"He must have preached a little too loudly then. Herod can take care of John, since he is a Jew. If Pontius Pilate has to do it, your whole nation will be screaming at the Romans again."

"When are you going to Galilee?" Mary asked.

"Early in the summer, I imagine," Gaius Flaccus told her. "My uncle has asked for more troops to keep down the riots that have been happening since he used the temple tribute to build an aqueduct. The way the Jews screamed about it, you would think they preferred dying of thirst to losing a little money. When the new troops are sent from Rome in the spring I will be commander. Then your countrymen will know what it is to have a strong hand at the helm, Joseph."

The young physician controlled his anger at the Roman's contemptuous tone. It would do no good to quarrel with him now.

"Confidentially," Gaius Flaccus went on, "Pilate believes some of this agitation is being stirred up by agents of Herod. If you are temple physician, Joseph, you know that Antipas is ambitious to rule both in Judea and Galilee, as well as in the tetrarchy of his cousin Philip. Herod is a fox, so it will not hurt to have fresh troops and a good hunter in Sepphoris, the capital of his kingdom."

What Gaius Flaccus said of Herod Antipas was true, as Joseph well knew. A group in Jerusalem called the Herodians, led by Jonathan, a son of the old high priest Annas, conspired constantly to have Judea ruled by a Jewish tetrarch rather than directly from Rome under a procurator. Jonathan, a vain and worldly man, had been passed over in the succession to the office of high priest in favor of Annas' son-in-law, Caiaphas. If Herod Antipas succeeded in convincing the Emperor Tiberius that Judea would be less troublesome under a Jewish king than a procurator, Jonathan would become high priest—hence the joining of forces.

Joseph turned to Demetrius. "You must be tired," he suggested again. "Let me take you home."

"Are you coming with us, my dear?" the old man asked as he got slowly to his feet, for his body was heavy with plethora and his strength was rapidly failing.

Before Mary could answer, Gaius Flaccus said quickly, "I would be honored if you would let me take you home in my private chair, Flamen. You must be tired after your dancing, and we could stop for some refreshment."

Mary smiled and shook her head. "I must rest tonight in order to be fresh for Plotinus' dinner in your honor tomorrow." She gave him her hand. "Until tomorrow then?"

Gaius Flaccus bowed gallantly and touched her fingers with his lips. "Until tomorrow.

"I will speak to the governor about you, leech," he said to Joseph. "He suffers with the gout, and I remember that you had some success in treating Pontius Pilate for that disease. The favor of the governor of Alexandria should be of great help to a physician."

The Roman was hardly outside the room when Demetrius burst out, "The arrogant swine! Just because he turns the heads of women, does he think he can insult men as well? And you!" He turned to Mary savagely. "Simpering and leading him on like a common strumpet. Have you forgotten what he did to you?"

The color slowly drained from Mary's cheeks, and her fingers clenched into the palms of her hands until the blood was pressed from the skin, leaving it dead white. "I have not forgotten," she said slowly, almost as if she were praying. "Before the Most High, I have not forgotten."

11

IF he had not loved Mary as he did, Joseph would have been tempted to leave Alexandria and return to Jerusalem rather than stay and witness the inevitable ending of the tragic course upon which she was embarked. But loving her, he could not desert her at a time when she might need him most.

And then there was Demetrius. The lyre maker was growing weaker, his body more and more swollen and distorted by the plethora and dropsy, which had grown much worse during the winter months. Actually neither Joseph nor anyone else could do much. When the accumulating fluid threatened to drown Demetrius in the secretions of his own body, Joseph dared to insert sharpened quills into the tremendously distended belly to let it out, but they both knew this was but a temporary measure.

Afterward, while the old man lay propped up in bed, they talked about Mary. The dangerous job of keeping both Plotinus and Gaius Flaccus at her beck and call without having them also at each others throats, took most of her time, so Joseph saw her only rarely on his visits to Demetrius. "Do you know any more about what Mary plans to do?" Demetrius asked him.

"No. But she said once that all of Alexandria will know the hour of her vengeance."

"Then she must plan to kill him publicly. And the most dramatic way of achieving revenge would naturally appeal to her. But when would all Alexandria know the hour? . . . By Diana!" he cried. "The festival of the Great Dionysia, of course."

"Why the Great Dionysia?"

"It is the greatest celebration of the year in Alexandria. For three whole days the people go wild."

"But the Alexandrians do not worship Dionysos?" Joseph protested.

"Dionysos was originally the same as Bacchus," Demetrius explained. "But here in Egypt he is regarded as almost the same as Serapis, who, as you know, is a combined god from Osiris and Apis, the sacred bull. His worship combines many religions, so they all join in this annual festival in his honor. It gives everybody an excuse to get drunk and celebrate the beginning of spring with a series of dramatic productions. I remember Mary telling me they are going to present the *Bacchae* of Euripides," he continued. "In the old festivals of the Great Dionysia, the god is represented by a man and is traditionally killed and resurrected from the dead. Of course the killing is only symbolic and so is the resurrection, but years ago an animal, and even sometimes a man representing the god, was actually torn in pieces by the Bacchae at the height of the ceremony."

"Do you suppose . . . ? But that would be fantastic."

"No more fantastic than Mary's believing she can kill a prominent Roman like Gaius Flaccus and escape the consequences," Demetrius said heavily. "Yes, I would wager that is what she is going to do. She can probably get Gaius Flaccus to portray the part of the god; he's vain enough to play right into her hands. In some of the Dionysia a ritual marriage between Dionysos and Aphrodite is celebrated just before the climax of the festival, when the god is killed and rises from the dead. And in Alexandria who else would be chosen for the part of Aphrodite but Mary?"

"Can we stop her?"

Demetrius shook his head. "If you report her to the authorities she will be imprisoned or executed. And you already know how futile it is to argue with her."

"But it would be murder."

"Would it? I think not. In the laws of the Jews a man who ravishes a young girl must be killed. Traditionally, the father or the brothers of the girl have a right to kill him. Having neither father nor brothers, Mary has elected that right to herself."

"Roman courts would not recognize that right," Joseph objected. "And certainly not when the man is of the ruling class."

"No," Demetrius admitted. "I don't think they would. Therefore it is up to you to see that she escapes when the act is done."

"To me!" Joseph looked at him aghast. "Why to me?"

"If Gaius Flaccus were a Jew it would have been your duty as her betrothed to cast the first stone at his execu-

153

tion. If you still love her, you must see that she gets safely away, where the Romans cannot harm her."

"But we could not go back to Jerusalem or anywhere else in the Roman Empire."

"Why not India? You can easily escape from Alexandria by way of the Nile and the canal that leads to the Red Sea. Even a small boat could easily reach Adana at its mouth, and Hadja could find a refuge for you among the desert tribes. Or you could take a ship from Adana to the cities of the Indian coast. With Jivaka's backing, you would be a success as a physician in any of the Indian cities."

Did he love Mary enough to help her commit murder? Joseph wondered. For that was what it really was. He could not fool himself into believing otherwise. And did he love her enough to give up forever the beautiful land of Galilee and Judea, his riches in Jerusalem, and his high position among his own people? Surely, he thought, no man had ever made a harder choice. And yet the thought of living without Mary, now that he had found her again, was a bleak prospect indeed.

"I have laid a heavy burden upon you, Joseph." Demetrius put his hand on the younger man's shoulder. "But I shall not live much longer, and I would like to be certain that someone I trust will be looking after Mary when I am dead. But do not decide now. Think of it and talk to Bana Jivaka. The prospect of life on the coast of Malabar may be more pleasant than you think, even though you love your own country. And you cannot stop Mary now. Think about this, Joseph, and tell me your answer in a few days."

Before making a decision Joseph went to Philo Judaeus. The Jewish leader was recognized as a high authority, not only upon the laws of the Jewish people, but also those of the Romans, and particularly the relationship between Roman and Jewish law. Because he could not mention Mary's name and thereby reveal her plans, Joseph was forced to pose the case to Philo as a hypothetical one of a girl without father or brothers who was raped forcibly.

"Was she betrothed?" Philo asked.

"Yes," Joseph said. "But the betrothal had not been published."

"That makes no difference," Philo said. "Did the act take place in the city or the country?"

"At the villa of Pontius Pilate in Tiberias."

The jurist frowned. "According to Jewish law, the girl in such a case could have called for aid. Therefore, she should be executed by stoning along with the man, since she is guilty of the same act of adultery."

"But she was unconscious at the time."

"Then she is free of blame," the jurist said promptly. "The rapist should be killed without the slayer's incurring thereby any liability. He should not be allowed to live a day, or even an hour."

"By whose hand should he die, then?"

"The law is very clear on that too," Philo said. "The accusers shall be the first to cast a stone. If her father or her brothers did not kill the man, the court could order it done."

"But where the girl is an orphan and is herself the accuser," Joseph interposed. "What then?"

"That is a difficult point," Philo admitted. "However, the laws of Greece as interpreted here in Egypt give such an orphan woman the right to act for herself. It is my view that she has a right to cast the first stone."

"Even to the extent of plotting the death of the man by her own hand?"

Philo stroked his beard. "You are asking me to make a distinction between murder and the right of execution, which is a hard choice. But the law is clear in saying that a man who seduces a betrothed virgin must die. Traditionally he has always been stoned to death by his accusers, but if I were the judge of this case, I would rule that the life of the guilty man belongs to the woman he has ravished." He looked at Joseph keenly. "This is not simply a hypothetical case, is it?"

"No. But I cannot tell you the details, for the woman involved is now in Alexandria."

"And the man to whom she was betrothed?"

"Myself," Joseph admitted. "But the criminal is not a Jew; he is a Roman. And you know well the Roman courts would not hold him guilty against a Jew."

"There is a law higher than Rome itself," Philo said gravely, "the law of the Most High. If you had killed the man when this thing happened, Joseph, no Jew in the world could have accused you of murder."

"But the Roman courts would have crucified me," Joseph pointed out. "Should a man bring on his own death merely to punish one who is guilty of a crime? Who will have gained thereby?"

"The law will have been upheld, and the law is above men themselves."

"I acknowledge no law that tells me I must kill my fellow," Joseph said firmly. "The tablets of Moses say, *'Thou shalt not kill,'* and so long as I live I will knowingly bring about the death of no man, whatever his crime. Let him be shut up somewhere as punishment; such a life must be worse even than death." He turned to go, but Philo Judaeus said, "Wait awhile, Joseph. Perhaps you are right, I do not know. What you say is very much like the teachings of the man called Jesus."

"Jesus? It is a common name among the Jews."

"But he is no common man," Philo said. "This Jesus is a young teacher of Nazareth, now preaching in the cities of Galilee. He followed John but is no zealot seeking to stir up the people against Rome. Instead he teaches forbearance, and love one for another, and the mercy of God to forgive sins."

"Esdras and Enoch spoke much the same thing," Joseph reminded him.

"It is no new thing he speaks," Philo admitted. "He might even be the Greek philosopher Socrates teaching in our own tongue, except that he is young and no one can understand from whence comes his wisdom."

"Why are you so concerned with him?"

"I have not told you all," Philo said gravely. "Many people in Galilee believe him to be the Messiah."

"The Galileans have always been prone to follow false leaders," Joseph pointed out. "They have done it before."

"But you have not seen this teacher of Nazareth, Joseph. How can you know he is false?"

"The Messiah would not come as an unknown teacher of Galilee," Joseph said positively. "Such a thing is unthinkable."

"You are undoubtedly right," Philo agreed thoughtfully. "Certainly no Jew expects the son of God in any such form. But no teacher in recent years has stirred up the people as does this Jesus, if my information is correct—not even John the Baptist. It would be bad indeed for the Jews if he were another Judas the Gaulonite."

Some twenty years before, at the death of Herod the Great, many Jews had resisted the setting up of a kingdom in Judea under his successor, Archelaus, and thousands had been slain in the fighting that resulted from this insurrection. A patriot band under one Judas, called both the Galilean and the Gaulonite, had even captured Sepphoris, the Roman capital of Galilee. In punishment for this affront to the dignity of Rome, Varus, governor of Syria, had conquered the rebels with twenty thousand men. Two thousand Jews had been crucified at one time, thirty thousand sold into slavery, and the city of Sepphoris destroyed.

A delegation of the leaders among the Jews had gone to Rome then and petitioned Augustus to discontinue the kingship in Judea and make it a Roman province. Thus the first of the procurators had come to rule the province in which Jerusalem was located. Sporadically rebellions broke out against these foreign rulers, usually under the leadership of self-styled messiahs. But although many of the Judean Jews would have liked to see the procurators removed from their land with the constant conflict over Roman emblems, dispositions of tax moneys, and the like, that had plagued Pontius Pilate's term of office, only the most fanatical nationalists, confined largely to the fertile province of Galilee, dared think of usurping the power of Rome by revolution and setting up their own king.

A more powerful and much better organized group, the Herodians of Jerusalem, worked to have Herod Antipas, Tetrarch of Galilee, made king of Judea as well. Joseph could understand Philo's concern over any self-styled messiah who might disturb this delicate balance and perhaps cause a revolution among the temperamental Galileans. Such a rebellion could lead to more bloodshed and possible retaliation by the Romans upon Jews throughout the Roman world. As acknowledged leader and spokesman for the largest group of Jews outside Jerusalem, the Jewish colony at Alexandria, Philo would be seriously concerned with such an explosive question.

"I had hoped you would be returning to Jerusalem soon," the old jurist said in parting, "so that you could report to me on this man Jesus of Nazareth."

"Surely you don't think this teacher could be the real Messiah," Joseph protested.

Philo shook his head. "Hardly, although Isaiah speaks of one who will come in humility and suffering. To us who have lived away from Jerusalem for many years, the Messiah has become a distant figure, perhaps more of a figure of speech than an actual person." He smiled then. "But do

157

not tell of this in Jerusalem when you return, Joseph. There are those who look every day for the Christ to descend from the heavens in glory. They would judge me blasphemous if they knew I had spoken otherwise."

12

As the winter months passed, Demetrius grew weaker and weaker. Soon the fluid accumulating in his body extended even to his lungs, so that much of the time he breathed with a rattling sound, as of air bubbling through water. It was becoming more and more difficult to remove the fluid through the sharpened quills, and finally a day came when the old lyre maker begged Joseph not to try any more.

"I have known for a long time I could live only a few more months at the most, Joseph," he said. "Nor do I dread to die. After all, as Socrates said, it is a great adventure. I have seen Mary triumph here in the theater, the thing I have lived for since she came to me in Magdala. And now that she is bent on her own destruction, I am not sure I want to be here to see it."

"But, Demetrius——"

"You need not argue, Joseph. In a way I welcome death, and I need only two things now to be able to die in peace. One is your promise that you will look after Mary, and the other to know that you two will be married as soon as this business is over."

"You have my promise," Joseph assured him. "I talked to Philo some time ago, and he agrees with you that Mary has a right, as an orphan, to the life of Gaius Flaccus."

"And you?"

"I will take no man's life knowingly, nor will I help her to do what she has planned," he said. "But when it is finished, I will try to help her escape."

"No one could ask more of you," Demetrius agreed. He rang a small bell that stood on the table beside the bed and immediately the slave who looked after him appeared in the doorway. "Ask my daughter to come here, please," Demetrius directed.

"B-but——" Joseph started to protest.

"It is better to get this settled once and for all," the old musician said firmly. "I know how it pains you to see her, knowing what she is doing, but this must be."

Mary came in a few minutes later. She had been dressing for the theater and was wearing the lovely Grecian robe in which she danced the story of the Galilean lovers. "I sent for you because I wanted to talk to you and Joseph together about something very important," Demetrius said. "Come sit here with Joseph beside the bed."

Gently the old man caressed Mary's shining hair. "I have known for a long time, dear," he said, "that I have only a little longer to live."

"No, Demetrius," she cried, and clung to him. "Don't say it."

"I am in no pain," the old musician continued. "And I am not afraid to die, now that I know someone will look after you when I am gone."

She raised her head from his breast. "W-what do you mean?"

"Joseph has promised me that he will stay here and watch over you."

"But he must not!" she cried, and turned to Joseph. "I told you to go to Jerusalem. Why should you be killed for me?"

"Do you expect to die after you have carried out your plan of revenge upon the Roman?" Demetrius asked.

"Joseph himself told me the chances of doing it without losing my own life are small," she admitted. "But I know what I am doing!"

"We know too," Demetrius told her.

She looked startled. "But I have not told you."

"You are planning to kill Gaius Flaccus during the festival of the Great Dionysia."

"I will tell you nothing," she said quickly, and looked away, but not before they had seen from her expression that their guess was correct. "This is my responsibility alone," she added grimly.

"But you have not said I am wrong," Demetrius insisted.

"Suppose you are right. Are you going to warn Gaius Flaccus?"

"No. Philo and Demetrius believe you have the right to take his life under our ancient laws," Joseph admitted.

"I told you I did. It is plainly written in the Books of the Law."

"I do not agree," he said, "but I had already planned to help you escape, even before Demetrius asked me."

"But why should you endanger your life for me, Joseph, when you don't believe I have a right to kill Gaius Flaccus?"

"You have been too long away from our people, Mary," he said simply, "else you would not have forgotten the words of a wise man who said, 'Hatred stirreth up strifes, but love covereth all sins.'"

Her eyes filled with tears. "Dear sweet Joseph," she said softly, and for a moment she was the girl he had been afraid had ceased to exist. "I think my love for you is the only good thing left in my heart by this demon of hatred. But you must have no part in all this," she added firmly.

"You cannot keep me from standing by in case you need help."

"What could you do? The might of Rome will be against me."

"With good rowers and a fast galley, we can be through the canal to the Red Sea and down to Adana in less than a week. Hadja could find a place for us with the desert tribes or at Petra. Or we could take ship to Malabar. Bana Jivaka would even go with us himself."

"Would you give up your position in Jerusalem and your riches there for me?" she asked softly.

"Have you forgotten the pledge of Ruth?" he asked. "It was given in love as a guide for all those who love each other."

"'Intreat me not to leave thee,'" she repeated softly, "'or to return from following after thee; for whither thou goest I will go; and where thou lodgest, I will lodge: thy people shall be my people, and thy God my God: where thou diest I will die, and there will I be buried: the Lord do so to me, and more also, if aught but death part me and thee.'" And suddenly she burst into tears and ran from the room.

Demetrius died two weeks later, quietly in his sleep. He was buried with his beloved cithara in his hands, as he had requested, on the shores of Lake Mareotis. And since he had made Mary promise to keep on with her singing and dancing as if nothing had happened, there was no mourning.

As she and Joseph walked home along the shore beside the great walls of the stadium, where the festival of the Great Dionysia would be held, Mary looked up at the huge building and shivered as if with dread.

"I hope you never know what it is to have hatred in your soul, Joseph," she said. "It is like a cancer, eating away at everything that is good in you."

"As a surgeon I would cut it out if I could."

"No one else can help me," she said firmly. "A part of me would do as you suggest, Joseph, and forgive Gaius Flaccus. But another part keeps repeating the words of the Most High. *'Eye for eye, tooth for tooth, hand for hand, foot for foot.'* How could I ignore God's commands?"

"You must do what your heart tells you to do. No one can do more. But be sure you are listening to your heart and not a demon of hate alone."

"Then I must go through with it," she said firmly.

"And you still refuse to tell me how you are going to carry out your plans?"

She nodded. "If you have no part in my guilt, Joseph, then you will have no part in my fate, whatever it shall be."

13

THE festival of the Great Dionysia in Alexandria was traditionally held at the end of March, when the chill of wintry breezes no longer attacked the city from the Great Sea and the air was already warm with the promise of summer. Flowers grew in great profusion everywhere then, and for the three days of the festival the public parks, the streets, the gardens along the shore of Lake Mareotis, and the islands off the shore were a riot of color.

Joseph had heard of this spectacle, when the people of Alexandria literally went mad in a surfeit of excitement and search for pleasure, but he could hardly believe it still, even seeing it with his own eyes. The racing season began several days before the Great Dionysia itself, and thousands thronged daily to the great Hippodrome beyond the

Canopic Gate. In the evenings the drinking establishments were crowded and there was merriment everywhere. Since Dionysos was considered by the Greeks to be the same as Bacchus, and by the Egyptians as Osiris and Serapis under another name, the festival of the Great Dionysia was a legal excuse for all sorts of bacchanalian celebrations. It was hard to believe that many people in Alexandria slept during the entire festival, for the streets were thronged both night and day with merrymakers.

Each day one of the great Greek dramas was presented in the theater, climaxed on the day before the symbolic marriage and death of the god by a presentation of the *Bacchae* of Euripides, in which Dionysos came to earth in the city of Thebes in human form and preached his own worship. Rejected by the women, he then used sorcery to arouse in them an ecstasy of adoration for the god Dionysos, the same ecstasy in which during ancient times women had torn men to pieces and sacrificed infants and later animals to the bacchant god. When, in the play, the king of Thebes, Pentheus, opposed the wild orgies of the cult, Dionysos, still disguised, used his magic talents to send the king among the Bacchae clad as a woman. And when he was discovered, the women, led by his own mother, tore him to pieces in a frenzy of ecstatic insanity.

Mary was dancing the part of Pentheus' mother, the leader of the Bacchae. As the tragic ending of the scene rose to its inevitable climax, she staggered from the place in the hills where the final tragedy had occurred, carrying the dripping head of the king who was her son in her hands. Joseph could not help shuddering with horror, so realistic was her portrayal, even to the last lines when she realized what she had done and, revolted, cried out against the god who had caused her to kill her own son.

Then the god spoke the line, "Ye mocked me, being God; this is your wage." And she answered, "Should God be like a proud man in his rage?" before beginning the tragic dance that ended the play, culminating in death by her own hand in expiation for her sin. As the applause of the crowd thundered through the great theater, Joseph realized that he had just witnessed what might well be the last performance of a superb actress in a real play, and perhaps, he thought with a shiver of dread, a preview of what would happen on the morrow.

Although Mary had consistently refused to tell him the means by which she planned to bring about Gaius Flaccus' death, Joseph was quite sure now that he knew. All Alexandria knew that the new *praefectus vigilum*, whose rank among the equestrian order placed him next to the imperial family itself in nobility, would be the god Dionysos. And that the most beautiful and beloved woman in all of Alexandria, the dancer Flamen, would naturally portray Aphrodite, the goddess of love.

By what diabolic genius Mary had been able to arrange her triumph of revenge during the culminating drama of the great festival, only she knew. Watching her these past few months, Joseph had seen how great a strain it was to pit two jealous and powerful suitors against each other in order to attain her own ambition. Now, like surging waters sweeping with inexorable force through a tidal rip, the currents were in motion. There could be no stopping now. And thinking of the morrow, Joseph felt a cold fear for the woman he loved grip his heart.

Joseph had no chance to talk to Mary the next morning before she left for the landing place on the shores of Lake Mareotis where the god Dionysos would arrive to claim his bride, the divine Aphrodite. Because of the size of the crowd, the festival was to be held in the great stadium instead of the theater. At one end of the amphitheater a stage had been built with dressing rooms beneath. Upon it were erected the throne of the god and the marriage bed, through whose thin transparent curtains the audience could share vicariously the ritual union of the wedded deities. There Dionysos would be symbolically killed to represent the seed as it died in the ground. And from the nuptial couch the dead god would then arise, symbolic of the seedling bursting from the fertile soil. Afterward would come the greatest and wildest celebration of all, climaxing the three-day festival of the Great Dionysia.

Joseph, Matthat, and Bana Jivaka attended the festival together. A great crowd of people was gathered on the shore near the stadium, where a landing had been built for private galleys and barges of the royal court when they visited the gladiatorial games. Here the god Dionysos would land and be met by his bride-to-be, the goddess Aphrodite. Following a triumphal procession through the streets of the city, they would repair to the stadium itself, where a great entertainment had been prepared in their honor preceding the divine marriage. And after that would occur the ritual death of the god, a make-believe tragedy that Joseph fully expected to be real.

The crowd was packed so tightly that Joseph and his friends were not able to force their way through it, but from the steps leading up to the stadium they were able to watch the events from a distance. The people were in a festive mood, as befitted the occasion, and shouts of "Flamen!" and "Aphrodite!" rose as an elaborate chair with closed curtains was carried down to the pier upon which the god would land.

From behind one of the eight islands in the lake a huge barge now appeared, rowed by a hundred slaves. Upon the great golden throne that had been built on the barge a man sat, while rows of beautiful dancing girls whirled and postured before him. Behind the chair a tall black slave held the traditional bull's-head mask of the god Apis when Dionysos appeared in that form.

At the sight of the barge the crowd set up a great shout, "Hail, Dionysos! Hail to the god of the vine!" And upon the floating dais the dancing girls whirled in a mad rhythm of adoration before the throne, until the barge itself was a mass of rippling color from their diaphanous garments. When the barge touched the pier and was secured against it, two tonsured priests of Serapis approached and knelt before it. One tinkled the sistrum, a rattle traditional in this service, while the other waved a palm frond of peace and welcome in his hands.

Next came two beautiful priestesses of Isis, the gold bands about their foreheads wrought into a likeness of the sacred cobra of the goddess. Behind them was the high priestess, with the sacred fringed mantle about her shoulders and the golden cobra upon her forehead. She carried before her a bowl containing waters from the great Mother Nile, so sacred that her hands could not even touch the container, it being protected from contact with her flesh by the fringes of a white drapery covering her head and hanging down over her shoulders and arms. As the priestesses of Isis knelt to welcome the god Dionysos in the name of their own deity, still another priest, waving wands, led a great chorus in chanting a hymn of welcome and praise to the divine visitor.

Now the slaves bearing the chair upon which Mary sat enthroned as Aphrodite lifted the carrying handles to their shoulders and moved to the pier, setting it down just behind the priests of Serapis and the priestesses of Isis. Beside the goddess of love marched the *gymnasiarch* Plotinus, who was to direct the festival, garbed in spotless white. "Welcome to Alexandria, O divine Dionysos!" he shouted. "Descend from thy craft, we pray, and join us for a celebration in thy honor."

A shout of approval rose from the crowd as Plotinus lifted aside the curtain of the chair and held out his hand to the lovely woman who stepped from it. "Flamen! Flamen! Aphrodite!" they roared again and again, and long minutes elapsed before Plotinus could be heard again.

"We have brought you this day a divine bride," he continued then, "with beauty and grace worthy of the gods. Hail, Aphrodite! Goddess of Love and Beauty! Hail, Divine One!"

Mary stood erect. She seemed in truth a goddess of love and beauty with her coppery hair, bound only by a white circlet, shining in the morning sunlight, the regal lines of the white gown she wore emphasizing the loveliness of her divine body.

"By the prophets of Israel," Matthat breathed. "There has never been so beautiful a woman. She is a bride fit indeed for a god."

In the morning sunlight Gaius Flaccus did resemble a god, with his handsome body and features, a gold chaplet upon his curls, and gold-laced sandals upon his feet. He wore no armor, and his short tunic, leaving his handsome muscular legs bare, was of a snow-white material, as was Mary's robe. The transparently costumed dancers advanced from the barge to the pier, escorting the god as he descended from his throne and marched with stately tread to meet the goddess. Before her he stopped, while Plotinus knelt to welcome him and the crowd shouted, "Dionysos! Aphrodite! Dionysos! Aphrodite!"

"Welcome to Alexandria, O Divine One," Mary said clearly. "I bow in homage before my husband-to-be." She dropped gracefully to one knee, but Gaius Flaccus, in the capacity of the vine god, reached out and took her hands, lifting her to her feet. When he drew her to him and kissed her upon the lips, the crowd shouted its approval again and again. Then, holding Mary's hand, he stepped with her into the waiting chair, whose curtains were now raised so that the whole city might see the divine visitor and his bride-to-be.

Slaves ran forward now with another ornately decorated chair for Plotinus, who would lead the procession. And at a word of command the great parade began. In the next few hours it would pass through all parts of the city before returning to the stadium for the celebration in honor of the divine visitor. The ritual marriage, consummation, death, and resurrection of the god would mark the beginning of another growing season in the earth's cycle of fertility, growth, harvest, death, and renewal of life from the seed.

First was the chair of Plotinus, and behind it the mummers, men and women in all sorts of fantastic costumes, representing the many gods worshiped in Alexandria, each in the form in which they were said to appear. Next a group of small girls in white strewed flowers along the way, followed by the dancing girls from the barge, their bright costumes of transparent bombyx a riot of color.

Now came the priests of Serapis, tonsured and bare to the waist, carrying the ritual palms and shaking sistrum rattles. The sacred mark of the god who took his name from both Osiris and the sacred bull Apis was on their foreheads. In their hands they carried golden tokens of the god, lamps shaped like Nile boats, tiny altars upon which the sacred bull was sacrificed, and even a veiled image of the god Serapis himself.

Behind the priests of Serapis marched the devotees of Isis, never very widely separated, for Osiris had been the dead and risen lord of Isis and father of her infant son, Horus, as well as father of the man-made god of the Ptolemies, Serapis. The priestesses of Isis were chosen for their beauty and were clad only in silken loincloths and golden chaplets bearing the sacred cobra. They, too, shook sacred rattles while they chanted a song of adoration to the goddess, and the crowd roared its approval as they passed in the bright morning sunlight.

The great chair in which the visiting god and his bride sat was borne next. Gaius Flaccus, quite evidently flattered at being the center of attraction, bowed and smiled at the plaudits of the crowd, but Mary sat erect, smiling mechanically, her cheeks as pale as her white robe. Watching from the crowd, Joseph wondered if she would be able to go through with what she had planned, and found himself praying that she would come to her senses and give it up at the last moment. Yet, remembering how the past five years had been a preparation for this moment of triumph over the man who had treated her so cruelly, he hardly dared hope that reason would prevail over the almost insane obsession that guided Mary now.

Behind the gods came hundreds of masquers, marching, dancing, cavorting in the streets. Satyrs and sileni, bacchantes, maenads, Bacchae, nymphs, victories, all the traditional celebrants of the Dionysian festivals held throughout the Empire thronged the street in the wake of the divine pair. And after them moved a procession of great floats drawn by sweating slaves pulling ropes covered with golden cloth, while overseers marched beside them cracking long whips.

On one of the floats a statue of Nysa, twice a man's height and marvelously lifelike, rose automatically to pour milk from a golden bowl. And upon another, satyrs cavorted amidst a great load of grapes, pressing out wine that streamed from spouts attached to the float, so that any who seized a cup from the girls distributing them could drink. Another showed the horned infant Zagreus being torn to pieces by the Titans at the front, while in the center Zeus, his father, held a glass jar in which the infant's heart continued to beat rhythmically, bringing cries of wonder from the crowd. The end of the float represented the bridal chamber of Semele, where she was impregnated by the living heart of Zagreus and gave birth to Dionysos himself.

On still another float the youth Dionysos played with a bevy of unclad nymphs in a cave, from which doves, pigeons, and swallows were let out to be caught by the onlookers. The last and greatest of the floats depicted the vine god. Upon it a great figure of Dionysos himself rode an elephant whose mahout was a satyr.

After the great floats came smaller ones bearing living tableaux depicting the other gods favored by the Alexandrians. Here was Alexander the Great, deified and attended by his patrons, Victory and Athena. Next in the procession was the deified Ptolemy I and his queen Berenice, then the Emperor Augustus and the living Roman god, Tiberius. Regiments of soldiers followed on horse and on foot, so that, all in all, it was more than three hours from the time the procession left the pier where the barge of Dionysos had come ashore until it circled the city and returned to the great stadium where the festival in honor of the visiting god would be held.

Enthroned upon the stage built at one end of the stadium, Dionysos and Aphrodite were now honored with a vast program of entertainment. Before them in the arena gladiators fought with sword and with net and trident, and charioteers battled from swiftly moving vehicles with naked swords. The grassy floor of the great amphitheater was soon slippery with their blood, but the crowd only shouted for even more spectacles and more carnage.

As the afternoon waned, skilled acrobats performed marvelous feats of strength and skill, interspersed between the acts of mimes depicting events in the life of both Dionysos and Aphrodite. And troop after troop of dancers of various nationalities performed the traditional dances of their people in honor of the divine betrothed pair.

In his seat near one of the *vomitoria*, the passages leading to the dressing rooms under the stands, from which the actors emerged into the stadium itself, Joseph watched the performances, sick with horror at this travesty of divine worship and tense with anxiety for Mary. And as the celebration wore its way toward the crowning event of the day, where the god and his divine bride would retire into the transparently curtained room at the very top of the stage, the tension of anticipation became almost beyond bearing.

Now the last mime was finished and the actors scampered off the stage. Somewhere off stage great drums rolled out a sonorous beat like the crash of summer thunder, and before the ornately decorated nuptial chamber a towering figure appeared, taller than any human Joseph had ever seen, wearing silver armor and bearing on his head the crown of the gods.

"It is Jupiter," Matthat said, "come to wed Dionysos and Aphrodite. I have seen that fellow play the part before."

At a command from the Father of the Gods, Dionysos and his bride-to-be knelt before him and joined hands. Over their heads the actor intoned the solemn words joining them in wedlock, and when he finished, Gaius Flaccus lifted Mary to her feet. Momentarily she swayed, and Joseph thought she was going to fall in one of the fainting spells that had troubled her as a young girl. She seemed to have become freed of them since coming to Alexandria, however, a not unusual occurrence, for girls often outgrew such conditions as they reached womanhood.

But Mary regained control of herself, and as the god Dionysos gathered the goddess of beauty in his arms and bent to claim her lips in the nuptial kiss, the crowd went wild. Now he took her hand and led her to the nuptial chamber, through whose transparent curtains their every movement would be visible to the audience. And as the curtains closed behind them, a torch set back of the room erected on the stage burst into flame, silhouetting their shadows in brilliant pantomime.

A great "Ahh" of pent-up emotion went up from the crowd as Gaius Flaccus lifted his bride in his arms and carried her to the great nuptial couch, taking her into the embrace signifying consummation of the divine marriage. A hush fell over the audience as they waited for the next act in the drama of marriage, fecundation, death of the seed, and rebirth into immortality.

Joseph turned his head away. Now, if ever, he knew, Mary must carry out her purpose. With Hadja somewhere backstage to take care of the details, it would have been a simple matter to substitute a real dagger for the one made of parchment or some similar flimsy material that would give the illusion of reality yet crumple when it stuck Gaius Flaccus' body. The victim would have no warning, before the blade found his heart, that the weapon was of steel, not paper.

Sitting there sick with horror and powerless to stop the rushing tide of tragedy, Joseph fought against the impulse to leap to his feet and shout a warning to the unsuspecting Gaius Flaccus. Nor would he have accomplished anything if he had, for in the great expanse of the stadium, with the crowd roaring its approval of the mock consummation and the symbolic death of the seed that was to follow, a single voice, even in warning, could hardly be heard. And if he had been heard, he would only have been lessening whatever chance Mary had to escape, once her revenge was achieved.

Every eye in the stadium was upon the dagger in Mary's hand as, outlined upon the gauzy screen of the curtains surrounding the nuptial bed as vividly as a picture painted in bold strokes, her arm rose above the body of the divine lover clasped in her arms. Even though the audiences of Alexandria were fully accustomed to such realism and knew that the dagger would actually crumple when it struck the body of Dionysos, a sudden tension gripped the crowd. When the blade finally plunged downward the pent-up suspense was expressed in a mighty groan from the onlookers, so real was the tense drama being played out there before them in the nuptial chamber where the marriage of the gods had just been ritually consummated.

Then a man's scream of pain rang through the great stadium, breaking the spell. The sound had hardly died away when Mary leaped from the nuptial bed and tore the curtains apart. Like an avenging goddess indeed she stood, silhouetted by the flaming torch behind the stage, a bloody dagger held high in her right hand. Blood was frequently spilled in the mock deaths of the Greek theater by means of small bladders filled with a red fluid, so the crowd still did not realize that they were witnessing a real, and not a pantomime, tragedy. But when Mary turned and ran for the wings of the temporary stage, instead of remaining to receive the resurrected god as her consort, a few of the onlookers realized that this was something more than the realism of the stage.

People began to surge to their feet then, caught up by the real-life drama they were witnessing. And now another figure appeared through the torn curtains of the nuptial chamber. It was Gaius Flaccus, no longer divine, for blood was staining his immaculately white tunic. "Help me!" he shouted, his voice hoarse with terror. "I am dying!"

Pandemonium broke loose then. In the midst of it, without pausing even for a prayer of thanksgiving that Gaius Flaccus was still alive and Mary was not yet, at least, a murderess, Joseph vaulted over the seats just below him and into the open passageway by which the actors reached the dressing rooms under the stage. He knew vaguely that the dressing rooms were somewhere below him, and as he raced through the corridors a deep roar from the crowd told him the people had at last realized how near they had come to witnessing a real murder.

Actors, actresses, dancers, musicians, and stage hands were milling about in the corridors beneath the great stadium. Most of them, not having been on stage, did not yet realize what had happened.

As Joseph hesitated for a moment one familiar face appeared among the crowd. It was Albina, and when he called to her she came over at once, her face grave. "Mary ran through to her dressing room just now, Joseph," she said hurriedly. "There was blood on her robe."

"She tried to kill Gaius Flaccus," he gasped. "Where is her dressing room?"

Albina wasted no time with questions but led him immediately to a door above which the torch symbol of Flamen had been painted. "I will wait outside!" she suggested. "If they come after her, perhaps, I can send them in another direction."

He nodded gratefully; there was no time for thanks. Hadja stood guard outside Mary's door. "Praise be to Ahura-Mazda that you have come, Joseph," he said fervently. "Did she kill him?"

"No." Joseph swept the corridor with a quick surveying glance. There was a large window at the end, large enough for them to escape through if they had time. "Open the window there," he directed. "I will get Mary and we will try to escape toward the lake."

As Joseph pushed open the door to Mary's dressing room, Hadja started toward the window. If they could get free of the stadium and reach the lake, it might be possible to hail one of the boats that plied for hire along the shore and make their escape before the audience in the great stadium had recovered from its momentary paralysis at the unexpected drama they had witnessed as a climax to the festival of Dionysos.

Mary stood beside her dressing table, her face devoid of color. Blood stained her fingers, her white gown, and the blade of the dagger still gripped in her right hand. Her eyes were dilated until they seemed to have no color, the wide pupils mirroring only a stark despair. By no act of recognition did she even so much as show that she knew Joseph was in the room.

When she did move it was so rapidly that Joseph almost failed to seize her wrist as the dagger plunged downward toward her own breast. He was not quick enough to save her a wound, but did manage to deflect the sharp point of the dagger so that it failed to find the target for which she had intended it, her own heart. Ripping through the white fabric of her gown, the dagger made a shallow wound in her breast before it dropped from nerveless fingers as she swayed and collapsed in Joseph's arms.

"I—I couldn't do it, Joseph," she sobbed in a sudden rush of words and tears, clinging to him like a terrified child. "Something held my arm back."

"The Most High would not let you commit murder," he told her. "We must go quickly. He will surely help us escape."

The voice of the crowd was a deep-throated roaring now, like a great pack of snarling animals. They were enraged at the affront to the god in whose honor the festival was being held, and the first target of their anger would

naturally be the woman who had tried to kill the imper-
sonated god.

"Hadja is waiting outside," Joseph told Mary urgently.
"If we can reach the lake in the darkness, we will be safe."

But she only shook her head. "I have caused enough
trouble already," she said almost in a whisper. "Leave me
before it is too late."

"I will never leave you, Mary," he said simply. "If the
crowd comes we will die together."

Bana Jivaka burst into the room then. "Hurry!" he
gasped. "The crowd was almost at my heels."

"You must go, Mary," Joseph pleaded. "All of us will
die if you stay here."

She moved suddenly and seized the dagger once more,
but Joseph gripped her hand, keeping her from plunging
the blade into her breast. "Please let me die, Joseph," she
begged. "It's the only way to save you now."

"Let me die! It's the only way!" The words exploded in
Joseph's mind with a burst of inspiration. Death—or the
appearance of death—might indeed be the best way now,
perhaps the only way, as Mary had said, of escaping the
fury of the crowd. Quickly he turned to Bana Jivaka. "You
told me once you could induce a trance so deep that it cannot be told from death. Could you do it now and make it
seem that she is dead?"

Jivaka's alert mind took in the situation at once. "With
that wound on her breast . . . and the dagger . . . Yes, it
might be the answer."

Joseph took the dagger from Mary's resistless fingers.
"You must do exactly as Jivaka tells you, dear," he said
quickly. "He may be able to save us all from the crowd if
you help."

She swayed against him as if she were about to faint,
and without waiting for an answer he lifted her in his
arms and placed her on the floor before the dressing table. "Look at Jivaka," he commanded. "And do exactly
as he tells you."

The Indian physician had already removed from his
pocket the emerald he always carried. As he held it before
Mary's eyes, the gem began to glow from the light of twin
tapers burning on her dressing table. "You must sleep,
Mary of Magdala," he started to chant in a deep mono-
tone. "You must yield yourself to sleep . . . sleep
. . . sleep."

172

14

ALBINA had done her work well, diverting Plotinus on a futile errand when he came raging backstage seeking Mary. It was almost five minutes before the *gymnasiarch*, with Gaius Flaccus and a pair of brawny soldiers carrying drawn swords, burst open the door above which a torch was painted. The Tribune was pale and his tunic was still bloody, but the shallow wound in his chest made by Mary's dagger had been controlled easily with a bandage. Behind the Romans, the forefront of the crowd surged into the narrow corridor, shouting with blood lust, but the soldiers held them at bay outside the door.

A dramatic scene greeted the eyes of the onlookers. Mary lay on the floor with the bloody dagger gripped in her right hand, the point touching the wound where the blade had penetrated skin and muscle. The red trickle of blood across her breast stood out sharply against the alabaster pallor of her skin, and closer observers than the angry and excited Romans would still have thought she had stabbed herself in the heart, pulling the dagger out again in the agony of death.

"By the gods!" Gaius Flaccus cried. "She has killed herself!" And the people behind him took up the cry, passing it back to the crowd outside. "Flamen is dead! Slain by her own hand!"

Plotinus seemed stunned for a moment, then he wheeled upon the two physicians. "Why are you here?" he demanded savagely, as if he blamed them for his not finding the woman called Flamen alive.

"I was her father's physician," Joseph said, "and her friend. I came after her immediately, afraid that she might do something like this. She tried to kill herself once before in Magdala."

"Then she really is a Jewess as you claim," the *gymnasiarch* said to Gaius Flaccus. "But why would she try to kill you?"

Before the Tribune could answer, Joseph said quickly,

"He betrayed Mary of Magdala long ago, when she was a girl. The life of the Tribune Gaius Flaccus has been forfeit to her since that time, according to the ancient laws of the Jewish people."

"And after five years she still wanted to kill me?" Gaius Flaccus swayed and held onto one of the soldiers for support. "Let us leave this place," he gasped. "The smell of blood sickens me."

"What drivel is this?" Plotinus snapped. "Romans are not governed by Jewish laws."

"This woman's father was a citizen of Rome," Joseph told him. "As such she is entitled to justice, even if she tried to kill the man who betrayed her."

Plotinus shrugged. "I dispense justice in the name of Rome here," he said coldly. "And I judge the woman called Flamen to be a murderess, even in death. Take her body away," he ordered the soldiers. "Let her be buried this very night on the shore of the lake, in the common ground for criminals."

Joseph paled. This was more than he had figured on, for he had planned that Mary's body would be turned over to him for burial. Then he and Jivaka would be able to revive her and escape from the city by way of Lake Mareotis and the Nile. "She was a Jewess," he said to the *gymnasiarch*. "Grant that I may take her away and lay her to rest after the manner of our people."

Plotinus did not even answer. "See that her grave is guarded," he told the soldiers and, turning on his heel, left the room, followed by his retinue. Two soldiers remained behind as guards until slaves could be sent with a litter to carry Mary's body to the burying ground of the criminals, but they would not let either Joseph or Bana Jivaka approach the body.

Led by two slaves bearing torches, a macabre procession filed from the stadium a short time later. Mary's body lay upon a litter borne by four slaves. So deep was the trance into which Jivaka had managed to place her that even Joseph, stealing a glance at her as often as he could and occasionally managing to come close enough to touch her skin, could still not tell that she was alive. Joseph and Bana Jivaka walked with Hadja at the rear of the procession, each cudgeling his brains for some strategem by which to get Mary's body away where Jivaka could release her from the stupor. But none of them thought of a way, and as each step brought them closer and closer to the grave where the Romans would bury her alive, their hopes for Mary's life grew fainter and fainter.

Through the turbulent streets of the city the little procession marched toward the dark, ghostly monuments of the Necropolis, across the Agathadaemon Canal. And still Joseph was able to see no way in which they could hope to save Mary from being buried alive. Then near the Necropolis Gate he spied a building before which a number of elongated boxes stood upended against the walls. It was the shop of a coffin maker, logically placed here at the entrance to the City of the Dead. "How long could she live in the trance if she were buried in a coffin?" he asked Jivaka in a whisper, seizing his arm and drawing him back out of earshot of the others.

The Indian's quick mind grasped his meaning. "I once saw a magician in India removed from a coffin alive after six hours," he whispered. "But the box was very large."

"Hold!" Joseph called to the slaves carrying the litter. "We must stop for the coffin."

"Plotinus said nothing about this," the soldier in charge of the guard objected as the procession halted.

"Would you rob the dead of a decent resting place?" Joseph demanded sternly. "Be sure her soul will torment yours throughout eternity if you do."

The soldier shivered. "It is true that the *gymnasiarch* did not forbid that she be buried in a coffin," he admitted.

"Then there is no reason why she should not." Before the soldier could object any more Joseph hammered on the door of the coffin maker's shop. "Wake up!" he shouted. "We have need of your wares."

The slaves had put down the litter, grateful for a chance to rest. In a few minutes the proprietor emerged from the building, rubbing his eyes, his sleeping cap still on his head. Joseph had already canvassed the row of coffins leaning against a building and selected the largest one he could find. "I will take this one," he said. "What is the price?"

"Why do you need such a large one?" the soldier grumbled. "It will only mean more weight to carry."

"This one has the best wood," Joseph explained. "It will last longer." He paid the coffin maker and called Hadja to help carry the rough wooden box.

Once again the little procession got under way. Now they were inside the City of the Dead itself, and as they moved through it toward the burial place reserved for paupers and criminals near the shore of Lake Mareotis, the shouts and sounds of revelry from the city across the canal grew fainter and fainter. Finally, almost at the water's edge, they came upon an empty space, and the soldier at the head of the party ordered a halt.

One could not dig very deeply here close to the water without having the grave turn into a well, so the pits were very shallow, with the sand piled up to cover the coffin if the dead were lucky enough to rest so luxuriously. Rotted fragments of wood sticking out of the ground all around them showed where others had lain, and sometimes bones projected from the soil, bleached white by the salt air from the sea that blew across the narrow tongue of land upon which the Necropolis stood.

A shallow grave was quickly dug by the slaves, barely deep enough to cover the coffin. Joseph did not insist upon its being deeper, for if his plan were to be carried out—and a desperate one it was indeed—every minute lost in uncovering Mary's body might mean the difference between life and death for her. He did not let himself think that his desperate plan might fail; the thought of his beloved smothering there in the darkness beneath the earth was more than he could bear. And yet he could see no other, no better, way, for the three of them, unarmed, would have no chance of overpowering the soldiers and the slaves. And if they were killed in a fruitless fight, all chances of saving Mary would be gone.

Joseph himself placed Mary's body in the roomy box. When it was covered, he managed to push a hole down to the wooden cover under the guise of placing a marker of driftwood at the head. He had purposely left the cover itself unnailed, hoping that some air would filter down through the loose dirt, at least enough to preserve life until his plan could be carried out.

When the burial was finished, the slaves departed hurriedly, anxious to be away from this realm of the dead. Joseph's heart lifted when he saw that only one soldier remained behind as a guard. It was like the Romans, he thought, to consider one armed soldier more than equal to three men, especially when one was a Jew. Actually, it was no part of his plan to attack the guard, for even if they managed to kill the soldier, another would come to relieve him in a few hours, soon enough to rouse the city and intercept them before they carried through their plan of escaping up the Nile. For all of them to be quite safe, it was important that Plotinus should think Mary was dead.

Joseph drew Bana Jivaka to one side, out of the guard's range of hearing. "How long do we have?" he asked anxiously.

"The coffin is large, and in the trance she breathes very lightly," Jivaka whispered. "She may have several hours. It is difficult to say."

Hadja clenched and unclenched his great hands. "Engage the soldier in conversation, Joseph," he begged. "And I will slip behind him and throttle him."

Joseph shook his head. "It is best if they do not know we have stolen the body," he explained. "We must wait a little while yet."

"But we cannot let her lie there in the grave and die from lack of breath."

"I am as worried as you are, Hadja," he admitted. "Believe me, my way is best, but I will hurry it."

The soldier paused in his steady pacing up and down beside the grave when Joseph approached. "What do you want, Jew?" he demanded, drawing his sword.

"This woman was my betrothed," Joseph explained. "Have you never loved a woman yourself?"

The guard relaxed. "She was very beautiful," he admitted. "I saw her dance once in the theater. But as for me, I prefer the women of the drinking houses who dance naked."

Joseph nodded toward the Rhakotis, only a short distance away across the canal. The sounds of singing and drunken laughter floated to them across the tombs. "There will be many such in the drinking houses tonight," he suggested. "Why should you not be with them?"

"I have been ordered to stay here until I am relieved."

"And when will that be?"

"Four hours at least. By that time my relief will probably be drunk and stop for another flagon."

"Surely no one will care if you quench your thirst in the Rhakotis for an hour while I watch beside the grave of my beloved."

"It would go bad with me if I were found out," the soldier said doubtfully, but Joseph realized with a rising sense of elation that he was wavering.

"Can the dead speak?" he asked. "I would pay well for an hour alone with her." He lifted his purse and let the man see that it was well filled.

The sight of money settled the soldier's doubts. He took the liberal handful of coins Joseph gave him and set off at a trot toward the gate leading into the city and the merriment of the Rhaktois. No sooner was he out of sight than Joseph whistled to Hadja and Bana Jivaka and, dropping to his knees, began to claw dirt from the shallow grave.

Quickly they uncovered the top of the coffin and removed it. Mary lay inside, just as Joseph had placed her, but the skin of her hands and feet were as cold as the marble they resembled, and there was no sign of life. "She is dead, Jivaka," Joseph said brokenly as they carried her to one side and laid her body upon their cloaks. "I waited too long to bribe the guard."

"Waste no time in self-censure," Jivaka said. "Place your mouth over hers and breathe into her body while Hadja and I cover the grave again. It is a method I have often used to breathe life into babies at birth."

Kneeling beside Mary and putting his mouth over hers, Joseph forced his breath between her lips. Steadily and slowly he breathed into her body, feeling her breast rise as the air distended her lungs. And when he drew away, a soft rushing sound could be heard as the air escaped from her nose and mouth. Over and over again he kept up the steady rhythm of inflating her lungs while Bana Jivaka and Hadja worked rapidly, covering the grave so the soldier would not suspect that it had been tampered with. When they finished, the Indian physician knelt beside Mary and felt for her pulse.

"Can you feel it?" Joseph asked anxiously.

Jivaka shook his head. "No. Have you seen any sign of life?"

"I cannot be sure. Her lips seem warmer, but it may be from my own."

"Wait!" Jivaka said. "I may be able to tell." Quickly he took from his pocket the green stone he had used to bring on the trance. Polishing it on his sleeve until it shone in the faint moonlight, he held it in front of Mary's mouth and nostrils for a few moments, then lifted it and studied the gem closely. "I believe I can make out a film," he said. "But we must get her to a place where we can warm her body."

"The Rhakotis is out of the question," Joseph said.

"Or anywhere else in the city," Jivaka agreed. "With so many people on the streets, we would certainly be seen."

"And there is no boat to take her to her own villa by water," Hadja added hopelessly.

"The catacombs!" Joseph cried. "Why didn't I think of them before?"

"Catacombs?"

"Achillas and his band live there. They are under an obligation to me."

"But could you find a thief's hiding place in the darkness?" Jivaka asked doubtfully.

"I am sure I remember the burial society whose name is on the entrance to the crypt," Joseph explained. "We will go there at once and look for it."

"What of the Roman?" Hadja asked. "He will give the alarm."

"The soldier will not know we have removed the body," Joseph pointed out. "That was the most important part of my plan. And he certainly will not tell that he was absent from his post."

Through the sepulchral City of the Dead the three of them carried Mary's unconscious body. The thieves would be busy tonight, Joseph knew, for there was much drunkenness in the city and purses could be lifted easily. But he did not believe Achillas himself would be out, for the old man had not completely recovered his strength from the long illness. He was counting on Achillas or someone to be at the underground headquarters.

Joseph's memory did not betray him, and without any difficulty he found the entrance to the catacombs where he had been taken to treat the old thief's empyema. But as he continued to knock on the inner door without receiving an answer, his hopes of finding someone there began to fade. Then a light shone inside and a face appeared at the small barred window. It was Achillas, and Joseph held up his own torch, taken from the rack just inside the outer door, so that the old thief could see his face.

"It is Joseph of Galilee," he said. "We need help."

The door was unbarred at once. "By Serapis!" the old man cried when he saw the burden they bore. "What is this, a corpse?"

"It is the dancer called Flamen," Joseph explained. "She is in a deep trance, and we must work to save her life."

Achillas did not waste their time with questions. He showed them where to place Mary, upon his own sleeping couch, and while Joseph started again to breathe into her body, he scurried about getting warm covers in which to wrap her and setting stones to heat on the always burning brazier. Bana Jivaka worked beside Joseph, chafing

179

Mary's hands and feet to restore the flagging circulation.

Long minutes passed without any evidence of success. The stones and the covers brought some warmth to Mary's body, but it seemed that she was past generating any sign of life within herself. Then suddenly, as he pressed his lips to hers and breathed gently into her lungs, Joseph felt a convulsive movement of her breast, as if she were trying to breathe against him. And when he felt for her pulse with trembling fingers, hardly daring to hope even yet that his senses had not deceived him, he detected a faint, swift flutter beneath his touch.

"She lives, Jivaka!" he cried exultantly. "Thanks be to the Most High, she lives!"

"It is a miracle!" The Indian physician's eyes were wet. "A miracle of faith, Joseph. Because you would not believe that she was dead, your God has brought her back to you."

Inspired by this promise of success, they renewed their efforts to strengthen the life now beginning to stir once again within Mary's body. Soon she began to breathe shallowly and rapidly, then more slowly as her body began to come alive again. "What about the trance?" Joseph asked. "Should we do something to bring her out of it?"

"I fear the shock of a sudden awakening," Jivaka said. "It is better to let her regain consciousness slowly and of her own accord."

Morning had come outside and the members of Achillas' band had long since returned from their night's adventures when Mary opened her eyes. "Where am I?" she whispered. "I don't remember this place."

"You are in the catacombs of the Necropolis," Joseph told her. "Some friends of mine who live here gave us shelter."

"I—I seem to remember having a bad dream. As if I were in a dark place like a—like a grave."

"Don't think of it now," he urged. "You have been very close to death, but we were able to bring you back. That is all that matters. We will be safe here until we can escape from Alexandria."

"Did I kill Gaius Flaccus?"

"No. It was a flesh wound. The dagger did not go true."

"My hand would not obey my will," she said slowly. "Something held it back."

"It was the power of the Most High. He would not let the devil that possessed you drive you to murder."

Her eyes moved around the room, to Bana Jivaka

standing by the couch, the tall smiling Nabatean, and Achillas blowing upon the coals of the brazier to heat more stones. The other members of the band hovered around the second brazier in the corner, upon which the usual pot of stew bubbled.

Everyone was happy at the return to life of such a beautiful woman, everyone, that is, except the son Manetho, who seemed constitutionally surly. When Joseph's eyes occasionally met those of the young thief, he was shocked by the hatred in Manetho's gaze. For a moment he could think of no reason for it, and then the truth suddenly came to him. After his father, Manetho would be the leader of the band. Achillas had come very near to dying several months before, only to be saved by Joseph's skill. And to a hate-distorted mind, the hand that had kept Manetho from becoming leader of the band, even though it saved his father's life, was lifted against him. Watching the glowering thief in the corner, Joseph felt a shiver of dread sweep over him.

"Achillas is the father of Albina, who dances in the theater," he told Mary. "These are his sons and the men who work for him."

Mary smiled. "Your daughter is a fine dancer. She will be the leader now."

The old thief bowed his head and lifted her pale fingers to his forehead. "No one will ever equal Flamen. I have said a prayer of thanks to Isis that you have been spared." None of them held the attempted death of a Roman against her; in a way it made her akin to them through a common enemy.

By midmorning Mary had recovered enough to drink a bowl of broth. While she had been unconscious Joseph had dressed the shallow wound in her breast, where the dagger had almost found its mark. Now, wearing one of Albina's robes, she looked little the worse for her narrow escape from death.

Early in the afternoon Hadja was sent into the city with a note to Matthat, asking him to give the money Joseph had left in his care to the Nabatean. With a part of it Hadja was to hire a swift galley which would wait for them at the mouth of the Agathadaemon Canal that very night. Tomorrow would find them far up the Nile on the way to where the canal from the Red Sea opened into the river. Once safely away from Alexandria, the way would be clear to freedom. Hadja was also instructed to stop at

Mary's villa for her clothes and her jewels and to dismiss her servants.

Joseph had not expected Hadja to return much before nightfall, but the musician was back in three hours. His face was grave and, noting that Mary was asleep on the couch, he drew Joseph out into the passageway leading to the underground refuge of Achillas and his band of thieves. "I have bad news, Joseph," he said at once. "Plotinus is using Mary's attempt to kill Gaius Flaccus as an excuse to persecute the Jews of Alexandria."

"But why? They are respected here."

"In the city they say Flamen has bankrupted the *gymnasiarch*. He owes much money to Jewish moneylenders and hopes to kill them in the riot so he will not have to pay."

"Did you find Matthat?"

Hadja shook his head. "A great crowd was going through the streets, breaking open the shops of the Jews. I saw them smash the door to Matthat's shop, but he was not there and I could get no money."

This was disquieting news indeed, for Joseph had deposited a substantial sum with the jewel merchant, and he had counted upon that money to pay their expenses until transfer of funds from his bankers in Jerusalem could be made to whatever city they settled in after escaping from Alexandria.

"I have only a few coins," Hadja added, "but they are yours." Joseph squeezed the tall Nabatean's arm gratefully. "There may be another way," he said. "Perhaps Achillas will make me a loan in return for a draft upon my bankers in Jerusalem."

Just then they heard the outer door creak open. With a muttered oath Hadja drew the long dagger he carried always beneath his robe, and they flattened themselves against the wall of the tunnel. In a moment a torch flared up, lessening the darkness of the tunnel, and began to move toward them. Joseph started to call to the visitors, but Hadja put his fingers to his lips and tightened his grip upon the dagger.

Soon two people appeared, a woman and a man. When Joseph recognized Albina and Matthat, he drew a long sigh of relief. He had been fairly certain that Plotinus would have no way of knowing about the strategem, but they still could not afford to be surprised by the enemy. When he stepped out into the corridor, in the full light of the torch, Matthat gave a cry of fear and dropped the torch, but Albina cried, "Thank the blessed Isis you are safe, Joseph. What of Flamen?"

"She is here," Joseph told them. "But what happened to you?" Their clothing was torn and mud-spattered, and Matthat's face was bruised and battered. He swayed there in the corridor, and Joseph took his arm to support him.

"Evil days have come to Alexandria," Matthat moaned. "Curses be upon all Romans." Supported by Joseph and Hadja, he managed to stumble into the room and collapsed upon a pile of rugs in one corner. "Speak softly," Joseph warned. "Mary is asleep."

Matthat could still only groan, and it was Albina who told them the story of what was happening in Alexandria. "I went to Matthat's shop this morning," she said, "trying to learn something about what happened after you left the stadium with Flamen's body. The crowd was already breaking into it, but I saw Hadja on the street and he told me the story."

She stopped for breath before going on. "I thought I might find out more about what Plotinus is going to do at the theater, so I went there." She stopped for a moment, as if reluctant to go on. "Manetho has gone to Gaius Flaccus and Plotinus with the story that Flamen did not die, Joseph."

"My son a traitor!" Achillas cried angrily. "I will kill him with my own hands."

"Fortunately Manetho did not tell where Mary is hidden," Albina continued. "He pretended not to know. Plotinus is wild with anger and has arrested Philo and the other Jewish leaders. He threatens to kill every Jew in Jerusalem unless Flamen is found."

Matthat had found his voice now. "He is taking them to the theater, where a mob has gathered," he managed to gasp. "The Forum would not hold the crowd. They had me, too, but I managed to slip away. Albina found me hiding and brought me here."

"Plotinus was already inflaming the crowd against the Jews before I got away from the theater," Albina added. "When the people are aroused he will turn them loose upon Philo and the others. Then they will start through the city."

Joseph looked at Mary, still sleeping on the couch. He had thought their troubles would be over when he rescued her from the living death of a criminal's grave. But now innocent people were suffering because of what they had both done, and more would lose their lives unless someone intervened. It was unthinkable to turn Mary over to Plotinus as a sop to his anger. Nor did he believe that would necessarily guarantee the safety of Philo and the other Jewish leaders, since it was to the *gymnasiarch's* interest to insure that the men to whom he owed large sums of money were killed by mob violence.

There was one other possibility, however. If Joseph insisted that the guilt was all his own, Plotinus might be forced to accept him as a hostage for the safety of Philo and the other Jews. With the letter he carried from Pontius Pilate to the governor of Alexandria, he could be certain of a fair trial in the courts. Roman justice was slow but fair, and once he was allowed to present the case against Gaius Flaccus and Plotinus in an open court, there was a chance that it might be decided in his favor. In any event, the proceedings would take a long time; enough, certainly, for Mary to be taken to a safe place. But first he must find money to hire a galley to take her safely away from Alexandria.

"Can you lend me five thousand denarii on a letter to my bankers in Jerusalem?" he asked Achillas.

"You can have it without any security," the old man said promptly. "After all, did you not save my life?"

"I had better give you the letter," Joseph insisted. "In case . . ." He did not finish the sentence, but they knew well enough what he meant. There were wax tablets on a table in the corner and, searing the surface of one of them quickly in the flame of a candle to smooth the wax of a former writing, he scribbled on it with the metal stylus, blowing the wax shavings away when he had finished. "When the riots are over," he told Achillas, "take this to a banker here. He will send it to Jerusalem and give you the money when it arrives."

Achillas went to a chest in the corner of the underground room to count out the five thousand denarii. While he was doing so, Joseph drew Hadja aside. "Listen closely, my friend," he said. "I am entrusting all that I love to you. Take the money Achillas will give you and hire a galley, the fastest one you can find. Tonight you must carry Mary aboard, with Bana Jivaka, and leave Alexandria at once. Take them both by way of the canal to Arsinoë at the head of the Egyptian Sea. I will meet you there when I am free."

"But you——" the Nabatean started to protest.

"Swear that you will do as I tell you," Joseph insisted.

184

Mareotis, with a torch flaring at its prow and four slaves at the oars. Reclining on the cushions was a fat Greek in a finely pleated robe, obviously a man of some substance. He probably lived in a villa on the shores of Lake Mareotis, Joseph thought, and therefore might not know of the happenings in the town. And besides, the Greeks and the Jews got along better than the other nationalities of Alexandria, for many Jews were part Greek.

If he hailed the galley, Joseph knew, he could probably gain a ride to the quays of the Brucheion itself, only about a block from the theater. But in doing so he would be crossing his own particular Rubicon, for once he was in the city itself, there could hardly be any going back. The torch at the carved prow of the galley was abreast of him now, and if he were going to hail, it must be soon.

A beguiling picture raced through Joseph's mind of himself with Mary, Hadja, and Bana Jivaka in just such a galley as this, only larger, speeding up the Nile toward the canal to the Egyptian Sea and freedom. But then another scene crowded the pleasant one aside, a scene that he knew was probably taking place right now within the great theater of Alexandria: the howling of a mob intent upon the murder of Philo and the patriarchs among the Jews, and the cold hard face of the *gymnasiarch* Plotinus stirring them up.

His decision crystallized, Joseph waited no longer. "Wait, please," he called to the galley, and stepped out where he could be seen. "I am a physician and a friend is desperately ill across the city," he explained. "Would you do me the favor of letting me ride with you?"

At a word from their master the slaves leaned upon the oars, stopping the boat. Joseph stepped down to the very edge of the water, into the circle of light cast by the torch on the prow. "I am quite alone," he said, holding up his hands. "If you help me it may mean the life of a friend." He was not telling an untruth, for he did indeed hope to save the life of his friend Philo.

"Bring the galley against the bank," the Greek ordered the slaves, and when the boat touched the earth, he gave his hand courteously to Joseph to steady him as he stepped aboard. "I am going to a dinner at the house of Alcibiades," he said jovially. "And if his food is no better than usual, I may need the services of a physician myself before the night is over."

The galley sped through the Agathadaemon Canal and

into the Harbor of the Happy Return, turning northeast-ward then to pass under the bridge of the Heptastadium nearest the city. At this time of day the great causeway leading to the Pharos normally thronged with people, but tonight it was almost deserted.

"Everybody must still be drunk from the Dionysia," the Greek observed. "I never saw the mall so deserted."

Joseph only nodded, although he knew the cause. Baiting the hated Jews would be a far greater attraction to the fickle tastes of the Alexandrians than the ordinary plea-sure of strolling along the causeway.

"Were you at the stadium yesterday?" the Greek con-tinued. "I hear Flamen tried to kill the Tribune Gaius Flaccus."

"Yes, I was there," Joseph admitted.

"That was one god who almost failed to be resurrected," the other observed with a grin. "A pity she did not suc-ceed."

"You approve her action?" Joseph asked, startled.

"A woman as beautiful as Flamen can do no harm. Any man should be willing to die in her embrace. They say she really didn't die, though. Some Jew worked a magic trick to save her when she appeared to be dead."

"I heard something of it." Joseph kept his voice non-committal.

"Where are you going?" the Greek asked. "I am for the barracks at the foot of Lochias Promontory."

"Anywhere on the quays will do."

"How about the Small Harbor beyond the Timonium?"

"That will be perfect." This was good fortune indeed, for the sheltered quays behind the half-moon-shaped is-land enclosing the Small Harbor were only a short distance from the Forum and the theater. With no farther to go than that, he should be able to reach the stage.

When the galley nosed in and touched the stone quay, Joseph leaped ashore and thanked his benefactor courte-ously. The quay here was also largely deserted, but from the nearby theater came a roar of many voices, and he soon came upon the outskirts of a huge crowd. People were pushing and shoving everywhere, shouting in every tongue, fighting with each other, laughing and snarling alternately, a truly savage spectacle. Joseph was quite unable to force his way any farther, and he realized that at any moment he might be recognized as a Jew. What would happen then, he was sure he knew, and the thought set a cold chill upon his heart. It was not too late to turn back to safety even now, caution advised. Philo and the others were almost certainly beyond help with a mob like this howling for their blood.

"What is happening?" he asked a tall man against whose body he was tightly wedged by the press of the crowd.

"Plotinus is baiting the Jews," the man said. "Blood will flow on the streets of Alexandria before this is over."

"Has he arrested them yet?"

"Arrested them!" The man snorted. "Why arrest bloodsuckers who take our money in usury? The crowd will take care of Philo and the others, you can stake your gold on that." He looked down, and suspicion gleamed suddenly in his eyes. "Why, you are a——" he began, but Joseph, filled with a surge of terror lest his identity be revealed here in the crowd, shoved the man fiercely so that he stumbled and would have fallen.

"A Jew! A Jew! Kill the Jew!" the man shouted, but Joseph lashed out at those around him and spun around. There was a flurry of excitement, and like a small whirlpool twisting in the midst of the current, he was pushed from hand to hand into another part of the crowd. The noise drowned out the man he had pushed, and he found himself, sweating and trembling, in another group of struggling people. He waited, paralyzed momentarily, for the cry of "Kill the Jew!" to be raised again, but to those around him he was only another person bent upon squeezing into the already overfilled theater.

With an effort of will, Joseph got control of himself. Looking back upon that moment of blind panic, he knew now that he could never have forgiven himself if he had yielded to it. And yet the memory of the savagery in the voices of the men around him as they had shouted for the blood of a Jew, himself or any other, left no doubt of his fate if he were set upon by the crowd. As Albina had warned, they would tear him to pieces more quickly than the lions tore helpless men and women apart in the games.

Faced with failure or death—and most likely both—Joseph did the only thing he knew to do, the only thing a devout Jew could do under the circumstances. He prayed silently to the Most High for direction. And standing there in the midst of a snarling, cursing crowd bent upon destroying any member of a hated race, the young physician suddenly felt as if he were alone, with all danger and all threats removed. It seemed then as if he heard a voice

189

speaking within him where no one else could hear, the voice of the prophet Isaiah, whose teachings he had learned as a child, saying:

"Fear thou not; for I am with thee:
Be not dismayed, for I am thy God:
I will strengthen thee, yea I will help thee;
Yea, I will uphold thee with the right hand of my
    righteousness."

Joseph felt a new strength and calmness flooding his soul now. The dangers still existed, but he feared them no more. And now that he was able to think clearly without fear, he saw how he could get into the theater.

"Take me to Plotinus!" he shouted. "I have news of Flamen."

The crowd took up the cry at once. Joseph was seized and passed from hand to hand until finally he was thrust before the guards at the gate leading into the theater. These lowered their swords to bar any passage, but when Joseph reiterated his desire to be taken to Plotinus with news of Flamen, they guided him along one of the *vomitoria* to a passage leading to the orchestra, from which Plotinus was haranguing the crowd in a stream of bitter invective against the Jews. Since the *gymnasiarch* was in the midst of the oration, the guards did not interrupt, but shoved Joseph up on the platform near where Philo and a dozen or more of the Jewish leaders stood under guard.

Looking around him, Joseph saw that Gaius Flaccus sat just behind the edge of the orchestra. The curtain had been raised, completely hiding the great stage and the machinery of the *skene* and *eccyclema* from the howling mob that filled every seat in the theater and spilled over into the aisles and the open space where the musicians ordinarily sat. Philo and the others had not been seriously hurt as yet, although several had bruised faces and torn clothing. The jurist faced his captors calmly, as did several of the older Jews, but some of the others were weeping, obviously overcome with terror.

On and on the tirade continued, accusing the Jews of all manner of fanciful crimes, the old shibboleths and stalking horses which were always exhumed when unscrupulous exhorters sought to inflame a mob for their own purposes. Plotinus, a skilled orator, was playing upon the fickle emotions of the crowd as a skilled musician plays upon the strings or pipes. With each new lie, each new accusation, they roared in an answering burst of fury, and when finally he chose to bring his flood of invective to a close, the howling continued for long minutes. Finally he turned and singled out the venerable doctor of the law from the other prisoners upon the platform. "Philo!" he shouted. "Confess your sins now to your peers if you are not afraid to move."

Contempt was written in every deliberate movement as the old lawyer shook off the hands of the Roman soldiers who started to jerk him forward and stepped out to face his tormentor. "Is there none of the vaunted Roman justice in Alexandria, Plotinus," he demanded sharply, "that you dare inflame a rabble against honest people? The Emperor is a just man; he will have your head for this."

The *gymnasiarch* struck the old Jew across the mouth with his hand, and a sudden hush fell over the crowd, for the name of Philo had always been a respected one in Alexandria. "We know the suicide of the Jewess called Flamen was a magic trick to escape a just punishment of death," Plotinus snarled. "Where have you cursed Jews hidden her?"

"I know nothing of the woman," Philo said quietly. "Nor do my people have anything to do with magic."

"You lie!" Plotinus screamed. "You Jews have hidden a murderess away, mocking the Roman justice you prate of so much."

"Who is dead by her hand?" Philo demanded contemptuously. "This man?" He leveled a finger at Gaius Flaccus. "He looks alive to me." The crowd roared with laughter at this shrewd sally. "Tell the people the truth," Philo went on scathingly. "That you borrowed money from lawful moneylenders to spend on women and wine, and now you cannot pay, so you seek to kill those you owe and escape paying just debts."

Plotinus raised his fist to strike the defenseless old man again, but before it could descend Joseph stepped forward. "Strike me, Roman," he said loudly enough for the crowd to hear. "I alone am responsible for the escape of Mary of Magdala, whom you call Flamen."

The *gymnasiarch* froze where he stood, and his fist dropped to his side. A sudden hush fell over the crowd at this dramatic change of events. "The woman is safe where you can never find her," Joseph continued. "Neither Philo nor the others here know where she is."

"But you know?" Plotinus found his voice at last.

"I know," Joseph said quietly. 'But you will never learn it from me, not even by torture."

Something in the quietness with which he spoke told the angry Roman that Joseph spoke the truth. And the knowledge that he could not learn the whereabouts of the woman he hated so bitterly for using him as a tool only infuriated Plotinus all the more. "Jewish dog!" he snarled. "Give me a reason why I should not thrust you through here and now."

Joseph turned to face Gaius Flaccus, and the crowd, sensing some new drama, grew quiet again. "Ask the Tribune Gaius Flaccus why the woman you call Flamen tried to kill him. He knows his life is forfeit to her."

Fear showed in Gaius Flaccus' eyes, for he well knew how easily the fury of the crowd—people from districts which had rebelled more than once against the Empire—could be turned against Romans. Nationalistic hatreds were easily fanned into flame, just as Plotinus was now using the traditional hatred of many people for the Jews, whose success as merchants and moneylenders throughout the Empire brought resentment from the people with whom they traded.

"It's a lie!" Gaius Flaccus shouted. "I owe the woman nothing."

Before Plotinus could intervene, Joseph said loudly to the crowd, "Flamen is both Jew and Greek." Between them the Jews and Greeks made up by far the largest population group of cosmopolitan Alexandria, and if he could drive a wedge between the Romans and the Greeks, a considerable portion of the crowd might swing to his side. "The *gymnasiarch* Plotinus hates her because he could not buy her favors with money he borrowed from Jews," he went on. "As a girl she was ravished by the Tribune Gaius Flaccus. And by Jewish law his life is forfeit to her and to her family, so she was within the law when she sought to kill him. The Romans talk much of justice when it suits them. Will you Greeks let a Roman murder just men to escape paying his debts?"

The crowd began to shout approval, but before Joseph could speak again Plotinus shoved him aside roughly and shouted, "Who rules in Alexandria? Rome or the Jews? Have you no pride, citizens of Alexandria? Or will you bow to moneylenders and merchants?"

Someone shouted, "No!" and the crowd took up the cry. Then a prompter—no doubt placed in the crowd by Plotinus for this purpose—shouted, "Kill the Jews!" and the shouting and cursing began again.

"Kill the Jews! Crucify the merchants and the money-lenders!" The beasts were growling for blood once more.

With a sinking heart Joseph knew that he had lost. Obviously Plotinus had been working toward just this. Now he could turn the prisoners loose to the fury of the crowd and, by pretending that matters had gotten out of hand and he could control the people no longer, escape blame for what happened when Roman justice, in its cumbersome way, finally got around to investigating the affair. Such things had been done before by Romans in order to destroy Jews to whom they owed money; undoubtedly they would be done again.

Those at the front of the crowd were already climbing upon the orchestra to seize the prisoners, when a sudden hush fell over the crowd. Joseph knew by the look of surprise in the faces of the men who were almost within reach of him, and the way they scrambled back, that something unusual was happening, but he had no inkling of what it was until a loud groaning of metal upon metal sounded behind him. He turned then and saw to his amazement that the great curtain, moved by no visible agency, was descending into its grooved niche. The look of startled surprise on the faces of Plotinus and Gaius Flaccus told him that this, at least, was no part of their plan.

The crowd was hushed while the curtain completed its descent and disappeared into the long slot in the floor, revealing the stage itself. This was entirely bare of scenery, but at the back four torches burned in the racks where they were placed to illuminate the stage after nightfall. And since it was almost dark now, the dancing pattern of the flames and shadows upon the floor of the stage gave the whole vast cavern revealed by the descending curtain an oddly macabre appearance, as if the audience were suddenly granted a glimpse of hell itself, complete except for the momentarily expected appearance of the demons who populated it.

Suddenly the crashing chords of a great cithara, an instrument whose notes Joseph would have recognized anywhere in the world, filled the great theater. And as the echoes died away a woman appeared at the very topmost level of the stage, silhouetted in the light of the torches flaming there. For an instant it seemed as if she had been born from the flames themselves, for through the diaphanous bombyx in which her body was wrapped, her flesh glowed as if it, too, were afire. And with her red hair unloosed to fall about her shoulders, the illusion of a living torch was so great that the crowd shouted in a mighty spontaneous roar, "Flamen! Aphrodite! Flamen! Aphrodite!"

For a long moment, while the waves of sound echoed and reechoed through the great theater, Mary stood poised there. Then her body began to sing a poem of love as only the Flamen of Alexandria, in all the world, could do. A deep, throbbing silence fell over the crowd; there was no sound save the crashing tones of the great cithara and the audible sigh of breathing from the audience.

Joseph had never seen this dance. In truth, no one had ever watched Mary dance it before, for this was its premier performance. She herself had witnessed it only once, when the slave girl Thetis had danced before Pontius Pilate and his guests, and she had watched from the dressing room beside the triclinium in Pilate's palace at Tiberias. But she knew how it would seize hold of the emotions of the men who watched it, until they forgot everything man seeks, but rarely finds, in the embrace of his beloved.

The performance of the slave girl Thetis had been an invitation to debauchery, a lewd thing of suggestive poses and writhing torso. But Mary was an artist first of all, and this was her greatest, perhaps her last, performance, as beautiful and as tender as any of the love poems she often sang on the stage. In the excitement of watching her, even the soldiers guarding the prisoners moved closer, forgetting their duties, until there was nothing between the doomed men and freedom but the door at the end of the orchestra and the open passage beyond leading down beneath the wings of the theater to freedom.

Joseph had looked away at the beginning of the dance when he realized that Mary was clothed only in the diaphanous swath of transparent bombyx. He knew what she was doing and why she was doing it, but he could not bear to watch her. Now, noticing that the soldiers had left the prisoners unguarded, he moved to the nearest one and said quietly, "Move out through the door there while the guards are not looking. Rouse the Jews everywhere and arm yourselves, then barricade the stoutest buildings."

With the large Jewish population of Alexandria, Joseph knew there would not be enough troops in the city to take them, once they were armed and behind barricades. Stirring up a crowd to kill during a riot was one thing, but ordering soldiers against innocent people who had broken no laws was quite another. The governor of Alexandria, even if he usually did the bidding of Plotinus, was not likely to go that far. Nor would Gaius Flaccus take such a chance either, when it meant probably incurring the displeasure of the Emperor Tiberius, who prided himself upon being a man of peace.

As the whispered order passed along the line of prisoners they began to file off the orchestra. It was quite dark now, and only the small portion of the stage where Mary danced was lit by the torches. But if it had been full daylight, the crowd would hardly have noticed the departing Jews, for every eye was held by the lovely figure there on the stage.

Now she was spinning like the torch for which she was named, her hair a cloud of fire about the gleaming column of her body. She had calculated shrewdly just how to hold the attention of the crowd, for, unlike the other dancers of the Alexandrian Theater, Flamen had never danced unclothed. Now, as the diaphanous draperies wrapped about her spun away one by one, floating like clouds in the half-darkness of the stage, her gloriously lovely body was gradually being revealed.

A deep sigh came from the audience when almost the last strip of bombyx wound around her body spun away. Now her flesh gleamed through the tissue-like fabric. And when she paused in the dance, still clothed in that wisp of cloth, a mighty roar came from the audience. "Flamen! Aphrodite! Flamen! Aphrodite!" they roared again and again, acclaiming her as the living counterpart of the goddess of love and beauty, whose worship was now largely confined to Alexandria.

A hand touched Joseph's arm, and he looked around to see only Philo standing where a file of prisoners had been a few moments before. The Jewish leader beckoned him to follow, but Joseph shook his head. Even with the crowd spellbound by the dance, Plotinus might still be able to turn their anger upon Mary. And since she had risked her life to come there, placing herself in the hands of the angry *gymnasiarch* and Gaius Flaccus, Joseph knew he could do no less than stay with her.

Quickly now the dance progressed to its climax, and as the last drapery spun away from her body, Mary poised, Aphrodite indeed come to life, her gloriously lovely body clothed only in the golden girdle that dancers wore about their loins. Then as the applause rocked the theater once more, she sank to the floor with her arms extended, and the flame of her hair enveloped her like a protecting cloak. From the wings where she had been waiting unobserved, Albina ran out with a long white cloak and wrapped it about Mary's body.

When she rose to her feet wrapped in the cloak, the applause was still roaring through the building, but Mary did not stay to acknowledge it. Instead she ran down across the stage to where Joseph stood alone, ignoring Plotinus and the others upon the platform, and threw herself into his arms. Clinging to him while she caught her breath, she told how she had awakened in the catacombs and learned that he had gone to the theater in the futile hope of saving Philo and the others from the wrath of Plotinus, and how she and Albina had arrived at the theater just as Joseph was thrust upon the stage by the guards. "It was the only way to save you and the others," she whispered, "even though I had to dance naked," and buried her face in his breast.

He kissed her, careless of who might see. With her slender, beautiful body wrapped in the white cloak and her hair tumbled about her shoulders, she was inexpressibly lovely. Too lovely to die, he thought, for that might well be the price they must both pay for saving Philo and the other Jews.

"Flamen! Flamen!" the crowd roared again and again. Nor would they quiet down until Mary went to the edge of the stage and bowed acknowledgment, throwing kisses to them with her fingers. Plotinus seemed stunned by this sudden change in events, but Gaius Flaccus was devouring her with his eyes.

When the applause finally began to die away, Plotinus turned savagely to where the captive Jews had stood on the platform. When he saw that they were gone, his mouth gaped with surprise. "Where are they?" he shouted to the guards, and as they, too, looked stupidly for the men who were no longer there, the crowd started laughing again. "You!" he wheeled upon Joseph. "Where have they gone?"

"To their homes to rouse all the Jews in Alexandria," Joseph said. "And Philo is demanding protection from the governor now in the name of the Emperor. You forget that many Jews in Alexandria are Roman citizens."

If anything, the sallow countenance of the *gymnasiarch*

became paler at this threat. "Then you two will die," he snarled. "And by my own hand." Suddenly he jerked a sword from the belt of the nearest soldier and lunged at Mary and Joseph with the blade upraised to cut them down. Defenseless and unarmed, they had no chance, of course, but Joseph did manage to throw his body across Mary's so that the knife would strike him first.

Help came fortuitously from another source. A strong hand gripped Plotinus' wrist before the sword could strike through their unprotected bodies. "Fool!" Gaius Flaccus snapped, holding the *gymnasiarch's* wrist. "The people will tear us to pieces if you attack her now."

A great roar of anger had come from the crowd at the first threat toward Mary, and even as the blow was stayed, men were starting to climb upon the stage, ready to attack Plotinus with their bare hands. "Kill the leech here, if you must have blood," Gaius Flaccus urged in a low voice. "The people will not care about him."

Slowly the crazed look went out of the Roman's eyes. "Were you responsible for the trick that made her seem dead?" he demanded of Joseph.

"I was," Joseph admitted. There was no use in involving Bana Jivaka, and the scheme had really been his. "She was under my spell when she tried to kill Gaius Flaccus," he added, hoping through the lie to turn their anger from Mary.

"That is not true," Mary protested. "The fault is mine. I wanted revenge for something he did to me."

Plotinus turned to Gaius Flaccus. "Is what this man said yesterday true?" he demanded. "Did you ravish her once?"

"It was a long time ago," the Tribune said lamely. "I— I had forgotten it."

"I take no other man's leavings," the *gymnasiarch* said contemptuously. "The woman is yours to do with as you wish."

"What will you do with Joseph?" Mary asked quickly.

"He must die," Plotinus said flatly, "for helping the Jews to get away."

"But it was I who gave them time to escape," Mary protested. "The fault is mine."

"Kneel, leech!" Plotinus ordered. "Your head will roll here and now, by my own hand!"

When Joseph stood proudly, refusing to kneel, Plotinus snapped an order, and two of the soldiers seized him roughly and forced him to his knees. Realizing that she could not influence Plotinus, Mary turned in desperation to Gaius Flaccus. "Save Joseph's life and I will be your slave," she pleaded. "If he dies, I will kill myself."

Gaius Flaccus hesitated. His rank was not so great as that of Plotinus, but he knew Mary well enough to be sure that she would carry out her threat. Seeing his hesitation, Mary added, "I am rich. You and Plotinus can divide my wealth if Joseph is spared."

Plotinus had been listening. It was no secret in Alexandria that he was always in debt. At the mention of Mary's wealth his eyes began to gleam, and he lowered the sword slowly to his side. "How much are you worth?" he demanded.

"A hundred Attic talents of silver. Perhaps more."

Plotinus swore under his breath, and the light of greed in his eyes glowed brighter. A hundred Attic talents was more than most rich men saw in a lifetime.

"Don't do it, Mary," Joseph begged. "I would rather let them take my life than for you to be a slave to Gaius Flaccus.'"

"The guilt for all this is mine alone," she said in a low voice. "You must not suffer for me, Joseph. What do you say?" she demanded, turning to Plotinus.

Plotinus handed the sword he was holding to the soldier from whose scabbard he had taken it. "It is agreed then," he said, obviously anxious to gain control of the money. "Flamen will be your slave, Gaius Flaccus, for so long as you shall live. And her possessions will be divided between us. Lift him up," he told the soldiers who were holding Joseph. "Take him to the waterfront and put him on the next ship bound for Judea. And tell the captain that I will hold him personally responsible if the leech is not guarded until the ship leaves the harbor."

"Come along, Jew," the soldier ordered, jerking Joseph to his feet. He had no choice but to obey and no opportunity to speak to Mary again. His last memory of his beloved was as she stood between the two Romans with tears streaming down her face, her arms outstretched to him in farewell. She had sold herself into slavery as a price for his life.

Book Three

EMMAUS

1

FALL had come again to Jerusalem. Upon the craggy hills, gray and bare in the chill breeze from the northeast, trees clung precariously to the thin soil, their limbs bare of foliage. Dawn was breaking, and the great white city slowly emerged from the shadows of the night. On the hilltops, the rising sun had already begun to gild the dome of the temple. And across the narrow Vale of Kedron the fortress of Antonia, grim reminder that Rome ruled even here in the Holy City of the Jews, towered like a threat above the sleeping city. On just such a morning as this several years before, the populace had awakened to find that Pontius Pilate, Procurator of Judea, had carried out this threat to display the eagles of Rome in Jerusalem, bringing them in under armed guard during the night and placing them upon the fortress.

Pilate had been clever enough not to come to Jerusalem himself then. And since only he could order the standards taken down, a great crowd had been forced to march over the mountains and through the narrow valleys, making the two-day journey to Caesarea by foot, to plead with him. For four days the Jews had waited patiently in the square at Caesarea before the palace of the Procurator, bemoaning this degradation put upon them in the name of Rome, since it was against the ancient laws handed down to Moses for "any graven image" to be raised in Jerusalem. Perhaps Pilate, in one of the black angry moods that assailed him at times, had expected the Jews to resist. Then he could have ordered the soldiers to cut the people down, as he had done on more than one occasion. But the resistance this time was only passive. Finally, unable to deal with people who only stood and mourned to their God for the affront that had been done to Him, Pilate had ordered the standards lowered.

Now, as the sun crept past the corners of the great fortress and into the courtyard, the eagles of Rome no longer flaunted themselves before the people, reminding them of their conquered state. But the ceremonial vestments of the high priest and his assistants were still kept locked in chests in the fortress of Antonia. And before every religious holiday the priests were obliged to march to the Roman headquarters and beg the authorities for permission to use them.

The Mount of Zion was first to emerge into full sunlight, for it rose above the other five hills upon which the city was built, its slopes studded with palaces and villas of the rich. The low ground to the northward, where the shacks and hovels of the poor clustered, was still dark, but people were stirring there, for a man needed all of the daylight hours to earn enough bread for his family, if he were lucky enough to have work, or to beg for it in the streets if he were not.

From the temple came the clash of steel upon steel, the tread of marching feet, and the sound of a sharp-voiced command as the Roman guard made the last tour of inspection for the night before marching across to the Antonia, where they were garrisoned. By night and by day the swords of the conquerors were drawn before the gates of the shrine of the Jews, lest they forget for a moment that, although their God ruled above the outer terraces, it was Rome who held the power of life and death outside the nineteen steps leading to the upper levels.

Slowly, as the sunlight penetrated narrow streets, the city came awake. Yawning and stretching men went to raise shutters and fold away screens which had hidden the open doorways of the shops during the night. Women appeared in the smaller courtyards where open pipes dispensed to all the water brought from distant springs through the aqueduct built by Pontius Pilate and paid for by the "temple tribute," another act of wanton ruthlessness for which the Jews would always hate the Roman Procurator. Filling their jars, they hurried homeward before the men could start to wash and find that their wives had been so improvident as not to bring water the previous night for the morning ablutions which no devout Jew dared omit.

A street vendor, followed by his mule, walked through the narrow streets, stumbling a little now and then, for the cobblestones were wet with dew of the night. He cried his olive oil, bread, and packages of figs and dates, so that no one who had failed to lay up a supply of food the day before need go without a crust of bread dipped in oil, a few figs or dates, or a cup of goat's milk from the bulbous skin attached to the mule's back.

In the shops the artisans were already setting out the tools of their respective trades and the materials upon which they worked during the day, hammers and punches, small anvils, awls for punching leather, waxed thread and sharp needles of Damascus steel for sewing, looms for weaving, and pots of rich dye. The scribes arranged on their tables wax tablets and papyrus scrolls for preparing letters and legal documents, small cups of ink, and metal styli for writing on wax. Everywhere the bustle of activity characterizing the day was beginning, and anyone listening from the mountaintop of Zion could have heard the voice of the city rising to him, muted still by the dregs of sleep, but steadily gaining in volume and pitch with the passing minutes as shown by the water clocks.

As soon as they awakened the Jews of Jerusalem began moving toward the temple, which was the center of the city's life, the very heartbeat of its existence. On the lower of the three terraces, the outer Court of the Heathen with its signs in many languages warning unbelievers not to climb the forbidden steps to the next level, a tinkling of coins filled the air as the money-changers began to set up their tables. There any pilgrims might exchange Roman gold, forbidden for use in the sacrifice because it carried the graven image of the Emperor, for an acceptable Jewish mintage, the "temple shekel." That he usually got sharply cheated in the bargain was casually accepted by all, for was it not true that part of the profits found their way into the temple coffers and thus also became an offering to Jehovah?

Built in a square five hundred ells to the side, the great temple would shortly be thronged by people of every nation, most of them Jews making the pilgrimage to the shrine in Jerusalem that every devout worshipper of Jehovah tried to make as often as he could. Not a few of the visitors were tourists, however, for Jerusalem was well placed on the caravan routes to Egypt and also on the great Central Highway traversing the highlands of Judea on its way northward.

Above the second level of the temple, restricted to

Jews alone, was the third and uppermost height, where only the priests might go. And there, sequestered from the sight of all but the most devout, was the Holy of Holies, where reposed the Ark of the Covenant. By the time the sun began to warm the priestly terrace the ones selected to officiate had completed the ritual washings and put on the spotless white robes of their office. The first sacrifice lay upon the altar, and the torch for kindling the burnt offering flamed in its socket. A prophet in Israel had once spoken against this rigid ceremony, often so detailed that its purpose was forgotten. His name was Micah and he had cried:

> "Wherewith shall I come before Jehovah, and bow myself before the high God? Shall I come before Him with burnt offerings, with calves of a year old? Will Jehovah be pleased with thousands of rams, with ten thousands of rivers of oil? Shall I give my first-born for my transgression, the fruit of my body for the sin of my soul? He hath showed thee, O man, what is good; and what doth Jehovah require of thee, but to do justly, to love kindness, and to walk humbly with thy God."

But the power of the Pharisees who put great store on form in the worship of the Most High was great in Jerusalem. And the Sadducees of the priestly class recognized the love of the people for form and ritual, so the solemn trappery of the temple went on every day.

Now the trumpets sounded a blast loud and clear from the upper level, the notes floating out over the city in the chill morning air. The great gates were opened just as the ritual knife in the hand of a priest descended unerringly to slash the throat of the sacrificial lamb. Blood gushed forth, and a sigh went up from the onlookers gathered to witness this beginning of the day's worship.

The music of harps and zithers and the clear high notes of trumpets poured down upon the awakening city from the eminence of the temple. Devout Jews bowed their heads, while those watching from the lower level prostrated themselves. The torch set the burnt offering aflame, and the smoke of incense rose skyward in the still morning air, while the Levites clashed their metal disks and a chorus chanted a poem of adoration to the Most High.

A new day had begun in Jerusalem, the Holy City of the Jews.

2

THE rays of the rising sun crept gently through Joseph's garden in Jerusalem. Fall had come, but the garden was still beautiful, for the oranges and lemons did not shed their leaves, nor did the olive trees, and much fruit still hung upon the branches. Bees hummed through the leaves, and the fragrance of spice wood filled the air. Although he was rich by the standards of the city and the time, Joseph did not live on the Mount of Zion in the Upper City, where the palaces of the very rich dotted the hillside. When he first came to Jerusalem he had purchased a plot of ground on the sun-warmed slope of the western hill of the Upper City from his uncle and namesake, Joseph of Arimathea. The old merchant was in poor health and had even gone so far as to have his tomb hollowed out of a massive granite outcropping at the corner of his garden. Joseph knew that he owed much of his success as a physician to the fact that his uncle had recommended him to Pontius Pilate and had also helped obtain for him the position of *medicus viscerus* in the temple. And so he had been happy when Joseph of Arimathea had offered to sell him a portion of his own estate in Jerusalem, so the young physician would always be conveniently close when the merchant suffered one of the attacks of pain and difficult breathing which sometimes threatened his life.

This morning Joseph was in the garden early, walking along the dew-wet paths between the trees and the grape arbors, talking to the old man who was his gardener. Since the death of his mother a few years before, he lived alone, and he loved especially these few moments in the morning, enjoying the trees and flowers and the waking songs of the birds that flocked here because they were fed daily. Another reason why he loved the garden was because it reminded him of another overlooking the Sea of Galilee from Magdala. One thing remained to make the scene complete, however—the voice of a girl lifted in song, a girl whose hair was as red as the pomegranates that grew here in their season.

It seemed longer than six and a half months, Joseph thought now, since he had been torn from Mary's arms on the great stage of the theater in Alexandria and hurried away to the harbor under guard. But the memory of her standing there, her lovely body wrapped in a white robe and her hair lying on her shoulders like a coppery cloud, would always be with him. Actually, she was much nearer to him now, for Gaius Flaccus had been sent to Sepphoris, the capital of Herod Antipas in Galilee, as commander of all Roman troops in the area, just as he had predicted. Sepphoris lay hardly three days' journey away by mule, and two by fast camel, but Joseph had not tried to see her, knowing that to do so would only open old wounds and create new unhappiness.

There was much going back and forth between the court of Herod and Jerusalem, however, so it was inevitable that he should hear of Mary from time to time. She was living, he had heard, as a mistress or common-law wife to Gaius Flaccus, a position hardly better than the slavery for which she had offered herself in return for Joseph's life and the lives of the Jews of Alexandria. The Galileans, he had been told, called her a concubine and accused her of adultery, since she was neither married to the man with whom she lived nor actually a slave.

From the reports Joseph received, Gaius Flaccus treated Mary badly, showing her off to his visitors not as a wife, but as a mistress, and never failing to remind her of her actual status in his household. Knowing Mary's proud spirit, Joseph sometimes wondered how long she could stand such treatment. At times, when his yearning for her seemed beyond bearing, he thought of going to Sepphoris and stealing her away from the palace of Gaius Flaccus. But such a gesture would have been foolhardy, for the power of Rome reached into the life of every person in this conquered country, and his rash act could easily result in death for both of them.

As Joseph was finishing his instructions to the gardener, the freedman Rufus who looked after his household came out into the garden. "The noble Nicodemus sent word that he would breakfast with you, sir," he said. "I have ordered two places set at the table on the terrace."

Nicodemus was already coming through the gate leading to the next estate, and Joseph hurried to embrace him. Older than Joseph by ten years, he was a brilliant student of the law and a member of the Sanhedrin, the ruling council of the Jews. His work with the law took Nicodemus to all parts of Judea, Galilee, Perea, and even as far as Antioch, the capital of the entire province, for he was respected by Jew and Roman alike. He was tall and commanding in appearance, his hair graying at the temples. Like Joseph, Nicodemus might have seemed overly reserved until he smiled, but then the warmth of his eyes showed the depth of his character and his understanding.

"Shalom, friend of friends," the lawyer said, looking at Joseph keenly. "You seem fatigued; perhaps you should take a journey too."

"I have no time to be running hither and yon as you do," Joseph told him, smiling. "It is enough that I have to visit Caesarea every month or so to look after the Lady Procula."

"She and Pontius Pilate are in Tiberias now. I hear they will stay for the winter."

Joseph's heart quickened at this good news. With Claudia Procula and Pilate in Tiberias, he might have a legitimate reason to visit Galilee again. And perhaps he would see Mary, if only from a distance. "What is the news from Galilee?" he asked. "Does Herod Antipas still plot to free Judea from the procurators?"

"Endlessly. But the more I see of that misbegotten spawn of Herod the Great, the more I respect the Romans."

"Even Pontius Pilate?"

Nicodemus shrugged. "There is no such thing as a good Roman, I suppose. They told me in Sepphoris that Pilate grows more moody and temperamental every day. And that nephew of his, Gaius Flaccus, is the most hated man in all of Galilee."

Joseph looked away, lest he reveal the turbulent feelings aroused by the mention of Sepphoris and Gaius Flaccus.

"I went to a dinner at Herod's palace," Nicodemus continued. "Gaius Flaccus attended and brought with him the most beautiful red-haired woman I ever saw. Some claimed she was a slave, but she was obviously a lady, and others called her his mistress."

"Is she known thus in Sepphoris?" Joseph somehow managed to keep his voice calm.

"And throughout Galilee," Nicodemus agreed. "Hating Gaius Flaccus as they do, the people of Galilee would hardly be expected to love a Jewess who lives with him, even if she were married to him."

"But she gave herself to Gaius Flaccus to save the life of someone she loved," Joseph cried indignantly.

"So?" Nicodemus' eyes brightened with interest. "How did you know all this?"

Joseph had no alternative then but to tell the whole story. "It is strange," Nicodemus said, "but I would have sworn Mary of Magdala no longer hates Gaius Flaccus, although she would still have every reason to do so, from the way he treats her."

Could Mary possibly have come to love a man she had hated bitterly enough to try to take his life? Joseph wondered. The very thought was disloyal to her, and yet his experience as a physician had taught him that the heart of a woman is something a man can never hope to understand. He remembered now what Demetrius had said long ago, that a woman never quite overcame the emotional shock of being possessed by a man, and that something deep within her, some savage instinct beyond reason, might draw her to him again.

"I wouldn't say she loves him as a woman does her husband, though," Nicodemus added. "In fact, her manner toward Gaius Flaccus was more like the way people behave who have come under the spell of Jesus of Nazareth."

"Did you see him?" Joseph asked in surprise. He would not have expected a doctor of the law from Jerusalem, such as Nicodemus, to pay any attention to the sort of Galilean rabble-rouser that was always causing trouble in that turbulent region. But Jerusalem had begun to buzz lately with talk of the Nazarene's doings, so Joseph was interested, if only from curiosity.

"Yes, I saw him," Nicodemus said slowly, his voice suddenly far away. "I saw him in Capernaum. And I was almost persuaded to follow him."

"Do you realize what you are saying?" Joseph demanded incredulously. It was one thing for the Galileans to make much over the man called Jesus. Everybody knew their emotions were fickle and had followed false leaders before, to their sorrow. But Nicodemus was an aristocrat of Jerusalem, a Pharisee of the Pharisees, and a member of the Sanhedrin itself. For him to accept the teacher of Nazareth, whose doings were attracting more and more attention in the Holy City, was almost like an endorsement from the high priest Caiaphas himself.

"It startles me too, when I think how close I came to giving up everything and becoming a part of the Galilean rabble that follows Jesus," Nicodemus admitted.

"This man must be a spellbinder indeed, to have you so bemused."

Nicodemus shook his head. "He is no zealot, like so many in Galilee. In fact, Jesus may really be what many of his followers believe him to be, the Messiah."

"Tell me what happened," Joseph suggested, for it was obvious that Nicodemus was not thinking clearly.

"I went to Capernaum to settle a legal matter for a man named Zebedee who runs the largest fishing establishment on the lake," Nicodemus explained. "Zebedee's sons and a man named Simon who was chief of the fishermen have all become followers of Jesus, so the old man was forced to sell his business."

"I once treated Simon for an arm broken in a fight over the Messiah. He has espoused radical causes before, and so have the sons of Zebedee."

"It was no zealot's plea that made Simon and the others follow Jesus," Nicodemus insisted. "The teacher came walking along the shore one day when Simon and Andrew, his brother, were casting their nets. All he said was, 'Follow me and I will make you fishers of men.' But it was enough to make them drop their nets and become disciples. The same thing happened with the sons of Zebedee, John and James."

"How does he cast this spell over people?" Joseph wondered.

"You must see and hear him to understand," Nicodemus explained. "What I was told by Zebedee aroused my curiosity, so I joined a crowd listening to Jesus. I tell you, Joseph, there were people among them not only from Galilee, but from the cities of the Decapolis, from Jerusalem and Judea, and even the country beyond the Jordan. The teacher had to go up on the side of the mountain so they could all hear him."

"Do you remember what he taught?"

"That is another strange thing. What he said is engraved in my mind as firmly as the texts I learned when Bar Mitzvah. They were simple things, like this:

"*Blessed are the poor in spirit for theirs is the kingdom of heaven.*

"*Blessed are they who mourn, for they shall be comforted.*

"*Blessed are the meek for they shall inherit the earth.*

"*Blessed are those who hunger and thirst for righteousness, for they shall be satisfied.*

"*Blessed are the merciful, for they shall obtain mercy.*

"*Blessed are the pure in heart for they shall see God.*

"*Blessed are the peacemakers, for they shall be called sons of God.*

"*Blessed are you when men revile you and persecute you and utter all kinds of evil against you falsely on my account. Rejoice and be glad, for your reward is great in heaven.*"

"It is a fine set of principles," Joseph admitted. "But they are not new. The Greek philosophers said much the same thing, and so did a writer of our own race in the Testament of God. I was reading it only last night." He went into the house and came out with a scroll. "Listen to this:

"*Hatred, therefore, is evil, for it constantly mateth with lying, speaking against the truth; and it maketh small things to be great, and causeth the light to be darkness, and calleth the sweet bitter, and teacheth slander, and kindleth wrath, and stirreth up war, and violence and all covetousness; It filleth the heart with evils and devilish poisons.*

"*Righteousness casteth out hatred, humility destroyeth envy. For he that is just and humble is ashamed to do what is unjust, being reproved not of another, but of his own heart, because the Lord looketh upon his inclination.*"

"Their doctrines are similar," Nicodemus admitted. "I thought of the Testament of God and the teachings of Esdras while I was listening to him."

"Here is something else," Joseph continued:

> *"And now, my children, I exhort you, love ye each one his brother, and put away hatred from your hearts, love one another in deed, and in word, and in the inclination of the soul.*
>
> *"If a man prospereth more than you, do not be vexed, but pray also for him, that he may have perfect prosperity. For so it is expedient for you. And if he be further exalted, be not envious of him, remembering that all flesh shall die; and offer praise to God, Who giveth all things good and profitable to all men."*

As Joseph rolled up the scroll Nicodemus rubbed his chin thoughtfully. "I recognize the teachings of Jesus are not new," he admitted. "But something about the man himself, something you can't put into words, makes you want to follow him."

"What is he like?"

"He is tall and well proportioned. And his face is full of kindness. He wears his hair long and has a beard like all the Nazarites."

"You could be describing almost any Jew with a pleasing countenance," Joseph pointed out smilingly.

"Actually, I thought of you when I first saw him," Nicodemus said. "You have the same kindness in your face. But Jesus' eyes are very striking too. They are blue and very brilliant, as if they could see into your very soul. And his hands are a healer's hands, Joseph, very much like your own."

"Did you see him perform any feats of healing?" the young physician asked eagerly. "If he is the Messiah, as some claim, he should be able even to raise the dead."

"As far as I could tell, Jesus claims only to teach the words of the Most High and the coming of the kingdom of God into the hearts and souls of men through repentance and right living. But it is whispered that when he gives the word, thousands of Galileans who believe he is the Messiah will rise against Rome, believing that the Most High will deliver His enemies into their hands."

"Those are dangerous teachings. Shouldn't you report them to the Sanhedrin?"

Nicodemus shook his head. "These are the things people say, Joseph, but Jesus teaches nothing of the kind. And I am sure he has given no encouragement to those who claim he is the Messiah."

"He lives in the territory of Herod Antipas," Joseph pointed out. "It would seem that Herod would be disturbed about this."

"He probably is," Nicodemus admitted. "Caiaphas asked me to investigate Jesus on this trip. I think he suspects Herod of planning to use the teacher to stir up the people and perhaps start a rebellion. By stopping it there, Herod might convince Tiberius that he should rule all the Jews."

"What are you going to tell the high priest?"

"Only what I am sure is true," Nicodemus said. "That Jesus is only a great teacher, or perhaps even another prophet, unless . . ." He stopped, then went on again, "Unless he is really the Messiah and the Son of God."

3

ABOUT a week after his conversation with Nicodemus, Joseph came home one evening to find a dusty, sweat-stained mule standing before his house. In the atrium a tall man in dust-streaked white robes was arguing with Rufus, the freedman.

"Hadja! My old friend!" Joseph embraced the Nabatean musician. "Where have you been?"

"I live in the house of Demetrius at Magdala so as to be near to the Living Flame."

"But everything she owned went to Gaius Flaccus and Plotinus."

"The house belonged to Demetrius. It was not listed among her possessions."

Joseph looked at Hadja's gaunt frame and the lines of hunger in his face. "Why did you not come to me for help?" he asked. "Do you think I would have let you want so long as I had a crust of bread and a roof over my head?"

Hadja smiled. "We men of the desert are tough. A little hunger will not hurt me. But the Living Flame needs you in Sepphoris, Joseph. She bade me tell you to hurry to her as quickly as you can."

"Is she ill?" Joseph asked, alarmed at once.

"She told me no more," Hadja said enigmatically. "But I know it is not for herself that she wants you."

Joseph wasted no time in questions. Mary had sent from Sepphoris to Jerusalem for him; that was enough. She would never have called for help unless there was a real need.

Travel by night was not advisable on the great caravan routes to the north, for the wild mountain country was frequented by bands of thieves and rebel Galileans. While Joseph and Hadja ate the evening meal Rufus was sent to purchase two swift camels. Dawn the following morning found them on the great Central Highway that traversed the mountain ranges of Samaria to the northward, past Beeroth, Shechem, and the city of Samaria itself to Engannim, where it joined the Way of the Sea from Joppa to the cities of the Galilean plain.

Late on the second day they came over the summit of a hill and saw the village of Nazareth lying near the top of a precipitous slope a few miles away in the hills of Galilee. Here they paused to let the hard-driven camels regain their wind.

Joseph was tired to the bone, for he was not accustomed to such rapid travel, but he could still enjoy the rugged beauty of this mountainous region between the lake and the sea. Westward, the heights of Mount Carmel showed the location of the seacoast less than fifty Roman miles away, and to the south lay the broad Plain of Esdraelon which they had just crossed. In the east towered Mount Tabor, and far to the north, shining in the afternoon sunlight, was the snow-capped crest of Mount Hermon. The peaceful and yet majestic scene brought to his mind the words of the Psalmist:

The North and the South, thou hast created them:
Tabor and Hermon rejoice in Thy name.

"There lies Sepphoris to the north." Hadja's voice brought Joseph back to the present. "You can see the theater easily from here."

Some five miles away a great city stood among the hills. The largest center of Galilee at one time, Sepphoris had been a center of government in the district for centuries. Judas the Gaulonite had captured it during his ill-fated aspiration to messiahship and the resulting revolution. On the hilly slope outside the city two thousand Jews had been nailed to crosses by the Romans in retaliation for the abortive uprising. Sepphoris had also been burned to the ground and its inhabitants sold into slavery, a solemn warning to the Galileans that Rome ruled here and would brook no disloyalty.

Herod Antipas had rebuilt Sepphoris in recent years, however, making it for a while the brightest gem among the cities of the fertile province. Then his desires, ever fickle, had turned to the newer city of Tiberias on the lake shore. Now the palace at Sepphoris was occupied for only a part of the year, but the city was still the headquarters of a large Roman garrison kept always ready in uneasy Galilee.

Farmers who went out to till the fields during the day crowded the roads leading to Sepphoris in the late afternoon, driving before them mules heavy-laden with produce for the markets. The camels were slowed to a walk as Joseph and Hadja threaded the crowded streets past the magnificent group of palaces forming the center of Herod's government and the quarters of the Romans. Before a villa of white stone second only in magnificence to Herod's own residence, Hadja stopped the animals. "This is the palace of Gaius Flaccus," he said. "The Lady Claudia Procula should be here, and perhaps the Procurator himself. The Living Flame had sent for them before I left."

Carrying the *nartik* containing his medicines and instruments under his arm, Joseph was ushered past two soldiers guarding the gate and into the broad cool atrium forming the center of the house. Almost immediately Claudia Procula came across the room to him, her hands extended in welcome. "Mary and I have been praying that your journey would be swift, Joseph," she said. "We will all feel better now that you are here."

"I came as quickly as I could," he said, bowing courteously.

"Pontius and I were glad to know Mary had sent for you. We knew that if anyone could help Gaius Flaccus it would be you."

"Gaius Flaccus?"

"But you knew he was ill, didn't you?"

Joseph shook his head. "I knew only that Mary needed me."

"He is desperately ill," she said. "I know you have every reason to hate Gaius Flaccus, Joseph. But Mary has forgiven him for what he has done to her, and I know you will save his life if you can."

"She has forgiven him?" This seemed to be a day of surprises.

Procula nodded. "The teachings of Jesus do seem to change people entirely, even though heard secondhand."

"Is Mary a follower of the teacher of Nazareth?" he asked incredulously.

"Yes. And there are more in Galilee who follow him than you would believe possible. If only I had the courage to admit what in my heart I know is true, I would be among them."

"Perhaps we had better go to the sick man," Joseph said a little dazedly. "I have heard words from your lips that I find hard to understand. And yet I know that the Lady Claudia Procula speaks only that which is true."

"Thank you, Joseph," she said gratefully. "May God give me strength to speak it to others as I have to you."

4

THE accident which had felled Gaius Flaccus, according to the story Procula told Joseph, could have happened to anyone. His horse had fallen during a chase after a stag, but the wound on his leg had seemed minor. Then a few days later the skin around it turned red and the limb began to swell. Chills and fever followed quickly, and for the past several days he had been raging in a delirium.

Claudia Procula did not enter the sickroom with

Joseph, but he did not notice, for he saw only the woman kneeling in a corner of the room, her eyes closed, her lips moving in prayer. It was a picture he knew he would never forget, for this was a new Mary of Magdala, a little thinner than when he had seen her last, her skin somewhat paler, but the copper-tinted glory of her hair still undimmed, and her face even more beautiful in sorrow than he had ever remembered it before. For now there was a quality of peace and serenity in those well-remembered features, an impression of confidence in some power he could not see.

When Mary opened her eyes and saw Joseph, her face lit up and color flowed into her cheeks.

"Joseph!" she cried, and his heart leaped with what he heard in her voice. "I knew you would come." She took him by the arms and kissed him on the cheek, holding tightly to him and leaning against him for a moment, as if she needed the strength and assurance of his presence.

Seeing her again and remembering the light that had come into her eyes at the sight of him, Joseph knew that her love still burned as warmly as did his own. "It is good to see you again, Mary," he said quietly. "Were you praying for Gaius Flaccus when I came in?"

"Yes. Do you find it so hard to believe?"

"We learned as children the admonition of the Most High, '*Thou shalt love thy neighbor as thyself.*' But were I in your place," he admitted, "I don't think I could find it in my heart to pray for him."

She smiled. "Jesus says, '*Love your enemies, bless them that curse you, and pray for them which despitefully use you and persecute you*'."

The man on the couch gritted his teeth and cursed. Two slaves stood by, and now they leaped to hold him. But Joseph waved them back and put his hand on the sick man's forehead. As if consciousness of the soothing gesture had penetrated his fevered mind, Gaius Flaccus quieted a little. His skin was hot and dry beneath Joseph's fingers, the pulse at his wrist racing and full, as if trying to burst the very skin beneath which it beat. The stertorous rasp of his breathing filled the room, and as he babbled and cursed in the delirium, his fingers picked constantly at the bedclothes and at his body, as if searching for unseen vermin.

A passage from the writings of Hippocrates came into Joseph's mind:

> *When in acute fevers . . . the hands are moved*
> *before the face, hunting through empty space, as if*
> *gathering bits of straw, picking the nap from the*
> *coverlet, or tearing chaff from the wall—all such*
> *symptoms are bad and deadly.*

Joseph laid his ear against the hot skin of the sick man's chest. He listened in several places and finally heard in the lower left side the sign he had been seeking, a dry sound as of leather rubbing together that betrayed a deep-seated pleurisy. And when he examined the abdomen, the grave light in his eyes deepened, for at the slightest touch Gaius Flaccus flinched with pain, even through his delirium.

In the left groin, above the injured leg, a large angry swelling seemed almost ready to burst with its own tension. Below this the entire limb was fiery red in color and the tissues boardlike to the touch. The skin wound seemed innocent enough in itself when Joseph removed the bandages. It was only a shallow cut, but the edges were ragged and discolored, and a thin serous discharge poured from the wound, in itself a far graver sign than a heavy flow of suppuration would have been.

His examination finished, Joseph rebandaged the cut and washed his hands carefully, for he knew from experience that inflammations such as this were easily transferred from one person to another, entering a cut or an abrasion as rapidly as they had invaded the original wound. He had often wondered just why this could be but had not yet found the answer, although it was true that the physician Marcus Terentius Varro had written several hundred years before:

> *Perhaps in swampy places small animals live that*
> *cannot be discerned with the eye, and they enter*
> *the body through the mouth and nostrils and cause*
> *grave disorders.*

This might well explain how some diseases were contracted, he was prepared to admit. But here it seemed obvious that whatever was causing the trouble had entered the wound, for it was the center of an angry inflammatory process. Was it possible for the tiny animalcules spoken of by Varro to enter the body through breaks in the tissues? he wondered. If so, this was a strong argument for the strict cleanliness in handling wounds that Hippocrates had advocated and that Joseph himself had always practiced rigorously.

"It is hopeless," Mary said in a low voice. "I can see it in your face."

"The poison has invaded his entire body," Joseph admitted. "I could hear the rubbing of inflamed membranes inside his chest."

"Can you do nothing?"

"The pulse is pounding, indicating an acute plethora. I will bleed him and wrap the lower body in hot fomentations. Sometimes that helps to quiet the delirium."

While Mary sent slaves to bring sheets and hot water, Joseph opened his *nartik* and removed a slender steel *nail,* the blade used to puncture veins. Then he showed one of the slaves how to squeeze Gaius Flaccus' arm above the elbow, distending the already bulging vessels. Quickly he plunged the blade with one stroke through the skin and the wall of the vein, turning it to separate the edges of the tiny opening. A thin stream of blood, dark and unhealthy in color, poured into the small bowl held by a slave. He kept the wound open until a full goblet had been drawn off, then removed the *nail* and bandaged the arm snugly.

Next Joseph wrung out sheets dipped in hot water and wrapped the sick man's limbs and lower body in a cocoonlike sheath of damp warm cloth. When this was finished, he managed to coax Gaius Flaccus into drinking a mixture of wine and poppy leaves, and shortly afterward the Tribune quieted down and slept naturally for the first time in days.

Mary and Joseph ate the evening meal together in a small chamber outside the sickroom. Although she was technically a slave, he noted that the entire household treated her with deference, and she was obviously very much respected and liked. "You have changed since you left Alexandria, Joseph," she said when the meal was finished. "Are you happy in Jerusalem?"

"How could I be happy when you are a slave?" he asked.

"Would it help if I told you that I don't mind being a slave any more?"

"But you still belong to another man."

She put her hand on his. "My body may be owned by Gaius Flaccus," she said simply, "but you know that my

217

heart is yours. It has been since one afternoon in Tiberias so long ago."

He smiled. "When you reminded me that I was not a physician but only a leech? And that I owed everything to my uncle, Joseph of Arimathea, besides?"

"You were a good leech," she said warmly. "Just as you are a good physician and a good man. The people need men like you, Joseph. You must try to be happy with your work."

"Just being here and seeing you has made me happy for a little while at least," he admitted. "But I wish we were back in those days at Magdala."

"I was at the house in Magdala for a few hours last week. I—I felt almost like the girl I used to be before all this happened."

"Has it been so bad, then?"

She shivered involuntarily at the memory. "Sometimes I thought I must kill myself, in spite of my promise to you. But Claudia Procula has been very kind. Pontius Pilate is troubled very much these days, but I think in his way he feels sorry for me too. You never really know with him, he is so moody most of the time. Lately, though, Gaius Flaccus has been drinking more than usual, and there have been times——" She stopped, and her hand went unconsciously to her throat. Joseph noticed then a dark bruise marring the white skin of her neck, near where the slow pulse beat in the hollow of her throat.

"He choked you!" he cried indignantly. "I can see the marks."

"I could hardly swallow for several days," she admitted. "Claudia Procula took me home with her until it was better. And while I was gone he went on his hunting trip."

"To think that I was living in comfort in Jerusalem while you were suffering such tortures because you sacrificed yourself to save me," he reproached himself bitterly. "How can I ever make it up to you, Mary?"

"I am the guilty one," she insisted. "It was on my account that you came so close to death in Alexandria. But I was another person then, Joseph. Something evil had taken hold of me."

"You were possessed by a demon. It was not your fault."

Mary shook her head. "Demetrius was right when he

said, 'The demons that possess man are born within himself.' As a child I hated my father because I could not have what I wanted so desperately, toys, happiness, clothes like other children, and all the things a girl loves even when she is little."

"You were right to hate him. After all, he would have sold you into slavery."

Mary shook her head. "God is right in telling us to honor father and mother, Joseph. Nothing is gained by hating anyone. I had to become a slave myself to understand that I could really forgive my father even that if I tried hard enough. I know now that I carried that burden of hate with me as a child and even when I had grown up to be a young girl," she went on. "What happened with Gaius Flaccus in Tiberias only made me hate more intensely, until my whole life was dominated by it."

"You might never have become the toast of Alexandria," he reminded her, "if your desire for revenge had not driven you on to achieve success."

"Another person lived in Alexandria, Joseph," she said earnestly. "And that person died months and months ago. Until I woke up in the catacombs there in the Necropolis and they told me you had gone to the theater to try to help Philo and the others, I had thought only of myself and my desire for revenge. But something came to me there in the theater. I felt as if the Most High approved what I was doing at last, even if most people would have called me a wanton for dancing naked before the crowd while Philo and the others escaped. A load of sin and guilt was suddenly lifted from my soul that day. I have been a different person ever since."

" 'Whoso findeth me findeth life,' are the words of God," Joseph reminded her, "and the Psalmist also said, 'To do justice and judgment is more acceptable to the Lord than sacrifice.' "

"I am sure I found the Most High again because I was willing to sacrifice myself for those whose lives were almost lost because of me," she agreed. "But I didn't really understand what had happened until I learned of Jesus."

"Tell me about him," Joseph begged.

Mary's eyes began to glow with a warm light. For a fleeting second Joseph felt a spasm of jealousy toward this man he had never seen, who seemed to have such a power over all who heard him. "We were passing through Capernaum one day," she said, "and were held up by the

219

crowd while the soldiers made a path for us. The people hate me because I live with Gaius Flaccus, but they are afraid to curse him, so they revile me because I am a Jewess and call me a fallen woman."

"But that is not true——"

"It would have done no good to tell them the truth. That day they were shouting 'Harlot!' and 'Adulteress!' at me because they knew the soldiers could not reach them through the crowd. I know Jesus did not hear them or see me, for I could barely see him. But somehow his words came to me as clearly as I hear you now, and he seemed to be speaking to me alone."

Nicodemus had said much the same thing, Joseph remembered. What strange power was it this teacher possessed that men could not forget the things he taught, when they forgot so easily what they learned as children from their parents and in the synagogue?

Mary's words recalled his thoughts. "I heard Jesus say: 'Blessed are you when men shall revile you and persecute you and utter all kinds of evil against you falsely!' . . . It was strange, Joseph," she added. "I had cringed when they called me 'harlot' and 'adulteress,' but now I didn't mind any more. It seemed as if he had given me strength to bear the insults and ignore them. . . . If you could hear him you would know what I mean. And Simon says——" She stopped suddenly, as if she were about to reveal something that should be kept hidden.

"What is it, Mary?" he asked. "Or would you rather I did not know?"

"I promised Simon I would tell no one, but I know he wouldn't mind your knowing. He says Jesus is the Messiah."

"But if the Nazarene is truly the Expected One," Joseph protested, "the good news should be proclaimed from the housetops."

"I think Simon wants him to get a much larger following before they reveal the truth."

Joseph shook his head soberly. "Judas the Gaulonite also claimed to be the Messiah," he reminded her soberly, "and Sepphoris was the center of his rebellion. But two thousand Jews were crucified here by the Romans and the whole city sold into slavery. That will happen again if the Galileans are foolish enough to follow another false messiah."

5

A few hours after Joseph's arrival, the condition of Gaius Flaccus changed sharply for the worse. He slept for a short while under the effect of the drug, and awoke in a frenzy of delirium, fighting the slaves who tried to hold him on the couch, and cursing at the top of his voice, while the rasp of his labored breathing filled the villa. When the frenzy was at its height, his head suddenly began to bend backward and his whole body became rigid and taut, while his arms and legs jerked in a continued spasm. Joseph looked at him and shook his head hopelessly. "The disease has reached the brain," he told Mary. "A convulsion like this means only one thing."

"Is it—the end?"

"Before very long. You had better send for Pontius Pilate and Claudia Procula."

"She was coming back with the Procurator after the evening meal. They should be here soon."

Gaius Flaccus was in the throes of another convulsion when Procula came in alone. The color went out of her face at what she saw, and her hand flew to her throat. "Is he dying?" she asked in a whisper.

"I have given him a sedative drug," Joseph exclaimed. "But the inflammation seems to have reached the brain. When that happens, it is——" He stopped, reluctant to say the fateful word.

"Then we can only pray to the Most High," Mary said quietly.

To Joseph's amazement, Claudia Procula knelt with Mary in one corner of the room and began to pray. Joseph himself dropped to his knees then and fumbled for some prayer from his childhood suitable for the presence of death. It was this scene that met the eyes of the Procurator of Judea when he came into the sickroom.

The two kneeling women made a lovely sight with their eyes uplifted to the ceiling, lips moving in a whispered prayer, each supremely beautiful in her own way, yet so markedly different. Claudia Procula was tiny, exquisite, and richly dressed, like a figurine shaped by the hands of a superb artist. Mary's gloriously colored hair was plaited and bound about her forehead. Her face was pale, but the inner fire that had always characterized her shone through the translucent skin. By comparison with Pilate's lady she was roughly dressed, and yet her beauty was far more striking than that of the Roman aristocrat whose ancestors were emperors.

Watching Pontius Pilate, Joseph saw the dark flush of anger rise in his face, but it was the hell in the Procurator's eyes that shocked him most. Utter despair was written there for an instant, as if Pilate were seeing something he had feared but, until this moment, was unwilling to admit. Then the look changed suddenly to one of cold, almost demoniac fury in one of the abrupt changes of mood that often came over him.

"Procula!" he snapped. "What are you doing?"

Claudia Procula got to her feet, trembling from the shock of the savage question. "We—I was praying for Gaius Flaccus," she stammered.

"This is your doing." Pilate wheeled upon Mary. But before she could speak Procula said firmly, "You are wrong, Pontius. I have prayed secretly to Jehovah for a long time. Mary had nothing to do with it, except to show me what believing in Him can do."

Mary showed no sign of fear before the anger of the Roman official. It was as if a power and a vision they could not know set her apart from all of them.

"We who rule for Rome worship the Emperor as divine, Procula," Pilate said sharply. "But the Jewish God acknowledges no other. When you pray to him, you blaspheme against the Emperor. And you." He turned upon Mary savagely. "You will henceforth worship the gods of your master's household."

"These are the words of Jehovah," Mary said quietly, *"'I am the Lord, thy God. Thou shalt have no other gods before me.'"*

For a moment Joseph thought Pontius Pilate was going to strike Mary, and moved quickly to place himself between them. His eyes met the hot angry stare of the Procurator, but his gaze did not fall while he waited, knowing fully the penalty if he were forced to resist.

A puzzled look came into Pilate's face. "What is the

punishment for striking one who rules in the name of Rome, Joseph?" he asked in a different tone.

"Crucifixion!" Joseph was surprised that his voice was calm and clear.

"And you would dare to strike me for chastising a slave?"

"She is a slave only to Gaius Flaccus," Joseph said quietly. "I owe her my life and would protect her if I could, even from the Emperor himself."

"What if she breaks the laws of Rome?"

"Rome has guaranteed to the Jew in his own country the right to worship his God," Joseph reminded him. "And Mary, being the adopted daughter of a Roman citizen, is protected by Roman law herself."

"You should have been a doctor of the law, Joseph," Pilate said then, but not unkindly. "At least you have a good mind, which is more than I can say for some of those I have to deal with in Jerusalem. But you forget that I can be judge as well as prosecutor under the law." He turned to the couch. "Can you help my nephew?"

Joseph took a long breath of relief. "I have drawn blood and tried to preserve his strength," he explained, "but the delirium grows worse. Just now he was taken with a severe convulsion."

"I have seen cases such as this from wounds incurred in battle," Pilate agreed. "There was no hope for him from the beginning, but I am glad Mary sent for you." He turned to her, and for a moment Joseph thought he was going to apologize, but he only said, "You have suffered much at the hands of this kinsman of mine, Mary of Magdala. How can you pray for him when his recovery means you are still a slave?"

"There is one who said, 'Love your enemies,' " she said simply.

"Can you Jews do nothing but quote texts from the sayings of your God?" Pilate asked sarcastically.

"This was spoken by a man," Mary told him. "The teacher, Jesus of Nazareth."

Before Pilate could speak, Claudia Procula said pleadingly, "Jesus is said to perform miracles, Pontius. If we would ask him to come here——"

"I will have no religious fanatics in the house of my kinsman," Pilate snapped.

"B-But——"

"Say no more, Procula! Joseph is the best physician

223

in this region. If he says here is no hope for Gaius Flaccus, there is no hope. Come. We will go back to Tiberias tonight. This mangy capital of Herod's does not appeal to me."

When Pilate and his lady had gone, Mary said softly, "You did a brave thing, Joseph, and I love you for it, but it would have been better to let him strike me than put your life in danger. I would not have minded the pain."

"He had no right to blame you for what Claudia Procula believes."

"Pilate is a troubled man, Joseph. Claudia Procula says he often seems beside himself lately, but she does not know what is worrying him. Sometimes he even accosts travelers on the road, asking, 'What is truth?'"

Joseph smiled. "Philosophers have done that since time began. It is their favorite question."

"I believe he knows the real truth, that everything comes from the Most High, but is afraid to believe it."

"Why should anyone fear to worship the living God?"

"Could Pilate acknowledge the Emperor as divine then? Or allow the eagles of Rome to be displayed before his palace? You can see what that would mean to a Roman."

"Yes," Joseph agreed. "But why did he object so strongly when Procula suggested that Jesus be asked to see Gaius Flaccus?"

"I think it was because of Pila."

"The boy with the twisted foot? I saw him when he was a small child but could do nothing for him."

"Since Jesus raised the daughter of Jairus from the dead, Procula has become hopeful that he might make Pila's foot straight," she explained.

"There was a Jairus who was a ruler of the synagogue at Capernaum. I treated him once."

"It is the same man," Mary confirmed. "Procula knew Jairus and his wife. When she heard about the miracle she wanted to take Pila to Jesus, but Pilate refused. Now she feels that he neglected the boy."

"Why did Pilate refuse to take Pila to the teacher?"

"It may be because Jesus heals in the name of the Most High. If Pilate's own son were healed by him, the Procurator would have to acknowledge the power of God."

"And he could not do that when he denies the very existence of the Most High," Joseph agreed thoughtfully.

"It must have been a hard decision to make, with his own son involved."

"I tried to tell Procula that," Mary said, "but she is Pila's mother, and things look different to her."

Joseph smiled. "Once I lectured you on your duty to God. Now you are teaching me humility."

"But everyone knows that you are good, Joseph."

He looked at Gaius Flaccus, who for the moment was lying quietly in a stupor, having exhausted his strength in the convulsions.

"Am I?" he said slowly. "I am sworn to think only of the welfare of the sick, but if Gaius Flaccus dies you will be free. I don't think I could pray for him as you did, Mary, when I know what it will mean for you if he lives."

"When you see Jesus," she said softly, "you will understand how I could pray for Gaius Flaccus' life, even though I knew that tomorrow he would flog me and give me to any man who visits this house. Just to look at Jesus and hear him speak can make you a different person."

During the night the sick man lapsed into a coma as the spreading poison of the infection completed the conquest of his body. Pontius Pilate and his wife returned to Sepphoris from Tiberias in the morning and were present at the end.

"Procula," the Procurator said when Joseph pronounced Gaius Flaccus dead, "we must follow the Roman custom, even though we are far from home."

She came over to stand by the couch, with Mary a little behind her. "Gaius Flaccus, arise!" Pilate called several times, and Procula repeated the summons. It was the ancient rite of the *conclamentio,* the "calling back" of the dead customary in Roman households.

"*Conclamatum est*—the cry has been raised," Pilate announced formally. "You may send for the embalmers, Joseph. In three days we will consign his body to the pyre with all honors befitting a military commander and send his ashes to Rome."

The embalmers were skillful and did their work well. First the body was preserved and dressed in a fresh toga decorated with the numerous military and civil insignia that the deceased had won in life. Then it was laid in state upon a funeral couch in the atrium, with the feet toward the door and a coin of gold in the dead man's mouth to provide passage money for the final journey across the river Styx.

Before the doors were opened to those who wished to enter and pay tribute to the dead, a wax impression of the Tribune's face was taken, called the *imago*. It would be sent later to Rome, where it would occupy a niche in one of the two *alae* at the rear corners of the atrium in the home of his family, along with an inscription, or *titulus*, telling of his accomplishments. The privilege of thus displaying *imagines* was limited to those of high rank.

Pontius Pilate had decided that his nephew should be cremated with full military and civil honors, just as would have been the case had he been in Rome. The ceremony, Joseph surmised, was also to serve as a reminder to Herod Antipas and the Galileans that Rome still ruled here. Herod Antipas did not dare object to honors given one who had been a favorite of the Emperor Tiberius, even if it entailed an mighty show of arms and a flaunting display of Roman authority and pomp in the capital of a Jewish tetrarchy.

Joseph was surprised, in the midst of the preparations, when he was summoned to visit the Procurator at Tiberias. Hadja accompanied him, as as they came down the steep and narrow road from Magdala to Tiberias, the whole panorama of the lake and the teeming, populous cities around it was spread out before them. To the north, beyond the city of Capernaum, lay the green carpet of groves and fields of the Plain of Gennesaret. From here in the spring came the first fruits and vegetables for the markets of Jerusalem, the finest of their kind in the world. So luscious indeed were they that the priests of the temple sometimes tried to keep them from reaching the markets on the feast days, lest the worshipers be tempted to enjoy the melons and other fruits, forgetting their duty to God.

A little way to the north of Capernaum was a place where springs of highly mineralized water burst from the rocks. Joseph had been there many times to bottle the water for medicine, expecially to treat those whose accumulated excess of humors needed purging. And beyond this area of springs was a small cove, almost semicircular in shape, a place of peace so quiet that a man standing on the shore could speak in a normal voice and be heard high upon the mountainside.

226

From where he stood well above all this Joseph could see that a large crowd filled the cove, even spilling over into the boats of the fishermen that floated, their colorful sails furled, close to the shore. At this height the fishing boats looked like toys and the people of the crowd hardly larger than ants.

"Jesus is teaching today in the cove," Hadja explained. "It is one of his favorite spots, for everyone can hear him there."

"That is the largest crowd I ever saw in Galilee," Joseph observed. "Does he always draw so many people?"

"The sick follow him everywhere," Hadja explained. "For he heals many."

"Have you seen this with your own eyes, Hadja?"

The tall musician nodded. "Once Jesus healed a man who was let down to him through the roof because a crowd filled the house. And at Gadara he cast out devils and drove them into swine, so they rushed into the lake and were drowned."

"Why do you follow him, Hadja?" Joseph asked as they guided their camels down the narrow road. "After all, you are not a Jew."

"In my country the nobles oppress the poor," the Nabatean explained, "just as they do everywhere in the world that I have been. The teacher of Nazareth tells me all men are equal in the sight of God. And since I know in my heart that this is a good thing, I believe what he teaches."

"Does he plan to remove the oppressors from power by force?"

"I do not hear that in the things that he tells me."

"Then how will he free men from those who hold them in bondage?"

Hadja smiled. "If everyone could be as good and kind in his heart as you and the Living Flame are, Joseph, there would be no injustice between a man and his brother. Jesus wants to change the hearts of men and set up in them the kingdom of God of which he speaks. Then all men will be free."

6

PONTIUS Pilate was in the garden between his villa and the water, reading from a small scroll in a summerhouse overlooking the lake. He looked up and smiled when the *nomenclator* ushered Joseph into the garden.

"Peace be upon thee, Joseph of Galilee," he said courteously, and held up the scroll he was reading. "Have you read the poems of Virgil?"

Joseph shook his head. "Treating the sick leaves me little time for anything else."

"In Rome physicians are often philosophers. I heard a very learned one say that more of man's ills come from his soul than from his body."

"The Greeks taught a similar doctrine," Joseph admitted.

"And you?"

"I would not deny that a melancholy spirit is often followed by a distemper;" Joseph admitted.

"I have proved that for myself," Pilate agreed. "It is no easy task to rule a contentious people like the Jews, Joseph. In Caesarea, where the burdens of my office are heavy, my gout is always more painful. And it is still worse in Jerusalem."

"It could be the climate."

Pilate shook his head. "The chill of winter is already in the air here, yet I feel hardly a twinge in my gouty toe. You must have noticed how much more peaceful it is here in Galilee beside the lake than in Jerusalem and Judea. A man can think here without having to listen to idle chatter from people seeking power." He picked up the scroll. "Listen to these verses: they were written of Italy, but describe Galilee just as well:

> "*But fruitful vines and the fat olive's freight,*
> *And harvests heavy with their fruitful weight,*
> *Adorn our fields; and on the cheerful green,*
> *The grazing flocks and lowing herds are seen. . . .*

> *Perpetual spring our happy climate sees,*
> *Twice breed the cattle and twice bear the trees,*
> *And summer suns recede by slow degrees."*

Pilate rolled up the scroll and turned back to Joseph. "You find me moody indeed today, Joseph," he said with a sigh, "but I have cares even here in Tiberias." He stood up and shaded his eyes against the afternoon sun. "I wonder where the fishing boats are this afternoon. They usually return with their catch about now."

"A great crowd has gathered at the other end of the lake," Joseph explained. "I saw many boats up there when we came down the road from Magdala."

Pilate's face took on a sober look. "When the Galileans come together in crowds, it brooks no good, Joseph. What were they doing? Shouting against Rome?"

"Hadja says they were listening to the teacher called Jesus of Nazareth."

"The one who claims to heal?"

"Yes. But many have made that claim in the past."

"I know," Pilate agreed. "Herod is trying to convince me that this man is stirring up the people to rebellion, but I must always seek two meanings in everything he says. Do you think I should take Pila to Jesus?" he asked abruptly.

Taken aback by the question, Joseph fumbled for an answer. But before he could speak Pilate said, "Never mind. You are honest enough to disagree with me if you felt that you should. And then I might be angry with you. I am resigned to the fact that my son will always be a cripple, Joseph. It is a part of the unjust fate that isolated me in Judea when I might have had a high place in the Empire. And yet——" He stopped and did not speak for a moment. "Did you hear that Jesus raises people from the dead?"

"I was told of the miracle," Joseph admitted. "If it really was one."

"Then you doubt it too?"

"I have seen many people die but none come to life again. If the girl was really dead, as they claim, and was raised, I would believe it a miracle."

"That is just why I sent for you," Pilate told him. "I want you to talk with this man Jairus in Capernaum and find out the truth. And while you are about it, you might listen to Jesus of Nazareth and tell me if he teaches anything against Rome. . . . No," he amended. "It would not be right to make you spy on one of your own race. I have ways of finding out those things myself. Just look into the raising of the child."

The funeral of Gaius Flaccus was held on the third day following his death. Long before it was to begin the city was filled with the carriages and chairs of Roman officers and civil officials. The dead Tribune's rank in the equestrian order and his office as commander of all Roman troops in this region had given Pontius Pilate an opportunity to make an impressive show of Roman military might, both to discourage the Galileans in any thoughts they might have had of rebellion and to remind Herod Antipas that Pontius Pilate, as the highest Roman official in this region except the Legate of Syria himself, still controlled considerable power.

Well before the hour for the start of the procession the *dissignator,* as the Roman official who acted as master of ceremonies was called, took his place before the house and began to arrange the order of march. Beside him were his lictors with their fasces, the universal emblem of Roman civil justice. The body of the dead commander was laid out upon the sumptuously upholstered bier in the atrium, with candles in tall golden candelabra casting flickering shadows upon wreaths of palms and flowers and ribbons lying on and about the body.

At the appointed time the trumpets of Gaius Flaccus' own personal troops sounded, and the pallbearers, officers of his own command, marched in and lifted the open bier to their shoulders. Outside waited the Tribune's chariot, drawn by the four swift horses he had loved to drive at breakneck speed through villages and towns, often leaving crushed and maimed bodies lying in his wake. A frame had been built on the richly ornamented vehicle to hold the shallow bier, which was now placed carefully on the chariot and lashed down by the handles, lest the spirited horses shake it loose as the conveyance bumped over the stone-paved streets.

Leading the procession was the chariot of the *dissignator* with six uniformed trumpeters marching before him to clear the way. Next came a double file of lictors and, behind them, the professional mourners, robed in white and chanting monotonously the solemn words of a dirge. Oddly in contrast to the mourners, many of whose faces were painted white and who beat their breasts in synthetic sorrow, were the dancers and pantomimists who followed. Some played on flutes while others portrayed in pantomine the triumphs of the deceased on the battlefield and in political life.

Next in the line was the elaborate chariot of Pontius Pilate himself. The Procurator stood erect, cold and haughty in his uniform and medals, looking neither to left nor right as the vehicle rumbled over the stone paving. In a funeral conducted in the deceased's home city, a long line of men would have followed in the uniforms of the deceased's illustrious ancestors, each wearing one of the *imagines,* the death masks that reposed between times in the *alae* opening off the atrium of his house. Thus the dead man would move to his funeral pyre preceded by a long line of his ancestors in effigy. But since the *imagines* of Gaius Flaccus' line were in Rome, small placards bearing the names and more important accomplishments of his famous ancestors were carried by a number of officers behind the chariot of Pontius Pilate. After them the Lady Claudia Procula rode in Pilate's own chair with the curtains drawn.

The elaborate sedan chair bearing the eagles of Rome was followed by Gaius Flaccus' favorite stallion, resplendent in golden trappings with an empty saddle on his back, led by the commander's equerry. A column of soldiers marched behind the battle charger, bearing the dead man's insignia and memorials of his trophies and his feats of arms in battle. And after the parade of the insignia strode fifty additional lictors, their fasces pointing downward, followed by another group bearing flaming torches, although it was daytime, relics of the old Roman custom of burying at night.

Next rumbled the funeral chariot itself, carrying the open bier. The embalmers had been skilled in their craft. Lying there, resplendent in full military uniform of the rich purple color favored by high officers, Gaius Flaccus might have been merely asleep.

Mary had chosen to walk with the other slaves who had become freedmen, as was customary, by the will of their dead master. She wore black and her hair was covered completely, but such was her beauty that she stood out among the others like a precious jewel in a pile of glass baubles. Joseph did not walk in the procession but followed along beside the slaves at the edge of the crowd.

The people of Galilee had not loved Gaius Flaccus, and so there was no mourning as the procession passed. Had there been less show of military might, some might have dared to jeer, but all were silent until the slaves and Mary came along. Then, to Joseph's surprise, a murmur of resentment ran along through the crowd, like a ripple in a pool. And as Mary passed, one woman spat out a word he had heard first applied to her years ago on the streets of Tiberias, *"Meretrix!"*

"Why do you call her that?" he asked the woman, a shrewish-looking housewife. "She is a slave like the others."

The woman looked at him suspiciously. "Are you a stranger in this region?"

"I am a physician from Jerusalem," he said truthfully enough.

"The woman in black there is called Mary of Magdala," his informant explained. "But she is no slave. She is a Jewess, a former dancer who chose to follow the Roman instead of living with her own people."

"How do you know this?"

"All Galilee knows it. Did not the Tribune Gaius Flaccus boast in the drinking houses, because he knew the Jews would be ashamed to know that one of them is an adulteress?"

"But she walks with the slaves," Joseph protested.

"It is only to hide her sin now that the man she lusted after is dead. Mary of Magdala should be stoned like any other wanton."

Mary had gone on while Joseph was talking to the woman, and the Roman troops were passing in review now, the thunder of their leather-shod feet upon the stones drowning out any further conversation. Century after century passed in full military equipment led by the centurions, captains of a hundred. And after them rode the cavalry with pikes upraised and colorful pennons fluttering from their points. Last of all creaked the siege trains, massive machines called ballistae that could hurl a stone ball of half a man's weight an eighth of a mile, the onager and the *catapulta,* giant bows that hurled great blazing arrows for long distances, and other equally formidable machines.

It was indeed an impressive spectacle, but Joseph was too concerned by what the woman had said about Mary to appreciate it. Had she come safely to freedom through the death of Gaius Flaccus, he wondered, only to have more trouble because the people whose very relatives she had probably saved in Alexandria still thought evil of her? It was a disquieting thought.

At the cemetery outside the city gates a great funeral pyre had been erected. Here the body of the dead man would be consumed by the flames and his ashes gathered and returned in state to Rome to rest in the *columbarium* housing the remains of his ancestors. As the funeral party reached the cemetery, it deployed according to the directions of the *dissignator* before a platform erected in front of the pyre. From this platform Pontius Pilate gave a lengthy oration of praise for the dead man, shrewdly adding a warning that the might of Rome thus displayed could also be used to bring the Jews to heel if they chose to rebel against Roman authority. The lesson was all the more pointed because, directly visible across from the cemetery, was the slope where Judas the Gaulonite had been crucified with two thousand Jews within the memory of many who watched and listened.

When the oration was finished, the elaborate bier was carried to the top of the pyre and set in place. At a command from the *dissignator* the chair of the Lady Claudia Procula was borne away, followed by the women of Gaius Flaccus' household. Pontius Pilate himself cast a flaming torch into the tinder prepared at the bottom of the pyre. It caught at once, and the flames raced through the dry wood, turning it into a fiery holocaust in a matter of seconds.

Joseph did not stay for the end of the ceremony, but hurried back to the city in the wake of the chair bearing Claudia Procula and the slaves who followed it. The press of the crowd was still great and he made slow progress, so that by the time he reached the villa Mary had gone to rest in the partly enclosed garden that was a prominent part of the houses in this pleasant climate. Dark shadows lay under her eyes and weariness showed in her face when he found her, for it had been a long hard day. But the smile she gave him as he came into the garden quickened his heartbeat. When she held out her hands to him he knelt and carried them to his lips. "You are free, Mary," he cried. "Free at last."

"Dear Joseph." She came into the circle of his arms as if she had longed to be there for all the months since he had left Alexandria. "What would I do without you?"

"You need never be without me," he said, kissing her gently.

"You don't know what it will mean to have someone to look after me and care for me again," she whispered. "How much simpler it all would have been if I had listened to my heart back in Magdala, when we first knew we loved each other. But then," she added, "you might have stayed in Magdala as a village physician and never have become *medicus viscerus* of the temple and the most famous physician in Judea and Galilee."

"I would give it all up today if you wanted me to. Come back to Jerusalem with me now," he begged, "or I will stay in Magdala, whichever you wish. Nothing must ever separate us again."

"What did you hear today that has disturbed you, Joseph?" She looked at him keenly. "Is something wrong?"

"It is nothing. Idle gossip."

"I heard them in the crowd saying I lived with Gaius Flaccus because I am a wanton. It is not the first time they have said it."

"Those who know you would never believe it."

"Yes," she agreed. "Anyone who knows me would understand. And as for those who do not, it does not matter what they say."

"Then you will come back with me now?"

She shook her head gently. "Not yet, Joseph. Being a Jew, you know what it is to be unclean. I must cleanse my body and my soul with prayer and mediatation after the manner of our people. Tomorrow Hadja and I will return to the house at Magdala, and through the winter I will live quietly and pray that I may be made whole again and understand God's will better. Besides, I want to listen to the teachings of Jesus, for they seem to bring peace to the soul. When spring comes to Galilee we will be wed as we might have been years ago. Then we can decide where we shall live."

"But Mary . . ."

"Give me these months to purify myself of the defilement I have known," she pleaded. "Then I can come to you clean and whole again, as I would have done had fate and the Most High left us in Magdala."

He argued no more for he understood the real reason for her wanting to wait. It was because she could not bring to him in marriage just now a body which had been contaminated by the seed of evil.

"Will you be safe in Magdala?" he asked.

"Hadja will be with me," she assured him. "And you know there is nothing to idle talk; it will blow over as soon as they have something else to gossip about. Are you going back to Jerusalem tomorrow?"

Joseph shook his head. "Pilate has asked me to investigate the raising of Jairus' daughter from the dead."

"Why?"

"I think he wants to be sure he was right in not letting Pila be taken to Jesus. After all, Pilate is human and he loves the boy."

"If Pilate would let Pila be taken to Jesus, it might help to settle the quarrel between him and Procula," Mary said thoughtfully. "I know she could forgive him his cruelty and moodiness, but not if he deliberately deprives Pila of a chance to be well. Try to find out the truth, Joseph," she begged. "If Jesus did truly raise the girl from the dead, there may be hope for Pila, and for Pontius Pilate as well. Then he would have to believe in the mercy of the Most High."

7

LEAVING Mary at the house in Magdala with Hadja, Joseph set out early the next afternoon to visit Jairus. It was only a short distance down the sloping hillside from Magdala and along the shore of the lake to the sprawling town of Capernaum. He found that he still remembered the way to the house, a few doors from the great synagogue of Capernaum, where Jairus lived. As one of the oldest and therefore the wisest men in the Jewish congregation, he was numbered among the elders, often called the "rulers of the synagogue," who sat upon an elevated platform of honor above the congregation itself. Respected and honored by all because of their piety and wisdom, they were often consulted by Jews outside the synagogue on matters of conduct and problems pertaining to observance of the law.

Jairus was at work in his shop when Joseph came in, but he courteously led the young physician to a shady arbor in the small garden around which both house and shop were built. "We here in the lake region are very proud of your success in Jerusalem, Joseph," the old man said gently. "Particularly so because you are a Galilean."

During the usual refreshment of wine and spice cakes, Joseph said casually, "I hear that your daughter has recently been ill."

"What seek you here, Joseph?" Jairus looked at him keenly. "Are those who govern the temple in Jerusalem concerned about the miracles performed by Jesus of Nazareth?"

"We have heard of Jesus in Jerusalem," Joseph admitted. "But I have another purpose in coming here. If the Nazarene truly raises the dead, as I have been told, he may be able to help the son of Pontius Pilate."

"The boy with the twisted foot? Yes, I can see that Pilate would want to know. But Jesus heals through faith in the Most High. Does Pontius Pilate have such faith?"

"I think not. But he asked me to come."

"The Procurator overlooks nothing that happens to the Jews, whether in Judea, Galilee, or elsewhere. Are you sure he has not sent you to spy upon the teacher of Nazareth?"

"I am no spy," Joseph said indignantly. "I seek only to know how Jesus cures the sick and if he can indeed raise the dead."

Jairus nodded. "You have the name of being a good man, Joseph of Galilee," he agreed. "What do you wish to know about my daughter?"

"Did Jesus of Nazareth really raise her from the dead, as I have been told?"

"You have asked me a question I cannot truthfully answer," Jairus admitted. "Let me tell you what happened and you can judge for yourself. My daughter was sick with what seemed to be a fever that made her sleep much of the time. You remember the physician Alexander Lysimachus, don't you?"

"Very well. I was his apprentice in Magdala."

"Yes. I remember that now. Then you know that he is a skilled physician and an honest man. Alexander Lysimachus could give us no hope for my daughter's life, so I went to where Jesus was teaching by the sea, intending to ask him to come and heal her as he had healed others. When I got to the teacher, I fell on the ground at his feet and said, 'My little daughter is at the point of death. Come and lay your hands on her so that she may be made well and live.' "

"What did he answer?"

"He said not a word," Jairus admitted. "But he looked at me as if he were seeing into my very soul, and then he smiled and stepped down from the rock where he had been teaching. He seemed to know just where to go, too, although he had never seen me before."

"The crowd knew you, since you are a ruler of the synagogue," Joseph pointed out. "He could have merely let them lead him."

"That is true," Jarius admitted. "I do not say that he knew the way, only that he seemed to know. Before we reached the house, some of those I had left there came to meet us, crying that the child had died."

"Did Alexander Lysimachus pronounce her dead?"

Jairus shook his head. "The physician was not here then. Those who were watching said life had departed from her, but when Jesus saw her, he said, 'Why do you make a tumult and weep? The child is not dead but sleeping.' "

"Are you sure those were his exact words?" Joseph asked quickly. Here, it seemed, was what he was seeking.

"I have told you just what he said. It is strange," Jairus continued. "I knew Jesus when he was working in Nazareth and Sepphoris as a carpenter and builder. Then he was like any ordinary person, but now the very power of the Most High seems to have come upon him. The people in the house laughed at him when he said my daughter was not dead, for they had already drawn the sheet up over her face. But when he took her by the hand and said, 'Little girl, I say to you arise,' she got up at once and walked."

"How is she now?"

"As well as you or I. The Master instructed us to say nothing about it, but so many people had seen her when she was dead that it could not be kept secret."

"Jesus himself said she was sleeping, not dead, according to your story," Joseph reminded him.

"That is true," Jairus admitted. "But when I looked at

her myself, I was sure that she was no longer among the living."

"Then you believe she was really brought to life again?"

Jairus nodded solemnly. "Some scribes and Pharisees came here the next day, trying to make me say she was not dead, but I told them just what I told you. They would like to trap Jesus if they could, by they got no help from me."

"Why would they want to trap him?" Joseph asked curiously.

"The Nazarene preaches forgiveness of sins, as did some of the prophets," Jairus explained. "But those who make a great to-do about the law seek to make him say things that are contrary to it, such as that those who sin should not be punished. If they could get Jesus to speak aganst the law, they would take him before the council and accuse him of blasphemy."

"But why would anyone seek to do him harm when he seems only to do good?"

Jairus shrugged. "To the Pharisees, the law itself is greater than good deeds, for by obeying it they think to assure themselves a life after death. If the people come to believe that the Most High will easily forgive their sins, who would follow after the scribes and Pharisees?"

Joseph knew from his own experience in Jerusalem that Jairus spoke the truth. Narrow minds, obsessed with the stern codes of the law handed down on Mount Sinai and the many conflicting details of what was called the "moral law," often overlooked completely the teachings of God in regard to loving each other and doing rightly. In their zeal they would not hesitate to stone to death even the best of men if he did not revere the law as they thought it should be revered.

Having learned all that he could from Jairus, Joseph started back up the hillside to Magdala. But hardly had he reached the outskirts of the city when he realized that something out of the ordinary was happening. The outer streets were strangely deserted, but from the Street of the Greeks he could hear the roar of voices and shouting, as if a mob had gathered there. Suddenly apprehensive, he pushed on and soon came to the edge of a crowd packing the streets.

No one seemed to know exactly what the excitement

was about, but as with all mobs, the tension was rising to a high pitch and could soon be dangerous for anyone against whom the fickle emotions of the crowd was directed. Finally, when he could get no farther, Joseph managed to attract the attention of a street vendor standing on his cart in order to see over the crowd. "What is happening?" he asked, tugging at the hem of the man's robe.

The peddler looked down and, seeing that Joseph was expensively dressed, answered respectfully, "The scribes and Pharissees have taken a woman accused of adultery and are inflaming the crowd against her."

"Who is she?" Joseph cried, remembering what he had heard in the crowd at the funeral of Gaius Flaccus.

"I know not, but her hair is as red as the copper of Cyprus and she stands before a house in the Street of the Greeks, with a tall man of the desert protecting her."

"Mary!" he cried, suddenly overcome with apprehension. Had she escaped from slavery, only to face the fury of a mob of Jews ready to punish an infraction of their precious law? This was what he had been fearing. Quickly Joseph took a gold denarius from his purse and pressed it into the hand of the man on the cart. "Tell me all you see," he said. "Have they started to stone her yet?" Stoning was the traditional method of execution for infractions of Jewish law, just as crucifixion was a practice peculiar to the Romans.

"Another man is with the woman," his informer called down, "and the accusers seem to be arguing their case before him. I can see him well now," he added excitedly. "It is the teacher they call Jesus of Nazareth. They must be asking him to judge her."

Joseph could understand how Mary would make a perfect case for those who sought to trap Jesus, since the Jews of Galilee believed that she had lived with Gaius Flaccus of her own accord, thus labeling herself truly an adulteress. Someone must tell the people the truth, he realized, and that could only be Mary, Hadja, or himself. They would hardly listen to Mary or Hadja, but Joseph of Galilee was widely known and they might let him speak in her defense.

When he tried to push his way through the crowd, however, it was like a wall. Those against whom he shoved kicked at him and cursed him without opening a way through. Only a battering-ram could make a path for

239

him, he thought, and with a flash of inspiration realized how it could be done. Quickly he took several gold coins from his pocket and held them up to the peddler standing on the cart. "Get me through the crowd with your mule," he urged, "and these will be yours."

The man nodded and scooped the coins from Joseph's hand. With the same movement he lashed the mule's backside with his whip. The young physician barely had time to seize the back of the cart as the pain-lashed animal lowered its head and butted directly into the mob. Cursing and shouting, the men gave way, opening a path into which the mule plunged. Jerked about at the back of the cart, Joseph was hard put to keep his feet, but only a few seconds elapsed before he found himself at the front of the crowd, looking upon a strangely dramatic tableau.

Mary stood with her back against the door of her house, where she had lived with Demetrius. Hadja was beside her. Her head was covered with a shawl and she wore the same dark dress in which she had walked yesterday during the funeral procession. But although she faced an angry and accusing crowd, no sign of fear showed in her face and she did not remove her gaze from Jesus during the commotion of Joseph's arrival. A strange look was in her eyes, a light of adoration, worship, and utter trust.

This was the first time Joseph had seen the young teacher, but Jesus was so like the description by Nicodemus that he felt as if he were looking at a familiar face. And he understood at once now why Nicodemus had said, "It is not just the teachings of Jesus that make you want to follow him. It is something about the man himself, something that cannot easily be put into words."

Jesus was standing quietly beside Mary and Hadja, listening to the impassioned oration of a tall man whose fringed robe labeled him a Pharisee. He was slender and slightly over middle height, with a face that was intelligent and kind. But the most distinguishing feature was his extremely brilliant eyes, as if the fire of the soul within his body burned more brightly than in ordinary men. He was rather pale, and his features were those of a scholar and dreamer rather than a man of battle and deeds of strength. And yet he had been able to draw men of action to follow him, such as Simon and the sons of Zebedee, who stood just behind him now. As he listened to the angry tirade from the Pharisee, Jesus' expression was thoughtful, with no hint of either censure or resentment at the half-contemptuous manner of the man who was denouncing Mary.

"Teacher," the Pharisee argued, "this woman was taken in adultery. Now in the law, Moses commanded us to stone such. What do you say about her?"

Jesus did not immediately answer. Instead he did a strange thing. Stooping, he began to write with the end of his finger in the dust of the street, as if he had not heard them and had quite forgotten where he was. The accuser craned his neck to see what the man of Nazareth was writing, but he was unable to decipher it and repeated impatiently, "What do you say about her?"

Jesus continued to write a moment longer, then straightened up and shook the dust from his fingers. When he spoke his voice was low, yet such was its peculiarly penetrating power that the whole crowd heard the words. "Let him who is without sin among you throw the first stone at her," he said gently. And stooping again, he began to write once more in the dust.

The Pharisee who had acted as prosecutor stared at Jesus for a moment in bewilderment. Then he looked uncertainly at those who had joined him in pressing the charge, as if asking which of them dared announce himself free from sin and cast the stone. The look of bewilderment on his face was so comical that someone in the crowd laughed at the discomfiture of the man who, a few minutes before, had been so arrogantly certain of trapping the teacher of Nazareth. And with one of those lightning-quick changes of emotion that happens to mobs, a roar of merriment rose from the onlookers.

One of the accusers started to sneak away, and at this the mirth of the crowd grew even louder and more pointed. The scribes and the Pharisees, realizing their cause was lost, started to move up the street, anxious to get away from this man who could, with a few simple words, set at naught their most elaborate schemes. And since the drama was ended, the crowd followed, until soon Joseph was left with Mary, Hadja, the teacher, and his disciples.

Jesus looked up then and said to Mary, "Woman, where are they? Has no one condemned you?"

"No one, Lord," she said in a low voice, and he said quietly, "Neither do I condemn you: go and do not sin again." And turning, he walked off down the street, followed by most of his disciples.

Mary remained just where she had stood throughout the whole dramatic episode, her eyes upon the slender figure in the rough robe of homespun, with the sunlight shining like a halo upon his uncovered head. Only when Jesus had disappeared did she turn, and Joseph saw that a great glory and a great wonder were in her face.

8

IT was like old times that evening in the house of Demetrius, except that they all missed the old musician with his massive belly and his humorous slant on life. Mary and Joseph insisted that Simon have supper with them. At first the huge fisherman argued that, since Jesus was going onto Nazareth that evening by foot, he should accompany the teacher, but when Joseph promised to take Simon there the next morning by camel, the fisherman agreed to stay. For the first time in many years the house of Demetrius rang with joyful music while Hadja played his cithara, and Mary sang the songs of the poets who had loved this beautiful region of Galilee. After they had eaten and were sipping their wine, without which no meal was complete in that day, Mary asked quietly, "What is Jesus like, Simon?"

"The teacher?" A note of reverence came into the fisherman's hearty voice. "The thing you feel about him is inside him and inside you. It speaks without words."

"When he spoke to me there before the crowd today all my fears melted away," Mary agreed. "It was as if he had opened the heavens and showed me the very throne of the Most High."

Simon looked at Joseph. "What did you think of Jesus?" he asked.

"He saved Mary from the stones," Joseph said simply. "If for nothing else but that, I would owe him my life."

Everyone was tired from the long day, and the dinner party broke up soon. When Simon and Hadja had gone to the Nabatean's quarters where they would sleep, leaving Joseph and Mary alone in the garden, he drew her into his arms. "How good it is to be back home again," she said softly.

"But will you be safe? They may make trouble for you again."

"Jesus will protect me," she said confidently.

"He has already left Magdala," Joseph pointed out.

"I am going to Nazareth with Simon tomorrow, Joseph," she said then. "When Jesus told me to 'go and sin no more,' I knew that I must follow him."

The announcement of her decision did not come as a real surprise. When he had seen the look in Mary's eyes as he watched her from the crowd that afternoon, Joseph had known that something more than just the saving of her from stoning was taking place. "Does this mean we must set aside our own plans?" he asked.

"Some things must be put above human wishes." Mary put her hand on his arm in a pleading gesture. "And we will both be happier in the end because we thought of someone else besides ourselves. Jesus is the Messiah, Joseph. Who else but him could forgive my sins?"

Joseph knew the answer to his question then. He had found her—and lost her again.

Nazareth lay in a natural cup in the hills above the Plain of Esdraelon, just off the Via Maris. They found Jesus teaching in the market place, but only a small gathering was listening to him, nothing like the great crowds that followed when he spoke in the populous cities along the shore of the lake. As they approached the crowd, Joseph noticed a little knot of men and women standing at the edge of the gathering, as if hesitant to come any nearer. They seemed distraught about something, and he realized the cause when a man came up to Jesus and said, "Your mother and your brethren are outside, asking for you."

Jesus lifted his head. "Who are my mother and my brethren?" His voice came to them quietly across the crowd.

The man who had brought the message looked at him incredulously, as if any man who did not know his own family, in the very city where he had grown up, must be demented. But Jesus only lifted his hands in a gesture that seemed to draw the crowd to him. "Here are my mother and my brethren," he said. "Whoever does the will of God is my brother, and sister, and mother."

When he made no further move to go to his family

and greet them, some of the crowd began to murmur against him. Their voices were low, but Jesus seemed to possess an uncanny faculty of hearing even a man's thoughts, for he said in a voice of gentle reproof: "A prophet is not without honor, except in his own country and in his own house."

The morning was hardly half gone when Jesus finished his teaching and, followed by his disciples, started along the road leading back to the Sea of Galilee. The crowd was disappointed, for they had expected some of the miracle working about which they had heard from people who had seen it in Capernaum and the other cities around the lake. But he did nothing to impress them.

"We must be going, Mary," Simon said. "Are you coming with us?"

She turned to Joseph, and her eyes were wet with tears. "I must," she whispered. "You know that I must, don't you?"

He could only nod, for the pain of knowing that he was losing her again would not let him speak. Gently he kissed her on the forehead and held her hands tightly for a moment before letting her go. Simon and Hadja had gone on a little way, and as she ran to catch them, Joseph thought of the last time they had been separated, seemingly forever. Then he had been carried away by the Roman soldiers from the stage of the great theater of Alexandria, leaving Mary standing there between Gaius Flaccus and Plotinus. And closing his eyes, he prayed silently to the Most High that, having brought them together again, he would not let this parting be for long.

The synagogue of Nazareth stood just off the market place in the cool shade of some tall trees. The appearance of Jesus' family at the edge of the crowd that morning and the teacher's apparent disowning of them had stirred Joseph's curiosity. Now that he was alone, it occurred to him that the *chazan* of the synagogue might be able to enlighten him about this strange happening and perhaps help him decide just what information he should bring to Pontius Pilate about Jesus.

An old man was puttering about just inside the synagogue. At the sound of Joseph's step upon the vestibule he came to the door and peered into the bright sunshine. "I am Jonas, the *chazan*," he said courteously to Joseph. "Do you come to pray to the Most High?" The *chazan* was sometimes also called the "apostle" of the congregation and was their spiritual leader.

Joseph introduced himself, and the two men chatted courteously for a few moments. Then the young physician asked, "What do they think of the teacher called Jesus here in Nazareth?"

The old man sighed. "That one has brought much pain to his family. Just today they came to me to ask what they should do about him."

"What do you mean?"

"Some of them believe he is demented and wish to shut him up somewhere, lest he come to harm. You must have heard that John the Baptist was killed by Herod because he stirred up the people? The family of Jesus fear that the same thing may happen to him."

"Then he is not called great here in Nazareth?"

The old man shrugged his thin shoulders. "Jesus grew up as a carpenter with but little learning. Where did this man get this wisdom he is reported to have? And the mighty works he is said to have done?"

"Some believe him to be the Messiah," Joseph pointed out.

The *chazan* shook his head. "It is written in the Book of the prophet Daniel, *'Know therefore and understand that from the going forth of the commandment to restore and to build Jerusalem unto the Messiah, the Prince, shall be seven weeks and three score and two weeks: the street shall be built again, and the wall, even in troublous times.'*"

"I remember the passage," Joseph admitted.

"This man called Jesus of Nazareth is a carpenter's son and not a prince!" The old Jew's voice rose with indignation. "Is not his mother called Mary? Are not his brethren James, and Joseph, and Simon, and Judas? And are not all his sisters with us?"

"I saw him first only yesterday and know nothing about him except what I hear," Joseph explained.

"I speak the truth," the *chazan* said with conviction. "Where did this man get all this? And how can the Prince of Peace come out of such a city as this?" The old man paused for breath, then went on, "Some see in everyone who lifts his voice in the market place a savior for Israel, because they look for God to speak to them through their ears and not through their hearts. But they forget the Books of the Law and the Prophets which foretell the true coming of the Expected One exactly as it shall be. Is there anything else you wish of me, young man?"

Joseph shook his head. "You have told me all I need to know. Shalom!"

"Shalom, my son! May the Most High give you wisdom and deliver Israel from false prophets."

9

IT was late afternoon when Joseph reached Pontius Pilate's villa in Tiberias. The Procurator received him in the garden overlooking the lake. "I expected you yesterday," he said abruptly. "Did you see Jairus?"

"Yes," Joseph told him. "But I wanted to see what I could find out about the teacher, Jesus of Nazareth, so I went to his home city of Nazareth this morning."

"What did Jairus say?" Pilate demanded impatiently. "Was the girl really raised from the dead?"

"There is a difference of opinion," Joseph explained. "Jairus and the people watching the sick girl are sure she was dead. But when Jesus came, he told them, 'The child is not dead but sleeping.' And then he raised her up."

A look of relief came into Pilate's face, and Joseph understood now why the Procurator had been so much disturbed. Had Joseph brought news that Jesus had indeed raised the girl from the dead, Pilate would have been forced, by his love for Pila and his wife, to take the boy to the healer, placing himself in the position of begging a Jew to help his son. To a proud Roman this would have been a hard thing indeed.

"Tell me the whole story in detail," Pilate ordered. "And be sure that you omit nothing."

Joseph gave a complete account of his talk with Jairus in Capernaum. "The girl was alive, then," Pilate said firmly. "The words of the teacher himself prove it."

"Unless Jesus was trying to keep the people from realizing what he had done," Joseph interposed. "Jairus says he cautioned them to say nothing about it."

"Would any healer want to keep people from knowing

he could raise the dead?" Pilate snapped. "It was because the child was not dead. He is a charlatan; what you have told me leaves no doubt of it."

"Jesus is not just another fanatic, I am sure," Joseph objected. "He has a strange power over people."

"Any zealot who climbs upon a high place and shouts to the people of Galilee will get a following," Pilate said contemptuously. "Look at the way the Jews flocked to the man called John the Baptist. I hear some even called him the Messiah that you are always talking about, but he could not save his head from Herod's ax."

"Is it true that John was killed to please a woman?"

Pilate shrugged. "John had to die. His following was too large, and he had begun to criticize Herod himself. But there were ways of getting rid of John the Baptist without putting him in prison or handing the man's head on a plate to that slut Salome. We can have no divided loyalties in those who live under the rule of Rome, Joseph. When people follow a leader who is not a deputy of the Emperor, that leader must be destroyed."

"Does that mean Jesus, too, will have to be condemned?"

"Eventually, if he continues to gain a following. But this time I hope Herod will be wiser. Prison and martyrdom are no fate for zealots." He smiled thinly. "You have heard of the *sicarii*, of course."

Joseph nodded. The professional assassins, called *sicarii*, were renegade fanatics. Many of them were remnants of the following of Judas the Gaulonite, and not all, by any means, were Jews. They infested the entire country and were a source of constant contention between the Romans and the Jewish authorities.

"Then you know that the daggers of the *sicarii* are at anybody's service for a fee," Pilate continued. "Herod's mistake was to have imprisoned John in the first place. If he is clever, he will have this man Jesus disposed of much more simply."

Early the next morning Joseph departed for Jerusalem along the valley highway that followed the western shore of the lake and the Jordan River to the south. A few miles south of Tiberias he passed through Hammath, whose medicinal hot baths were famous throughout the entire region. Already the sick, many of them bent and crippled by inflamed and stiffened joints, were making their way painfully toward the rock pools of the baths.

Farther north, near where the city of Capernaum nestled against the shore, Joseph could plainly see the sparkling gush of water from the rocks called the Seven Fountains, a favorite watering place for travelers along the Via Maris.

As he continued southward along the shore of the lake toward Tarichae, the pungent odor of drying fish soon met his nostrils at the edge of that city. In the great white sheds by the shore hundreds of women worked, cleaning, splitting, and salting fish by the tons for the markets of the world. The chattering of many feminine tongues gave the city a voice of its own.

On the eastern rim of the cup in which the lake lay, across the sparkling emerald green of the water in the morning sunlight, row upon row of lovely Roman villas lined the steep slope, each with its luxurious courtyard and terraced gardens descending to the water. Boats of all kinds rode at anchor by the landings of the foot of long marble stairways leading from the houses to the level of the lake, and many of the villas were all but hidden by trees and vines growing in riotous profusion along the terraced hillside.

Farther back in the hills was a great Roman camp, housing the garrison over which Gaius Flaccus had been commander, with the tents of the legions arranged in geometrical lines upon the slopes and the white houses of the officers nearer the lake itself. Beyond the Roman camp Joseph could glimpse parts of the Greek cities of Hippos and Gadara in the hills, with their palatial theaters and amphitheaters, their colonnaded forums and wide market places, and the white domes of temples shining in the sunlight. Although a part of the Decapolis, as the ten Greek cities to the east were called, they were closely allied with the towns of Galilee. The Greek influence from this closely related region had materially affected the lives of the people of that populous province far more than in Judea and Jerusalem, where the Pharisees in particular stubbornly resisted any infiltration of foreign thought and custom.

No wonder those who had lived for even a few days in this earthly paradise loved it ever after, Joseph thought as he sat his rangy camel in the narrow pass where the Jordan tumbled over the rocks, carrying the waters of the lake onward to the Dead Sea far to the south. No matter how far he traveled, he always looked forward to returning to the Sea of Galilee, which he loved so much, and the thriving, turbulent cities around its shore. Now he was reluctant to urge his camel into the pass, shutting the lake from sight.

More than just a nostalgia for earthly beauty drew him back to the lake, however, for there was here a feeling of peace and contentment that he had never known in Jerusalem. And looking back across the years, he could see that for all his riches and his high position he had been happier as a youth, driving his mule up and down the steep roads circling the lake, his bottle of leeches and his *nartik*, filled with bandages, instruments, and medicines, bumping against the patient animal's flanks.

10

JOSEPH was not surprised, a few days after his return to Jerusalem, when he received a call to visit the old high priest Annas in his home near the temple, nor that the indisposition turned out to be a trifling one. Although several of Annas' sons had occupied the position of high priest since his own retirement and now his son-in-law Caiaphas was in the same position, it was well known in Jerusalem that Annas himself held the reins and the others did his bidding. One son, Jonathan, had been passed over, however, and was known to be constantly plotting with Herod Antipas to make that wily ruler of Galilee king in Jerusalem. Very little happened to Jews, even in Galilee, that was not reported to the old high priest immediately.

Elias, the doctor of laws before whom Joseph had qualified as *rophe uman*, was in Annas' house with Caiaphas and several others when the young physician arrived. After Joseph had prescribed a soothing mixture for the old man's cough and closed his *nartik*, Caiaphas cleared his throat portentously. He was a tall, lean man with a harsh cast of countenance and eyes that hardly ever looked directly at the person to whom he was speaking, so that one rarely had an opportunity to divine the thoughts back of his cold exterior. "You were recently in Galilee, I believe," he said to Joseph when the formalities of greeting had been observed.

"I was called to attend the Tribune Gaius Flaccus in his last illness."

"Did you speak with the Procurator Pontius Pilate?"

Joseph told of his conversation with Pilate and his mission to Jairus. He could see the interest of his audience quicken, and when he finished Caiaphas asked, "Do you know positively, then, that the girl was not raised from the dead?"

"I have only the word of Jairus," Joseph pointed out. "According to him, everybody thought the girl was dead, but when Jesus came he said that she was not."

"Do you remember the exact words the Nazarene used?" Elias interposed.

"I have them only from Jairus, not from Jesus himself."

"Jairus is a good man and a ruler of the synagogue in Capernaum," Caiaphas said impatiently. "He would have no reason to lie about this."

"According to Jairus," Joseph told them, "Jesus came into the house and asked, 'Why do you make a tumult and weep? The child is not dead but sleeping.' Then he said, 'Little girl, I say to you arise.' She got up at once from the bed."

Caiaphas looked around the small circle of bearded men. "I told you we could not depend upon the reports of the crowd," he said heavily. "They would make a miracle of anything. Obviously the girl was not dead."

"Did you see Jesus of Nazareth yourself?" Elias asked.

"Yes. I heard him teach at Magdala and also in Nazareth—"

"You say you heard Jesus speak?" Caiaphas interrupted. "What did you think of him?"

"He has a great power over the people. But I heard nothing from his lips that our own prophets and teachers have not taught before."

"He preaches revolution against Rome and the legal heads of the temple," Caiaphas snapped.

"I heard no such things," Joseph insisted.

"How do you explain then that this Nazarene has among his followers a man named Simon the Zealot, who is known to have been a follower of Judas the Gaulonite and the Galilean revolutionaries?" Caiaphas demanded scornfully. "And there is another man named Simon who was a frequent troublemaker when he was a fisherman of Capernaum, along with the sons of Zebedee, James and John. They are called Sons of Thunder by the Galileans for the same reason."

"I heard some people say Jesus is the Messiah," Joseph admitted, "but no talk of rebellion."

"Are you absolutely sure you heard no blasphemy?" Annas asked again.

"None," Joseph said firmly. "He taught only such things as I have heard spoken before by teachers from the Porch of Solomon here in the temple."

When Joseph told Nicodemus of his visit to the house of Annas, the lawyer said promptly, "You were before the political Sanhedrin."

"I think you are right," Joseph agreed. All Jerusalem knew that there were actually two ruling councils of the Jews, although only one was provided for legally. The Great Sanhedrin was the traditional council called upon to settle religious matters. It could, if it saw fit, impose the legal sentence of death under Jewish law by stoning, subject, of course, to the approval of the Roman governor. The other group had no official status but much power. It dealt mainly with matters of state as they concerned the relationship between the priestly hierarchy and the rule of the Romans. Naturally it was composed of Sadducees, from which the priests came.

"Caiaphas dominates the political Sanhedrin completely," Nicodemus continued. "Even Elias, who is completely honest, believes that peace under Rome and Caiaphas is better than striving for freedom. And of course the merchants, the priests, and the tax gatherers want no change in Judea, so long as Rome leaves them free to enrich themselves."

"Why do you suppose they are so concerned about the report that Jesus had raised the dead?"

Nicodemus shrugged. "You have studied Greek logic, Joseph. Would a mere man be able to bring the dead back to life?"

"No. Only the power of the Most High could do that."

"Then if Jesus had the power to control death, it would mean that he is sent from God."

"And therefore that he is the true Messiah," Joseph agreed thoughtfully. "I can see now why they were so relieved that he did not claim to have raised the girl."

Nicodemus nodded. "Caiaphas wants to stay in power, of course, and so he courts the favor of Pontius Pilate. But he would not dare to oppose the true Messiah, who will come from the Most High."

"The girl may have been in a stupor," Joseph admitted. "Sometimes they come out of such states for no apparent reason, so the case proves nothing."

"To you, perhaps not. But Caiaphas does not want to believe that Jesus of Nazareth is the Christ, so he accepted your evidence readily. The high priest can attribute no good motive to the Nazarene because he dares to tell the people the truth about the priests themselves," Nicodemus continued. "But Caiaphas also knows that the people are following Jesus in great crowds, so he will do nothing himself. I imagine he even hopes that Herod will make another mistake with Jesus, as he did with John the Baptist, for anything Herod does to anger the people also lessens his chances of sitting upon the throne of Judea."

"Should we not warn Jesus about Simon the Zealot?" Joseph suggested. "He may not realize how dangerous a person like that could be."

Nicodemus smiled. "Somehow I think the Nazarene already knows what is in the hearts of the men who follow him, Joseph. On my last visit to Rome I listened to Seneca speak in the Senate. He said something about Diogenes that I have often thought of lately in connection with Jesus:

"'It is worth a kingdom to be, in a world of cheats, murderers, and kidnapers, the only person whom no one can injure.'"

11

LIFE in Jerusalem seemed somehow to have lost its zest for Joseph, and so he was not at all unhappy when a message came several weeks later from Tiberias, asking that he come at once to attend the Lady Claudia Procula. He kept a swift camel in his stables now against the time when Mary might need him, and so he accomplished the journey to Galilee in little more than half the time it would have taken by mule. Although still confined to her bedchamber from a severe attack of asthma followed by a mild lung congestion, Pilate's lady was quite out of danger when he arrived, but he had no difficulty in persuading himself that he should stay in Galilee for a few days to be sure his patient suffered no relapse.

Pontius Pilate was in an evil temper when the young physician saw him that evening. The Procurator was having trouble again with his gouty toe, and while Joseph superintended the application of leeches to it, Pilate fumed against Herod Antipas and the Galileans, and against Jesus of Nazareth in particular for stirring up the excitable people of the lake region. "I would put the *sicarii* upon the Nazarene myself," he stormed, "but then Herod would send word to Rome that I was interfering in his kingdom. Nothing would fit in better with his plans to sit on the throne of Judea himself, with Jonathan as high priest, than to influence the Emperor against me."

"Then you know?" Joseph asked, startled.

"Roman gold can always buy spies." Pilate smiled grimly. "I even know that you appeared before the high priest, Joseph, and tried to convince him that Jesus intends no revolt."

"But I am certain that he does not."

"Good men like you are easily deceived," Pilate said, not unkindly. "How do you explain the presence of men like Simon the Zealot and Judas Iscariot among Jesus' disciples? Judas even controls the moneybags, the most important part of any revolt."

This was exactly the argument Caiaphas had used in Jerusalem, Joseph remembered. And Pilate had known in detail of his interview before the political Sanhedrin, which meant that the relationship between Pilate and the high priest was as close as it was generally believed to be. "Why doesn't Herod arrest Jesus then?" he asked.

"The noble Antipas is suffering the pangs of conscience," Pilate said contemptuously. "They even tell me he thinks he hears in Jesus the spirit of John the Baptist come back to haunt him. What he really wants is for the Nazarene to go to Jerusalem. Then it will be Pontius Pilate who must deal with him. But I have handled Galileans before," he added sharply. "Once I even had to cut down a gang of rebels on the very steps of the temple."

"I heard of it," Joseph admitted as he removed a fat leech and applied a lean one. The occurrence had taken place before he had come to Jerusalem to live. It was but another in the long list of reasons why the Jews hated Pontius Pilate.

"If you would save your Galilean friends from a similar fate," Pilate warned, "you had better remind them of what happened to the others. They will be treated differently in Jerusalem if they ever make the mistake of trying to stir up the people there."

Early the next morning Joseph set out for Magdala to see Mary, but the house was empty and the door barred. From a neighbor he learned that neither Mary nor Hadja had been in Magdala for more than a week.

"Mary of Magdala follows Jesus," the neighbor volunteered. "And he teaches his disciples to take no thought for where they will eat or sleep. But they manage to eat," he continued. "Just last week the Nazarene and his disciples fed five thousand people with a few loaves and fishes."

"Five thousand!" Joseph was startled. Crowds of that size were almost unheard of, even in this populous region. "Did you see this miracle yourself?" he asked.

"Not with my own eyes," his informant admitted. "But it was told to me by one who heard it from lips that tasted the bread and the fish. They say all were satisfied and afterward twelve baskets of broken pieces of bread and fish were gathered up for the poor. Since then his

254

followers have taken to calling themselves the Company of the Fish."

"It was indeed a miracle," Joseph admitted, "if it happened as you were told."

"Every day more and more people tell in the market place of the wonderful things the Nazarene does." The man lowered his voice, as if to tell a secret. "Many say he is the Messiah and that when the time comes people will rise up everywhere and proclaim him king."

He must find Mary soon, Joseph realized, and warn her of what people were saying about Jesus. Talk like this would convince Pilate and Herod even more strongly that the Nazarene was indeed stirring up the people to revolution.

"A man was here several days ago looking for Mary of Magdala." The neighbor's voice intruded in his thoughts. "It was Chuza, one of Herod Antipas' stewards."

Joseph remembered that Mary had mentioned how kind Herod's steward and his wife were to her during her stay in Sepphoris in the household of Gaius Flaccus. If she were still in Galilee, Chuza or his wife might know where she could be found, he thought, and turned his camel toward Sepphoris.

Chuza's house was only a little way from Herod's ornate palace in Sepphoris. He was a small man with quick nervous movements and an air of deep sincerity. His face brightened when Joseph introduced himself. "My wife Joanna and I are very fond of Mary of Magdala," he said. "We have heard her speak of you often."

"I was told in Magdala that you were looking for Mary."

"Yes. My wife went yesterday to warn her."

"To warn her?" Joseph asked, his apprehension rising. "Is she in danger?"

The steward hesitated; then, evidently deciding that he could trust Joseph, he explained: "Herod may act against Jesus at any moment. I hope Mary can persuade the Master to cross over the Jordan into the territory of Philip."

"Do you mean the teacher will be arrested?"

Chuza shook his head. "No prison in Galilee could hold him; the people would tear the very stones from the walls with their bare hands. Herod has been hoping Jesus would go into Pilate's territory, but he is afraid to wait any longer. It is told everywhere that Simon Zelotes and the others will proclaim Jesus king in Galilee any day now, and if Herod lets that happen, the Romans will take over his kingdom."

"I heard the same rumor in Magdala today."

"The stories are true. I know these zealots, Joseph. They would risk anything to free the Jews from Rome."

"But would the people of Galilee follow Jesus if he led them against Herod and Pontius Pilate?"

"I believe they would. Such a rebellion would be like a raging fire, once a spark ignited it. That is why Herod has hired the *sicarii* to kill the Nazarene."

"Can you tell me their plans?" Joseph asked quickly.

Chuza shook his head. "I heard no details, but the simplest way would be to start a riot in the crowd. Then it would be easy for the assassins to kill Jesus during the fighting."

"I will go and warn Mary at once so she can tell Jesus," Joseph decided. "Do you know where I can find her?"

"They were at Capernaum until yesterday," the steward said. "But if Joanna found them, they may already have moved to Bethsaida, in the territory of Philip. Look for the crowds and there you will find Jesus healing the sick and teaching."

Riding northeastward on the Roman Highway, Joseph wondered what would be the outcome of this rapidly developing drama. Now, if ever, it seemed, Jesus of Nazareth must proclaim himself—if he were indeed the Messiah.

12

THE city of Bethsaida—colloquially known as "Fish Town"—was situated on a small bay at the northern end of the Sea of Galilee, to the east of where the cold waters of the Jordan tumbled into the lake. Near Bethsaida the springs of Ain-et-Tabighah poured their water through a Roman aqueduct into the lake, striking the cold stream of the Jordan from the north and setting up a swirling current that brought fish in huge numbers. As he rode along, Joseph could see them leaping in great schools that made the very water seem alive. Fishing boats swarmed to this region, and sometimes the fishermen could barely haul in their nets, so heavily were they loaded with fish. Oddly enough, however, he saw few boats upon the water today.

Just beyond Capernaum, where the road to Damascus turned northward toward the snowy cap of Mount Hermon and the Ford of the Daughters of Jacob, stood the customhouse marking the boundary between the tetrarchies of Herod Antipas and his brother Philip. Joseph carried nothing on which a duty should be paid and so he was allowed to pass through and continue on toward Bethsaida.

Chuza had been right, he saw, in saying he would have no trouble finding Jesus for he came upon the edge of the crowd while still about a mile from Bethsaida. Looking over the heads of the people as his camel moved slowly along, Joseph was impressed by the variety of faces that made up the crowd. Jews thronged everywhere, of course, most of them the strong, vigorous peasant stock of Galilee. But here and there the lean ascetic faces of Pharisees and scribes from the more educated levels could be seen along with merchants, artisans, fishermen, travelers, Romans in togas or in military uniform, Bedouins from the deserts to the south and east, Syrians from the region of Antioch to the north, a few swarthy Egyptians from the caravans that passed nearby on the Via Maris, Persians, Phoenicians, and even an occasional Nubian, far removed now from the shores of Africa. This was almost as cosmopolitan a group as would have been found on the quays of Alexandria, and the row of boats drawn up on the shore side by side told him why there had been so few upon the water.

As always wherever Jesus went, the sick made up a substantial part of the crowd. Beggars crawled along in the dirt, their hideous, oozing sores caked with filth. Men with joints drawn by the inflammations of rheumatism hobbled along on sticks or rude crutches. Some, unable to walk, were carried by their families on improvised litters. The blind led each other, bumping into those who could see, and these, in turn, cursed them and shoved them rudely away.

To one side a small group occupied a little open space

of their own in the crowd. Their very isolation would have betrayed the nature of their unclean disease, had not withered limbs, fingerless hands, and gaping face wounds exposing open nostrils named it even more certainly. Word had gone out that Jesus healed lepers, and every one for miles around now followed him, hoping for his touch. A little way beyond the lepers another group carried a man bound hand and foot, cursing and slobbering with insane fury as he fought against the bonds protecting the crowd from his ragings. Women with all manner of infirmities dragged themselves through the crowd, some marble-pale from the issue of blood, some hiding with dirty cloths the stinking cancers that ate into their bodies.

The whining of beggars, the screams of pain from those jostled unmercifully in the crowd, and the babbling of the insane made a harsh cacophony of sound, equaling in its repulsiveness and horror the very sores of the lepers. Looking at the mass of miserable, suffering, cursing, and pleading humanity that made up at least half of the crowd, Joseph could understand why Pontius Pilate, naturally intolerant of people like this, could have come almost to hate the man whose followers cluttered up good Roman roads. Such things violated every sense of order that came so naturally to the military mind. Particularly galling to Pilate would be the knowledge that his wife, a Roman patrician with the blood of emperors in her veins, also secretly believed the teachings of this carpenter of Nazareth.

As he rested his camel in the press of the crowd, Joseph could easily see Jesus, for the teacher sat on a small outcropping of rock above the shore that formed something of a natural pulpit. Mary was not visible, nor was Simon Peter, but Hadja stood near him. A group of Pharisees, distinguishable by manner quite as much as by dress, were gathered around Jesus. "Will you give us a sign, good teacher?" Joseph heard one of the Pharisees ask. "A sign from heaven to show that the Most High has endowed you as his prophet?"

Jesus raised his head, and Joseph was shocked by the change in him since the day he had first seen the Nazarene before Mary's house. His body and his spirit seemed bowed down as if by a great sorrow or disappointment. Yet Joseph could not understand why, for never before had he seen so great a crowd in Galilee. It must be, he thought, even greater than the five thousand whom

Jesus was said to have fed with a few loaves and fishes.

When Jesus did not answer immediately, the Pharisee who was questioning him said insistently, "The prophets of olden time gave us signs. Moses brought forth water from the rock and fed the children of Israel upon manna from heaven."

"Why does this generation seek for a sign?" Jesus said quietly then. "Truly I say to you no sign shall be given to this generation."

Another group of Pharisees had been working their way through the crowd, and now they approached the rock where Jesus sat. "Get away from here," one of them said loudly, "for Herod wants to kill you."

A deep growl of anger came from the crowd, but Jesus raised his hand and it subsided. "Go and tell that fox," he said to them, "behold, I cast out demons and perform cures today and tomorrow, and the third day I finish my course. Nevertheless, I must go on my way today and tomorrow and the day following; for it cannot be that a prophet should perish away from Jerusalem." Then his voice changed and became a cry of anguish. "O Jerusalem, Jerusalem! Killing the prophets and stoning those who are sent to you! How often would I have gathered your children together, as a hen gathers her brood under her wings, and you would not! Behold your house is forsaken! And I tell you, you will not see me until you say, *'Blessed is he who comes in the name of the Lord.'* "

Joseph was startled by Jesus' impassioned cry. Just so, he thought in a flash of inspiration, might the true Son of God, the Expected One, have spoken if he had come to lead the Jews and been rejected by their rulers, as he was indeed being rejected now by the scribes and Pharisees who questioned him everywhere he went, seeking to ferret from him some statement in violation of the law. For the first time Joseph's conviction that Jesus could not be the Messiah was severely shaken. Moved by a sudden impulse, he got down from his camel and started to push through the crowd, hoping to reach Jesus himself and ask him a direct question which must reveal the truth.

Just then, however, Jesus stood up, as if impatient with the righteousness of the Pharisees and their endless demands for signs. The crowd parted before him as he went down to the water's edge. Only when he stepped into one of the boats drawn up there on the shore did they realize that he was leaving, and they began to howl angrily for him to remain and perform his miracles of healing. Some of them even tried to seize the boat and hold it back, but the boatmen leaped aboard and pushed it into deeper water with their oars. Hoisting the sails, they moved away toward Bethsaida.

The crowd was in an ugly mood. The sick who had not been able to get close to the Nazarene cursed and grumbled, and the well, their movements obstructed by the slow-moving sick, pushed and struck those around them. Sporadic fights broke out, and the people milled about aimlessly, grumbling and even cursing the teacher himself.

What had happened? Joseph wondered. Jesus' sadness, the disappointment that he made no attempt to hide, and now the petulance of the crowds who had followed him blindly before—all of this seemed to signify a change of some sort. Logic asserted that it was only the natural dissatisfaction of the people with one whom they expected to perform miracles and heal all who came to him if he did not do so. But did the refusal of Jesus to give the Pharisees a sign mean that he did not possess the power? Or did he possess it, as he must if he were truly the Expected One, yet for some reason of his own refuse to use it?

Hadja spied Joseph with his camel and came over to greet him. "What brings you to Galilee again so soon?" he asked.

"The Lady Claudia Procula was ill and sent for me."

"We heard of it. Mary has prayed for her recovery daily."

Joseph looked at him in surprise. "Why do you not still call her the Living Flame?"

"The one called the Living Flame was another person," Hadja explained simply. "Now she is only Mary of Magdala, one of the women who serve Jesus."

"Chuza told me she is chief among the women now."

"It is true. Perhaps because she loves him more than the others."

For a moment Joseph felt a spasm of jealousy toward the Nazarene teacher. But he put it from his heart at once, for he knew that Mary's love for him and her love for Jesus were two different emotions. One was the love of a woman for the man to whom she is betrothed, the other that love which a person gives only to God.

"We are camped in the hills just back of Bethsaida,"

Hadja said. "Mary will be glad to see you." The crowd had thinned out somewhat, and they were able to walk along the road that led eastward to the city.

"I have come to warn you that Herod is plotting to kill Jesus," Joseph told the Nabatean. "But the Pharisees who spoke just now were before me."

"We know Herod has hired the *sicarii*," Hadja admitted. "That is one reason why we came into the kingdom of Philip. I now stay close to Jesus always when he is teaching," he added grimly, "with my knife ready at my belt."

Hadja guided Joseph up into the hills above Bethsaida. As they walked along they could see below them the boat in which Jesus had left the shore, sailing on past the town. Soon they approached a small building around which a number of goatskin tents had been pitched. Several women were working at the outdoor ovens back of the house, but none of them had Mary's red hair. "She may have gone into the city for something," Hadja suggested. "I will go and ask the women."

Joseph had seen many camps like this outside the towns through which the caravans passed. People usually traveled in groups on the highroads of this turbulent land, joining together for protection against the thieves and brigands who infected the hilly country. The leader and his own family would sleep in the house, which they might have rented for the short period of their stay, while the others slept in the tents in winter or on the ground in summer, wrapped in skins and woven coverlets or rugs, for it was chilly on winter mornings and even on summer nights the air became cool before morning.

Suddenly the voices of several people talking together reached Joseph's ears from the small building near which he stood. He recognized the booming tones of Simon and moved closer, sure that his old friend from Capernaum would be glad to welcome him. Just outside the door, however, he stopped, for he realized that the men inside were quarreling.

"I say proclaim him king tomorrow," a deep, angry voice said. "Philip is weak and will not oppose us. Before he knows what has happened, we will have gathered enough of a force to descend on Galilee and take it by storm."

"But if the Master refuses?" Simon asked.

"Can he refuse to be king in Israel when we set the crown upon his head?" the deep voice said.

"I tell you, Jesus does not want to be king." Joseph started, for it was Mary's voice. "Can't you even try to understand his purpose?"

"He must be king," the deep voice said positively. "Is it not written in the Psalms of Solomon:

"Behold, O Lord, and raise up to them
    their king, the son of David,
At the time in which thou seest, O Lord,
    that he may reign over Israel, thy servant.
And guide him with strength that he
    may shatter unrighteous rulers.
And that he may purge Jerusalem from
    the nations that trample her down to destruction.
With a rod of iron he shall break in pieces
    all their substance.
And shall destroy the godless nations, with
    the word of his mouth."

"It would seem that we do have the promise of the Most High that Jesus shall be king," Simon admitted.

Joseph had realized by now that he was eavesdropping upon a plan to force Jesus into becoming king in Galilee, preparatory, no doubt, to marching upon Jerusalem itself. He knew that, as an outsider, he had no right to listen. But Mary was in there, and what concerned her, he told himself, concerned him.

"It would seem," the deep voice parroted sarcastically. "Is your faith so small, Simon, that you doubt Jesus is the Messiah?"

"No man can name me disloyal to the Master," the fisherman shouted angrily. But before he could go on, Mary said firmly, "Simon called Peter followed Jesus long before Simon the Zealot. Neither of you have a right to settle this. The Master himself must decide."

"But he has said he will go into Tyre," the man called the Zealot objected. "It would be disastrous to leave Galilee now. The people are ready to crown him king."

Suddenly Joseph felt an iron hand grip his shoulder. At the same moment the sharp point of a dagger penetrated his robe and pricked the skin. "Make no move," a harsh voice ordered.

He could not see his captor, nor did he dare cry out to

Simon Peter and Mary inside the house, lest the man who held the dagger plunge it into his back. "Who sent you?" the harsh voice asked. "Herod Antipas?"

"My name is Joseph of Galilee," the young physician managed to stammer.

"You are of the *sicarii*. Else why would you listen when honest men speak among themselves?"

"Take me into the building," Joseph begged. "Mary of Magdala and Simon Peter know me well."

"Walk, then," his captor directed. "But make no false move."

When they went through the door Joseph got a glimpse of the man who held the dagger. He was a Jew, and tall, with prominent cheekbones, a jutting beak of a nose, burning eyes, and hair already turning a little gray at the temples. It was not a face easily forgotten, especially when met under these circumstances.

Mary was the first to see them and moved quickly to seize the tall man's arm. "Put up your dagger, Judas of Kerioth!" she cried indignantly. "Joseph is my betrothed and a friend to all of us."

Simon stared at them in amazement, but it was to the other man that Joseph's eyes turned. The man called the Zealot, or "Zelotes," no doubt to distinguish him from Simon the fisherman, was short and thickset, with broad shoulders and long arms. His neck was short and his head small, giving him an oddly formidable appearance. He got to his feet now with a muttered curse. "What is this, Judas?" he demanded.

The man Mary had called Judas of Kerioth sheathed his dagger reluctantly. "I found him listening outside the door," he explained.

"Then he heard everything we were saying," Zelotes growled. "Are you the Joseph of Galilee who is *medicus viscerus* for the temple and a friend of Pontius Pilate?"

"Joseph does not eavesdrop upon other people's conversations," Mary cried indignantly. "He can explain anything he was doing."

"Hadja and I had come from where Jesus was teaching by the lake," Joseph explained. "He went looking for you, Mary, but I heard yours and Simon's voices from this building and started over to speak to you. When I realized that you were talking to someone else I didn't come in."

"But you remained outside where you could hear,"

Simon Zelotes pointed out. He turned to the other Simon. "What if he goes to Pontius Pilate?"

"Joseph is no informer," Mary insisted. "But I almost wish he were. What you are plotting is evil. The Master will tell you what to do; you will not tell him."

"I have known Joseph of Galilee for a long time," Simon Peter agreed. "If he has heard anything he should not and we ask him to keep it to himself, he will do so."

"Whatever I heard will be told to no one," Joseph said. "I swear it by my honor as a physician."

Grudgingly the other two men accepted Joseph's word, but he knew that their suspicions were not entirely allayed. Judas of Kerioth was also known, he learned, as Judas Iscariot. Both he and Simon Zelotes belonged to the group of Galilean fanatics called Zealots, many of whom had been with that other Judas, the Gaulonite, who had brought down the wrath of Rome upon the city of Sepphoris. Joseph wondered if he should reveal to them that Pontius Pilate knew their intentions already, but decided that to do so would only increase their suspicions of him. Perhaps Mary might be able to convince Jesus that he should not follow them upon what must inevitably be a foolhardy course. And yet he was somehow sure the gentle carpenter of Nazareth was quite able to take care of himself.

13

THE camp was filled with tension that night. Judas and Simon Zelotes were waiting for Jesus to return to urge upon him their projected uprising, and Simon Peter was of more than half a mind to support them. Then a thunderbolt struck. James and John, the sons of Zebedee, returned from Bethsaida with news that their leader had sent them back and had gone up into the hills to pray. And they also revealed that the teacher was adamant in his decision to leave Galilee at once and go into the region of Tyre, near the seacoast.

When the evening meal was over the others went away

for a conference on this new development, but Simon remained behind for a while with Joseph and Mary.

"I saw Jesus on the shore this afternoon," Joseph said. "What has happened to him? He seemed to be sad."

"He is disappointed because his disciples do not understand him," Mary said promptly. "They think in terms of earthly kingdoms, but Jesus wants only to change men's hearts."

"But he is the Christ," Simon insisted. "The Messiah sent from God to free the Jews from oppression."

"What proof do you have, Simon, that Jesus is really the Expected One?" Joseph asked.

"What proof do I need save his own words?"

"He told you that himself?"

Simon nodded. "It was here at Bethsaida some time ago. Jesus asked us, 'Who do you say that I am?' And I answered, 'The Christ, of God.' Then he commanded us to tell this to no one."

"Why did you say just that?" Joseph asked.

"It was something I knew," Simon said simply, "like I know that I am sitting here with you and Mary tonight."

"I feel it too, Joseph," Mary said. "The very first time I saw him, I knew who he was in my heart."

"But if Jesus is really the Messiah," Joseph protested, "why does he not announce it publicly?"

"Until now the time had not come," Simon explained. "But we are ready. If the Master had not left us, we would proclaim him king and march on Sepphoris and Tiberias tomorrow. Jerusalem would be next, and then the Anointed of God would reign over all of Israel."

"Then you think Jesus really plans to establish an earthly kingdom?"

"Why else would the Messiah come?" Simon looked at him in astonishment. "Is it not written that he will free the Jews from bondage and set them over all the people of the world?"

"But the soldiers of Rome—"

Simon stood up, his face suddenly flushed with anger. "Take care, Joseph," he warned. "When you say the power of the Most High cannot prevail over any earthly power, even Rome, you blaspheme against God." And without waiting for an answer, he stalked from the room.

Joseph started to rise and follow Simon, but Mary put her hand on his arm. "You can't argue with him," she said. "He and Simon Zelotes and Judas Iscariot and the sons of Zebedee think of nothing but setting up an earthly kingdom."

"I know you don't agree. Why?"

"The Pharisees once questioned Jesus about when the kingdom of God would come. He told them, 'The kingdom of God is not coming with signs to be observed. Nor will they say: Lo! Here it is! Or, There! For, behold, the kingdom of God is in the midst of you.' The message of Jesus is not for our eyes or our ears, Joseph," she said. "It is for our hearts."

He was tempted by her calm conviction and his love for her to agree. And yet the man he had heard speak from the rocks beside the shore that afternoon was utterly different from what he had been taught since childhood to expect of the liberator who would be known as the Christ.

"Come walk with me by the shore, Joseph," Mary said, getting to her feet. "Jesus may return later. If he does, I must be here to wash his feet and anoint his head with oil and see that a fresh robe is ready for him in the morning, but we can have a little time together until he comes."

The moon had already risen above the precipitous hills to the east where lay the Greek cities of the Decapolis. A broad band of silver lay upon the water, broken occasionally by thousands of tiny wavelets when a fish leaped to shatter the mirror-smooth surface. Joseph took Mary's hand and they walked along the shore close together both in body and mood.

"Do you remember when we last talked by the water?" she asked.

"It was at Alexandria by Lake Mareotis, in the garden of your villa."

"You tried to persuade me then not to kill Gaius Flaccus." She lifted his hand and put it to her lips. "Dear, good Joseph," she said softly. "If I had only listened . . ."

"You could have been one of the richest women in the world."

"But then I might not have known Jesus."

"Is knowing him worth giving up everything you might have had?"

"If I were as rich now as I was in Alexandria," she said simply, "I would still give all of it in exchange for the privilege of serving Jesus. Deep down inside me, in my very soul, I know this is what I was intended for."

"Teach me to know Jesus as you do, Mary," he begged

impulsively, but she shook her head. "I can only show you the way to see for yourself, Joseph. Today you are like those of whom Isaiah said, '*You shall indeed hear, but never understand.*' Perhaps only a woman can really understand the inner heart of Jesus," she continued. "The love he has for the world is like that of a mother for her child, a thing that all women feel inside them." She turned her eyes to the hills back of Bethsaida. "Somewhere up there he is alone, Joseph, praying to his Father that men's eyes shall be opened, so they can see him for what he is. So many look to him only to be healed, and the Pharisees seek a sign from heaven, while Simon the Zealot and Judas only see him leading the Jews to triumph over Rome. None of them seem able to realize that through believing and following Jesus their very hearts can be changed until they see the glory of the Most High here on earth itself."

"Then he has failed in his mission?"

"No, Joseph. The Messiah cannot fail, but those he loves have failed him. His family name him a madman and would shut him away. His disciples—even Simon Peter, whom he loves more than the others—can think of him only as an earthly king. And Pontius Pilate and Herod Antipas call him a criminal but dare not arrest him because they fear the consequences."

"What can he do then, except go away?"

"I don't know," Mary admitted. "But I am sure he has come to some sort of decision and that our going away from Galilee at this time is a part of it. He told us not so long ago, 'The Son of Man must suffer many things, and be rejected by the elders and chief priests and scribes, and be killed, and on the third day be raised.'"

"What sort of man prophesies his own death?" Joseph asked incredulously.

"Who could prophesy it? Who else but the Son of God."

Jesus did not return to the camp that night, and early the next morning a messenger came from him bidding the others follow along the road to Tyre. Joseph watched them break camp and start the march northward. Judas, the two Simons, and the sons of Zebedee were angry, but they could do nothing except obey the command of their leader. To proclaim a king when there was no king to crown would have been worse than folly.

Joseph bade Mary good-by and turned his camel toward Capernaum and the road to Jerusalem. He had not gone far when he noticed that he was being followed. Obviously Simon Zelotes and Judas of Kerioth were taking no chances that their plans would be betrayed to Herod Antipas or Pontius Pilate.

All that morning the Zealot rode behind Joseph. Only when he was well into the Plain of Esdraelon on the Central Highway and past Sepphoris, did the other man stop. Watching the distant figure sitting his mule on a little hill where he could see him on the road, Joseph thought with a sudden flash of insight that Simon and the rest of the band of revolutionaries called the Zealots were a far greater threat to Jesus of Nazareth and the seed he was trying to implant into the hearts of men than Herod or Pilate could ever be.

14

WINTER was a busy time for a physician in Jerusalem and particularly for the *medicus viscerus* of the temple. The stone floors of the great sanctuary were cold and damp, and the feet and legs of the priests, usually corpulent men addicted to feasting, often swelled and cracked open. This condition, known colloquially as "temple foot" or "priest's foot," was an exceedingly painful one. Joseph had been outstandingly successful in treating it with snug bandages and soothing balms, but the bandaging took time and had to be replaced often, so he spent long hours in the quarters of the priests. The winter climate in Jerusalem was damp and raw much of the time, too, and there was much sickness in the city, particularly among the pilgrims who came here from warmer climates and were ill dressed for the weather.

Joseph thought of Mary often but had little news from her. From information picked up by Nicodemus on his travels about the country, it appeared that Jesus was avoiding Galilee, perhaps fearing that a return to the site of his more successful ventures would cause the revolutionary spirit of his disciples and the people who followed him to flare up anew.

A devout Jew, Joseph had always viewed the temple as a symbol of everything sublime in the worship of the Most High, a holy place dedicated to a holy purpose. But now he began to see things which, in his concern with the higher principles of God's worship, he had never noticed before.

The booths of those who sold animals, spices, and other precious objects to be offered as sacrifices to the Most High were, he knew, a necessary and natural part of the temple worship. But now he saw the cheating that went on. A tender and pure lamb sold this morning to a pilgrim of Cyprus and delivered over to the priests to be killed and burnt upon the altar often appeared in the same seller's stall that very afternoon, while a mangy animal costing less than a third as much as the pilgrim paid was killed in its stead.

The lower court of the temple swarmed with peddlers selling all kinds of curios to the pilgrims who thronged here. And since only temple shekels could be given as offerings, the money-changers did a thriving business turning money from the hundreds of cities of the Empire into approved coin, at a tremendous profit to the changer. Daily Joseph saw messengers from synagogues of Israel in far-distant cities of the Empire pour into the temple, bringing the "tribute" required of all Jews, which they were happy to pay as their duty to God. But while the priests lived in magnificence and luxury, the poor who had scraped up their last denarius for the temple tribute went hungry and often without shelter. And meanwhile the priestly hierarchy grew richer and richer every year.

In moments of self-examination—which his profession gave him all too infrequently—Joseph admitted to himself that there had been no change in the temple and its practices. These injustices had been going on for centuries. What had happened was a change within himself, a new vision that let him see through the outward gloss to the pettiness beneath, the outright thievery masking under the guise of worship, and the constant political plotting among the Sadducean groups who controlled the temple and therefore the religious life of Israel.

Nor were the Pharisees really any better, he saw now, although he had always prided himself upon belonging to

269

that select group. In their pettiness over details they had completely lost sight of the fact that the individual man was important in the sight of God.

"What is man, that thou art mindful of him?" the Psalmist had asked. And then had gone on to say, "Thou hast made him a little lower than the angels." Now Joseph knew what it was that appealed to people so much in the teachings of Jesus. It was the act that the Nazarene brought to them an assurance that the Most High loved each of them as individuals. There could be no greater assurance of his concern for the individual than the words of Jesus: "Are not five sparrows sold for two pennies? And not one of them is forgotten before God. Why, even the hairs of your head are all numbered. Fear not; you are of more value than many sparrows."

What a comfort such an assurance of the love of God for every man was to people bowed under the burden of the law that the Pharisees worshiped so devoutly. It was easy to understand now why they would follow one who assured them of the forgiveness of their sins and the concern of the Father for each of them.

More and more as the months wore on, Joseph was tempted to leave all this sham and pretense, the thievery, gluttony, and luxury in the guise of the worship of God that characterized Jerusalem and the temple. If he had thought Mary would join him, he would gladly have given up his successful career and returned to Magdala to live with her. And the more he thought of the quiet garden at Demetrius' old house overlooking the lake and Mary's happy voice singing there, the more he was convinced that only in Galilee would he find the peace he seemed to need more and more.

Nicodemus returned from one of his trips late one afternoon in midwinter. Joseph had just come home from visiting the sick, and when he saw his friend's retinue before the house he hurried over to greet the lawyer. "I traveled fast so as to reach Jerusalem before nightfall," Nicodemus said, embracing Joseph, "for I bring bad news."

Joseph caught his breath. "About Mary?"

"No. She was well when I saw her last. Jesus is on his way to Jerusalem, Joseph." Nicodemus' face was grave. "He is walking directly into the hands of Pontius Pilate and Caiaphas."

"But I thought he was still in Tyre."

"He left there several weeks ago and traveled through Galilee without attracting the attention of the crowds."

"Did Herod Antipas know he was in Galilee?"

"He may have. But Jesus was careful not to stir up the people, and Herod may have been content to let him pass."

"Did you see him yourself?"

"Yes, I came upon the Company of the Fish, as they call themselves now, by accident at Tarichae, at the south end of the lake. Jesus was starting down the valley road with his disciples. Your betrothed was with them and sent you her love. She hopes to see you here within a few days."

Joseph felt a warm glow of happiness rise within him at the thought of being with Mary again.

"I listened to Jesus teach for a while," Nicodemus continued. "And when he stopped, something made me ask him, 'Good teacher, what must I do to inherit eternal life?' "

"What did he say?"

"He just looked at me for a moment," Nicodemus said. "And then he asked, 'Why do you call me good? No one is good but God alone. You know the commandments: Do not kill. Do not commit adultery. Do not steal. Do not bear false witness. Do not defraud. Honor your father and mother.' Then I said to Jesus, 'Teacher, all these I have observed from my youth.' "

"That is true," Joseph said loyally. "There is no more pious man than you in all Judea."

"The strangest thing happened then," his friend said. "I felt Jesus' love for me, as if it were an arm put about my shoulders to support me, or the hand of God reached out to me. 'You lack one thing,' he said to me. 'Go, sell all that you have, and give it to the poor, and you will have treasure in heaven; and come, follow me.' I wanted to follow him, Joseph," Nicodemus said earnestly. "I wanted it more than I have ever wanted anything in my life. But my riches were like fetters about my ankles, holding me back."

"Did you see him any more?"

The lawyer shook his head. "No. I had to come back by way of Sepphoris to finish up some business with Herod's stewards. But all the way back to Jerusalem I kept thinking about what he said and the way his love encompassed me." He stopped and took a deep breath. "I've made my decision, Joseph. I am going to do it."

"You are going to sell all this?" Joseph asked incredulously.

"Yes. An accounting will be made of everything I possess. When it is finished, I will sell and give all to the poor. If Jesus will take me then, I shall become one of his disciples."

"But you are a rich man," Joseph protested. "You employ many people and give much to the poor. Who will defend the poor without pay in the courts of law if you leave Jerusalem?"

"None of that is important now that I know the truth," Nicodemus said earnestly.

"The truth?" Joseph frowned. "What do you mean?"

"Jesus is the Messiah, Joseph. I am convinced of it now."

15

THE more Joseph thought about his talk with Nicodemus, the more certain he became that he should warn Simon Peter and the others about the dangers inherent in their coming to Jerusalem. The people of the capital city were not like the Galileans, fired by a patriotic nationalism which could burn more strongly than caution. Long accustomed to being ruled by Rome, and profiting by that rule, the Judeans would not easily be stirred up against the Roman masters from whom they made an excellent living. Nor would the priests wish to disturb the temple worship, except to welcome the true Messiah, which they certainly did not consider Jesus of Nazareth to be.

All in all, Joseph was sure that a visit by the Nazarene to Jerusalem could mean nothing but trouble, so he decided to leave the next morning and travel eastward toward the Valley Highway, hoping to meet the Company of the Fish and perhaps persuade them not to come to Judea.

The road to the Jordan from Jerusalem led northeastward to Jericho. It was still before noon when Joseph's swift camel pushed into the resort city. A mere village before Herod the Great had transformed it into a popular watering place, Jericho had now been taken over largely by the Romans as a winter resort. Herod had erected a winter palace here and brought to it the healing waters of the hot springs at Callirhoe near the Dead Sea by means of an aqueduct. A large theater, public markets, and the inevitable forum betrayed the Roman influence, and the streets were always crowded with people of widely different nationalities.

Joseph paused only to munch bread and dates and cheese from a pack he carried and to find water for his camel and himself before pushing on northward along the road that paralleled the Jordan. He had not gone far before he saw a group of people beside the road in a little glen. The presence of large numbers of sick and demented would have told him he had found those he sought, even if he had not seen Jesus himself in the center of the group and spied among the women a graceful figure whose hair, glowing like fire in the midday sunlight, could belong only to Mary of Magdala.

Tying his camel to a tree at the edge of the crowd, Joseph made his way to where Mary was standing. She kissed his cheek and took his hand but put her fingers to her lips, warning him to be silent, for Jesus was speaking. The lesson was soon finished, and when the crowd began to disperse, the teacher came over with his disciples for the food that Mary and the others had prepared.

Joseph had never been so close to Jesus before, except that day before Mary's house when he had fought his way through the crowd to try to help her. As he waited with the women, he studied the man of Nazareth. Once, when he raised his eyes, Joseph found himself looking directly into the eyes of Jesus, and suddenly he felt the same thing that Nicodemus had described to him, a feeling as if a loving and protecting arm had been put around his shoulders. It was a strange feeling, this sudden sense of peace and certainty that came over him, one he did not remember feeling since he had been a child in Galilee years ago and his father had spoken approvingly of something he had done.

When he finished eating, Jesus stood up and walked to the edge of the glen, where the road to Jericho passed. And as Simon Peter and the others followed, he turned and spoke to them.

"Behold," he said, "we are going up to Jerusalem; and the Son of Man will be delivered to the chief priests and the scribes, and they will condemn him to death, and deliver him to the Gentiles; and they will mock him and spit upon him, and scourge him, and kill him; and after three days he will rise."

Just then James and John, the sons of Zebedee, pushed forward importantly. "Teacher," James said, "we want you to do for us whatever we ask of you."

"What do you want me to do for you?" Jesus asked.

"Grant us to sit," James said promptly, "one at your right hand and one at your left, in your glory."

Jesus raised his head. "You do not know what you are asking," he said quietly. "Are you able to drink the cup that I drink, or be baptized with the baptism with which I am baptized?"

"We are able," the sons of Zebedee said in chorus.

"The cup that I drink you will drink," Jesus promised them. "And with the baptism with which I am baptized, you will be baptized. But to sit at my right hand or at my left is not mine to grant; it is for those for whom it has been prepared."

A murmur of anger arose from the other disciples, who resented the preferred position which John and James had always claimed because they were among the earliest followers of Jesus. But before anyone could speak out against them he said reprovingly, "You know that those who are supposed to rule over the Gentiles lord it over them, and their great men exercise authority over them. But it shall not be so among you. Whoever would be great among you must be your servant. For the Son of Man came not to be served but to serve, and to give his life as a ransom for many." He turned then and went on toward Jericho.

Joseph walked along with Mary, letting Hadja load as much of the tents and cooking gear as he wished upon the camel. "Why did you come, Joseph?" Mary asked. "I sent word by your friend Nicodemus that I would see you in a few days."

"I want you to tell Jesus that there may be trouble if he goes to Jerusalem," he explained.

"Why didn't you tell him just now? I saw you looking at him."

"Something happened to me back there. I felt as if Jesus had reached out and put his arm about me, although he was at least twenty paces away, and then I seemed to forget about everything else for a moment."

"Joseph!" Mary cried, her eyes shining. "I had been hoping this would happen. Now you know what he means to those of us who love him."

"I do feel somehow different, perhaps closer to him," Joseph admitted. "But if he is really the Messiah, should I not have recognized it suddenly, like a burst of light?"

"The recognition of Jesus comes to each of us in a different way," Mary said quietly. She looked over the crowd walking along behind Jesus, chattering, grumbling, and quarreling, and added sadly, "To some it never comes."

"Don't they understand him any better yet?"

Mary shook her head. "Simon Zelotes and Judas keep them stirred up all the time. They can think of nothing but an earthly kingdom."

"Do they still expect to crown Jesus king in Jerusalem itself?"

"Yes. And most of the others believe it now."

"But Jesus must know what they think. Why does he not teach them differently?"

"I think he has decided there is only one way to make people understand why he came into the world," she explained. "You heard him just now; he has said the same thing several times before."

"But why is he going to Jerusalem if he knows it may cost him his life?"

"Don't you see?" she said. "Jesus is willing to die if it means that people can be shown the way to God again only through his death."

Joseph remembered the things he had observed in the temple and Jerusalem the last few months since his eyes seemed to have been opened. The Jews had indeed moved far away from God in their emphasis upon form

275

and ritual and upon the worship of the law itself instead of the Most High, Who had made both man and those laws. "Then I came here to no avail," he admitted sadly.

"What happened to you there in the glen today is more important than whether or not you were able to warn Jesus," Mary said quickly. "It means that you and I can live together in life and after death, even through all eternity—with him."

Jesus and his party spent that night in Jericho, and in the morning they set out again toward Jerusalem, now only about fifteen miles away. Just outside Jericho a man who had been sitting quietly beside the gate, with a stick in his hand such as blind men carried to tap themselves on their way, called out, "Jesus, Son of David. Have mercy on me!"

"What do you want me to do for you?" Jesus asked him.

"Master," he begged, "let me receive my sight." And Jesus said, "Go your way; your faith has made you well."

For a moment the blind man seemed not to understand, then he dropped to his knees on the ground, crying, "I see, I see! Blessed is the name of him who comes in the name of the Most High!"

The people began to crowd around him, eager to see this miracle, for many of them were from Jericho and knew the man, but Jesus stepped around them and went on his way toward Jerusalem.

"Stay back and look at him closer if you wish, Joseph," Mary suggested. "You can easily catch us on the road."

Joseph did indeed want to examine this seeming miracle more closely. When the people around the once-blind man moved away, he said, "I am a physician. Can you tell me anything about how you were cured just now?"

The beggar stood up. He seemed to gain stature and no longer groveled. "Are you one of the Pharisees who doubt everything done by Jesus of Nazareth?" he demanded suspiciously.

"I too love Jesus," Joseph explained. "But there will be those in Jerusalem who will ask me, 'What cures have you seen the teacher perform?' and I would like to answer them for certain."

"Tell them the truth then, that Bartimaeus, the son of Timaeus, received his sight again. All who pass this way between Jericho and Jerusalem know me."

"Then you were not blind from birth?"

"Ten years ago, in a time of great sinfulness on my part, the Most High struck me blind as a punishment for my sins. Today, when I heard that the Expected One was passing, I knew he could heal me if he would. And so I shouted, 'Son of David, have mercy on me!' You heard what he said then?"

"He told you your faith had made you well."

"It was as if scales had fallen from my eyes, and suddenly I was able to see."

"And you can tell me no more?"

"What more is there to say? Jesus has healed me, and I will follow him to the end of the world. Are you going with him to Jerusalem?"

"Yes."

"Then we will walk along together, for I am no longer sure of the way. It has been ten years since I have seen this road."

Bartimaeus was unable to travel fast, and so Jesus and his party were almost to Jerusalem by the time they caught up with them. From Bethpage and Bethany, suburbs of the temple city itself, a great mass of people had come out to meet him, and his entry into the city was a triumphal procession.

Joseph made his way with difficulty through the crowd, but Mary saw him coming and ran to seize his hands. Her eyes were shining. "The people know him, Joseph!" she cried. "God has shown the people of Jerusalem who he is."

Joseph could not help being infected by the enthusiasm and the ecstasy which gripped the rest of them. Simon the Zealot marched along with a broad satisfied smile on his face, as if this were the culmination of what he had planned. And even Judas Iscariot, who was rarely known to smile, seemed happy at their reception.

Simon Peter saw Joseph and strode through the crowd to slap him on the back. "Your doubts were needless, Joseph," he cried, "just as I told you they would be." He threw up his arms, and his voice rolled out across the crowd. "Listen, ye people of Jerusalem," he shouted. "Listen to the words of the prophet Zechariah:

"*Rejoice greatly, O daughter of Zion! Shout, O daughter of Jerusalem! Behold thy king cometh unto*

277

thee! He is just and having salvation; lowly and riding upon an ass, and upon a colt, the foal of an ass.

"And I will cut off the chariot from Ephraim, and the horse from Jerusalem, and the battle bow shall be cut off: And he shall speak peace unto the heathen: and his dominion shall be from sea even to sea, and from the river even to the ends of the earth."

There was an instant of silence before the meaning of the prophecy struck the minds of the crowd. Then they understood that Simon Peter was proclaiming Jesus the Expected One, the Messiah predicted by the prophets, who would lead Israel to dominion over all the people of the earth. And when Simon the Zealot shouted, "Hosanna! to the Son of David! Blessed is he who comes in the name of the Lord!" the crowd took up the cry in a mighty roar of exultation.

Thus, in triumph, did Jesus of Nazareth enter Jerusalem.

16

NICODEMUS and Joseph both turned over their houses and estates to Jesus and his followers, but the Master preferred to stay in Bethany, on the outskirts of the city. In the days that followed, it did seem that the successes in Galilee were repeating themselves.

On the morning after his entry into the city Jesus went to the temple and taught from Solomon's Porch, which was reserved for teachers and their students. But whereas the other teachers were surrounded daily by a set group of devoted adherents, those who came to hear Jesus overflowed the porch and the steps of the lower terrace, spilling out into the streets. And as always the sick outnumbered the well.

During the hours that he taught, all temple functions were forced to come to a halt, for the crowd was so great that pilgrims could not pass in and out of the temple.

The flow of money died to a mere trickle, and when the high priest appeared to inspect the gathering hardly anyone noticed him. To a man like Caiaphas, this was the ultimate insult, an even greater one than that a lowly Nazarene dared to usurp the place of Jerusalem's most famous exponents of the law.

As they had in Galilee, the priests, Pharisees, and scribes gathered around Jesus seeking to trap him. "By what authority are you doing these things and who gave you this authority?" they demanded of him.

"I also will ask you a question," Jesus told them. "And if you tell me the answer, then I also will tell by what authority I do these things. The baptism of John, whence was it? From heaven or from men?"

Joseph was standing nearby, for he was curious to see whether the religious experts of Jerusalem, who prided themselves on their detailed knowledge of the law and the history of their religion, would be any more able to trap Jesus in an argument than those of Galilee had been. He could hear them conferring among themselves: "If we say, 'From heaven,' he will say to us, 'Why then did you not believe him?' But if we say, 'From men,' the crowd will turn on us, for the people themselves believe that John was a prophet." Finally one of the priests admitted, "We do not know."

"Neither will I tell you by what authority I do these things," Jesus said to them. He spoke to the crowd for a little while, then turned back to the Pharisees who were still pestering him. "Truly I say unto you, the tax collectors and the harlots go into the kingdom of God before you. For John came to you in the way of righteousness, and you did not believe him. But the tax collectors and the harlots believed him; and even when you saw it, you did not afterward repent and believe him."

The crowd murmured its approval of his thrust at the smugness and self-sufficiency of the Pharisees, who were not always popular with the common people because of their constant hemming in of man's normal activities by their interpretation of the law. But the men of the law were accustomed to this dislike and kept boring in, ignoring the disapproval of the crowds. "Teacher," one of them asked, "which is the great commandment in the law?"

Jesus smiled faintly, and Joseph could see that he understood the purpose of the question. Once he admitted that one portion of the great mass of rules by which the strictly pious Jews lived was more important than another, he would be exposing himself to endless questions on minor details.

"You shall love the Lord your God with all your heart, and with all your soul, and with all your mind," he said simply. "This is the great and first commandment. And a second is like it. You shall love your neighbor as yourself. On these two commandments depend all the law and the prophets."

On another day when Joseph was listening to Jesus teaching from Solomon's Porch, he heard him ask some of the Pharisees who were plaguing him as usual, like a gnat plagues a man in the summer, "What do you think of the Christ? Whose son is he?"

"The son of David?" one of them answered at once.

"How is it then," Jesus said, "that David, inspired by the Spirit, calls him Lord, saying:

> The Lord said to my Lord,
> Sit at my right hand,
> Till I put thy enemies under thy feet.

If David thus calls him Lord," Jesus continued, "how is he his son?"

The Pharisees looked at each other in astonishment, but none tried to answer.

"The scribes and the Pharisees sit on Moses' seat," Jesus said, turning to the crowd and to his disciples, who sat on the steps at his feet. "So practice and observe whatever they tell you, but not what they do; for they preach but do not practice. They bind heavy burdens, hard to bear, and lay them on men's shoulders; but they themselves will not move them with their finger. They do all their deeds to be seen by men; for they make their phylacteries broad and their fringes long. And they love the place of honor at feasts and the best seats in the synagogues, and salutations in the market places, and being called rabbi by men.

"But you are not to be called rabbi," his voice rang out. "For you have one teacher and you are all brethren. And call no man your father on earth, for you have one Father, Who is in heaven. Neither be called masters, for you have one master, the Christ. He who is greatest among you shall be your servant. Whoever exalts himself shall be humbled, and whoever humbles himself shall be exalted."

And now his voice was that of a judge imposing sentence upon wrongdoers: "But woe to you, scribes and Pharisees, hypocrites! Because you shut the kingdom of heaven against men; for you neither enter yourselves, nor allow those who would enter to go in. Woe to you, scribes and Pharisees, hypocrites! For you traverse sea and land to make a single proselyte, and when he becomes a proselyte, you make him twice as much a child of hell as yourselves."

The Pharisees squirmed and their faces were red with embarrassment. Jesus was pointing out with inexorable logic the pettiness and unimportance of the very things they had elevated upon an equal plane with the worship of God Himself. The crowd was enjoying this lecture to these superior beings, too, chortling with delight at each point that Jesus made, and shouting their approval when the voice of denunciation continued:

"Woe to you, scribes and Pharisees, hypocrites! For you tithe mint and anise and cumin, and have neglected the weightier matters of the law, justice, mercy, and faith. These you ought to have done, without neglecting the others, you blind guides, straining out a gnat and swallowing a camel!"

The people roared their approval of this apt comparison, and for a moment Jesus could not continue because of the tumult. It was the first time Joseph had seen the Nazarene really angry. His eyes sparkled now with indignation as he made his points one by one, denouncing the cringing Pharisees, priests, and scribes who had dared decide for themselves what constituted the true worship of God.

"Woe to you scribes and Pharisees, hypocrites!" The damning phrase lashed the men around him like a whip. "For you are like whitewashed tombs, which outwardly appear beautiful, but within they are full of dead men's bones and all uncleanness. So you also outwardly appear righteous to men, but within you are full of hypocrisy and iniquity."

Jesus paused, and when he spoke again, his voice was sad, all anger gone. "Therefore I send you prophets and wise men and scribes, some of whom you will kill and crucify. And some you will scourge in your synagogues and persecute from town to town, that upon you may come all the righteous blood shed on earth, from the blood of innocent Abel to the blood of Zechariah the son of Barachiah, whom you murdered between the sanctuary and the altar. Truly I say to you, all this will come upon this generation.

"O Jerusalem! O Jerusalem!" It was the same cry Joseph had heard him utter on the shores of the lake, when the Pharisees had tormented him for a sign. "Killing the prophets and stoning those who are sent to you! Behold, your house is forsaken and desolate. For I tell you, you will not see me again until you say, 'Blessed is he who comes in the name of the Lord.'" Jesus stood up suddenly and swung his arm in a wide sweeping gesture that encompassed the great temple upon the hill, with its gleaming marble and gold, and the beautiful white city around it. "You see all these, do you not? Truly I say to you, there will not be left one stone upon another, that will not be thrown down." Then abruptly he left the temple, descending the steps without looking to either side or speaking.

Mary and a number of the other women were staying in Joseph's house, while the men, except a few who were closest to Jesus and remained with him always, were quartered on the adjoining estate belonging to Nicodemus. Although the lawyer had definitely become a follower of the Nazarene teacher, he still kept his position in the Great Sanhedrin. Nicodemus came over that evening to where Joseph and Mary were walking in the garden. His face was grave as he greeted them.

"Why so sad?" Mary asked him, smiling. "Joseph tells me you are one of us, and those who follow Jesus know a joy to be found nowhere else."

"The whole temple area is seething with the news that the Master administered a tongue-lashing this morning to the priests and to the scribes and Pharisees," Nicodemus said. "Now they will hate him more than ever."

"I was there," Joseph volunteered. "He flayed them mercilessly, but justly."

"The smaller the soul, the greater the hatred for those who show up that smallness for all to see," Nicodemus said. "The political Sanhedrin met this afternoon. They would bring Jesus before the council and stone him if they dared."

"The crowd would not let them," Mary protested. "The people who love Jesus outnumber the priests and the scribes, and even the Pharisees. They would drive the Sadducees from the temple and from the city if they tried to harm a hair of his head."

"Fear of the crowd is all that holds Caiaphas back," Nicodemus agreed. "That, plus the fact that Pontius Pilate is not in Jerusalem."

"Would he dare send for Pilate?" Joseph said quickly.

Nicodemus shook his head. "The Procurator hates Jerusalem in winter; only the Emperor himself could make him come here before the Passover. Then he always arrives with extra soldiers, in case the crowd becomes unruly."

"What can Caiaphas do?" Mary asked. "We guard the Master so closely that even the *sicarii* cannot get to him."

"And besides," Joseph added, "a hired killer would be torn to pieces by the crowd as soon as his knife had struck. They all know that, so they are not likely to make an attempt upon his life here in Jerusalem."

"Caiaphas knows all those things," Nicodemus agreed. "Yet he can hardly let Jesus keep on building up a following when so many Zealots are in Jerusalem. Particularly since they now have a leader."

"Simon Zelotes!" Mary cried. "In Bethsaida he was ready to proclaim Jesus king."

Nicodemus shook his head. "Simon the Zealot is not the real leader. You forget the man of Kerioth."

"Judas? But he says little. It is always Simon who speaks."

"And tells what Judas orders him," Nicodemus added. "But I think we can be sure what the high priest will do."

"What is that?"

"The law is a bludgeon that the priests and the Pharisees hold over the people, since only they can intrepret it legally. Jesus cannot speak very often as bluntly as he did today without breaking at least some of the oral law. And when he does, they will accuse him of blasphemy. Nothing excites the crowd so much as a charge of blasphemy or of speaking against the temple."

Joseph felt a sudden chill of premonition, for he was remembering the words of Jesus that very morning, "Truly

I say to you, there will not be left one stone upon another, that will not be thrown down."

When he told Nicodemus and Mary of it, the lawyer's face became very grave. "Let us pray that Caiaphas does not learn the Master's exact words," he said. "Even Jesus might not be able to save himself if he is accused of blasphemy against the temple of God."

Mary shivered, and Joseph put his arm around her. He knew that she was remembering the day when Jesus alone had saved her from the stoning. Both of them knew what the fury of a mob could mean. Nor, as Nicodemus had said, would the present favor of Jesus with the common people of Israel necessarily save even him from such a fate. Against him would be arrayed the hangers-on around the temple, the keepers of the stalls that infested the lower level, the money-changers, the animal and spice sellers, even the sellers of scrolls, and all the hundreds of others who lived by the temple and the business that came to them as a result of it. They were wealthy and influential people, and once a sufficient mob of them had been gathered together to make a common front against a man they had every natural reason to hate, violence could break out at any time.

"What do you think we should do, Nicodemus?" Mary asked.

"Jesus must leave Jerusalem," the lawyer said emphatically. "I see no other answer."

"But the people are flocking to him, and he gains new followers every day."

"I know that," Nicodemus admitted. "But most of them are either Zealots or sympathetic to the Zealot cause."

"You are the closest to him of all the women in his following, Mary," Joseph suggested. "Perhaps you could persuade him to leave. Jesus must realize that you are one of the few who love him for what he is, without any thought of gain."

"Both of you love him unselfishly," she pointed out.

"You have accepted him as the Christ," he pointed out. "But for some reason I cannot yet be sure in my heart that he is the Expected One."

"When the time comes for you to see the Messiah in Jesus, you will be sure," Mary said confidently. "It is something each of us must experience for himself. The Master will be returning from Bethany in the morning," she went on, "and I will try to persuade him to leave Jerusalem. But somehow I think he may already be planning to go."

Nicodemus looked at her in astonishment, but Joseph had learned how reliable was this deep understanding she seemed to have of the Nazarene teacher and his purposes.

"Why do you say that, Mary?" Nicodemus asked.

"Jesus' success here in Jerusalem is great, perhaps greater than it ever was in Galilee," Mary said. "But who comes to him? The Pharisees who seek to trap him. The priests of the Sadducees who hate him. The sick who want to be healed. And the Zealots, who see in him a Messiah to lead them against Rome. Only a few follow him because he teaches a kingdom greater than anything that could be established on earth, the kingdom of God in men's hearts."

The men were silent, for no one could deny the force of her logic. "Once before," she continued, "Jesus went away when they would crown him king in Galilee. I think he will do the same again. Unless——" She stopped, and a look of great sadness came into her face. "Unless he knows he can show men the meaning of the kingdom of God only by dying for it himself?"

"Being the Messiah, he must know it," Nicodemus said logically. "If that is what must take place."

"He has predicted it himself," Joseph pointed out. "And you have all heard him say a prophet should not die outside of Jerusalem."

"This must all be part of a pattern," Mary said thoughtfully. "Being the Christ, Jesus could save himself if he would. But having decided that he must die to make people understand why he came to earth, he will not use that power."

"Then we can do nothing," Joseph said sadly.

"You may be right," Mary agreed. "But I will speak to him as soon as I can. Perhaps he will tell me what is to happen."

"In any event, Caiaphas dares not arrest him now," Nicodemus added. "So we will have time to make plans to protect the Master if he refuses to leave the city."

But there, as it happened, Nicodemus was in error.

17

ALTHOUGH he spent most of every day listening to Jesus, Joseph had still to carry out his duties as *medicus viscerus* of the temple. This he usually did early in the morning, immediately after the opening sacrifices. He was in the temple as usual the morning after Jesus had so bitterly denounced the Pharisees from Solomon's Porch, binding the feet of priests suffering from "temple foot," treating those whose digestion had been overtaxed by too much feasting, and otherwise looking after the health of the temple population. Just as he was finishing one of the tight starch bandages used to treat "temple foot," a sudden hubbub arose on the lower terrace, sometimes called the Court of the Heathen. Seconds later one of the Levites ran past on the way to the room where the high priest spent most of the day. "The prophet of Nazareth is overturning the tables of the money-changers," he shouted. "There is fighting on the lower terrace."

Joseph dropped his *nartik* to the floor, assailed by a sudden dread. Could this be the beginning of the disaster they feared? Quickly he turned and ran across the terrace and down the steps to the lower level. From the steps he could see a mass of pushing, shouting, cursing men filling the lower terrace. And when he reached the alcove where the tables of the money-changers were located, he came upon a dramatic tableau.

Everywhere there was confusion, except in the center of a small circle where Jesus moved calmly along the terrace, turning over the small tables upon which the money-changers kept their coins piled, spilling the money upon the floor and leaving the tables themselves to be trampled into pieces by the people who fought each other and groveled on the stones picking up the coins. When he came to the stall of the animal sellers, Jesus broke them open, too, and so continued around the terrace, wrecking the places where the merchants and money-changers bilked those coming to sacrifice and shared their profits with the officials of the temple.

The priests seemed paralyzed by this unheard-of thing, and the faces of the small knot of disciples around Jesus showed their horror at what he was doing. Once or twice one of them put out a hand as if to restrain their leader, but drew back in the face of the Master's anger.

Joseph had never seen Jesus so angry before, not even when he had tongue-lashed the Pharisees. His eyes burned and his movements as he tumbled the flimsy tables to the floor and wrecked the stalls were purposeful and strong. Only when he had made the circuit of one side of the terrace did he stop and face the crowd. Those nearest him quailed before his wrath then and tried to back away. "It is written," he shouted at them, " '*My house shall be a house of prayer,*' but you have made it a den of thieves!"

By now a group of the same Pharisees he had denounced yesterday had managed to get some temple guards together. They pushed through the crowd, and one of them, more brazen than the rest, demanded loudly, "How long will you keep us in suspense? If you are the Christ, tell us plainly."

"I told you." Jesus' words lashed at them like whips. "And you do not believe. The works that I do in my Father's name, they bear witness to me. But you do not believe because you do not belong to my sheep. My sheep hear my voice, and I know them, and they follow me. And I give them eternal life, and they shall never perish, and no one shall snatch them out of my hand."

He paused and looked out over the crowd. Joseph saw that the anger had faded from his eyes now, to be replaced by a look of sorrow. "My Father, Who has given them to me, is greater than all, and no one is able to snatch them out of the Father's hand. I and the Father are one."

For a moment the full implications of that statement did not penetrate the minds of the men who were questioning him. When it did, the Pharisees suddenly began to shout, "He has blasphemed! Stone him! Stone him!" Some of them even pushed forward to seize Jesus, but he raised his hand, and the force of his calmness and certainty of purpose held them back.

"I have shown you many good works from the Father," he said. "For which of these do you stone me?"

"We stone you for no good work but for blasphemy!" the spokesman for the Pharisees shouted. "Because you, being a man, make yourself God." The common people understood little of the minute points of the law so beloved by the Pharisees, breakage of which was called blasphemy. But in matters of religion they were accustomed to look to the Pharisees for leadership, and when the cry of blasphemy was raised, many of them took it up.

Jesus looked scathingly at his tormentors. "Is it not written in your law, *'I said you are gods'?* If he called them gods to whom the word of God came (and scripture cannot be broken), do you say of him whom the Father consecrated and sent into the world, 'You are blaspheming' because I said, 'I am the Son of God'?" He paused, then went on, "If I am not doing the works of my Father, then do not believe me. But if I do them, even though you do not believe me, believe the works, that you may know and understand that the Father is in me and I am in the Father."

"Blasphemy!" the Pharisees took up the cry again. "He has blasphemed against the Most High. Let him be stoned."

Simon Peter and the sons of Zebedee were close beside Jesus, but they seemed stunned by this sudden happening. Joseph had not seen Mary, but when the crowd began to bay for Jesus' life she pushed forward as if to protect him. Quickly, then, Joseph elbowed his way through the crowd until he stood beside her, putting his own body between Jesus and the crowd. "Jews of Jerusalem!" he shouted. "You know me, Joseph of Galilee. I have bound up your wounds and nursed you back to health when you were sick. Listen to me!"

A momentary hush fell over the crowd, for many of them had been healed by his medicines and his skill, and they respected him and trusted him, as a man naturally trusts his physician. "You all know that I have kept the law from my youth," Joseph told them. "These Pharisees would have you stone a good teacher because he has shown you what they are, whited sepulchers, hypocrites, liars. Then they can say, 'We have not done it, but the crowd.'"

"He lies," the leader of the Pharisees shouted. "Joseph

of Galilee is bewitched by the woman of Magdala who follows Jesus. Look, there she stands now."

With her bright hair and her beauty, Mary stood out from the crowd, as a lily would stand out among thistles. And many a man in the crowd, seeing the light in her eyes as she looked at Joseph, envied him and hated him for his good fortune at the same moment.

"Stone the blasphemer!" the Pharisees shouted again. "To the gates!" And the mob once more took up the cry.

Clawing hands were already tearing at their clothing, and all seemed truly lost when Joseph heard the sound of marching feet. He looked up and saw a group of soldiers led by a centurion passing along the lower terrace on their way back to Antonia from the first guard period of the day. The officer he recognized as a man named Trojanus, whose wife Joseph had cured of a severe fever only a few months before.

"Trojanus!" he shouted in desperation. "Trojanus! Would you see the physician of Pontius Pilate killed by the mob?"

The Roman turned, and his eyes quickly took in the situation. The entire garrison knew that Joseph was a friend of Pilate and his wife and also served as physician to the Roman troops. At a sharp command from Trojanus the soldiers lowered their shields and, using the butts of their swords as bludgeons, plunged into the crowd. Like a battering-ram, the column easily forced its way through the cursing, snarling mass of humanity and surrounded the small group who were the target for the buffeting of the mob. "What is the trouble here?" the centurion demanded.

"The Pharisees seek to have us stoned," Joseph explained breathlessly. "Can you guard us as far as the road leading to Jericho?"

Trojanus looked doubtful, until Joseph added, "I will be personally responsible to Pontius Pilate for your actions!"

"Make a good story of it then," he said, grinning, and Joseph knew that he had won. "Tell him how I saved your life when it was in great peril."

Guarded by the soldiers, the small party left the temple and crossed the city to the gate where the road from Jericho entered. Not many of the crowd followed. It was one thing to drag a defenseless Jew accused of blasphemy

289

outside the gates and stone him to death, but quite another to attack Roman soldiers and bring down the wrath of Pontius Pilate upon all the Jews in Jerusalem. By the time they reached the gates, only a small crowd of the curious followed, and when the party set out toward Jericho they were unmolested.

Jesus had not spoken during their dramatic rescue. Looking at the sadness and disappointment that showed in his face now, Joseph thought Mary must indeed be right. Jerusalem had failed him, just as had Galilee, and Jesus must be glad to be away from it.

The Master walked ahead on the road, alone and lost in his thoughts, while the disciples followed along behind, quarreling among themselves at the ill fortune which had forced them to leave Jerusalem just when it seemed that they were near the height of their success. None dared blame their leader for precipitating the controversy that morning, but a few upbraided Joseph for taking them out of the city under the Roman guard, insisting that they might have been able to hide inside the walls and thus continue their plans for making Jesus king in Jerusalem.

At Jericho, when he was sure there was no pursuit, Joseph turned back to Jerusalem. He and Mary both felt that it was important now to have someone they could depend upon in the temple city, to keep informed about what was happening there. "Take care, Joseph," she begged as they were saying good-by. "You have made a bitter enemy in Caiaphas by saving Jesus. He may try to punish you."

"I think not," he assured her. "Jesus answered the Pharisees this morning and proved that there was no blasphemy in what he said. They were trying to arouse the crowd to stone him, so they could get rid of him without being blamed for his death. Caiaphas would have to bring me before the Sanhedrin, and then it would come out that he tried to have Jesus murdered by the crowd." He stopped, but Mary saw that something was troubling him and asked, "What is it, Joseph?"

"One thing troubles me," he admitted. "The Christ could have stopped the riot and walked through them without being touched, but Jesus made no move to do so. It is not so much that I doubt, Mary. I only want to understand what really happened."

"Cleansing the temple may have been his last act in

Jerusalem before putting the city behind him," she said. "Remember that he did not object to leaving Jerusalem, so he must have been ready to go."

"But the prophecy——"

"That he would be killed in Jerusalem? Yes, I have thought of that too. But remember, he did not say when. He merely said, 'The Son of man will be delivered to the chief priests and to the scribes, and they will condemn him to death, and deliver him to the Gentiles; and they will mock him and spit upon him and scourge him and kill him.' We cannot always understand the will of God, Joseph, but we can obey it because it is always just and right."

He thought of these words of Mary's many times in the months that followed, while winter faded and the first budding signs of spring began to show once again. But he had more pressing things than reverie to occupy his mind, for on the day after his return to Jerusalem he received a cryptic summons to the apartment of the old high priest Annas. Correctly surmising that he was to go before the political Sanhedrin, Joseph took the precaution this time of taking Nicodemus with him, lest Caiaphas and the others try to trap him on some minor point in the law.

The same group were waiting, but it was the high priest Caiaphas, cold-eyed and furious, who opened the attack upon him even before the short exchange of greetings demanded by courtesy was finished.

"Why did you not stay with the blasphemer they call Jesus of Nazareth?" he demanded.

"I heard no blasphemy uttered by Jesus," Joseph said stoutly.

Caiaphas brushed his denial contemptuously aside. "You are a spy sent back here to keep contact with the Zealots who plot with the Nazarene. What will your friend Pontius Pilate think when I send him word of this?"

"Pontius Pilate knows I speak only the truth," Joseph said quietly. "He will believe me when I deny such a false charge."

Caiaphas whitened and bit his full upper lip until it seemed that his teeth would penetrate the flesh. To ease some of the tension Elias asked, "Where has Jesus of Nazareth gone, Joseph?"

"I left them at Jericho. But they spoke of going to Peraea."

"As we thought," Caiaphas snapped. "He has run to the territory of the Tetrarch Philip."

"Jesus did not have to leave unless he wished," Nicodemus said quietly.

"Why?" Caiaphas wheeled upon him.

"Because he is the Christ," the lawyer said simply. "Jesus could have stricken you and your hirelings dead where you stood if he had wished."

"We know where this man comes from," Caiaphas thundered. "He is a carpenter of Galilee. When the Christ appears no one will know where he comes from."

"Have you forgotten the prophecies of Isaiah?" Nicodemus reminded him.

Caiaphas shrugged. "Is the Christ to come from Galilee?" he demanded. "Do not the Scriptures say that the Christ is descended from David, and comes from Bethlehem, the city where David was?"

"Many prophecies refer to the coming of the Messiah," Nicodemus pointed out. "Some we understand, some we do not. How can you say he can be only of one place and not of another, when you cannot be sure of the meaning?" It was a telling point, for even the most learned Pharisees often quarreled over the meaning of many things in the Books of the Law and the Prophets.

"Jesus is a blasphemer," Caiaphas said flatly. "That is enough to earn him a sentence of death."

"Why did you not bring him before the council then," Joseph asked, "instead of sending men to inflame the mob and have him stoned? Does our law judge a man without first giving him a hearing and learning what he has done?"

"You are from Galilee," Caiaphas sneered. "Search and you will see that no prophet is to rise from Galilee."

"You accused Joseph just now of being a spy, Caiaphas," Nicodemus said evenly. "It is a charge not lightly made. Let us take him before the Great Sanhedrin and have all this brought to light. There are many just men among the council who will not like to hear that you sent your hirelings among the Pharisees to stir up the crowd against Jesus. To bring about a man's death outside the law is murder and punishable by death. Even the high priest is not immune from the justice of the Most High."

Caiaphas blanched before this threat. He knew well that Nicodemus, as one of the most respected among the doctors of the law, and Joseph, the *medicus viscerus,* would be heard carefully and their charges thoroughly weighed by the Sanhedrin. "I—I spoke in anger," he admitted lamely. "No one charges Joseph of Galilee with breaking the law. You may both go."

"Be careful, Joseph," Nicodemus cautioned when they were outside the building. "The high priest is a venomous man and he is close to Pontius Pilate. We have no way of knowing what lies he will tell the Procurator, or what plots he will make against you."

A few days later word came to Joseph that Jesus had gone beyond the Jordan to teach in a town called Ephraim, where John the Baptist had achieved some of his greatest success. With the Nazarene now so far from Jerusalem, the ferment over his appearance in the temple city seemed to have subsided. Many Zealots still remained in the city, and Joseph heard in roundabout ways that they were actively working for the time when they could proclaim Jesus king in Judea. But they did not consult Joseph or Nicodemus, doubtless because they knew that these two had little sympathy with such a movement.

And so the rest of the winter passed uneventfully. Joseph had already given up all hope that he and Mary could be married any time soon. To ease some of the pain of loneliness, he threw himself into his work and into keeping alive, through teaching and ministering to the sick and to the poor, the loyal band of followers that Jesus had developed during his short stay in Jerusalem. Among the believers were counted several members of the Sanhedrin and many influential teachers, as well as merchants and artisans, devout Jews who saw in the pretensions of the Pharisees and the emphasis upon form and accumulation of wealth that characterized the rule of the priests a veritable travesty of the things that the worship of the Most High meant to the really devout Jew.

With the coming of spring, the whole city began to prepare for the greatest of all the religious celebrations, the Feast of the Passover, for which Jews came to Jerusalem by the thousands from even the farthermost cities of the Empire. It was then that the children of Israel traditionally buried any differences they might have had with each other in a common giving of thanks for their deliverance from Egypt centuries before. Called the Passover, because it commemorated the sparing of the first-born when God passed over the houses of the Jews in Egypt and took the sons of the Egyptians instead, the holiday was characterized by eating unleavened cake, symbolizing the deliverance from Egypt according to the promise made by God to Moses, their leader, and bitter herbs, a sign of the bitterness that had been the lot of the children of Israel as slaves of the Pharaohs.

In the temple and in the synagogues the ceremony of worship would include a prayer of thanks and recitations of praise to *"Him Who wrought for us and for our fathers all these miracles. He brought us out from slavery to freedom, from sadness to joy, from mourning to festivity, from darkness to great light, from oppression to deliverance."*

And as always before the Passover, Pontius Pilate returned to Jerusalem with a large reinforcement of the normal garrison of Roman troops, lest the excitable Jews, stirred to a new fever of nationalism by this week of celebration, in which they were reminded daily of the time when they had freed themselves as a nation from the heavy hand of another oppressor in Egypt, be tempted to revolt.

Joseph paid a call upon the Procurator as soon as he was installed in his palace. The discomforts of the journey from Tiberias had stirrred up Pilate's gout, even though he had ridden in the royal chariot, and he was even more than usually moody and irascible. While Joseph applied leeches to the swollen toe, Pilate fumed against Herod Antipas, the population of Jerusalem, and this part of the world in general.

"I trust the Lady Claudia Procula is in good health," Joseph said courteously when Pilate paused for breath.

"She has spent a better winter than usual," Pilate admitted. And then added testily, "But she attributes it to faith in the teacher, Jesus of Nazareth, instead of the climate, which has been more favorable than for a long time."

"I have noticed that those who are calm in spirit are ill less often than those who are distraught."

Pilate shot him a surprised glance. "Even with such a thing as a gouty toe?"

"It is possible."

"Absurd!" Pilate snapped. "What possible good can it do to go mooning around about eternal life and doing good to others? Power is the only thing that counts in this world, or any other that I know of."

Joseph was familiar with Pilate's way of thinking and wanted nothing less than to get into an argument over his philosophy of power. To change the subject he asked, "Did the Lady Claudia Procula come with you to Jerusalem?"

Pilate shook his head. "She wished to stay in Jericho until your feast is over and we can go on to Caesarea. Herod Antipas offered us the use of his palace there, but I prefer to be here, in case there is any trouble."

"Jericho is pleasant at this time of the year. And the baths will no doubt be good for her health."

"She did not stay for the baths," Pilate said laconically. "Jesus of Nazareth is in Jericho again. . . ."

"In Jericho!" Joseph was so startled that he dropped the leech he was taking from a jar. "I thought he was in Ephraim."

Pilate looked at him quizzically. "Is what I have heard true, Joseph? Are you really one of his followers?"

"Yes," Joseph admitted. "I am sure the teachings of Jesus are the best way of life for all men."

"I am not talking about philosophy," Pilate said testily. "Many others have said the same things. Do you believe he is the Christ that you Jews have been expecting?"

"I don't know," Joseph admitted.

"Did you ever hear him claim to be the Messiah?"

Joseph shook his head. "No, I have not."

But Pilate was persistent. "Has anyone heard him make such a claim to your knowledge?"

"Not to my knowledge."

The Procurator stared at him speculatively, his lips pursed. "You would not lie to me, Joseph," he said, "I am sure of that, and whatever they say about me, I am a just man. If I listened to Caiaphas, I would arrest Jesus and execute him tomorrow for proclaiming himself king of the Jews. Yet is he does make that claim, I have no choice. There can be but one ruler in Judea or anywhere else, Joseph, the Emperor in whose name I govern."

"I am sure Jesus does not desire to be king of the Jews," Joseph said earnestly. "He is only trying to change the hearts and souls of men, not their political beliefs or their government."

"What you say may be true of the man himself," Pilate

295

admitted. "To me he is just another fanatic, like the one Herod killed. But the Zealots were ready to proclaim him king in Galilee last fall, when he suddenly withdrew into the hills. And they were preparing to do the same here in Jerusalem, until he left the city for Peraea."

"You seem to know a great deal about his actions."

"It is my business to know such things. Judea has had peace for many years because I usually know what is going to happen before it happens."

"Does not Jesus' withdrawal at these times prove that he does not wish to be a temporal leader?" Joseph suggested.

"Perhaps." Pilate shrugged. "But you could also argue that his followers had become too enthusiastic before the time was yet ripe for the rebellion they plan."

"What are you going to do?" Joseph asked, trying to make his tone noncommittal.

Pilate laughed. "You would never make a conspirator, Joseph. Your thoughts show in your face. But you may tell Nicodemus and the rest of those who follow the Nazarene that I have no desire to destroy him, so long as he is not so foolish as to let the hotheads among his disciples proclaim him king. Then I would have no choice. The Emperor Tiberius rules in Judea, Joseph, with Pontius Pilate as his deputy. Always remember that."

18

WITH the Feast of the Passover only a week away, Jerusalem teemed with travelers and pilgrims from every part of the Roman Empire. The lodging places within the city were quickly filled, and the overflow of travelers spilled out into the surrounding villages, Bethpage, Bethany, and others, even as far as Emmaus, about seven miles away. Here Nicodemus had a country villa, a lovely place at the head of a small valley, to which he liked to go in the spring, when the flowers and the fields were just beginning to awaken to new life. When Joseph received a call to visit his friend at Emmaus, he was glad to have an opportunity to get away from the clogged streets of the city and the constant babel of voices in every language that characterized Jerusalem at Passover time.

Nicodemus was not very sick. Joseph's diagnosis was merely one of the intermittent fevers that came and went here, often being worse in the spring with the onset of warm weather. He prescribed a bitter draught and hot spiced drinks to bring on a sweat and lessen the fever, and started back to the city, for he still had many patients to see that afternoon.

The hills were covered with the flowers of spring as Joseph rode along. Daffodils bloomed everywhere, interspersed with clumps of sea leek, the "flower of Sharon" with its star-shaped blooms of purest white. Occasionally a patch of "cuckoo flowers," with blossoms shaped like a lady's smock, set the bright color of lilac against the white. And everywhere were the thistles and the burnet, with its thorns and tiny leaves of darkest green and red blossoms like drops of blood. The burnet was both useful and beautiful, for it was used to make the hot blast of the lime kilns as well as to heat the cooking fires upon the rude hearths of the countryfolk.

Riding along the road over the hills toward the great city visible in the distance, Joseph was lost in thought and did not notice at first the crowd ahead of him near the gate leading into the city itself. Then he head the shouts. And because they were somehow familiar, his heart quickened its beat and he pushed the camel he rode onward.

"Hosanna!" the crowd was shouting. "Blessed be he who comes in the name of the Lord!" cried the people as they spread their cloaks and leafy branches cut from the fields upon the road. He did not need to see the solitary and somehow lonely figure riding a mule at the head of the small procession to know what had happened.

Jesus of Nazareth had returned to Jerusalem.

Joseph's heart was beating quickly as he guided his camel into the back of the procession marching into the city, for he had glimpsed a familiar graceful figure, a woman whose copper-red hair could not be hidden by the shawl over her head. And yet he could not repress a feeling of dread and apprehension, for this was no such spontaneous acclamation by the multitudes as had greeted

Jesus on his visit to Jerusalem only a few months before. If any further evidence was needed as to how quickly the people had forgotten the Nazarene teacher whose followers believed him to be the Messiah, it was in the question Joseph heard asked again and again by curious onlookers beside the roadway, "Who is this?"

Only occasionally did someone answer, "This is the prophet Jesus from Nazareth of Galilee."

The procession had already entered the city by the time Joseph reached Mary. She seized him by the arm, and he saw that her eyes were red as if she had been weeping, but her happiness at being with him again shone in her face.

"Why did he come back, Mary?" he asked, yet he knew the answer before she spoke.

"The time is now, Joseph," she said simply. "He has come to fulfill the prophecies."

"But Pilate is in Jerusalem. He and Caiaphas will certainly take Jesus' appearance here now as a sign that he intends to be proclaimed king."

"Perhaps he dies," she said. "The death of a king means more than the death of a prophet."

With Jerusalem swelled almost to bursting by the pilgrims, the procession that accompanied Jesus was swallowed up quickly in the sea of humanity surging back and forth through the city. At the steps of the temple the disciples began to raise again the cry of "Hosanna in the highest! Blessed be the kingdom of our father David that is coming!" And when some of the Pharisees at the lower level of the temple rebuked them for their noise, Jesus himself said, "I tell you, if these were silent, the very stones would cry out."

Upon the steps leading to the second level he stood and looked out over the crowd. In his face there was a great sorrow, not for himself, Joseph was sure, but for the callousness and greed and pretentiousness of this city that called itself holy, yet had rejected him and his teachings. Then he turned and went on up to pray.

Joseph had expected some disturbance when Jesus visited the temple, especially from the Pharisees and the priests who had baited him and tried to trap him here before. But the Nazarene only stayed long enough to pray and look around, as any other pilgrim might have done; then, followed by his disciples, he descended the steps to the lower level and went down into the city. Watching Simon Peter and the others as they followed their Master, Joseph could see that they were puzzled and uncertain. Even Simon the Zealot seemed to have lost much of his assurance and fanatic zeal.

At the very end of the group of disciples one man walked a little apart. It was Judas Iscariot, his brilliant cold eyes and sharp profile as striking as ever. But a different look showed in his eyes now, a look that seemed both disappointment and decision, although it was hard to reconcile the two.

"Judas has changed, Mary," Joseph said quickly. "What has happened?"

"He has stayed apart from us more than usual lately," she admitted. "I think he finally realizes that Jesus will not let himself be proclaimed king."

"The others seem subdued too."

"They are all disappointed because Jesus will not be part of a rebellion," she explained. "Simon Peter and the sons of Zebedee and Simon Zelotes most of all. Judas never shows his feelings much, but he is the leader of those who planned it, and I suppose, in a way, he has the most to lose—except Jesus." She clung to Joseph's arm, as if to draw strength from him. "Help me to pray, dear, that our faith will be strong enough for whatever—for whatever happens."

Although he reassured her, Joseph did not at the time understand what she meant. Later, however, he was to know.

Now, if ever, would have been the time for Jesus to whip the crowded city into a religious frenzy by means of some startling miracle that might well have culminated in his being proclaimed the Christ and king of Judea, but he did nothing to attract attention to himself. Still, when he sat down to teach, his audience was far larger than that gathered around the other teachers who drew crowds at this season of religious enthusiasm. He did not lash the Pharisees and the priests for their sins, as he had done before, however. Nor did he disturb the operation of the temple, which had gone back to its former practices almost as soon as he had left after overturning the tables of the money-changers some months before. Following Jesus as he went about the city, Joseph was puzzled. It seemed almost as if the Master were waiting for something, and yet he could not understand what that could be.

Joseph did not think for a moment that Caiaphas, hating Jesus as he did, had given up hope of arresting him and having him executed. But the crowd that followed the Nazarene teacher, although much smaller than before, was still large enough to make it unsafe for the high priest to arrest him in broad daylight. For then the people would swarm to the trial before the Sanhedrin that must inevitably follow, and with as much sentiment as there was in the Sanhedrin itself in favor of the gentle teacher of Nazareth, Caiaphas would stand little chance of convicting him of blasphemy. Those who were regarded as prophets had always been allowed to speak more freely by far than those who could claim no such divine inspiration. And Jesus was already acclaimed a prophet by many of the Jews.

And so nothing happened for almost a week. In a few more days the Passover season would be finished and many of those who thronged the streets and listened to the teachers upon Solomon's Porch would depart again for their homes. The day before the Passover itself, Mary joined Joseph as he was going down into the city early in the morning to visit the sick. She had remained at his estate most of the time, for only the inner circle of the disciples accompanied the Master on his nightly visits to Bethany. Joseph was surprised to find her moving toward the city now with several of the women who traveled in Jesus' retinue.

"You are out early," he said, taking her hand as they walked along.

"Jesus asked us to help Mary, the mother of Mark, prepare a supper for him and the twelve tonight," she explained. This Mary was the sister of Barnabas, a leader of those in Jerusalem who followed the Nazarene. Her son Mark was still only a lad, but he, too, believed along with his mother. Often when in the city Jesus and the twelve rested there before going out to Bethany in the evening.

"But why tonight?" Joseph asked in surprise. "The Passover feast is not until tomorrow evening."

"I don't know," Mary admitted. "The Master insisted upon eating tonight with the twelve at Mary's house." She gripped his hand tightly. "Have you looked in his eyes lately, Joseph? I am terribly afraid of what I see there."

"Nothing that we feared has happened," he protested. "And the Passover season has almost ended."

"What if Jesus knows his time has come and this is the farewell meal with his disciples?"

"Prophets often speak parables that we cannot understand," Joseph comforted her. "He may have meant something else when he spoke of being killed."

"Promise that you will watch outside the house where he eats tonight," Mary begged. "It will be the only night since he returned to Jerusalem that Jesus has remained in the city."

"I will watch," he promised her. "And Hadja will be with me. If anyone comes, we can give the alarm."

Darkness had already fallen when Joseph and Hadja took up their watch outside the house. It was warm, and the curtains of the windows of the upper room where Jesus sat at supper with his disciples had been drawn aside. From time to time the voices of those at the feast grew loud enough for Joseph to hear as he waited nearby in the shadow of a clump of bushes. Hadja was on the other side in order to command a view of the street from another direction.

Mary came out to bring food and a small flask of wine to Joseph and Hadja. She clung to Joseph for a moment in the shadows, as if seeking to draw strength from him as she had so many times in the days since Jesus had returned to Jerusalem. "Watch well, Joseph," she begged. "I have a feeling that the end is near."

As the feast in the upper room went on and nothing happened, Joseph began to be more and more certain that they had wrongly interpreted Jesus' words about being arrested in Jerusalem and put to death. Then suddenly the Master's voice rose above the others in the room. "Truly I say to you," Joseph heard him say, "one of you will betray me, one who is eating with me."

Immediately there was a babble of questioning as one after another of the disciples asked, "Is it I?"

"It is one of the twelve," Jesus said, "one who is dipping bread in the same dish with me."

Joseph felt a sudden dread grip his heart, for Jesus' voice had been resigned, as if, with his prophetic insight, he already knew exactly what was going to happen. Could Mary's fears really be justified? Could her intuition have been really a forewarning of some terrible thing that was to happen here in Jerusalem at the Passover season?

Soon they all began to sing a hymn, by which Joseph knew that the supper was over and the group was breaking up. He drew a sigh of relief, for now they would leave the city, and whatever threat hung over Jesus would be averted, at least until tomorrow when he returned.

Joseph was on the point of calling Hadja to draw back into the shadows so that the others would not know they had been watching, when the door of the house burst open and a man plunged from it. The tall figure with the hawklike profile and the iron-gray hair could not be mistaken, and as the man of Kerioth ran past him, Joseph got a glimpse of his face in the light of a lamp that burned outside the door of Mary's house. It was set in an even harsher cast than usual, and he realized suddenly that something important had happened in the upper room to fill Judas with such a fiery purpose. As he plunged on up the street, half running, Joseph obeyed a sudden impulse and followed him.

Across the now quiet city Judas went almost at a trot with Joseph close behind, hard put to keep up. Judas never looked back, and only when he reached the palace of Caiaphas and was challenged by the armed guard that stood always before the door did he stop. The challenge was perfunctory, however, and he was admitted as soon as the guard was able to see who he was. Obviously, Joseph realized as he drew back into the shadows lest the guard see him, Judas was expected.

Now Joseph became conscious of the sound of men moving about and talking in the courtyard of Caiaphas' house. Some were Jewish voices, but the rattle of arms and rough words used by Roman soldiers betrayed the fact that a party of Pilate's troops was included among those who had been waiting, perhaps for a man who would lead them to their prey. Judas had come to betray Jesus, Joseph was certain now, to inform Caiaphas where the Nazarene teacher could be captured, by night when there were no crowds to interfere.

But why had this moody, strange man called Judas Iscariot chosen to sell the knowledge of his Master's presence in the city this night to the high priest and his minions? Joseph wondered. The man of Kerioth had changed lately, Mary had said. Perhaps, Joseph thought, it was because he had realized at last that Jesus had no intention of allowing himself to be proclaimed a king in

302

Judea and Galilee, as the Zealots planned. Or it might be that Judas hoped, through Jesus' arrest, so to provoke the teeming thousands of the city into action that they would tear him from the hands of the soldiers and set him upon the throne of Judea in defiance of the high priest and Pontius Pilate. And Caiaphas, it seemed, was acting in collusion with the Procurator. The presence of Roman soldiers in the party waiting for Judas' arrival could mean nothing else.

Now the gates of the courtyard opened and a burly Roman officer emerged with a captain of the Jewish temple guards beside him. Behind them was a party of at least fifty men, more than half of whom were soldiers of the cohort manning the Roman garrison of Jerusalem. When Judas emerged from the house and joined the leaders before the gate, Joseph knew with a desperate urgency that he must no delay here any longer. Jesus and the disciples might not yet have left the city, and at all costs they must not be caught within the gates tonight. Winded as he was, Joseph knew he must race back across the city to warn them, hoping to be able to arrive far enough ahead of the slower-marching troops to hide Jesus in some safe place before they arrived at the house where the supper had been eaten that night.

But when Joseph reached the house, Jesus and the disciples had gone. Mary was with the other women, clearing away the remains of the feast. She came quickly to Joseph. "Hadja said Judas ran from the house and you followed," she told him. "I was worried for you."

"Judas is bringing Caiaphas and the Romans here," Joseph gasped. "I came to warn Jesus."

"Judas!" she caught her breath. "Of course. He would be the one."

"Have they gone to Bethany?"

Mary shook her head. "The Master will not return there tonight. As they were leaving Simon told me they were going to the Mount of Olives instead, to pray in the Garden of Gethsemane."

"The soldiers will be here soon, we must send them in another direction," Joseph said. "Go tell the women not to reveal where Jesus really went, and I will run to the garden and warn them."

"But Judas knew Jesus was going to pray with the disciples in the Garden of Gethsemane, Joseph."

"Then he is leading the soldiers to the garden and not here!" Joseph cried. "If only I had stayed to watch where they went," he added bitterly, "but it is too late now."

"You could not have possibly warned Jesus and the others in time," Mary pointed out logically. "Don't you see? It is just as Jesus said. One of the disciples has betrayed him and he will be taken to the chief priest and the scribes. It had to happen this way, Joseph."

And that, as they discovered when they met the soldiers returning with Jesus bound in their midst near the foot of the Mount of Olives, was exactly what had occurred. Led by the traitor Judas, the temple guards and the Roman detachment had surrounded Jesus while he prayed in the garden and had taken him prisoner without resistance. Of the eleven who accompanied him, not one stood by him in this hour of trial or offered to share his fate.

19

SURROUNDED as Jesus was by nearly fifty guards, any attempt at resistance would have been foolish. Mary and Joseph followed as closely behind as they could, while the party retraced the way by which it had come and entered again the courtyard of Caiaphas. Only a few people could get into the chamber where the priests were questioning Jesus, but Joseph was recognized by the guard, and he and Mary managed to push their way in with the crowd where they could see and hear the trail, if indeed it could be called such.

This was no formal hearing before the legally constituted Sanhedrin. Caiaphas and Annas, the old high priest, with Elias and several others of the same group who had questioned Joseph after his return from Galilee, made up the tribunal before which Jesus was brought. It was what Nicodemus had called the political Sanhedrin, the small body of influential priests and doctors of the law who, although having no legal existence, yet ruled the people, in so far as the Jews ruled themselves at all, with an inflexible hand.

Jesus stood quietly with his manacled hands before him. Already dark bruises showed on his fair skin where he had been man-handled by the guards, and blood trickled from a small cut on his wrist where the irons had been roughly applied. The sorrow that Joseph and Mary had noticed so markedly in his face these last few days was gone now. It was replaced by a look almost of exaltation, as if God had indeed given him some special source of strength in this hour of trial. He showed no fear, nothing indeed but a calm resignation for whatever was to come.

The witnesses, Pharisees whom Joseph recognized as having been among those who questioned Jesus whenever he taught, stood to one side. When Caiaphas nodded to them, the leading one said eagerly, "I heard him say, 'I will destroy this temple that is made with hands, and in three days I will build another not made with hands.' "

Caiaphas was obviously triumphant at thus establishing blasphemy against the temple, but when Jesus looked at the Pharisee who witnessed against him, the man began to stammer a different version of his story. Angrily Caiaphas sent him back to the group of witnesses, but when one after another tried to tell how Jesus had blasphemed, only to have their stories become more and more confused, the crowd began to murmur among themselves at this travesty of a trial.

Caiaphas flushed at the reaction of the crowd and said sharply to Jesus, "Have you no answer to make? What is it that these men testify against you?"

Jesus did not speak, and the high priest said sharply, "Are you the Christ, the Son of the Blessed?"

Slowly the eyes of the prisoner swept the room and the elegant person of the high priest who was tormenting him. Before the calmness in his glance even the confidence of Caiaphas seemed to wane a little. When Jesus spoke, his voice was loud and distinct, as if he wanted not only those in the room to hear, but also the small crowd that filled the courtyard. "I am," he said, "and you will see the Son of Man sitting at the right hand of power, and coming with the clouds of heaven."

Then Caiaphas, suddenly triumphant, tore his robe and shouted, "Why do we still need witnesses? You have heard his blasphemy. What is your decision?"

And as they had been coached, the members of this mock council answered, "He deserves death!"

"Bind him and send him to Pontius Pilate for sentencing," Caiaphas ordered exultantly. This was his hour of triumph. The man who had dared to mock the priests and the Pharisees before the people was at his mercy, condemned by his own words.

The soldiers converged upon Jesus once more, but before they took him from the room he looked around and saw Joseph and Mary standing there, distressed at this mockery of a trial and yet unable to do anything. A smile seemed to warm his lips for a moment, a smile of encouragement for them although his life, not theirs, was in danger.

As Joseph's eyes met those of Jesus it was as if a sudden light burst in his brain. And in a blinding revelation that could come only from God Himself, he knew now that the one thing he had lacked, he lacked no more. For he had looked into the eyes of the Son of God and seen there the glory of a revelation he had sought but not been able to find, until the moment when he had heard Jesus proclaim himself the Christ.

The shock and the glory of the revelation made Joseph reel a little, so that it was he who clung to Mary's arm for support now. And she, realizing what had happened to him because she had experienced the same blinding glory, put her arm about him and held to him tightly while tears streamed down her cheeks. They remained thus while the soldiers took Jesus from the room and the crowd filed out, leaving them alone.

"He is indeed the Son of God, Mary," Joseph whispered as they went out into the courtyard. "I saw it just now, as if the Most High had opened a page and let me look upon the words themselves written there."

"I know, dear," she said softly. "I always knew that when the time came Jesus himself would reveal the truth to you." And then her voice broke with grief. "But what can we do, Joseph? Pilate will sentence him in the morning and they will crucify him. It is the Roman way."

Joseph straightened his shoulders. "I must speak to Pilate tonight. Perhaps I can still persuade him of the truth."

But he was foiled there, too, for a double guard had been placed around the Procurator's palace and strict orders given that he was not to be disturbed under any circumstances. If they had needed any further evidence that the whole thing had been planned by Caiaphas and Pilate together, it was this.

For a while they could think of nothing that would help Jesus. Then Joseph had an inspiration. "Claudia Procula is in Jericho," he said. "If I ride there and ask her to come at once to Jerusalem, she may be able to influence Pontius Pilate."

"You can try," Mary agreed. "I know she loves her husband enough to do anything she could to help him from crucifying the Son of God."

Dawn had broken long before Joseph's swift camel entered the courtyard of Herod's palace in Jericho where Claudia Procula was staying. But the guard was a member of Pilate's household troops and knew him, so he was admitted immediately. The *nomenclator* informed him that the Procurator's lady was still asleep, but at Joseph's insistence she was awakened. A few minutes later Claudia Procula came into the room, wrapped in a rich dressing robe, her face still flushed from sleep. When she saw who her visitor was, her eyes widened and her hand went to her breast. "Why are you here, Joseph!" she cried. "Is Pontius ill?"

"The Procurator is in good health, I am told." He knelt before her. "I come to beg that you save Jesus of Nazareth."

"To save Jesus? What has happened?"

"Caiaphas arrested him for blasphemy and they have condemned him to death. The Procurator will pass sentence on him today."

"Crucifixion!" she gasped.

"It is the Roman method of execution."

"But why? I thought they had decided he was harmless."

"Caiaphas fears Jesus," Joseph explained, "lest his teachings break the hold the high priest has on the people. He must have convinced the Procurator that Jesus' death is best for the state."

Claudia Procula's eyes fell. "He required little convincing, Joseph. Pontius ordered me not to listen to Jesus and I refused. That is why I did not come to Jerusalem."

"You must come now," he urged, "or your husband will crucify the Son of God."

She looked at him closely and saw that he was confident of the truth in what he said. "I know Mary has believed he is the Messiah for a long time," she said. "But I did not think you believed it. What made you change your mind, Joseph?"

"This morning it was revealed to me," he told her simply. "I no longer doubt."

Claudia Procula took a long breath. "And if he really is the Christ——" Her face grew pale. "Pontius must not do this thing, Joseph!" she cried. "Go order a chariot made ready. We will drive at once to Jerusalem."

The great crowd gathered around the *praetorium* where the Procurator held court while in Jerusalem indicated that the trial of Jesus, if trial it was to be, was already in progress. But the eagles upon the chariot in which they rode, as well as the sight of Pontius Pilate's wife standing straight and lovely in the vehicle, opened a way for them through the mass of people. Looking around him, Joseph saw many of the same faces that had been in the mob that morning several months before when Jesus had almost been stoned and Trojanus had rescued them.

These were not the simple people of the city who had listened to the Nazarene teacher and loved him. The high priest and his sycophants had obviously sent word that Jesus was to be judged to the people who would be most interested in seeing him destroyed, the money-changers whose booths he had overturned in the temple, the sellers of sacrificial animals whose stalls had been ripped apart, the lesser priests who lived luxurious lives on the temple tribute, the stiff-necked Pharisees in long fringed robes, and the haughty scribes, carrying the curved inkhorns, symbols of their trade, slung over their shoulders. At the hands of such as these, Jesus would receive no mercy, for all of them hated him.

They went directly to Procula's apartment and found Mary waiting there. As the two women embraced, Claudia asked, "What must I do to stop this terrible thing, Mary?"

"Jesus is before the Procurator now in the *praetorium*," Mary told her. "If you go to him he might still order a lesser sentence."

"Pontius would resent my interfering in public," Procula demurred. "I will write a note to him. There is an alcove behind the throne. We will watch from there, and one of the servants can give it to him."

She wrote quickly upon a wax tablet and, calling a soldier, gave orders for it to be given to the Procurator immediately, even if the proceedings must be interrupted. Then she guided Joseph and Mary to an alcove near the throne from which they could see the entire room where the hearing was being held.

Pontius Pilate sat upon an elevated dais with the clerks beside him. Flanking them were the lictors, whose upright fasces indicated that this was a civil court. The actual proceedings were just beginning, and while they watched, Jesus was brought in, his hands still chained together, between two Roman soldiers. Joseph could see that the Master had been cruelly treated during the night, for his face was puffed and bruised, and the marks of scourges were on his body. But the same light shone in his eyes, as if he were seeing something far beyond the vision of those around him, and the same half-smile of pity was upon his lips. After him came the priests led by Caiaphas, his thin-lipped mouth tightly drawn and his eyes cold with hate for the prisoner.

"What charges do you make against this man?" Pilate asked the high priest formally.

"He claims that he is king of the Jews," Caiaphas said, and looked around at the others. "All of us heard him say it."

A chorus of voices continued the statement.

"Are you the king of the Jews?" the Procurator asked Jesus directly.

Jesus turned to look at him, but for a moment he did not speak. Then he said quietly, "You have said so."

Pilate was obviously taken aback by the answer, and his uncertainty plainly showed on his face. Caiaphas and the others at once broke into a babble of charges against Jesus, lest the Procurator be influenced by the prisoner's calm demeanor, but Pilate silenced them with an uplifted hand. As the babble was dying away, the soldier came up to the throne and handed him the wax tablet upon which Claudia Procula had written. Pilate glanced at it quickly, and a startled look came over his face before he turned and looked into the alcove. Seeing his wife standing there, pleading with him wordlessly to have mercy, he seemed to waver for a moment.

Watching the Procurator, Joseph could almost read his thoughts. For Pontius Pilate, in spite of his cruelty, was not a man of direct and consistent action. Twice he had deeply affronted the Jews by insisting that the customs of

Rome take precedence over their ancient laws. And each time when they had resisted passively he had been forced to give in. Watching him now, Joseph saw that Pilate was strongly tempted to turn Jesus loose, even though it would mean a break with Caiaphas, with whom he had planned the destruction of this man who threatened so much trouble for the high priest and his group, and also for the Romans, if the ever-bubbling caldron of revolt against Rome should once boil over.

Pilate turned to Jesus again and asked, "See how many charges they bring against you. Have you no answer to make?"

The prisoner did not answer, and the Procurator frowned and looked at Caiaphas, as if for advice. Something in the high priest's eyes, perhaps his contempt for the Roman's uncertainty, seemed to sting Pilate, and a faint flush rose in his sallow cheeks. Then his face hardened and he straightened his shoulders and drew himself more erect, as if he had come to a decision.

"Pontius! No," Claudia Procula cried in a broken voice. But just then a man shouted from the crowd, "Release to us a prisoner as is the custom on this day," and the sound of her plea was drowned out by hundreds of voices that took up the cry, demanding that the Roman governor observe the custom of the Passover, when traditionally he released whomever the crowd demanded from prison.

Pilate's face cleared. Here was a way out of the difficulty, for if the crowd demanded the release of Jesus, he would have good reason to grant them the request. "Do you want me to release to you the king of the Jews?" he asked.

Now the final working out of Caiaphas' plan showed itself. For the high priest knew his co-conspirator and his weakness and had cleverly prepared against it. From the front row of the crowd a group of the temple hangers-on shouted, "No! No! Release to us the man called Barabbas."

Barabbas was a hardened criminal, a known revolutionary who had murdered a man during one of the brawls between Zealots and the temple guards that happened so often. Pilate was obviously startled by the vehement request. "Then what shall I do with the man whom you call the king of the Jews?" he asked.

"Crucify him!" those in front shouted. "Crucify him!"

The dread words rolled back over the crowd, magnified again and again by the shouts of a hundred bloodthirsty throats glad of a chance to punish this man who had dared to expose how they had made a mockery and a shameful thing out of the worship of God and His holy temple.

Taken aback by the fury of their demand, Pilate asked again, "Why, what evil has he done?" But his question was drowned out by the answer, "Crucify him! Crucify him!"

"So be it!" he said then resignedly. "Let him be scourged and taken to the place of execution." He signaled to the soldiers and they led Jesus away.

20

DARKNESS had fallen, and although it was the season of the Passover, when all Jews rejoiced to eat the ritual meal together, thousands still gathered on the slopes of the hill called Golgotha beneath three crosses outlined in the light of torches carried by the watching Roman guard. These were not the bloodthirsty group who had crowded into the *praetorium* that morning, demanding that Pontius Pilate release to them not Jesus of Nazareth, who was innocent, but a known criminal, Barabbas. These were Jews who had loved Jesus and heard in his teachings a new hope, a new evidence that God loved them for themselves, not for their sacrifices, their minute observance of the law, as the Pharisees claimed, or the pretentiousness of their piety. They prostrated themselves in the dust of this place of execution and wept for the pale white figure on the center cross whose hands were nailed to the beam called the *patibulum*.

The Roman soldiers who had carried out the order of execution had tried to make Jesus bear the beam of his own cross, as customary, but he was not strong enough, and it had been transferred to the broad shoulders of Simon the Cyrene. They had beaten Jesus and taunted him before they put on a purple robe to mock him. And they had then jammed a crown of thorns down cruelly upon his head until the sharp points penetrated the scalp and framed his face in a halo of blood.

Above his head now hung the placard which Pilate had ordered put there, bearing the jeering charge, "The King of the Jews."

Joseph and Mary had been near the foot of the cross from the beginning of the end. They had flinched as the nails were driven one by one into the tender hands which had brought surcease from pain to so many of the sick and afflicted. And they had marveled when Jesus had prayed for those who tormented him, "Father, forgive them, for they know not what they do." Even the rough soldiers who were casting lots for his garments had been silenced for a while then.

And finally Joseph and Mary, with some of the others who had found their courage and come to watch the death of their master, had heard the pathetic cry from the cross, "Eloi! Eloi! lama sabachthani!" the cry of the dying man who in his last agony felt utterly forsaken, even by the Father. After that Jesus had seemed to lapse into unconsciousness. He had not even roused when one of the soldiers, thinking to do the doomed man a kindness, reached up to thrust a spear into his side and thus relieve his suffering by hastening the inevitable end.

During the afternoon Joseph had sent a messenger to Pontius Pilate through his uncle and namesake, Joseph of Arimathea, asking that he be allowed to prepare the body for burial and lay it in a tomb. And now, seeing that Jesus had ceased to breathe, he and his uncle approached the centurion in charge of the guard and asked that the cross be taken down and the body turned over to them according to Pilate's order.

The centurion himself helped them to lift the broken and wounded body from the cross and lay it upon a clean cloth placed on a litter. As he straightened up the Roman said quietly, "Truly this man was the Son of God." He hesitated for a moment, then added, "When you have placed him in the tomb, flee the city. I heard talk among the temple guards. They hope to take all who were close to the teacher tonight and put them to death."

"We will be careful," Joseph promised. "And be sure God will bless you for warning us."

Mary and Joseph followed behind the litter as it was

312

borne down the hill by four strong men of his uncle's household and across the city to a tomb hewn from the rock in the corner of his garden. Mary's hand stole into Joseph's as they walked in the darkness behind the litter upon which lay the body of the man they knew now to be the Son of God. "Do you still believe he will rise, dear?" he asked gently.

"I know he will," she said confidently, "for he once said: 'They will mock him, and spit upon him, and scourge him, and kill him; and after three days he will rise.' "

Those of the followers of Jesus who had dared to watch his death followed the litter with their Master's body. They stood around the entrance to the tomb while Joseph arranged the body upon a clean white cloth and applied the spices and herbs that were customary until it could finally be prepared for burial after the Sabbath, which would come on the morrow, had passed.

The wounds were painfully evident on Jesus' body as Joseph prepared it for burial with his own hands in the light of torches held by those at the mouth of the tomb. All who watched could see the prints of the nails in his hands and his feet, and the tiny prick marks of the thorns where the cruel crown had been pressed upon his forehead until the points penetrated the skin. The slight gash on his wrist where the irons had cut was also visible, and in his side was an ugly gaping wound made by the mercifully intended spear of the Roman soldier.

Joseph had almost finished, when a commotion arose outside and a big man rushed in to throw himself on the stone floor beside the bier upon which Jesus' body lay. At first Joseph did not recognize Simon Peter, for his clothes were torn and covered with dirt and he was sobbing wildly. He continued to weep while Joseph finished preparing the body, and when he was through the young physician lifted the big man to his feet and led him from the tomb. "Jesus has promised that he will rise, Simon," Mary said comfortingly, putting her arm around him as they left the tomb. "We have that assurance still before us."

A great retching sob shook the big man's body. "But I denied my Lord," Simon groaned. "I denied him thrice in the courtyard of the high priest last night."

"Perhaps it was not Jesus himself you were denying, Simon," Mary said with that strange insight of hers in regard to the Master that seemed to come from the depth of her great love for him.

"But I was looking at him myself," the big man protested. "And still I denied him."

"You were denying the same thing that Judas denied when he betrayed Jesus," Mary explained. "The thing that you wanted him to be, not what he really was. Now you know what the Christ really means and why he came."

Simon Peter looked at her uncomprehendingly for a moment, then a light of hope, almost of joy, began to burn in his eyes. Seeing it, Joseph said quietly, "The centurion warned me that our lives may be in danger, Simon. You were the leader after Jesus. Call the others and we will go to Nicodemus' house at Emmaus where we will be safe.

It was a new man who turned to the little group of huddled figures there in the shadows and spoke to them. And like sheep following their master, they fell in behind the tall, commanding form of Simon Peter, their new leader, as he started along the road to Emmaus.

"If I did not already know why I love you, Joseph of Galilee," Mary said softly, "I would know it now." With fingers intertwined they followed the new leader.

The next day was the Sabbath, so the scattered followers of the crucified leader remained at Emmaus, some seven miles outside Jerusalem in the hills. Nicodemus' country place was small, however, so Mary and Joseph, with Simon Peter and some of the others, stayed at the home of a man named Cleopas, who was also a follower of Jesus.

Early on the morning after the Sabbath, Joseph and Mary, with some of the others, set out for Jerusalem for the final tribute to their crucified Master, the embalming and preparation of his body for final burial, after which the tomb in the garden of Joseph of Arimathea would be sealed. There had not been time on the night of the crucifixion to carry out these final details, for according to Jewish law they could not be done on the Sabbath.

Mary was no longer downcast as they walked along the road to Jerusalem from Emmaus, for flowers were blooming everywhere and the trees were putting forth the first green leaves of spring. "I see now why Jesus chose this time for his death," she said softly. "Like the seed that is sowed in the spring, he had to die in order that he may rise again to show everyone the way to eternal life through him."

Joseph looked at her, startled once again by her insight where Jesus was concerned. "But what if he does not rise again?"

"He will," she said without hesitancy. "He has promised us that he will, and the Son of God cannot lie."

"Would that I had your faith, dear," Joseph said with deep sincerity.

She smiled and squeezed his hand. "You do, Joseph, but where I believe what I know in my heart is true, you believe what your senses and your mind tell you is true. Do you doubt any longer that Jesus is the Son of God?"

"No. I know that beyond any shadow of a doubt."

"He will rise from the dead," she said confidently. "And you will be just as certain of his rising when he chooses to reveal it to you."

They walked on a little while in silence, their eyes upon the great white city that clothed the hills ahead of them. Then Joseph said a little hesitantly, for he feared what the answer might be to his question, "What about us, Mary, now that Jesus has been crucified?"

"He has fulfilled his purpose," she said simply, "and no longer needs me." Then she smiled. "See, the flowers are blooming, the leaves are coming out again, and we are together—just as I promised that we would be."

"Will our lives ever be the same as before?" he wondered.

Mary shook her head. "No one can follow Jesus and ever be the same again, Joseph. But who would want to be? After what he gives to us?"

Joseph's eyes were upon the city shining before them in the morning sunlight. To a pilgrim approaching Jerusalem, fired by the adoration with which every devout Jew regarded the Holy City, it must have been a sight next only in magnificence to the throne of God itself. But he knew only too well what lay behind that glittering façade of marble and gold, the lust for power and greed for wealth, the misery and the suffering, the rapacity of those who were rich in goods but poor in spirit, the exploiting of pilgrims in the name of a corrupt temple hierarchy whose greedy fingers reached out to exact tribute even from the lowliest seller of curios in the outer Court of the Heathen, the false pride of the Pharisees who debased the worship of God into the worship of rule and cant and creed, the scribes who spent endless hours in fruitless arguments, when they might have been serving their fellows—all these made up the Jerusalem seen by the adoring eyes of the pilgrims. And those same men had crucified the Expected One who had come to show them again the higher purpose which had been gradually lost during the centuries since the Jews had smeared the blood of the paschal lamb above the lintels of their huts, so that the avenging wrath of their God upon the people who oppressed His children might be fully vented.

"Would you like to go back to Galilee and start anew?" Joseph asked suddenly.

His answer and his reward were in the glory that shone suddenly in his beloved's eyes. "I was hoping you would say that, Joseph," she said, reaching out to take his hand in hers. "But we will not really be starting anew. We will be merely turning back to the beginning of the road we started to travel on a day like this in Tiberias."

At the gates of the city Joseph left the others and went on to the shops of the spice sellers to buy the things necessary to prepare Jesus' body for burial. He made his purchases quickly and turned his steps toward the tomb where the body of Jesus lay.

Nor was he at all sad at the thought that this was one of the last times he might be walking through Jerusalem. The memory of the green jewel of the Sea of Galilee, the rich vineyards and groves of Gennesaret, the leaping schools of fish that shoaled before Bethsaida, and the bright-colored sails of the fishermen coming home in the late afternoon was a far lovelier picture than anything that now met his eyes. And of course with Mary there, nothing would be lacking.

As he turned into the gate of his uncle's estate with his bundles Mary came running through the garden from the tomb, her arms outstretched, a great glory shining in her face. "Joseph!" she cried. "It has happened! Jesus is risen!"

21

IT was a simple story that Mary told of the miraculous thing which had happened, while tears of joy streamed down her face and the light of a glorious knowledge burned in her eyes. She and the women had come to the tomb, wondering who they would get to push aside the stone for them. But the stone was already rolled away, and when they found the tomb empty and the body of Jesus removed, some of the women ran to get Simon Peter. He also had looked into the tomb and had seen only the cloth upon which Jesus had lain.

The others had gone on into the house then, but Mary had remained by the tomb, weeping, afraid that Caiaphas, or perhaps Pontius Pilate, had stolen the body in order to exhibit it later as proof that Jesus was not able to carry out in death the promise he had made in life to rise from the dead.

After a while—as Mary told the story to Joseph—she had looked again into the tomb and seen that it was still empty. But when she turned around a man was standing beside her. "Woman, why are you weeping?" he asked. "Whom do you seek?"

She did not recognize him and, thinking he might be Joseph of Arimathea's gardener, she said, "Sir, if you have carried him away, tell me where you have laid him and I will take him away."

Jesus had spoken to her in his own voice then and she knew him and cried, "Rabboni!" But when she would have touched him, he said, "Do not hold me, for I have not yet ascended to the Father, but go to my brethren and say to them, I am ascending to my Father and your Father, to my God and your God."

When Joseph reached the tomb he saw that the stone had indeed been rolled away, although it had taken several strong men to put it into place blocking the entrance when they had laid the body there. And the print of

Jesus' body was still upon the cloth in which Joseph had wrapped him, while the marks of blood from his wounds still stained it.

None of the others besides Mary had seen Jesus, and Joseph knew that no court of law would accept her unsupported evidence that she had seen him, for she was known to have loved the Master deeply and to have been firmly convinced that he would return. Whether or not, in her intense desire to know that Jesus was not dead, she had seen a vision, no one could say. As for himself, Joseph was tempted strongly to believe that she had indeed seen Jesus in the flesh, but deep inside him he felt the same lingering uncertainty he had experienced concerning the Messiahship, until it had come to him with the blinding light of a revelation as he watched the Master himself at the trial.

"You think I saw a vision," Mary said quickly, "as mad people sometimes see things that are not there."

"I know that Jesus was there—for you."

"But not necessarily in the flesh?"

"It is the way others will think," he pointed out.

"But if he could appear to me," she cried, "he can make himself visible to any of us when he wishes."

"Let us pray that our faith be given final strength then through him," Joseph said simply. "Meanwhile we must protect you."

"Protect me? From what?"

"The others are already running everywhere in the city, proclaiming that Jesus is risen and has appeared to you. Think what this will mean for Caiaphas and Pontius Pilate."

She caught her breath. "Since I am the only one who has seen Jesus—— "

"They must silence you at all costs. For if the people come to believe that Jesus has indeed risen from the dead, they will know without question that he is the Christ and will insist upon crowning him king in Judea."

"But he will not remain here," Mary objected. "His words to me were, 'Do not hold me, for I have not yet ascended to the Father, but go to my brethren and say to them, I am ascending to my Father and your Father, to my God and your God.' Jesus is leaving the earth, Joseph. He told me that himself."

"Will Pilate and Caiaphas believe it without seeing him in the flesh themselves?"

"No," Mary admitted sadly. "You are not sure of it yourself, so we could not expect them to understand."

"There is only one thing to do," he said urgently. "You must leave Jerusalem before word of this gets to Pontius Pilate and he sends to arrest you."

"But what of the others? And you?"

"You are the only witness to the resurrection of Jesus in the body. Until he appears to the rest of us, we will be in no danger."

"Come with me, Joseph," she begged. "I don't want us ever to be separated again."

"I will settle up my affairs in the city and come to Emmaus this afternoon," he promised. "Tomorrow we will go on to Galilee. If Herod Antipas will not give us refuge, we can go on to the territory of Philip or even to Antioch. The legate there will protect us; he is in debt to me for curing his son of a distemper."

"But I have committed no crime," Mary protested. "Why should I hide like a criminal?"

"You possess a knowledge that can set the world afire," he pointed out soberly. "And we must guard that flame lest it be quenched before it can begin to burn more brightly."

"I will go back to Emmaus and wait for you at Cleopas' house," she promised then. "But be careful, Joseph. I would die if anything happened to you now that Jesus is going to the Father."

All day long the city hummed with the news that the man who had been so shamefully crucified had risen. Hundreds came to the garden to see the empty tomb, with the cloths still upon the bier showing the print of his body and the marks of his blood. Some scoffed, naming it a trick to make them think the dead had been raised. But many who had known and loved Jesus believed and were convinced that he was the true Messiah whose coming had been predicted by Isaiah.

It was late afternoon before Joseph was finally able to leave for Emmaus. Cleopas went with him, and as they walked along they talked over the exciting events that had occurred within the past few days.

Neither of them noticed the man who shortly fell into step beside them, until they looked up from their earnest conversation and saw him there. He was slender, dressed in a long robe, with a hood about his head that kept his face almost hidden. His hands, too, were hidden by the long full sleeves. Something about him was familiar, Joseph thought, but could not tell exactly what it was.

Joseph and Cleopas gave the stranger a pleasant greeting. "What is this conversation which you are holding with each other as you walk?" he asked politely.

"Are you the only visitor to Jerusalem who does not know the things that have happened there in these days?" Cleopas asked, astonished.

"What things?"

"Concerning Jesus of Nazareth, who was a prophet mighty in deed and word before God and all the people? And how our chief priests and rulers delivered him up to be condemned to death and crucified him?"

Watching the stranger while Cleopas told the story of what had happened that morning, Joseph could not put aside the odd conviction that he knew this man, perhaps well. If he could have seen his eyes he thought he would have been able to recognize him, but the stranger kept the hood pulled well over his face.

"Was it not necessary that the Christ should suffer all these things and enter into his glory?" the stranger asked when Cleopas finished the story of Mary's having seen Jesus.

"I believe they were necessary," Joseph said earnestly. "For I know that Jesus of Nazareth is the Christ."

The stranger did not speak, but Joseph felt his own heart suddenly warm and fill with a strange feeling, a sensation oddly like the one he had experienced when he had met the eyes of Jesus across the room in the palace of Caiaphas three days ago and had been flooded with a divine assurance of his identity.

"How can you say he is the Christ, Joseph, when you saw him die from the spear thrust in his side?" Cleopas argued. "And when with your own hands you laid his dead body in the tomb?"

"I know he is the Son of God," Joseph said simply. "And who is of God cannot be overcome, even by death."

When he spoke again, the stranger's voice was more gentle, and as they walked along the road he discussed with amazing learning the prophecies contained in the books of the Law and the Prophets concerning the Christ that was to come, showing how they applied, like a garment cut to one's very measure, to Jesus of Nazareth.

Cleopas' home was at the edge of Emmaus, on the road leading to it from Jerusalem. When they came to the path leading up to the door, the stranger started to go on, but Joseph said impulsively, "Stay with us, for it is toward evening and the day is now far spent."

When Cleopas added his entreaty, their still unknown companion finally acquiesced and went with them up the path and into the house. Cleopas went immediately to bring wine and a basket of bread to refresh them from the long walk as was fitting when guests entered one's home. When he put it upon the table he said courteously, "Will you bless and break it for us, sir?"

The stranger reached out and took a piece of bread from the basket. As he did so, the sleeves of his robe fell back from his hands and Joseph saw them for the first time. And now he knew why the man who had joined them on the road to Emmaus had seemed familiar. Even if there had been two pairs of hands in the world with those same marks where the nails had been driven through, it was hardly possible that the identical wound would also be upon the wrist, where the manacles applied by the guards that night on the Mount of Olives and the Garden of Gethsemane had cut into the skin. As Joseph stared, still hardly able to believe his own eyes, the visitor reached up and pushed back the hood. And now Joseph saw again those same gentle, loving eyes he remembered so well, and the little row of puncture marks across the forehead where the thorns of the crown pressed down so roughly by the soldiers had penetrated the skin.

He started to rise from the table, but just then Jesus began to bless the bread and the wine, and he was forced to hold his tongue. When it was finished, he heard Mary's voice in the outer room and, excusing himself quickly, went to tell her the glad news and bring her to Jesus, so that they might fall down and worship the risen Lord together.

"Jesus is here, Mary," he called to her. "He joined us on the road and is in the other room."

"Oh, thank God," she cried, her eyes shining. "I have prayed that he would reveal himself to you."

"I saw the nail prints in his hands, the cut on his wrist, and the pricks of the thorns upon his brow." He held out his hands to her. "Come. We will go and worship him together."

But when they came into the room only Cleopas was there, looking at them a little foolishly from the cupboard where he had gone to get the wine. "The stranger left, Joseph," he said. "I turned around for only a moment to get the wine, and when I looked back he was gone."

"He was here when I went to get Mary," Joseph said dazedly. "I knew it was Jesus by the prints in his hands." He turned suddenly to Mary. "You don't doubt that I saw him, do you?"

"I knew he would reveal himself to you when he was ready for you to know the whole truth," she cried, her eyes shining, while tears of joy streamed down her cheeks.

"But Cleopas was in the room and he did not recognize him."

"That was what the Master intended," she said softly. "You are a physician, Joseph. You knew that he was dead, for you put his body in the tomb. But now you know that he lives again, for you have seen in his resurrected body the very wounds in his hands that we saw as you laid him in the tomb. Together we must proclaim to the world the truth that has been revealed to you on the road to Emmaus. The truth that Jesus, being crucified, has indeed risen from the dead. No man can fail to know now that he is indeed the Son of God."